THE BOZ TRILOGY, #1

SEADOCK

or

THE LAST BATTLE OF BERKELEY

a novel

Thomas Givon

White Cloud Publishing

The Boz Trilogy, #1
SEADOCK
or
The Last Battle of Berkeley

A novel
by Thomas Givon

Copyright © 2011
Thomas Givon

Library of Congress Control Number: 2011900118
ISBN: 978-0-615-42843-7

Cover graphics: Mikey Quiver

Published by White Cloud Publishing
Durango, Colorado

Printed in the United States by Morris Publishing®
3212 East Highway 30
Kearney, NE 68847
1-800-650-7888

To Mike Lindquist, who told me a strange tale;
to Christopher, who showed me a gorgeous sunset;
and to Karin and the Midnight Mine Marching Band
in fond remembrance of times past.

To Jackie
& Bud — —
Enjoy Leo & the
gang!
As ever, Tomás

I. TOO LATE FOR THE REVOLUTION

It is all perfectly true. Well, almost, given the vagaries of story telling. Am I proud of myself? Hardly. For so much of this reflects poorly on my own person. Still, I have resolved to tell it like it is, or was. Let it all hang out, the ugly kinks, the ungainly mess. For I am who I am and have always been, alas, a colossal fuckup.

I have been known to embellish. Not this time. A perverse pride demands that I let the chips fall as they may, let them point their incriminating finger at yours truly. I am the born scapegoat, *Qui Tollis Peccata Mundi,* he who bears the shame. Often with a wince, ever with fortitude. Say dignity? Say panache? But above all with resignation, born of having been told off too often in no uncertain terms.

Though as in all tales of sin and redemption, there is a saving grace here too. But I am jumping ahead of myself.

1. People's Park

(Berkeley, May 1968)

"Do you mind?" says Mad.

Her voice carries the barest hint of North Country brogue, an improbable affectation given the time and place. She must have picked this up from our *Contemp Cult Crit* prof, a gin-pickled Brit, an asshole who nevertheless gets the credit for bringing us together and thus, by a leap of inference, for Mad now straddling my bare loin, her spare frame gyrating like a charmed snake, her lips peeled wide in an inward-gazing smile of utter bliss. She is--urgently, relentlessly--bearing her perfumed garden-of-heavenly-delights down upon my erect pride-and-joy.

She is here and now and yet light-years away, launched upon her galactic ride. I am to call her Mad, short for Madeleine. She knows what she wants and most often gets it, as I was advised early in our union, just in case I had missed the point. But what she seems to want right now makes no sense--she wants off her joyride, summarily, prematurely.

Neither of us has come yet, I certainly haven't. And just for the record, I do mind. For my monstrous erection is embedded in Mad's succulent depths, where it is being ground down slowly to sweet pulp. My tattered jeans are slipped down below my knees, my bare ass is mashed into the damp grass, and my souped-up blood is coursing madly in my veins.

I hail, on my father's side, from a long line of rum-guzzling Norsemen, veritable Hagars each and every one. Our putative family tree, embossed on pre-aged parchment, is mounted above my father's red-oak desk, where it is flanked by the cornucopia of his degrees, memberships and testimonials. One of which sanctions Leo Swenson, Sr., MD, PhD, to minister to the guilt-ridden psyches of his affluent flock. Which reminds me--Holy Jesus--I had better call my mom.

I am wearing no underpants. Like my sea-faring forebears, I come ready to hoist the ensign when lust beckons, what with life being so brutally short as I have recently come to suspect. What with my future prospects dwindling and Vietnam looming large over the horizon. What with Mad all juiced up and hellbent on Eden.

Once again, I oblige. For charity begins at home, and my joystick has just been cleansed of the dose of the clap bequeathed by Mad's immediate predecessor. After three weeks of enforced celibacy, I am raring to go, as is Mad. We have been sniffing at each other's rump like a pair of randy felines, in and out of the one class--*Contemp Cult Crit*--we share with four-hundred hormone-pumped, draft-deferred, state-subsidized strangers.

I do mind, though it is rather beside the point. For if my long tenure under the exacting yoke and, occasionally, baffling generosity of the female gender has taught me anything, it is this: One must resign oneself to the serendipity of their minds. I strive to divine their every whim as I stray into their temple. I praise their oracular wisdom, I worship at the altar of their lush bounty. And I labor mightily to temper my chagrin when--spiteful, savage, serene--they cast me down like a worn-out sock as they unfailingly do.

Often, I shut my eyes tight letting the red glow on my lids illuminate the mind's dark screen. On which I run and rerun the wild transformations that come over their taut faces when the mood for ground-zero lovin' swoops upon them like a predatory Texas twister. I wallow in their sweet mana, soaked to my armpits in sweet hog heaven, happy and buoyant, secure in the transitory majesty of their divine glory.

Just don't ask me to explain the mysteries that rules their orbits.

And so, in spite of my ardent member risen to full tilt and the blood pounding my temples, I relent and help Mad down onto the damp grass beside me.

"What's the matter, babe? You cold?"

The flimsy green lace sheathing Mad's slender bosom affords little protection against the chill elements. My solicitude is but a gambit.

"Let's finish up in there" she says.

"Gate's locked" I tell her. "The demonstration starts

in just three hours, the cops must be on their way over right now".

"Good" she says. "Better hurry then".

"Why in there?"

"We gonna to make a statement, Leo".

"Well..."

My ardor is not yet fully extinguished, but even I have my limit. For I know what Mad has in mind, I have seen this reckless gleam in her eyes before, and for once I would just as soon beg off.

"You wanna fuck, don't you?" she says.

"Sure, babe".

"Well shake a leg then. And one more thing".

"Yes?"

"Don't call me babe. I have a pretty cool name. Use it".

She has half-risen to her elbow, fixing me with a hopped-up squint. Sure I know her current *nom-de-guerre*, why else should I avoid it?

Having driven her point home, Mad rises--barefoot and bare-assed, her damp hair flailing behind her--and sprints across the grass to the cyclone fence just next to the chained gate with the sign proclaiming, under the neon floodlight:

UNIVERSITY OF CALIFORNIA

PRIVATE PROPERTY

NO TRESPASSING

VIOLATORS WILL BE PROSECUTED

The small print below ticks off the appropriate municipal codes. Above, sprayed in spidery red letters, the crux of what

6

is soon to take place is boldly proclaimed:

PEOPLE'S PARK!

FUCK OPPRESSION!

ALL POWER TO THE SOVIETS!

Mad is half the way up the wire mesh by the time I catch up, my fly not quite zipped. I know I should turn back and run, leave Mad to enact on her own whatever fantasy that may be consuming her. But once again, my sense of the absurd--coupled with the lingering erection--gets in the way.

"What the fuck..."

And so I follow her up the eight-foot wire mesh. By the time we are down on the forbidden ground inside, both my hands are badly scored from the barbed wire on top, my right knee is grazed, and my Reed College sweatshirt, souvenir of another squandered year, is in tatters. Mad's flimsy lace shift is unscathed.

The cracked dirt of People's Park, littered with weeks' worth of revolutionary garbage, is not all that conducive to resuming our *conjunctus interrumpus*.

"Gee, Mad..." I survey the desolation over which fierce armies will soon do pitched battle. "This is kinda rough, don't you think?"

"Stop whining, Leo" she says.

She is casting about thoughtfully, her brow furrowed.

"I've been meaning to tell you" she says, "I hope you'll take this in the spirit in which it is offered.

In the five weeks we have known each other, I have

yet to see her think twice. Or once. Her reckless ferocity is her most salient trait. Reticence is not part of her social tool-kit.

"Try me" I say, my heart sinking.

Mad brings her face close to mine. The pupils of her large brown eyes are still dilated from the Afghani hash we consumed earlier in the evening.

"Whoosh" she says, "whooshy whoooosh... guess I will".

Her eyes assess me, searching for the hidden fissure.

"I worry about you, Leo" she says. "I think I've just figured out why. It's serious, so pay attention willya?"

"Serious like terminal?"

She glares at me.

"Don't patronize me with your East Coast shtick" she says. "And yes, it may be terminal. You're suffering from a crippling lack of imagination".

Her ferocious gaze fixes me for a brief moment, then shifts.

"I don't know..." she says. Her eyes are casting about in the shadows midway up the forlorn plot of hallowed revolutionary ground.

"Maybe, with luck.... Come!"

She grabs me by the hand and leads me back to the gate, where she turns to face me, her back flat against the wire mesh, right under the back side of the City's warning sign.

"Come to mama" she says.

And she pulls me roughly to her, and before I know it

her free hand is groping expertly at my crotch, where my pride-and-joy has alas regained its modest everyday dimensions.

"Shit, you've shrunk... Guess we'll have to fix that. Quick, drop 'em..."

By way of inducement, she hikes up the front of her shift.

"Come on, Leo" she says, "show some life, willya..."

"Christ, Mad!" I plead. "Not right here..."

"It's here and now" she says, "or nowhere and nevermore".

The demonstration is scheduled for 8:00 AM, an improbably early hour for the denizens of our Shangri-La by the Bay. It must be five now, the fog-bank is rolling in from the bay, casting an unearthly pallor over People's Park. A dog has just burst into a fit of irate barking somewhere in the bowels of the Victorian crash-pad across the street.

We are standing in the bright wash of the neon. In spite of Mad's urgent ministration, my deflated alter ego is not in the mood.

"Have a heart, babe" I plead. "How about over there by the back fence? It's a bit more private..."

"No way José" she says. "We gonna make a statement, you and I, right here where it counts. So crank it up, hey? Shit, you'd think I've asked you to swallow a fuckin' pill..."

And I shrug and relent, co-opted once again. My reticent junior partner is--somehow, miraculously--coaxed back into life, with Mad's knowing fingers kneading it against the moist petals of her swollen labia.

Christ in Heaven, how they can keep going! In my next incarnation, I shall come back as one of *their* elect gender. Then, armed with their superior vision, I may yet decipher the mysteries of life on this planet, something I have been meaning to do ever since my mom first clued me into the radical--and grossly unfair--disparity between the two principal sub-species.

And so, with the flesh again willing, I draw Mad's legs up, one after the other, and she twines herself around my hips. Soon she is breathing hard again, as I thrust my resurrected implement all the way home. And we are at it again, the sweet business of indulgence.

Which is when the police cruisers--three of them, on loan from the Oakland PD--sneak up on us out of the mist. They switch on their flashing lights and crank up their sirens, then come at us with drawn sidearms.

Which is how I wind up being too late for the revolution. Caught *in corpus flagrante*, with Mad at my side screeching bloody murder:

"Don't you dare touching me, you dirty old prevert pig!..."

We are hauled unceremoniously down to the holding pen near the Emeryville dockyards. We are finger-printed and charged with LLPE--lewd and lascivious public exposure (section 617). At eleven o'clock, released on our own recognizance, we hitch a ride back to the Av just when the

10

innocent frolic is over and the ugly mess begins.

I miss it all---Jerry Rubin's incendiary diatribe, Abby Hoffman's wild histrionics and, worst of all, Mario Savio's frenzied recap of his Dirty Speech harangue of 1966. How could I ever forgive myself?

I also lose Mad. On the lam, alone and thoroughly disgusted, I watch the fun and games go sour. First from a back-row perch across the street, half a block down from the Park. Then as a captive observer-participant in the bowels of the hopped-up multitude, which by now has transformed itself into a mean-spirited mob.

In the bargain, I get a lungful of teargas; I get doused by a high-pressure fire hose; I get clubbed on the kidney by an Alameda County motorcycle cop in his shining armor. Shrieking in agony, I spit at him in mad defiance, utterly unlike me. In response, the cop breaks rank and comes at me on his gleaming machine. I turn and run for dear life into--my luck--a cul-de-sac, where I find myself in the company of a black giant sporting a gothic Afro. The cop on his rumbling Electra Glide is breathing fire down our necks, his dark visor gleaming like the exterminating angel.

Just when it seems like the trooper has gotten us trapped, the black giant barks out:

"Watchit, whiteboy!"

And we turn back in tandem and--like a well-drilled team of angry jackals--jump the hapless trooper with a pair of empty garbage cans. Before the guy has noticed, he is trapped.

11

His gloved hands are desperately steering the bike, too busy to go for his service revolver. In a mad dash to turn his mount around, he skids, crashes into a utility pole and overturns.

In a flash the two of us are upon him. My companion renders him breathless and gagging with a well-placed kick to the chest. Before I know what has gotten into me, I am all over the prostrated cop, stomping and cussing.

Soon the prone man has ceased struggling. I lean over and almost gag at the sight of blood welling in his slack mouth. I strip off his helmet and hand it over to my companion. As an afterthought, I pull off the leather gloves.

"Not too shabby" the black giant says. "For a honkey".

I look up. The buff blue face looms over me like the night, inscrutable, eyes in full eclipse behind the wraparound shades. I can only hope I am not next on his agenda. By way of propitiating, I say:

"Right on, bro' ".

"Wes" says the giant, offering his hand.

"Cool kick, Wes. I'm Leo".

"I'm Libra. See you around".

We shake hands in silence. Mine is almost crushed in the giant's vise-like grip. Down on the pavement, the prostrated cop is moaning. The two of us, our rage dissipated, turn and back-track down the alley, leaving the cop to fend for himself as we dash for the safety of numbers.

●　　●　　●

A panicked human avalanche dumps me in the alley behind the Piccolo. With the fleeing multitude, I try to loop back toward the neutral grounds of the campus, only to discover we are trapped in a war zone, with all retreat routes severed. Around me, hysteria is rising into bedlam, in the midst of which I struggle to avoid being trampled. I am deflated against the worn brick wall, nearing suffocation, when a resolute hand reaches out from behind a metal door, grabs me by the scruff of my neck and pulls me into the pitch dark.

"There. I knew if I'd just waited long enough, you'd turn up with the roused rabble".

The voice of my friendly neighborhood dealer.

"Boz..." I croak. "Perfect timing..."

"To judge by the color, you were about to give the ghost".

I nod. He may have saved my life.

"Thanks" I tell him. "How come you're here?"

I don't expect an answer. The Boz treads the borderlands of mystery. To my surprise he says:

"I live here".

"Above the Piccolo? Wow, I didn't know that".

"No reason you should".

Nobody I know has ever tracked the Boz down to his lair. The conventional wisdom veers from *he lives somewhere* to *nowhere* to *here and there*.

The Boz leads me slowly upstairs.

"Thanks again" I say.

"Never mind. I need something in return".

"You got it".

A little voice tells me I may live to regret the gesture. As we reach the landing, he says:

"Listen". He fumbles for his keys in the dark, then throws the door open. I am blinded by bright daylight.

"Wow!..."

I follow the Boz into a well furnished loft. The wall-length lace-curtained window gazes down upon the Av. In silence, we watch the cops mop up the last of the stragglers. Paddy-wagons are flashing their blue strobe lights. The smell of tear-gas filters through. The silence renders the scene below sinister. We survey the pandemonium together.

"That's some sound insulation you got" I tell the Boz.

"They'd have me thrown out long ago if I didn't".

After which he wanders off into the back of the loft. I follow to find him sitting at a vast grand piano. He tilts his head as if to listen, then launches into a *brillo* rendition of the Bach-Buzoni variations.

I listen, entranced, through a seamless transition into Debussy's Children's Corner. After which the Boz glides effortlessly into Scarlatti's Spanish partitas, their formal white-lace architecture shot through with dark strands of Flamenco. He stops. I am speechless.

"Shit Boz" I say at last. "Christ, I'll be damned..."

"Foul mouth and all".

"I wouldn't have guessed in a hundred years..."

14

"Good".

I wait. The Boz lowers the lid and turns to face me.

"Now shut up and listen, Leo. I got a job for you. Two days, three max. You leave tonight, soon as the cops strike down the barricades".

"Hold it, Boz" I tell him, "I'm still at school, you know".

The Boz skewers me with his liquid brown eyes under arched brows that are almost feminine. He shakes his head. His grey-streaked curls are as long as mine.

"Don't bullshit me, Leo" he says. "You haven't been to class in weeks. That little bitch you been humping won't let you outa bed".

"Have a heart, Boz. Finals are up in a week".

"Nothing's up in a week, Leo. Take it from Uncle Boz. Campus is locked up tighter than a virgin's ass, nobody coming, nobody going. Off limit till the fuz finish sorting out your revolution, two weeks min. You really hot to sit for your exams, you'll be back in plenty of time".

"Gee, I don't know..."

"You seldom do, Leo" says the Boz, "so pipe down willya. This whole mess ain't good for business, case you haven't noticed. Who's gonna buy all that Thai shit with the cops camped in everybody's yard?"

I have come to appreciate the uncanny reliability of whatever information the Boz elects to share. I have done a few short hops for him, and have yet to be stiffed. Still, three

15

days is a long haul, either up north over the Siskiyous to Eugene, or south over the Tehachapees to LA. Anything can happen.

I decide to throw a feint:

"I'll need to talk to Mad..."

"If you can find her. Chances are she's either in the hospital with a busted head or in the county pen. More likely, she's fucking Mario's brain out up Grizzly Peak".

"Now, Boz..."

He beats me to the punch, and to my great surprise relents.

"Okay" he says, "I take it back. No hard feelings, hey? Cunt's all yours, go talk it over with her. There's some real bread in this one, Leo. You can split it with her when you come back, if she's still around".

We are back at the window. An army of grey-blue-and-gold is setting up camp on the Av. The Boz is right on the money.

A shutdown campus is but the least of my woes. I am flat broke and would be panhandling on Sproul Plaza with the rest of the riffraff but for Mad and her like-minded Revo groupies. They have been keeping me in tofu and brown rice, not to mention crash space, ever since my rude eviction from a North Oakland dump for falling two months behind on the rent.

Then there's Nam.

16

"Can I use your phone, Boz?" I ask.

He is standing next to me, surveying the apocalypse below with curious satisfaction.

"Local?"

"Yes. If not, I'll reverse the charges".

"Be sure you do. I'm not into charity this week".

"No sweat".

I dial Mad's number and get one of her roomies, who recognizes my voice and doesn't seem overjoyed. Mad hasn't been back since early last night.

I put the phone down. The Boz is still at the window, where his trim silhouette is framed in the incandescent white lace. The mid-afternoon sun has finally broken through the fog, and is flooding the room with brilliant shafts of gold. It is practically summer, if only for a day.

I sigh, pick up the phone, dial the operator and give her the familiar ten-digit number. Then I wait for my call to go through.

Three rings, a click, then the familiar voice-- cultivated, businesslike, melodious. My mother's voice, transforming the monosyllable into a drawn-out triple mora, the last trace of an otherwise thoroughly eradicated Texas honey:

"Ye-ae-asss?"

I cup my hand around the mouthpiece and say, as softly as I can:

"Hi Mom".

My mother's voice transforms immediately into a vivacious exclamation:

"Leo honey, thank God! Where are you?"

"Berkeley".

"Are you alright?"

"Sure, why?"

"We've been watching TV, I could swear I saw you being clubbed... Your father's been calling the hospitals. Are you alright?"

"I'm fine, Mom".

"You're not joshin' me are you, honey-chile?... Leo?"

"Honest, Mom, I'm fine".

"Then why are you calling?"

Not much wiggle-room there.

"I gotta get outa here, Mom. Place's a madhouse, you saw it on the tube. They shut down the campus, we can't take our finals. It's a f--... it's a mess, mom".

There is a long pause. My mother is considering my news in light of all the other times and places. When she speaks again, we are back to our old fencing grounds.

"I'm not holding you there, Leo" she says. "It wasn't *our* choice".

Berkeley was to be my last free ride, subject to the grimmest stipulations, which we both remember.

"Cool, Mom. I need money for the bus".

"The bus where?"

"Home".

18

"You mean *here*?"

My mother's antennas are keen, and now fully extended. She has been a pillar of the same small community for over two decades, and is the last one in need of reminding where home is. I sigh. In the art of negotiating with the superior gender, my mother is my first and best tutor, an acquiescent early victim but also the most accomplished graduate of the Leo Swenson school of devious ploys and wild tacks. My bag of tricks have been honed down to a fine edge on the whetstone of her wary patience. I am in equal measures her crowning glory and her crushing defeat.

Into the receiver I mumble:

"Where else, Mom?"

"Well... I better talk it over with your father".

A straight *no*, that one. Still, I would hate for my mother to think I have lost my touch.

"It's kinda urgent, Mom" I tell her, "I'm being squeezed".

"Squeezed?"

We have been here before.

"It's a long story, Mom. Maybe when I get home, if you really want to know. In a nutshell, the pigs have shut down the campus. I've been kicked out of my apartment. I'm flat broke".

"I see" she says. "Tell you what, honey. We'll wire you the ticket, you pick it up tomorrow at the Albany Greyhound".

Checkmate in one move.

"Mom" tell her, "it'd be easier if you just sent the money".

Indeed.

"Leo honey" she says, "are you all there?"

"What do you mean?"

"Are you listening?"

"Sure".

"What I mean is, are you listening to yourself?"

"Well..."

Now, as sure as the rain, comes the dread litany of my past infractions.

"Was it Bennington first, Leo?"

"Well..."

"Then Williams, right? Then Oberlin?... Oops, I forgot Emory, that must have been before, right?"

"Yes, Mom".

My mother recites the rungs of my descending ladder with practiced ease, never mind the deliberate lapse on Emory, where I lasted all of seven weeks with my tuition never refunded after a number of indignant letters from the Dean of Student Life.

"St. John's of Santa Fe, was that next?"

The silent immensity of the High Desert, the sharp sting of the snow-capped mountains, my first introduction to the magic cactus.

I shoot a quick look at the Boz, who is still at the

window.

"Yes, but..."

But my mother is enjoying herself.

"Then Reed?"

Hard living in a leaky barge on the Willamette river, the brilliant halo of acid-colored haze.

"Have I left any out, Leo?"

"No, Mom".

I sigh inwardly. My mother must be doing the same at the other end. Berkeley will be my seventh straight strikeout. Also a fluke, since for once it is--actually, genuinely, certifiably--not my fault. I have been making an honest-to-goodness attempt at, and have come perilously close to, graduating. Eight years.

"Never mind, Mom" I tell her. "Gotta run".

"Hold it, honey. The ticket will be there tomorrow at ten. You gonna use it?"

"I don't know, Mom. I gotta think".

A long pause.

"I love you, honey-chile".

"I love you too, Mom".

"I'll tell your father you called".

"Sure. Tell him I said *hi*".

Let sleeping dogs lie. I know my mom is close to tears, as I am. She must be thinking of Nam too.

The Boz eyes me speculatively from his vigil at the window.

"We're in business then?"

"Guess so. When do you want me to leave?"

"Tonight. Soon as things cool off".

"I'll need to stop by Mad's to pick up some clothes".

"Let me make sure first the coast's clear. The cops might be looking for you".

"What do you mean?"

"This long-hair dude they showed on TV, beating up a motorcycle cop in an alley off Durant?... Sure looked like you".

"But that was--"

So that's what she saw on the tube. Shit.

The Boz shakes his head:

"Don't tell me" he says, "You don't want to know what I think either".

"But it was..."

The Boz's dark locks bounce to some hidden rhythm.

"Makes no difference" he says, "not if the cops think it's you on the newsreel. So far nobody's mentioned a name. Still, if I were you, I'd pack up while I'm at it, case you decide not to come back".

"That's ridiculous".

The Boz shrugs.

"It's your life, Leo. You fuck it up whichever way you want. Now go take a nap".

The Boz points in the direction of his bedroom. I go in and am down and out in a jiffy.

•　　•　　•

This is how I find myself driving a beat-up 1957 Plymouth down US 101 at three AM, wide awake and still shaken, past the shuttered fruit stands south of San Jose toward Gilmore. The Boz's beat-up brown suitcase is stashed in the trunk, a crisp C-note roosts in my wallet. I also have an LA phone number memorized.

"You ask for Gary" the Boz said, "he'll tell you where to deliver. Payoff at the other end".

"How about the car?"

"Keep it. My treat".

"Is it hot?"

"Lukewarm".

"Meaning?"

"Body's hot, plates are good for three more months. Long's nobody takes too close a look at the serial number, you're alright".

"I better dump it then".

"If you like. Just make sure to wipe off the wheel and doors".

Some treat.

Just before Salinas, on an impulse, I make a right turn and, skirting the sleeping town, head for Carmel and Highway One. If the cops are serious, they will be looking on 101.

The scenic route slows me down, which is just as well, I am in no hurry. And the Boz has gassed me up to Morro Bay. I tune in to a Fresno redneck station on the AM and soak up a bellyful of cowboy heartache. The plaintive music cheers me up.

Daybreak overtakes me on the cliff just north of Big Sur. I stop for breakfast at the Nepenthe station, where the barefoot hippie waitress flirts with me as I load up on carbs and Tabasco. By noon I regain 101 at San Louis Obispo, only to let go again south of Oxnard. From there I wend my way down the wave-beaten coast, with the road hugging the chaparral hillside.

It is nearly five when I pull into the sand-packed parking lot of a rundown motel, just past the spot where the highway widens up to four lanes north of Malibu. I've got the phone number written on the inside of my wrist now.

A woman answers. I ask for Gary. She wants to know who. I tell her nevermind. A male voice comes on line, gruff lower-register:

"Yup".

"I bring good cheer from the far north" I tell him.

"Another Berkeley bozo" says the voice, "just my fuckin' luck. Where are you?"

"Within range".

"What's the matter, you hot?"

"Let's just say between me, the car and your lousy suitcase, you could melt buttons".

I am tense, dirty, dog tired. I have just driven thirteen hours straight and my hands haven't quite stopped shaking.

"Lemme think" says the voice.

The sun is just fixing to set. The phone booth I am conducting my business from, on the edge of the parking lot, overlooks the shimmering water. The coastline has somehow transposed itself into an east-west axis. A fog-bank is rolling in from beyond the horizon, spicing up the red dusk. I am wilting fast.

"Wake me up when you're done thinking" I tell the guy.

"Hey, no need to be sarcastic. Here's what you do. Check yourself into a motel right where you are and have a good snooze. Call me back around midnight, I'll let you know what's next".

"Can't I just pull off down to the beach and crash in the car?"

"Don't be an asshole. It'd be the first place they'll be checking. Get a motel. Talk to you at midnight".

The phone goes dead.

With the last of the Boz's C-note I check into the motel and ask for a midnight wake-up buzz. Then I toss and turn and fret as faceless men chase me across a vast dreamscape. The harsh ring at midnight is a relief.

When I call again, the woman has my instructions, which take me down 101 through the coastal cities all the way to Laguna Beach. I am expected just before sunrise.

"Park off the beach when you hit the bottom of the hill" she says, "then take a walk up the coast. He'll find you".

"How am I going to recognize him?" I ask.

25

"Just walk on north, he'll be there".

Omniscient mystery men make me nervous.

I hit the bottom of the hill in Laguna just after four. The sky is clear and crammed with limpid white stars. I park the car near the all-night hamburger joint, shuck my shoes and walk out on the sand. I am apprehensive. For over twenty-four hours now I have been stuck with a hot car and a suitcase full of God-only-knows-what-species-of controlled substance. How long will my luck hold?

I strike out due north. Even at low tide, the dark cliffs to my right crowd into the edge of the water. I clamber over the slippery rock to the other side, traversing a succession of small coves. The waves plop their small burdens in rhythmic thumps onto the hard sand. I have the entire coast to myself.

Soon the beach opens up into a wide swath of dry sand. The bright lights of Corona Del Mar are beckoning from the north. I retreat back to the last outcropping and find a precarious shelter in the thin moonshadow, where I crouch and wait.

The western sky bears a faint pink imprint when I give up and start walking back. I clear the first rock barrier and hit the sand. A lone figure is standing at the edge of the water, swaying to a slow contemplative beat. The arms are raised and lowered, swinging dreamily like windmills. A long cape whirls around the limber body. The figure keeps rocking too and fro, the hip-long hair swishing. It calls to mind a giant heron about to take flight.

I watch, transfixed. After a short eternity, the figure pauses, its back to me. A deep baritone calls out:

"You the Boz's clown, ainit?"

"Well..."

"Got a name, bozo?"

"Leo".

"Check. Keep your hands where I can see them. Drag your carcass over here. Real slow, like".

I do as I am told, advancing toward the dark figure who seems frozen in mid air, his back still to me. When I am twenty feet away, he turns around slowly. In the thin light, I make out the gaunt face, framed in stringy dark hair that runs in two cascading torrents down his shoulders. The dark cape is clasped tight under his face. His lids half-droop over impassive dark eyes that crowd together above the thin aquiline nose.

"Gary?"

"Suppose it is?"

"Then it's fuckin' time. I got something belongs to you. I'd like to dump it and haul ass. Boz says you got my bread".

The impassive dark eyes are not looking at me but scanning the cliff above, where a faint yellow band of dawn is slowly blooming.

"Whoa, not so fast".

"What now?"

27

I left my coat back in the car and am beginning to shiver. My companion is snug in the folds of his cape.

"Now we get acquainted" he says. "If I like you, we do business. Think I will?"

"How the fuck'd I know?"

The gaunt head shakes solemnly.

"You got no manners, man".

"Sorry" I say, "but the Boz said it was a done deal, that you'd know what to do".

"I do. But how do I know you ain't trailing a string of narcs? Them guys're devious".

"Guess so".

" 'Sides, nothing's a done deal till the woman says so".

A new wrinkle.

"What woman?"

"All in good time, man. Right now, the woman's said to check you out. So I'm checkin' you out. *Comprendes*?"

I stand there, my apprehension mounting, as my companion proceeds to circle around me slowly on the wet sand, his bare feet stomping a ritual hoop. I crane my neck, conscious of the low humming sound that emanates from his mouth.

"You packin', man?"

Last time I heard this was in a B western.

"You mean, like, a gun?"

He nods slowly, still circling.

28

"Like".

"Do I look that stupid?"

"Hard to tell. Not enough light".

My tall companion comes to a stop facing me. His impassive face looms a good six inches above mine.

"Woman says to bring you in if you look harmless" he says. "You harmless, Leo my man?"

"Pretty much" I tell him. Which is, I reckon, near enough.

"Ever done state time? Rap sheet flapping behind you?"

"Nope".

"You a tough guy? Bite rusty nails? Skin little puppies?"

"Never hurt a fly" I tell him. "I'm as harmless as they come, soul of sweet reason. Didn't the Boz tell you?"

"But are you truthful?"

I got a philosopher on my hands.

"That's a stupid thing to ask". Just in case he's heard of Zeno.

"Bravo" says my companion. "Woman says to bring you over if you're not a total asshole. Reckon maybe you ain't".

He turns and beckons for me to follow. We walk together in silence back to the public beach near the parking lot, where he motions me to a halt. We stand in silence, our backs to the water, watching the brilliant chromed cage of the burger joint. It is empty except for the sleepy burger-wala.

"This's where they'd be waiting, wearing their fake city-crew coveralls" says my companion. "Reckon they're not on your tail?"

"I hope not".

My companion exhales in mock exasperation.

"Just like the Boz to pack a green mule. At least you're not a pro, so maybe you're not on their list. Now go wait in your jalopy. I'll be crossing the highway over there. You see me clear the next light, start up and follow, real slow like. If I raise my hand, stop for me. Got it?"

"And if you don't?"

"Then don't".

"Is all this really necessary?"

I get the slow once-over from the hooded dark eyes.

"Boz hasn't taught you much, has he?"

Not really a question. I shrug and proceed to the Plymouth. I slide in. In the back mirror I watch Gary's caped figure crossing the deserted Coast Highway and walking in my direction. I let him overtake me in silence. His cape is keeping beat to the long graceful strides. When he is almost to the next crossing, I start the engine and follow. As I pass him, he signals casually with his hand and I stop and let him in.

"Where to?"

"Just keep going".

In the unfolding early dawn, we thread our way slowly across the shuttered town. We rise up Laguna Canyon, then hang a left and proceed all the way up to a dead-end crowned by a ramshackle Victorian clapboard in a grove of ancient oaks. The cracked asphalt of the serpentine drive has seen no repairman in years.

Deep in the hills above Laguna, the house stretches out without clear beginning or end amidst a wild proliferation of outer pods. Some, I discover later, are burrowed deep into the hillside. Others extend into the green canopy, where tree houses have sprouted like oversized acorns. Others yet cluster around the shaded packed-dirt yard, where makeshift greenhouses, vegetable beds and strung-out hammocks intersperse among the rusting vans, decommissioned school busses and stripped-down chassis.

"Far fuckin' out".

"Home sweet home" says Gary. "Park any place you like".

I ease the Plymouth deep under the thicket at the fringe of the compound, where it may rot in perpetuity. I hop out, open the trunk, and pull out the Boz's suitcase. It is bulkier than I remember and infinitely more sinister. I am anxious to terminate my affiliation with the decrepit brown cardboard and its cracked-leather straps.

"Let's see" says Gary.

He pries the suitcase out of my hand and, with practiced ease, hoists it on top of the hood and loosens the straps.

"Wanna know what it was all about?"

Under a layer of pale-green hospital towels, the suitcase is packed with plastic-wrapped rectangle bricks.

"Light up half of Orange County for a week. Wanna sample?"

"Now?"

"We wait till the rest of them are up, there won't be much left to sell. Greedy slackers... Thing is, Leo my man, how else would we know what I'm paying for?"

"I thought you were in business with the Boz".

"Sure. Me 'n the Boz go back a long way, all the way back to Nam. Know where that is?"

Holy cow.

"You mean Vietnam? The Boz was in Vietnam? In the Army?"

"Who says Army?"

"I thought..."

"Nevermind. Thing is, I seen the Boz Man pull fast ones that'd put a Cholon opium dealer to shame. I'll follow the Boz Man to hell, but that don't mean I gotta trust his supply chain".

"Guess not".

We get thoroughly trashed, the two of us leaning onto the hood of the old Plymouth, rolling joints out of five random bricks and sampling them in rapid succession. The Boz's stash is rare vintage.

The shaded yard is slowly being pierced by the first rays of the rising sun. Shimmering patches of color dance in the air above us, transforming the green canopy into a bright kaleidoscope.

"Wow" I say, "Maui Zowie".

"Thai" says Gary. "Boz's gone done it again".

We watch the color show in silence. Then, when I least expect it, my companion pulls a thick wad of green out of a deep fold of his cape and proceeds to peel off ten crisp C-notes.

"Here".

"I thought you were going to have the woman check me out first".

"What the fuck, let her sleep. She was up late. Reckon I can size you up by myself".

I tuck the money into my pocket.

"Thanks" I tell Gary.

"Nevernmind. You stick around, I might have use for you".

"How about the car?"

"Leave it where it is".

"Boz says it's hot".

My companion surveys the assorted vehicles that litter the yard.

"Ought to be in good company then. You hang on. The Woman will be up soon. She put out a dynamite breakfast. If she likes you".

2. Serena

(Laguna Hills, June 1968)

Apparently, she like me. On the evidence of the sweet greeting I receive when she finally emerges into the central courtyard in all her glory at nine o'clock, her thick honey curls trailing behind her like a serpentine halo, her bare feet striding the compacted dirt. A Rubens Amazon in martial progress, her dark-grey eyes surveying the reigning chaos with dispassionate approval.

"You must be Leo".

A deep musky voice that sits well with the rest of her.

I mutter a garbled response, at loss for words, overwhelmed by her presence.

"Gary says you'd be shy" she observes. "Come inside have some chow".

I tag along and am soon rewarded with the most delicious blueberry pancakes since leaving home. In the course of our leisurely breakfast, watching her preside deftly over the giant wood-burning stove, I am smitten, seduced, imprinted with this awesome being. Like a hapless duckling hot to trail his mama.

As is, I soon discover, everyone who has strayed into her crowded orbit. With the rest of them, I now pine for

35

morsels of her benign attention.

"You can crash downstairs" she tells me, as other denizens drift in. "Just find a free corner. Gary says you'll be dog-tired".

"Gee thanks--"

I have yet to discover her name, but I am hers for the taking. As if reading my mind, she says:

"You can call me Serena. Everybody seems to".

"Serena..."

I taste her name tentatively, rolling the delicious syllables over my tongue slowly to protract the pleasure-- Serena, Serenata, Serenissima--as I go about liberating my pack and sleeping-bag from the Plymouth. Then I descend gingerly into the dark basement, where I grope for a free corner and crash. The celestial syllables of her name spice my descent into dream.

Tacitly, with no words spoken, I have been admitted-- inducted, seduced--into the labyrinthine order of the oak-shaded Victorian in the hills above Laguna. Gradually, I discover its teaming multitude of rabbits and goats, cats and dogs, adults and children, male, female and ill-sorted others. They sway in perpetual slow-mo, coming and going at leisure, at all hours of day and night, forming and reforming into human bundles that flop together or just hang out, their fluid bonds lubricated by the triple sacrament of food, flesh and dope.

The latter runs the rainbow gamut from plants to pills

to nameless potions, sniffed or smoked or--I discover with a pang of initial recoil, soon mitigated by shared folly--injected. I succumb without thought, striving to fit in, eyes glued upon the honeyed Amazon that brightens my days and wets my dreams.

She treads the earth like an summer storm, in equal parts seductive and alarming. Everybody comes to her for succor, love or justice. The adults, the runaway teens, the kids, the animals. The household is implicitly governed by the triumvirate of herself, Gary, and his buddy Troy, who is still away on an errand. There is little doubt, though, who the hub is around which our lives spins. She may be old enough to be my mother, but one free and wild and immeasurably seductive.

The five boys, whose ranks seems to swell at times to a baker's dozen, are all hers, each, it seems, by a different father. The oldest, a shy strapping of fifteen, hangs out with the runaways. The youngest, a curiously quiet but perpetually mobile two-year-old who delights at being underfoot, may or may not be Gary's. Together with the three rambunctious ones in-between, they run the gamut of American ethnicity.

● ● ●

It is early in the morning. I have been here for a week and a day, a count that is beginning to loose sense. An insistent hand is shaking me out of my dream.

"Rise 'n shine".

"What the fuck..."

I sit up and blink. In the dim shadows I make out Gary looming over me.

"Shush" he says, "you'll wake up the whole bloody world".

"Wha's happenin'?"

"Action time".

I follow into the yard, where we seem to float inside a damp cloud. The vegetation overhead is spraying us with a fine drizzle.

"What's the rush?" I ask.

"Tell you later".

We hop into my car, start and descend down the narrow canyon in the fog. The windshield clouds up in a minute, the defroster is out of commission, not that I'm surprised.

"Where're we headed?" I ask.

"Dana Point".

"What's there?"

"Troy".

The coast highway, once we regain it at the light, is free of traffic. Everybody else must be smarter. We proceed cautiously, our headlights plowing through the grey soup.

"This is unhealthy" I tell Gary. "How far do we have to go in this crud?"

"Ten, twelve miles".

"Couldn't we just wait till it burns off?"

"We can't see, they can't see".

I would like to know who *they* are, but Gary clams up. We crawl onward in silence. Time stretches. Eventually, Gary points to a barely-visible turnoff sign. We drift to the right. In a minute, we emerge in what seems to be a small town. Street lights pop out of the fog and sink back almost immediately. The pounding surf just ahead suggests we are still on the coast.

Several blind turns follow, leaving me disoriented. We cruise into a parking lot, I proceed slowly past the parked cars till I spy an empty space. I maneuver the Plymouth in, barely missing a pickup crowned with a large cab-over camper.

I turn the ignition off. In the ensuing silence, I can hear the surf swatting itself on a wooden surface nearby. Otherwise, we are engulfed in a blanket of fine mist.

"Wait here" says Gary, diving into the void.

He rejoins me ten minutes later. We circle the parking lot twice before he points to an alley that leads out along a wooden wharf lined with a tangle of masts and sterns.

"That one" he says, pointing.

I see nothing and say so.

"She's easy to miss" says Gary.

When we finally pull to a stop, we are parked across the plank from what appears to be a thirty-foot sloop. Her sails are piled at the bottom of the boom. On the curved aft I make out the faded name:

Serena-II

Long Beach

We wait. Presently, a burly figure materializes on

board and leans over the rail. Gary and I get out of the Plymouth and make our way slowly up the swaying plank. A short hop, and we are aboard and following our silent guide. In the downstairs galley I watch Gary and our host exchange an elaborate handshake.

"This here's Leo" Gary says, "refugee from the north".

The man who now crunches my fingers is stocky and of medium height. His facial features are concealed in the vast dark-red beard that reaches half-way down to his waist. The narrow blue eyes above the snub sun-burned nose scrutinize me wearily.

"Troy" he says, finally releasing my hand. "Gary says you're okay. How's the Boz?"

"Flyin' high, last time I seen him".

"Cool cat, that Boz, hey?".

I nod. The two of them, standing next to each other, are a study in contrast. One dark and streamlined, vertical and eerie, the other hairy and squat, a sun-bleached mossy rock.

The rock turns to Gary:

"Sure they're not tailing you?"

"In this fog?"

"How would you know?"

"No way".

"You say so".

In the protective cover of his thick foliage, it is hard to make out whether Troy's faded blue eyes, now fixed on Gary, signal assent or challenge. The two of them seem to transmit over a private channel. Gary's dark eyes deflect the challenge.

"Wha'd'ya wanna do?"

"Shit" says Troy, "they would've hit me by now, I was sure they were on to me right when I left Ensenada. Got real spooked, almost dumped the load just before dark. I think I lost them in the traffic though. No way they could've hung on to me in this weather".

"That so?"

The two of them are again communing in silence.

"I'm clean's a whistle, man" says Troy. "Are *you*?"

Gary shrugs.

"There's one sure way of finding out".

"How's that?"

"Where's the Bronco?"

"Coupla slips down. It's cool, guy's away".

"How long would it take to load up?"

"Ten minutes, top".

"Okay" says Gary, "here's the deal. If they followed us from Laguna then they're hip to Leo's rig. So we load up the Bronco then let Leo pull out ahead of us. We wait five minutes, take the Bronco and split. Ought to work".

Troy's blue eyes are scanning his partner's face.

"You think so?"

"A cinch".

This is when I finally get over the shock and regain my voice. These guys are bartering away my life.

41

"Now hold it you two. Am I supposed to run you a decoy?"

I watch Gary, then Troy. Both are eyeing me speculatively, the way one contemplates a choice cut of sirloin about to be slapped on the grill.

"Didn't I tell you this car was hot?" I almost shriek at Gary.

A long, silence ensues. Presently Gary nods. A good sign? Does he understand? Sympathizes?

"See?" says Gary.

"Perfect" says Troy.

"The fuck it is!" I tell them.

I am about to lose my cool when Gary intervenes.

"Don't you see the beauty of it, Leo my man? These guys are after us and the dope. They're narcs, *comprendes*? They don't give a shit about you and your hot car, you ain't on their radar. They stop you, they see you got nothing, they let you go, then try and chase after us".

"Says who?"

"Says your uncle Gary. It'll be a coupla hours, tops. All you gotta do is act natural".

"Be cool, play dumb" says Troy.

I let it pass. My relationship with Troy seems destined to the dump.

I turn to Gary.

"Suppose they call the DMV? Or the Alameda County Sheriff? I was on the fuckin' tube last week. For all I know, there's an APB with my mug on it in every post office by now".

Gary pats me reassuringly on the shoulder.

"Have faith, man" he says. "These guys are Feds out of Tucson. They don't give a shit about Berkeley, rich hippie kids getting even with daddy. They stop you, what've they got on you? You're a sweet college kid driving to visit your aunt in San Diego. You pulled off to wait out the fog, you don't even know where you are. They'll cut you loose once they find nothing in the car. Just make sure you got nothing there. Here--"

Gary peels off five fresh C-notes from his ubiquitous wad and hands them to me, his dark eyes unblinking, free of guile or remorse.

"Have yourself a big breakfast, then come on back to the house. We make it, we cut you in on the deal. Alright?"

"Shit" I say. But I've already taken the bills. "You should've told me".

I must sound like a wimp.

"You're going to drive out anyway, right?" says Gary. "So what's the big deal? We're the one stuck with the dope, right?"

Unassailable logic.

"Tell you what" he says.

He is talking to me now like one would to a child needing a firm hand, a pat on the back, maybe a spanking.

"Instead of going back up north, you turn right and

43

drive south. If they ain't stopped you by the time you hit Seaside, you're in the clear. Hang a huey and come back to the house".

Under the protective guise of the grey mist, I help them pull the plastic-wrapped bales off the sloop and load them into Troy's Bronco, now parked next to the Plymouth. In ten minutes, they wave me off.

I crawl out blindly, all alone, groping my way back to the highway. I am shivering uncontrollably. My gut is knotted tight with premonition.

●　　●　　●

It all reels out just like Gary said it would. Ten minutes after I regain the Coast Highway, just before the turnoff to San Clemente, there are red lights flashing in my rearview mirror, a siren's crescendo pierces my eardrums. I pull over onto the shoulder and turn off the engine, cussing myself and preparing for the worse. Three cars brace me almost immediately. I am yanked out at gunpoint, spread-eagled on the hood, cuffed and body-searched. They march me into the closed van in front, from the back of which I watch them as they trash the Plymouth and toss my meager possessions out onto the shoulder. Then I watch the three Feds mill around the Plymouth, kicking gravel. When I've had enough of watching them getting nowhere, I turn to the clean-cut guy behind me:

"Maybe if you guys tell me what this is all about,

I might be able help?"

I get no response. The guy's ice-blue eyes are scanning the deserted highway to the south, where the fog is now beginning to lift.

Presently the whole crew converge back on the van. They are clearly disappointed, but the grilling I receive is half-hearted.

"Where is it?" the stocky one asks.

"Beg your pardon?"

"Where's the stuff?"

"What stuff?"

"Don't be cute with us, scumbag".

We go at it back and forth for a desultory forty minutes, in the course of which I trot out my putative aunt in San Diego. They hardly notice, their heart is set on the missing cargo, now tucked away safely somewhere in the hills to the north. Incredibly, just like Gary said, they've got nothing either on me or the Plymouth.

I thank the Good Lord for strict compartmentalization and need-to-know. An old gem out of Lao Tse floats by:

> *When the rulers are dull and lazy,*
> *The people are snug and content.*
> *When the rulers are smart and busy,*
> *The people are bitter and restless.*

Just as abruptly as they pounced out of the fog, the Feds depart. I stand by the old Plymouth--doors pried open, seats ripped apart, hood and trunk flapping forlornly--and watch them make their U-turns in unison across the wide median, like trained Orcas. When they are gone for a few minutes, I gather my possessions slowly. I have no idea which way I should be heading.

●　　●　　●

It is almost dark when I glide down the hill to the traffic light, make the right turn and head up Laguna Canyon. I have spent the day on the beach south of town, waiting for a sign. None forthcoming. By the late afternoon it becomes clear I could not stay away from Serena.

As I reach the turnoff, my excitement mounts, as does my apprehension. I stop, pull the Plymouth off the road and try to clear my head. Nothing doing, I am drawn uphill like a helpless magnet seeking its boreal destiny. As a half-assed concession, I leave the car at the bottom and hike the last three miles up, slowly, cautiously.

Nobody there. The house is dark, the vast yard under the oaken canopy is an abandoned battleground, the contending armies having decamped to live and fight another day. The scene is shrouded in eerie silence.

I peer out cautiously from the shelter of the rocks in the back of the house. Nothing is stirring. Then a damp nose on the back of my knee startles me to palpitations. I jump, then crouch and grope about. A small mutt is wagging its scruffy tail at me.

"Shit, puppy" I say, and I crouch and pet him, immensely relieved. His hair is thickly matted. He licks my hand.

"Good puppy", I tell him, "sweet puppy".

We seem equally relieved to have found each other, both alone in the world, left behind with the gutted car-hulks under the dark canopy, with the dirty clothes and garbage and mutilated children's books near the TV, whose opaque eye glares blankly as we scout our way from one deserted room to the next.

"It's you and me against the world, pup" I tell him, pulling my sleeping-bag off the floor and rolling it in a bundle.

I could crash there for the night. Maybe for eternity? But the plug has been pulled out of the place.

"She's not here" I tell my companion.

Together, we shuffle back down the road, the mutt keeping pace beside me. We reunite with the Plymouth at the bottom. I open the door and the mutt clambers in with a well-practiced hop. I dump the sleeping bag in the back seat, start the car, and am about to pull away when a tall figure detaches itself from the thick chaparral and hails us.

"I wondered how long it'd take you to make up your mind" she says, as she pulls the door open and seats herself next to the pup.

For a moment I am dumbfounded. Her mere presence next to me in the dark is overpowering. A wave of great relief washes over me, I feel weak. The puppy has clambered onto her lap, and is busy wagging his tail and licking her face.

"Sweet Jesus..." is all I can finally manage. My heart is thumping like an unruly yo-yo, I can't believe she is right there next to me.

"Leave Divinity out of this" she says. "And make a U-turn next chance you have, we're going the wrong way".

I slow down, pull into a narrow driveway and turn the Plymouth around.

"Where are we heading?"

"East" she says, "then north on 395. Ought to make it to Hemmet before crash time. How much gas you got?"

"A little bit".

"Better fill up at the Union station in Irvine".

I am trying to process her directions.

"How did you know I'd be back?" I ask her.

"Let's say I had a hunch".

"Where's everybody?"

"Gone".

"Did Gary and Troy make it back?"

She pauses. There's more to it than she will share.

"They called from Lake Elsinore".

"Where's that?"

"Out in the sticks, east of here".

"What are they doing there?"

"They're on their way" she says cryptically, "they said the house might ge t busted. At least they had the decency to call..."

A long silence follows. She must regret losing her home. As if reading my mind, she says:

"I suppose it was time to move on. Happened before, best way to get rid of the garbage. We've been there for almost two years. Fuckin' lifetime..."

Regret? Resignation?

"How about the rest of the troops?"

"Hauled ass. Just as well, it was time to cut the herd size, grazin' was getting lean".

"Where're the kids?

"With Gary and Troy. I sent them over with one of the refugees".

As we reach the top of the canyon, the country opens up. We gas up at the Union station, where the sleepy attendant is glad for the company and would love to talk through the night. We seem to be in a hurry, tho.

We are past Irvine, climbing slowly east into the foothills, when I finally get down to asking her:

"How come you stayed back for me?"

"Don't be silly".

"They didn't tell you to forget it?"

"They did".

I hear the note of barely-suppressed fury in her voice. In the dark, I have a strong urge to stop the car and turn the dash light on, so I can see her face.

"Steady now" she says.

Then she adds:

"Yeah, they told me".

"How come you waited then?"

"Let's say I didn't like it. Say I thought you got a bum rap? Does it matter? Besides, I need a vacation from all those kids. Gets to you after a while, especially the big ones".

I wait.

"Those two jerks..." she says presently. "They said the Feds followed you, said not to worry, that you'd be alright. Fuckin' bullshit. Someone had to make sure... You walked right into a bust, took the heat for them. Someone's gotta care..."

I wait.

Her next comment is blunt, almost derisive:

"You don't know those two" she says, "or you wouldn't trust them further than you can pitch a dead mule".

"Well..."

I find myself ready to defend Gary and Roy, but she cuts me short.

"Men" she says. "Just like kids, only much worse".

She is about to say more, then checks herself. I wait. After a while she says:

"There's a hamburger joint at the next intersection. I'm starved".

●　　　●　　　●

And so we embark upon our Odyssey across the Western desert due north and then east, in the Boz's medium-hot '57 Plymouth whose engine sounds like it is about to give up the ghost. With the mutt and Serena snug in the seat next to me and my meager possessions in the back seat. And, this time courtesy of the Feds, no incriminating evidence in the trunk.

We traverse the dreaming Orange County in short order and hook up with US 395 north of Elsinore.

"Just remember" says Serena.

Remember what?

It is past midnight. We have settled down in a nondescript one-room motel cabin on the outskirts of Hemet, where we have been making love for an eternity. I am flat on my back, deliciously sated, light-headed and limp like a puff of lint. Serena has just turned to me in the dark, rising on her right elbow, smoking. The three of us are bunched together in the middle of the sagging queen-size bed.

"Just remember" she says, "once we get there, none of this has happened. Nada, zilch. Don't ever think about it, and it won't happen again. So don't go all gooey-eyed on me, hey?"

She may be prophetic, tho too late to do me much good. For I had fallen in love with her, head over heels, that first morning under the canopy of the oaks.

In the dark, I fumble for a better deal:

"Why?"

"As a rule" she says, "I don't two-time my ol' man. Took years to learn it's bad medicine. Still, you and I have three days of hard travel ahead of us, even if your jalopy doesn't quit in the middle of nowhere just like every goddam car I've ever been stuck with. So we might as well settle this sex business before it gets out of hand, okay?"

I am about to protest but she cuts me short:

"Never mind" she says, "it's really my fault. You're kinda cute, you know".

I sit up to better see her face. She is smiling. What I really want to do is pull her down and start all over again, but there is more talk coming.

"Besides" she says, "I owe Gary some for two-timing me with anything in skirts this side of Cabo San Lucas. The jerk thinks I don't notice, as if I can't smell the cheap Mexican perfume on his chest, doesn't even bother to shower..."

"You mean, you know but still?..."

"Still what? Shit, men are so goddamn obvious. All of you. You fall in love at the whiff of ripe pussy, sweet-talk us into letting you in, wallow in the trough like pigs, treat us real nice... Then you get smug, you go sniffing around for fresh pussy. Like fuckin' dogs... Ain't nothing special about Gary that I ain't seen before, I've had worse. Guess we must be asking for it, or we wouldn't be putting up with all of your bullshit..."

I am blushing in the dark, for I am an old hand at the game, having loved and left without looking back countless times. But there is still something I don't understand, a mystery that has always eluded me.

"Why then?" I ask Serena.

"Why do you think?"

"Beats me".

"Beats all of you" she says. "See, you don't get attached, but we do..." She pauses. "Then there's sex. Then, there's the kids. You keep hoping the knuckle-head will care about them if not about you... Plus all other things being equal, it'd be nice for a kid to know her daddy. Some daddy. Any daddy. So Gary'll do, as long as he doesn't abuse the privilege too often".

"You must have walked out on some" I observe, hoping I haven't offended her.

But Serena is through talking. Her large, veined right hand is stroking my chest, sliding down. With her other hand she offers me the tail end of the roach she has just re-kindled, as she proceeds to massage my deflated member.

"There" she says, pausing to admire her handiwork, "this is more like it.... now..."

"Serena..." I whisper, tasting her name again.

"Take it easy, you oaf, slow down..." she says as she slides on top of me. "Be a shame to let this gorgeous hard-on go preemie..."

"I love you" I tell her as she slithers down to envelop me.

"Don't be silly".

53

Her gray eyes are looming over me like twin half-moons.

"Remember?" she says. "Besides, I'm old enough to be your mother. Shit, I got a daughter your age..."

"No way" I protest.

"Twenty five. I was all of sixteen when I had her. My first".

"That's incredible" I tell her. I mean it, too. "Where is she?"

"Gone, split when she turned fourteen. You won't believe what she's doing now".

"What?"

"She's an Army nurse, in uniform".

"No shit".

"I told you you wouldn't believe it. I didn't either. Ain't got nothing against nursing though, would've done it myself if I'd had half her brains. She must've gotten hers from her dad, one thing he did have..."

"But Army?"

"Got that from her dad too. He was a marine, served with McArthur in the Philippines, used to tell me stories. Boy was a bullshitter, I must be a sucker for bullshitters. Are you one too, Leo?"

Her eyes twinkle over me, whether of mischief or genuine wonder.

"I take the Fifth" I tell her.

"That figures. You're either one already, or will be

some day when you grow up. Christ, what am I doing here?"

What she is doing is a slow rhythmic squeeze that is so delicious it threatens to launch me into higher orbit.

"See what I mean?"

Her voice has turned dark and husky.

"What?"

"I'm contributing to the delinquency of another minor... You'd think I would've learned... ooooh... this is divine..."

She is rocking gently, I have to fight hard to stay in the game. She moans, I reach up for her breasts.

"Not quite a minor" I remind her.

"You think you're a man, hey?" she says, "just because you can jack up a hard-on?..."

And who am I to contradict her? Not when she rises slowly and props herself above me and it becomes impossible to resist her sheer abundance, her lush inevitability.

Before I know it, we are back into heavy-duty sex, sliding and hurtling into delectable outer spaces, with the mutt's plaintive whine playing treble to Serena's moaning base. Yes, life may be short and brutal, but God is it sweet.

•   •   •

We make it to Vegas in the waning cool hours of late morning and linger in the air-conditioned paradise of a back-street casino through the scorching mid-day, sipping beers and blowing quarters on the chromed machines.

"No sense tempting the Goddess" says Serena, "your car deserves the charity".

When the burgundy sun tilts low over the horizon, with the red rock glaring at us from a safe distance and the sunset almost too heart-wrenching to bear, we hit I-15 again, heading north through Henderson.

"You watch now" says Serena.

"What?"

"Just keep watching".

The night overtakes us slowly, in small increments, on the deserted Interstate. The immensity of the extinguished sky is underscored by Venus rising on our left. The still-scorching wind is rushing in through the open window, blowing wild in Serena's gorgon hair. The mutt lies contented in her lap.

"Wow" I say, "wow".

"Hush".

We ply our way through the darkening void.

In Mesquite, just short of midnight, we call it a day and make furtive camp in the dry riverbed, in a thick clump of the place's namesake. I build a small fire, we sup on pop and munchies from the all-night store. Then we light up and get royally stoned. The red desert is our backdrop, the grey sagebrush our pillow, the dust-blown sky our covers.

She is crouched on my sleeping-bag, her hair hanging down like a weeping willow. I hike up her denim skirt. As I've suspected, no underwear. I mount her from behind as she bucks, seeking me impatiently.

"I saw these monkeys fuck on PBS once" she says.

We align ourselves slowly, leisurely, and I lose myself in her depth. An earlier hunch is at long last confirmed--there is no bottom to her. No matter how deep I scour, there is more. Tho I keep trying, for by now I suspect her boundless inner space may lead straight into the earth's molten core.

Just before our joint fusion, she yanks me out of my reveries with the dry observation:

"You got potential".

Her voice is almost muffled in the wild tangle of her hair, flung down on my face.

"Someone must have taught you the mechanics" she goes on, "kinda nice, ainit?... Now if you could only stop confusing the mechanics with the real thing..."

"Didn't you say love was out?"

"Dumb puppy love is" she says, "but serious fuckin' love ain't..."

For a while there she just moans. Then she says:

"There, let me show you... First thing, slow down... relax... let *me* do the heavy lifting... right... Now get comfortable, we're in no hurry to go anywhere..."

I follow her lead as best as I can. I arch back, hanging on to her prodigious hips. I fling my head back and the stars zoom right in on me, garlanding my head with a zircon halo. Thus crowned and mounted, I hurtle with her into outer space, clinging piggy-back onto Serena's majestic rump.

Somewhere along our timeless trajectory, she whispers her patient instructions:

"Gotta remember... the whole idea's not how to get there, but how not to get there... ever, if possible... well, near-ever... just hang on to the rim, balance, then climb higher... higher... just hang on in there... ooooh... you're getting the knack, see...?"

I am not sure what I'm getting, nothing I can put my fingers on. Except, I am getting laid, royally, exuberantly, body and soul, down to the marrow. In the process I am also falling deeper in love, Serena's injunction notwithstanding.

We scale the parapets in tandem and crash the sound barrier, our rhythmic convulsions twining into a sweet seizure. Soon we are hurtling downward through the sage-scented night that has just begun to chill in the pale hint of early dawn.

I drift into dreamless slumber, drained and sated, only to be awakened an hour later by a businesslike Serena, who has already gotten the coffee going and is prodding me to rise and shine.

Christ, I hope she never meets my mom. And Christ again, I hope we never get to wherever it is we are going.

●　　●　　●

We strike camp in silence, in a jiffy we are out of the mesquite and back on the interstate, streaking past the slumbering St. George, Utah, before the sun finally vaults over the jagged granite rims of the Kaibab. We have been slowly gaining altitude, and are back in cedar-and-pinyon country whose stunted denizen--dark, erect, detached--stand their silent vigil like estranged kin nursing their ancient grievances.

"Some day, if you have a chance, try to hit the sunset at St. George" she says. She is taking her turn at the wheel. "The whole place goes nuclear".

"What do you mean?"

"The town's downwind from Yucca Flats. It does something to the air, must be the dust. You can tell when they've just popped a big one, the place glows in the dark for hours like a pumpkin. Lasts for days, till the wind blows it out east".

"You've been up here before?"

"Up and down and sideways".

Her face softens up in recollection of times and men past. I would give an arm and a leg to have shared all her ups and downs, her sideways too. Not for the first time, I try to imagine what she was like at twenty. Or sixteen.

"You stop back in St. George ten years from now" she says, "see the kind of monsters they'll be hatching... When all them blond Mormon cuties hit breeding age, crawl out of the LDS pews into the back seat of their daddy's chevy and start fuckin' for Gosh-Golly real... Bet you could stand in

59

front of the church, sell tickets for the freak show..."

Serena's apocalyptic flight cheers neither of us, tho likely for different reasons. I am acutely jealous of her wild past. She may be grieving for its imminent passing. And so we lapse into silence and, in the gathering heat, make it to Spanish Fork just before noon and take our leave of the Interstate. In a gas station on the edge of town, we stock up on pop and munchies as the young attendant lusts silently after Serena's unrestrained breasts. She has tied them up with her shirt tails, so that her bare bronze midriff, belly-button and all, is exposed, driving the poor kid bongo as he pumps our tank full.

As I pay him, she says:

"There's a coupla serious uphills the next thirty miles. Think your car's up to it?"

"I don't know". Another way of saying, I am afraid not.

"Thing is" says Serena, "I was hoping to make it past Green River today, maybe all the way to Grand Junction".

"We can try" I tell her. "Might have to hitch the rest of the way if the beastie croaks".

If truth be told, I'd rather we took our sweet ol' time, like forever, to get to where it is we are going. I throw a sidelong glance at Serena.

"I miss the kids" she says, "I could never stay away for more than two days at a stretch... It's not that I don't trust the guys, they do just fine bossing them around, sometimes I think they're better at it than I am... It's just that, I get real tense if the whole pack is not within hailing distance".

The Plymouth does its grudging best till the radiator boils over just below Soldier Summit.

"Perfect timing" says Serena.

We pull over to the unpaved shoulder, park and lock up. Then we walk downhill into the ravine, looking for shade, the mutt in the lead. The scrub oak on the hillside rises taller as we progress, and is now studded with an occasional cluster of Ponderosa pine.

In the shade of one of those, with Serena's back leaning onto the rough bark and her bare legs coiled around my hips, we pick up where we left off the night before. She has lit a joint and, one hand on my shoulder, is feeding me tokes. My jeans are tangled around my boots, Serena's long skirt shelters our joined bottoms like a scaled-down tipi. In the sanctuary of this protective tent, my hands are kneading her divine ass as I scour her garden of heavenly delights. I am leaning forward into her, my face all but buried in the tangled mass of her mesquite-scented hair.

"Back home to mama?" she says.

We bide our sweet eternity. By the time our heat has fully dissipated, so has the Plymouth's. We nurse the car slowly uphill to the pass, then roll down carefree all the way to Price, the three of us cooling off in the dry wind whose bite now carries intimations of the snowcaps high above.

We make it out of Carbon Canyon and hit the flats, where the desert reclaims us with a vengeance. It is almost five and the heat is relentless. We consider briefly waiting it out right there. But Price is not the most welcoming little burg on earth, and Serena is impatient.

"What the fuck" I say " the old wreck might just make it".

I am rewarded with a beatific smile.

The Plymouth does make a valiant run, but the terrain has proven deceptive, concealing its treacherous ups and downs in the fine desert haze. We do alright on the flats, but the long haul up from the dry river-beds to the top of the mesas drives the temperature gauge into meltdown territory. It takes the entire downhill glide to nurse the needle back down to near safety.

And so we seesaw our way and in time rumble into Green River, right about eight o'clock. The Plymouth is giving clear indications of having had it. At the public park, right on the river, we pull in for an overdue pit-stop. Steam is billowing out from under the hood, the switched-off engine emits strange metallic rumbles.

"Let the poor beastie rest a while" says Serena.
"Yeah".

We are both near exhaustion from nursing the Plymouth through its ordeal of successive close calls. While the mutt goes to investigate the prairie-dog city down the riverbank, we plop down to the grass and are out in a jiffy.

Serena rouses me out of my reveries just after midnight. The air has barely cooled off, the town of Green

River is silent under its pale neon haze. A yellow quarter moon has just cleared the eastern horizon.

"The Chevron is open" she says, "let's gas up. Shall we try for Grand Junction?"

"How far's that?"

"Another hundred miles".

"Maybe" I tell her without much conviction. "We better see about that radiator while we're at it, buy a water can if they've got any".

• • •

The Plymouth gives up the ghost in a terminal high-pitch grind just before we hit the defunct desert outpost of Thompson. The two of us alight and push the car into a former gas station, the town's earlier *raison d'être*. We sit down on the hood to catch our breath. It is three in the morning.

The concave moon is suspended directly above us, spraying the decrepit remains of Thompson with fine silver dust. Next to me on the hood, Serena's sweat smells of sage and molasses. We are both wide awake. The mutt is scurrying about.

"Perfect, hey?" says Serena.

I am about to voice my dissent, then I catch her drift. She has spread-eagled herself over the hood, her skirt hitched up, looking back at me, grinning hugely in the moonlight:

"You up to it? Might be your last chance".

And sure I am up to it, tho my ardor is tempered with despair.

"Wow..." says Serena.

Her heavenly ass on the still-warm moonlit hood is wiggling in search of its naked prey.

"Make it last, Leo sweetheart" she says. "It might be a while before our ride shows up".

After which she lets me in and proceeds to transport me slowly, methodically, into wild abandon, my feeble attempt at control notwithstanding.

I cling to her beatific frame for dear life, riding her raging roller-coaster, shrieking with joy. And, *mysterium mysteriorum*, we still wind up clearing the top together. After which we plunge downward sweating and wheezing and hollering in sheer ecstasy like a pair of hogs bound to slaughter.

A minute later, a pair of headlights probe our horizon from the west. Soon we hear the approaching growl of the engine. Serena nudges me to dismount her. I do, reluctantly.

"Get busy, Leo" she says, "our ride's a tad early".

"How do you know he'll stop?"

"You silly" she says. "Just watch".

I disengage and watch Serena as she swings into action. She pulls down her skirt, grabs her handbag out of the car, pulls out a brush and has a quick go at her hair.

"Reckon I'll do" she says. "Now listen--pack your

stuff and be ready".

She darts to the roadside, the mutt in her wake. I am still rummaging in the back seat for my stuff when a mammoth eighteen wheeler screeches to a halt. I grab my pack and the sleeping bag and rush over to join Serena.

By the time I am there, a deal has been struck with the two burly cowboys in the cramped cab, who are willing to take only one of us, guess who.

My heart is screaming bloody murder, I am assailed by separation panic.

"Are you sure it's safe?" I blurt out after Serena.

She is clambering up the giant cab, the mutt riding in the crook of her elbow.

"Don't worry" she calls down to me, "you'll be alright. We'll send a tow-truck from GJ, they'll do it for the salvage. You can catch the bus from there".

All I can see of her is her backside looming high above me, and the honeyed tangle of her wild hair.

"Where to?" I scream after her as the truck revs up. "Serena!..."

"Aspen, stupid" she calls back.

"How am I gonna find you?" I holler after her, my voice choked with the intimations of doom.

"It's a small town, just ask around. We'll be either in Basalt or Old Snowmass, maybe Cow Creek..."

"Wait" I call after her, "I don't..."

The redneck in the middle, who must be panting for

her to join them, chimes in:

"Lady..."

His voice rumbles low. It carries the rough imprint of a thousand smoked-out barrooms along the Texas Interstate.

"Cut the cord, willya?" he says. "We gotta make it to Denver before noon".

"Don't worry, Leo" is the last thing Serena says, just before she slams the door shut. "We're still on the same planet".

3. Rocky Mountain High

(Aspen, July 1968)

My first few days in Aspen are spent looking--desperately, frantically--for Serena and her troupe. Alas to no avail, the earth seems to have swallowed them whole. The last of the cash I received from the Boz and Gary is soon gone. I check out of the motel and make cold camp out in the woods across the river. After two rain-soaked nights I give in and sign up as a dishwasher at the Jerome Hotel. The job goes with complimentary crash space in the dank basement, shared with a host of itinerant strangers. I subsist on leftovers from the kitchen and the occasional charitable joint from a fellow traveler.

Another week goes by, I am desperate enough to contemplate calling home. I come real close before, instead, putting in a collect call to Mad's pad at Berkeley. One of her roomies still remembers me, not too fondly.

"She doesn't live here any more" she says. She sounds gleeful.

"Did she leave a number?" I ask

"No".

"Did she say where she was heading?"

"No".

"Any hints?"

"Well..."

She obviously knows more.

"Have a heart" I tell her.

With women, I do best as the supplicant, on my knees. Must be the Goddess thing. This one hesitates but then, bless her heart, relents:

"Last we heard, Mad's hooked up with this new Swami. Took off in his entourage. She still owes us a month on the rent".

I try to digest the news. Somehow, I am not shocked.

"You know where they're heading?" I ask.

"Points east. Someone said Boulder. Who knows?"

"I see..."

Do I feel disappointed? Should I? Near as I can tell, I feel deserted.

"Tell you what" I tell the roomie, "if she calls, could you tell her I'm in Aspen?"

"If she does".

She doesn't seem to consider the probability overwhelming.

"If you see her first" she adds, "tell her her check bounced".

Her voice carries a clear ring of finality. I thank her and hang up. God, am I aching for Serena. I am also--somewhat to my surprise--pissed off at Mad. Also worried about Vietnam. And I may still have to call home.

68

At the end of the third week, my predicament is simultaneously relieved and compounded. It all starts innocently enough with hand-bills stapled to every utility post in town, alerting us to the impending visit of the new Enlightened One, Ultimate Perfect Master, thirteen-year-old Guru Maharaj-ji, lately of Bombay. He is, it appears, to grace the Roaring Fork valley with His Divine Presence, Friday night at the Community Church.

I get dispensation from my shift boss and, having fortified myself with an early cold-cut dinner, head out across the bridge toward the fork. By the time I am near the church, scores of others are trekking up the road beside me. Many more are converging on the church from all across the countryside.

I squeeze my way into the hall through the milling hordes, and am immediately assailed by a familiar cacophony. The place is jam-packed with beaded longhair folk of every age and persuasion. Bright banners fly above, leather backpacks are slung over rugged shoulders, incense sticks and votive candles waft away, their scent mingling with the acrid sacramental smoke of the good weed.

Kids in tattered overalls, patched in all colors of the rainbow, scurry about shrieking and snacking and having the time of their life. The tribal hosts in their rioting tie-dyes and sparkling amulets, out from under their high-country rocks.

An anorexic--or macrobiotic--blonde in a psychedelic sari who couldn't be a day over fifteen offers me a joint. I accept and am soon pleasantly sedated, righteously right on.

That is when I see Serena. She has just paused inside the door, surveying the crowd, her myopic gray eyes squinting. Her kids are in the process of scattering all over the compass. Gary and Troy bring up the rear.

I turn to hand the joint back to my sweet neighbor.

" 'S cool" she says, "you keep it".

My thanks are somewhat perfunctory as I plunge into the crowd, aiming for the door. My eyes are glued on the three of them as they wade their way slowly along the center aisle, pausing here and there to chat. They seem to know everybody. As I approach, I have to restrain myself from jumping all over Serena. Tho my face must betray my delight.

"Why, here's Leo" she says, feigning mild surprise. "We've been wondering how long it'd take you".

"I've been here for two weeks" I blurt out.

I am torn between lingering resentment and an immense sense of relief, keenly aware of Gary's tall frame directly behind Serena. The hooded dark eyes take me in silently. I had better prepare for the worse, but Gary steps forward and grabs me by both shoulders.

"Leo my main man" he bellows, "how's tricks?"

He seems pleased to see me. Hasn't he just dispatched me on a four-day spin across the Western desert with the sexy amazon standing at his side, the woman I am hopelessly in love with?

God, I wonder what she told him.

"Cool, man" I tell Gary, "righteous, like".

"Thanks for keeping the lady company" he says.

His eyes are on me, as are Troy's and Serena's. This is, I think, frantic with worry, where I will surely blow it. Where crude emotion will burst my near-transparent exterior. Still, if I go down now it won't be for lack of trying.

"My pleasure" I tell Gary, tell the three of them.

"We owe you one, dude" he says. "You handled the Man like a fuckin' pro. Ain't been for you, they'd have busted us for sure. Fed rap too, the worst. Was a tight spot wasn't it, Troy?"

"Was".

Troy's unwavering eyes squint at me from above the heraldic feral beard. In my unease, I turn to Serena for reassurance. Wrong move, but I am saved by the bell. Well, the cymbals.

A light-complexioned black man in white *dhoti* strides out to center stage, holding a cordless mike.

"Watch out now, time for the freak show" Gary's voice rasps behind me.

"Brothers n' sisters" say the black man, "His Holiness Guru Maharaj-ji sends his love to one and all. He thanks you for coming down to be with Him tonight. He's had a rough flight in, and is still in deep meditation. We know you'll understand, so in the meantime let me share with you the infinite blessings that have befallen on me upon meeting the Perfect Master".

71

He pauses to scan the crowd. It may have finally dawned on him he's the only black person this side of Denver. Still, he is determined to give us his best shot. Must be a strain, I can see the perspiration gathering on his forehead.

"I used to be a drug fiend" he announces, pausing for dramatic effect. "I used to be a willin' slave of the Devil, boozin' 'n whorin', shootin' 'n fornicatin'! Ten years of mainlinin' the hard stuff! Doing coke, poppin' candy, doin' hard time--you name it, I done it... I used to steal from my poor ol' grandma, used to pimp my own ol' lady... Shoot, I once turned the sweet woman in for a deal n' a plea... I was a major sinnin' dude, brothers n' sisters! I was down and out, rock bottom! The peee-its!..."

The black man pauses, nodding his smooth-shaven head. The last falsetto note of his pitch is trailing high under the vaulted beams as he waits for the punctuating *Amen* that, alas, never comes.

"Far fuckin' out, man" someone calls out.

Others join in:

"Right on, bro!"

"Keep on truckin', bro!".

"Keep on fuckin', bro!"

"Keep on suckin', bro!"

The black man does a full-turn shuffle, nimble and graceful, beaming and strutting, blowing kisses.

"Thank ye all, brothers n' sisters! Thank ye and God

bless!... So there I was, whorin' 'n sinnin' 'n shootin' away, till one day, by the grace of God, I chanced upon the Perfect Master... Better still, the Perfect Master, he found me!... Pickin' me up n' raisin' me high! Pullin' me to His Shinin' Bosom! Openin' His Infinite Heart to meeee!... He--opened--my--eyes--an'--made--me--seeeee!..."

His high note screeches over the crowd, who remain singularly unmoved.

"Well" demands the black man, "how 'bout that, brothers n' sisters? How 'bout that?..."

A lone voice floats out to intercepts him:

"Nothin' we ain't heard in church, man!... Now when's the main dude gonna show up?"

In response, the black man unleashes his *piece de resistance*, ticking off the wages of instant bliss:

"I been with His Holiness the Perfect Master for three weeks now, and look at me, I am a changed man! Healthy, Happy, Holy!..."

"Get lost, brother!"

"Clean as a whistle, my friends! Purged to my innermost membranes! No more booze! No more dope! No more nookie! I been reborn in the bosom of the Perfect Master!..."

Loud catcalls and piercing whistles drown the rest of the testimonial. The blissed-out multitude makes it crystal clear where it will draw the line--it will not be separated from its triple sacraments.

73

On the other side of Serena, Troy's *basso profundo* sums up the prevailing mood:

"Dude's bad for business".

"Fuck off, Troy" says Serena, "give the poor spade a chance".

The man on stage must have heard their exchange. He takes a mock bow at Serena, valiantly trying to outwait his tormentors. But his fifteen minutes in the sun--let alone his momentum--have expired. He has met his nemesis, our drug-shorn attention span.

As the man smile grows strained, his gestures turn disjointed, a puppet gone limp on his strings. Food missives and a hailstorm of pennies are landing all around him. Bowing to the inevitable, he beats an apologetic retreat, cheered on by the crowd, who are bellowing in unison:

"We want the Perfect Master! We want the Perfect Master!..."

Out of the blue, inside my head, I hear the utter non sequitur: *Not this man! No, not him! Not this man! Give us Barabas!*

No matter, we still get three more testimonials from like-minded fresh converts who come and depart in rapid succession. Soon even Serena's boundless generosity has run its course. Troy and Gary are sent to round up the kids. At last, we are alone.

"I thought you dumped me" I tell her. "Nobody knew where you were..."

"We had to lay low, Leo. The friggin' Feds were breathing down our ass..."

Which conjures up--how could I help it--a sharp vision of Serena's divine rear end. Nothing I'd care to share with the narcs.

"You could have left word" I chide her. "I was sure I lost you".

"Cool it, Leo. I ain't your mama".

"Who said you were?"

She eyes me evenly.

"I thought we had something special going" I remind her.

"We did" she says, "while it lasted. I told you, didn't I?"

"But that was before--"

"Don't be silly. Before, after. Same difference".

God, the difference should be obvious, most of all to her.

"I love you" I tell her.

Serena squints at me, her smile bemused, reflective. When she speaks again, it is hard to decide who has won.

"Poor Leo" she says, tracing my cheek with her forefinger. "What two weeks without decent pussy can do to a man. We better find you some of your own, mine's taken up for the duration" .

I cannot keep the sulk off my face.

"Hey, take it easy" says Serena. "We had us some real fun, didn't we? Don't kill it".

In the hush that suddenly descended upon the auditorium, I can see Gary and Troy herding the kids in our direction. I look up. In a parting of the multitude along the right aisle, a small procession is slowly plowing its way toward the stage, led by a business-suited mahogany-skinned man walking backward, loaded to the gills with video equipment aimed at the advancing entourage.

The others follow slowly, led by a diminutive silver-bearded Sikh in immaculate floor-length white regalia and head-wrap. He is pacing himself rhythmically, dancing in manifest joy. His head, on a thin rubber-neck, is shifting from side to side like a back-window doll.

Next comes a stout Indian woman in bright pink sari, her heavy makeup underscoring the harsh eyes and the frozen smile. The crimson dot at the center of her forehead floats over two deeply-etched vertical frown creases.

Trailing behind the woman in a dispirited shuffle is a pudgy brown-skinned teenager in a brilliant saffron robe. Whatever space might have once existed where his neck should have been is garlanded with a thick jasmine lei.

"Ouch" says Troy, right next to me.

I turn to look at him, but Serena's hand is patting my shoulder urgently:

"I think *that one* will do, Leo" she whispers in my ear.

Which one? Do what?

In my confusion, I turn back to look at the slow

procession, and my eyes fall on the skinny figure bringing up the rear. Her head is close-shaven. She is sheathed in a chaste white robe, holding a thick wand of wafting incense in her right hand and copper cymbals in her left. Her slim frame and graceful long neck crane protectively over the squat Perfect Master.

That's when it finally hits me:

"Christ almighty!" I blurt out, much too loud. "That's Mad!..."

"You know her?" says Serena. "Far out..."

"Shushh..." I implore.

Too late. For Mad has already spied me. She stops. In a flash, she changes course and is slicing her way through the crowd in our direction.

"Leo!" she bellows.

Next to me, Gary says:

"Better grab her and split. Them Gurus can be possessive. Here--"

He hands the three kids to Serena, as does Troy with the remaining two.

"You guys head for daylight" says Gary. "Troy 'n me'll tackle".

In the ensuing commotion, nobody seems to consult me.

"Leo!" shrieks Mad. Unnecessarily, for she is now right at my side. "I've been looking for you for ages!..."

Then she drapes herself over me and, in my

frustration, I grab her and head for the door in Serena's wake. From behind, a hectoring screech emanates from the Indian matron:

"Madharyana! Come back immediately!..."

Her piercing high-C is followed almost immediately by what must be directed at either Gary or Troy or both:

"Get your dirty paws off me, you filthy infidel brute!"

We reunite outside and rendezvous at the fork with Gary and Troy, who seem inordinately cheerful.

"Fuckin' Paki cunt almost scratched my eye out" says Troy.

In the gathering dusk, Serena says:

"Are you gonna introduce me to your friend, Leo?"

I fumble, then spurt out:

"Uh... Serena, this is Mad... Mad, Serena... Gary, Troy... kids..."

I am not at my most articulate. Once again, I have been trumped by the wilier gender.

"Might as well head back to the mine" says Gary. "You bring your cutie-pie up, Leo. It'll be easier to keep an eye on you while she's around".

Next to me, Mad has recovered her voice:

"Say, could anybody spare a 'lude? Fat Cow took my stash away, put me on some *ghoulish* herbal shit... My hands've been twitching for weeks..."

"Here" says Gary, fishing a handful of pills out of the deep folds of his cape. "Help yourself".

Mad goes for a generous helping, popping three in rapid succession.

"Thanks" she tells Gary. The smile she lavishes upon him is plainly intended to dazzle. "Sheee-it..." she says, letting out a long-held breath. "Thanks you, guys, I thought I was gonna die in captivity".

I give in and trudge along with the rest of them up the steep dirt road, sulking away in my misery, a steer led to the slaughter. Mad is hangings tight to my arm, chattering all the way up to High Noon Mine.

●   ●   ●

The lost tribe has been squatting for the past two weeks at High Noon Mine with the tacit approval of the owner, a scion of a spark-plug fortune who owns the alpine landscape for miles in all directions. The small basin is nested at ten thousand feet in the palm of a dry glacial depression, on the backside of High Noon Mountain. It is a steady two-hour trek straight up the twisting dirt road. The hard-rock mine shafts are flooded all the way to the top and haven't been worked since the VJ Day 1945, when the price of nickel crashed never to quite recover. The snow in the north-facing basin is yet to melt. I am told it seldom does before August, and is back with a vengeance by early October.

Serena is out of reach, occupying, with Gary and the kids, the one-room log cabin that squats half-buried into the

79

scree at the lip of the basin. The damp twilight inside their lodge is commanded by the lone piece of furniture, a large cast-iron wood-burning stove. The rest of us drift in daily to scavenge for food and dope and, above all, warmth. All three are in short supply up the High Noon slopes, as is money. The latter only temporarily, I am told.

I have yet to see her alone. Banished in plain sight, stymied, finessed, my frustrated passion smoldering like a barely extinct volcano. I am seldom more than a hundred yards away, but she is never alone and neither am I, what with Mad glued to my side like a long-lost twin.

The two of us, along with an gaggle of crashers whose comings and goings remain a mystery, reside in a cavernous decrepit coal shed next to the flooded mine. We are here at the sufferance of Troy, who had staked his prior claim to the large sleeping loft, where he is shacked up with his current old lady, a honey-blonde snake dancer answering to the name of Wahini. Under the steep corrugated roof, the rest of us roost among piles of rotting lumber and rusted scrap metal.

Our first night up the mountain, Troy lays down the law, one of the few times I hear more than a grunt out of him:

"I don't know what your game is, kid" he tells me. "All's I know, you did alright back on the coast. Big Guy says you're okay. Big Lady seems to like you. So I'm going along. You stay, your little bitch stays. Pick yourself a corner, take care of your own shit. House rules. Just remember, I ain't yet made up my mind about you. You a college kid, right?"

"After a fashion..."

"Fashion my ass. Fuckin' draft dodger more like it, like the rest of them rich kids sucking up to Big Guy 'n the Lady. Well lemme tell you something, smartass--I don't trust nobody ain't been to Nam. Got no clue why Gary trusts you enough to let you traipse all over the wild West with his ol' lady".

"Now wait a minute--"

"I ain't finished yet, Bozo, case you ain't noticed. You don't know Gary like I do, you ain't been in the same fuckin' mud hole with him like I been... Too many fuckin' mud holes, can't hardly remember... So you better start praying you ain't got the hots for his ol' lady, 'cause if you do, you'd better wish I ain't heard about it".

Troy's diamond-hard pale-blue eyes pin me down. I do my best not to whimper.

"See" he says, "you mess up, it don't matter he likes you, it don't matter she likes you, ain't none of that gonna save your sorry ass. So just remember, I'm watching".

"Gee thanks, Troy" I tell him. "I appreciate the confidence".

"Nevermind the college crap" he says. "Just don't forget what I said".

"I won't".

"Good. Now, Big Guy says you done some chem'stry in college. That fact?"

I am taken aback by the sudden shift. Truth be told, I was a chemistry major at Emory, tho I didn't get very far with either the subject matter or place, where my record was strewn with Incompletes, some of which took considerable give-and-take, on the long-distance circuits between Decatur, Georgia and Salt Point, New York, to expunge. That, and a solid pledge to the Emory Campaign from Leo Swenson Sr., MD, PhD. The very last time he got directly involved.

But that was four colleges and eons ago. And, shit, how did Gary know? I smell a rat.

"Gee, Troy" I tell him, "I was a chem major once, briefly, but I hardly remember any of it. See, I was stoned most of the time, hardly went to class. Why're you asking?"

"Think you can still find your way around a pharmacology library?"

"I suppose I could" I tell him, "if you gave me enough time..."

I am not enchanted with the drift of our conversation, Troy's improved manners notwithstanding.

"Good" says Troy. "We might have some use for you yet".

"What kinda use?"

"Good use".

"Nearest real library is either in Denver or Boulder" I tell him.

"I reckoned as much. Come time, we'll fly you up there. Now get lost".

82

I beat a hasty retreat and join Mad in constructing our nest.

The first week cements my new routine. I rise alone at the first hint of dawn on the western escarpment, fumble for my clothes in the dark, then slip and slide to the bottom, from where I hitch a ride to town and make it to the Jerome for my nine-to-six shift. By the time I am back, it is almost dark again.

The other denizens of High Noon Mine seem disinclined to come off the heights, for reasons that must run the gamut. Troy, Gary and Serena are still dodging Federal warrants. Serena's five boys glory in their freedom, roaming and scavenging up and down the steep wooded slopes. Serena is still undecided about the local schools.

Most of the crashers divide their time evenly between sleep and dope, trooping down to town at rare intervals to cash their welfare checks or put in a collect call home. Their feeding habits boil down to a simple rule--whoever is the hungriest at any given time is charged with buying the next bag of munchies.

•　　•　　•

When I come back to the mine the first evening, Mad is in her hyper manic phase that suggests recent access to Gary's rainbow stash. I pop the two leftover reds while she polishes off the last benny. The way I see it, the reds would make it easier to put up with her, also with my misery.

To make conversation, I ask her about the Perfect

Master.

"Shit, what a creepy scene" she says, shivering in reminiscence. "Fat Cow kept bossing me around like I was her fuckin' slave..."

She is picking her way distractedly through the large bag of cheetos I brought up with me, pacing about and munching and talking at a furious clip:

"Hey, this is divine!" she says, waving the bag like a pennant. "I don't care if I ever see another macrobiotic rice curry for the rest of my life... Wow, I don't know what I'd have done without you, Leo. I was getting desperate..."

I grunt amiably, though the accolade leaves me depressed.

"How did you hook up with that Hindu bunch?" I ask.

"The whole scene went dead after the demonstration... Campus closed off, pigs cruising the Av. Real pain... Plus my mom was on my ass to come home, yanked my allowance, fuckin' bitch... Nobody would advance me any dope, and I was already a month behind on the rent..."

"That's what your roomie said".

"Suzy?

"Whatever her name was".

"When did you talk to her?"

"A while back".

Mad stops chewing her Cheetos long enough to make her sentiment crystal clear:

"Fuck that bitch" she says, "I owe her nothing".

"Sure babe".

I can see she is having a heck of a time keeping her train on track. Our conversation has been lurching from one jump-start to the next.

"Well?" I say.

"Well what?... Oh, anyway... shit, I was running all over looking for you. Nobody knew where you'd gone..."

She stops and looks at me in genuine surprise:

"Where the fuck *did* you go, Leo?"

"I was doing a gig for the Boz".

"Shit, the fucker could've told me, I would've gone with you..."

Now that.

"Anyway" she says, "I saw this ad for the Guru, free demo at Golden Gate Park... So I hitched over and--shit, I was ready for something new..."

"How'd you like him?"

She ponders for a long moment.

"Fatso's alright" she says, "really... reminds me of my pet lizard..."

Mad's face breaks out in fond reminiscence.

"They let me edit his speeches" she says, "didn't mind that. Fuckin' Fat Cow can be harsh, tho... Right off the bat she invites me to travel with them. Before I knew it, I's part of the household... Madharyana do this, Madharyana do that, like I was her fuckin' slave... I figured, what the fuck,

I'd hitch my way East with the friggin' freak show as far as it goes... But then Fatso started getting sweet on me... Didn't really mind, 'cept for the fat bitch... She's got him on a short leash, him and his older brother... She jerks, they jump... You should hear her screaming and cussing like a fuckin' trucker..."

Mad pauses again.

"Oh, before I forget" she says, "the Boz wants you to call".

"He does?"

"Yup".

"When was that?"

"Lemme see... I bumped into him in Golden Gate Park, musta been two weeks ago... He said he hadn't heard from you..."

"Did he say what he wanted?"

"Nah... just said for you to call".

"Oh".

This doesn't bode well. But at the moment my more urgent concern is that Mad has settled next to me on the floor and seems to have sex on her hopped-up mind. I do my best to deflect her, but the devil between my legs, nasty little bugger, is being sorely tempted. If she keeps it up, I might just have to oblige.

I am again saved by the bell. For in the nick of time, Mad pauses to pop two more reds, which even for a person of her prodigious tolerance scotches immediate carnal pursuits. The two of us drift off into sleep.

●   ●   ●

Friday I get home early and the place seems shaken out of its stupor. I can feel the buzz from half-way down the mountain. I make it up just in time to turn right back. With mounds of accumulated laundry, we all troop down the slope together, then drive ten miles up the road to the hot springs in Conundrum. Once there, Gary and Troy take off in the old Bronco. The rest of us settle in for a long-overdue communal dip.

The crashers and the kids soon band together, splashing and horsing around in a merry pack. Soon Mad detaches herself to join them. For the first time in over a month, I am alone with Serena. Alone and, under the bubbling sulfurous surface, stark naked.

"How you holding on, Leo?" She says.

"Not so good" I tell her.

It is nice to have someone to confess to, however forbidden. She is a few feet away, her shoulders glistening in the moonlight. When she raises her arms to untangle her wet hair, her breasts float to the surface like a pair of killer whales at play. The near-full moon is right behind her, so that her face is in the backlit shadow. I am choking with lust.

"Poor baby" she says. "She ain't taking care of you, is she?"

87

"Shit" I tell her. "You know exactly what it is".

Under the water, Serena's big toe is tracing slowly up my thigh, and has just made exploratory contact with my exuberant erection.

"Wow" she says, "no shit... I better have a serious girl-chat with the wench".

"Don't you dare!"

She laughs. In the phosphorescent moonlit bubble, her toe is probing its target with delicate precision.

"I told you how it was gonna be, didn't I?" she says.

"You did".

She ponders for a moment. On the fringe of the pond, the kids, the crashers and Mad are raising a wild ruckus.

"Tell you what..." she says.

And before I know it, she has pulled herself over right next to me, so that her lush belly flattens itself against mine. Her burning bush is rubbing against my thigh, driving me into near frenzy. She grabs hold of my startled junior partner and, with gentle, expert fingers, rubs it to and fro in her matted *mons veneris*. Her eyes, very close now, are holding mine steadily across the steaming surface.

We must have turned around, for now Serena's face is bathed in gossamer. I can see her pupils, dilated like the full eclipse.

"Are you on something, Serena?" I ask.

"What do you think?"

"I think you're fuckin' zonked out of your gourd".

"Pretty good guess... Want some?"

I am about to answer in the affirmative, for I would share anything with this glorious *divinissima*. But her expert ministrations have finally done me in.

"Shit..." I say as I erupt, wildly, convulsively, my entire body contracting in sweet agony. With Serena's hand pressing me tight to her tangled love-mat, I blow my hot wad onto the lush surface, where it congeals almost immediately in the hot water.

When I open my eyes again, Serena is looking right at me.

"There" she says. "That was easy, wasn't it? Feel better now?"

"That's not what I had in mind" I say.

"I know" she says. "You're a hopeless romantic, Leo. But this's all you're gonna get".

I am about to protest when Mad finally remembers me and paddles over to join us.

●　　　●　　　●

Gary and Troy never make it back to the hot-springs that evening, and in fact seem to have dropped off the face of the planet for the balance of the week. I watch Serena for clues, she seems unruffled. And High Noon Mine is as peacefully sedated as ever.

As it turns out tho, not for long. For the two

musketeers resurface at daybreak when the road has dried up enough for them to coax the old Bronco all the way up the mountain. And since it is my day off, I am there with the rest of the denizens to swarm out and greet them.

Their venture must have been a roaring success. Soon the place is jumping with excitement and fresh dope. Before the day is gone, the entire tribe--minus the crashers, who remain behind long faced and are conceded the run of the cabin and some fresh dope, a consolation prize--packs up and roars down the mountain. We relocate in style at a ski lodge just outside Snowmass Village.

Several days of non-stop partying follow--daily shopping expeditions, late-night bar-crawls, traffic jams in the motel parking lot, people knocking on the door at all hours. Gary and Troy play Big Men On Campus to all comers. Their wadded rolls of green peel off periodically to dispense the largess. Everything is on the house.

Serena and the kids now sport new clothes. Wahini is freshly bedecked in a dazzling Navajo turquoise squash-blossom. Even Mad and I are beneficiaries of the trickle-down largess.

In the course of the revelry, needles make their discreet rounds, alongside sniffing implements and glassine bags of assorted white dust. I balk at first, but both Mad and Serena brand me a party pooper. Eventually. I succumb and join in.

In a last-ditch effort, I drag myself to my job at the

Jerome one more time. No use. I give it up with a shrug. Nirvana or oblivion, as long as it is to be had right here and now, I'm game. Come and get me. I am all yours.

I have just about lost track of time when Gary walks into our room one early morning. His face is deeply lined and--dark as it normally is--pallid. His long mane has lost much of its gloss, and is indifferently bundled at the nape of his neck. He waddles listlessly across the room and plops himself on the floor next to our disheveled bed.

Incongruously, the TV across the room burst into a loud detergent commercial.

"Quick, kill it! Kill it!" Mad screams next to me.

I turn the sound off.

"Go take a hike, little lady" Gary tells Mad.

"What the fuck..."

As spent as Gary seems to be, there is no mistaking the ring of authority in his voice:

"Go on. Serena's fixin' breakfast. Might have some left for you. My treat".

We watch Mad prance about stark naked in search of something to wear. Her minuscule breasts bounce on her wiry tomboy frame. She tucks herself into a white slip and bangs the door behind her.

I wince. We savor the silence together.

"Some lively pussy you got there" says Gary.

"You like?" I ask him.

"Might".

"Be my guest".

His eyes focus slowly on me.

"Share and share alike, hey? Old Injun custom. You dig, *kemo sabe*?"

The multiple ways one could parse his remark fly way over my drug-addled head. Did he just tell me he knows about Serena? Appearance notwithstanding, this cartoon Breed is neither dumb nor harmless.

Prudently, I deflect:

"Whatever".

"Just a thought, *kemo sabe*. Now listen, Troy says you can swing it".

"Swing what?"

"The chemistry bit".

Oh, shit.

"How did you find out?"

"Nevermind, that's another story. Wanna go up to Boulder? Visit the library, check things out?"

"Check what out?"

"Mescaline".

"Shit".

"Pipe down, Leo. This's just a recon job, know what I mean? Check out the procedures--extraction, purification, that kinda stuff... Lab equipment, chemicals, the works".

This is getting way too heavy.

"I don't know" I tell Gary, "it's been years. Besides,

I've never been all that good at it".

"That's not what the Boz says".

So that's how. It all figures, tho how the fuck would the Boz know? The whole setup carries an ominous ring. I smell a truckload of rats.

The gangly figure slouched next to me in an ungainly heap under his soiled cap--like an emaciated cormorant--is oblivious to my misgivings.

"I'm gonna level with you, Leo my man" he says. "We got this guy says he could get us cactus buttons by the truckload... Says he can cart it up from Sonora, says it's a cinch... Now Troy and I've been peddling them buttons one at a time for fifteen, twenty a piece max... Fuckin' stuff's hard to handle, too much bulk... Plus the customers ain't happy, shit's harsh on the stomach, got that bad poison in it, strychnine, ainit?... Takes four-five buttons to boost you into low orbit... So way before you get there, you're puking your guts out behind the squaw bushes... Now clean powder, that's something else. You boil it down to pure dust, no more mess, no bulk transport, no pukin'... Stuff weighs next to nothing, easy to stash, spots good on paper. Everybody's happy, we charge the limit. You 'nstand?"

I do. That is why I would rather not get involved. Tho it is imprudent to say so out loud.

"I don't know, man" I tell Gary.

"What's there to know? You go on up to Boulder, case the joint, visit the library stacks, ain't nothing illegal in that.

No need to check anything out, just take notes...You come back 'n tell us what's what... You like, we cut you in on the deal. Shit, you come in with us at the bottom, sky's the limit. It's a growth industry, man, we can blast the whole country sky high. Here--"

The ubiquitous green wad comes out of the cape, nine crisp C notes peel off. They are in my hand before I can get a word out edge-wise.

"You take the evening flight to Denver, rent a car and drive to Boulder, check into a motel, then call me. Figure on two-three days, hey?"

"Well..."

"Take your time, man. Shit, take a week if you like. Here..."

Another sheaf of C-notes changes hands.

"Case the joint real slow, have some fun" says Gary. "Place's a fuckin' playpen, ought to remind you of Berkeley. Shit, I wish I could take the time off, come along, show you around. Big Woman says you're miserable, says you're fadin' fast".

"Shit".

"Whatever, none of my business. You call back when you're done, let me know your flight number. I'll get someone to pick you up".

●　　●　　●

That's how come I am not there when the shit hits the fan.

Like Gary said, Boulder is a cinch. I get my library chores done in less than a day, once I figure my way around the reference section. I use another day to call supply houses and get estimates, presenting myself over the phone as a high school science teacher from Leadville, picked up at random off the map.

I stay clear of the night scene. Well, almost. I do let a mendicant Buddhist hustler--just off campus, in saffron robe and shaved head--talk me into sinking the balance of Gary's C-notes into two baggies of near-pure coke. Easy come easy go.

I take another day to come down. On the tail end of a pitch-dark low, I call home. It is late morning and my dad has already left for the hospital. My mom's voice comes on line:

"Yeae-sss?"

"Hi Mom".

"Leo!"

She takes a moment to get a grip. Once again, I cannot help but admire the resolute way she regains her feet.

"Where're you calling from?" she says.

"Boulder".

"Boulder?"

You would have thought it was Timbuktu.

"Colorado. It's near Denver, mom".

95

"I know where Boulder is. But what are *you* doing there?"

"Nothing. Visiting the campus".

"You're not thinking...?"

Her query requires no completion.

"Don't worry, Mom" I tell her, "I'm just visiting. Been staying in Aspen, mostly".

"I didn't know you skied, Leo" she says.

"Nobody skies in the summer, Mom".

"I should think not. When are you coming home?"

"I'm getting closer".

"Are you okay, Leo?"

"I'm fine, Mom".

Why do I bother faking? My mom know I never call home unless I am in a jam. What's the point, being a creature of my times and peer-group?

At the other end my mom is no doubt reminding herself the very same thing, tho her hard-earned realism is forever tinged with regret. I can only hope she is not being too hard on herself.

"I wish I could believe you, Leo" she says at last. "When are we going to see you?"

"Soon, Mom. I've got to go back to Aspen first".

"Are you in trouble, Leo?"

"Nothing I can't handle, Mom".

"You got any money?"

Technically speaking, I don't. But that is only a small

detail, given Gary's expansive projections.

"Sure, Mom, I'm loaded".

Again, it is a moot question whether she believes me. Or how she would feel about it if she did.

"Which airline flies out of there?" she asks.

"Aspen, Rocky Mountain... Why?"

"I'm going to wire you a ticket".

Again?

"Thanks, Mom" I tell her, "I don't need it".

"It'll be there just in case. You never used the one I sent to Albany".

"I didn't need that one either".

"Never mind" she says, "you take care now, honey-chile, y'hear?"

Something clicks home. The syrupy meltdown of South-Texas vowels. Faint echoes of our early intimacy, you and I kid in the big empty house?

"I will, Mom" I tell her.

"I worry about you, Leo" she says. "I know it's no use, but still I do. I'm not going to tell your dad about this. He's got enough on his mind as it is. He's on the draft board now, you know? He's not enjoying it".

Sending poor suckers to Nam? My dad?

She will tell him though, sooner or later. My parents' union is founded--always has been--on a distressing amount of information flying over my head in both directions. Information proffered, pondered, digested, sometime regurgitated in long self-revelatory binges.

For the record, I tell her:

"Thanks, Mom".

"We love you, Leo".

"I know. I love you too, Mom".

"We'll be looking forward to seeing you soon".

"Sure, Mom".

The line goes dead. I feel like crying.

I call the lodge back in Snowmass, just before my flight takes off. Nobody answers from the room, the desk clerk says. There's something funny in her voice when she tells me the previous occupants are there no more. I dismiss the thought. The party must be over, must've gone back to the mine.

I am still not worried when nobody shows up to meet my late-evening flight. I make it to the luggage ramp and wait. I almost jump out of my skin when Serena's discorporeal voice floats over from behind me:

"Don't look" she murmurs as she passes, "just get your stuff 'n walk out to the road... Make like you're going to hitch a ride. I'll pick you up, just make sure nobody's following..."

I am so startled, I wind up sneaking a look at her in spite of her admonition. She is wearing dark glasses and her hair is stuffed under a yellow shawl. I watch her walk out slowly, deliberately, clearing the sliding doors and disappearing into the ill-lit parking lot.

I retrieve my pack, make sure nobody shows undue interest, then head out nonchalantly. Serena picks me up in an old wreck I don't recognize. It reeks of gasoline, the upholstery is trashed. We drive into town, where she proceeds to meander at seeming random, circling the same block several times, parking and taking off and parking again.

"What's going on?" I ask.

She bides her time. At long last we are off again, heading back out of town on Colorado 82. All I can see of Serena's face is the dark silhouette illuminated briefly by traffic lights. She is still wearing the shades.

We turn left at the fork and proceed west. The dark Community Church looms on the right.

"Trouble" she says.

Like the rumbling flow over a burst dam, it all comes out in Serena's matter-of-fact rendition:

"They crashed the door with drawn guns" she says. "No knocking, no warrant, just kicked in the door... Kids started screaming, they were all in the front room watching TV... Gary ran in from the bedroom to see what the ruckus was all about... That's when they shot him, point blank... Hauled us all in, didn't even let me go in the ambulance with him... We spent the whole night in jail, me and the kids and Wahini... Lawyer finally showed up, ten in the morning, bailed us out..."

I can tell there's more. The car slows down.

"They got Troy" she says, "one bullet through the

heart. Barely missed Wahini".

I am afraid to ask, but still:

"How about Gary?"

"In the hospital in Denver... They flew him out the next morning for surgery. They say he's paralyzed from the waist down, won't let me visit him... I'm under court order to stay in Pitkin County... Besides, we're not married".

That, too.

"Where're the kids?" I ask.

Her voice almost cracks there.

"Family Services got them in the County shelter. They say they'll have to check me out, I may be an unfit mother... I have to go to court to get to see them".

We are approaching the turnoff. I struggle to assimilate the information.

"Where're the rest of the guys?" I ask.

"Split. The fuz drove up and trashed the mine, same time they busted us in the motel... Scared the shit out of the crashers, sent them packin'... God what a mess..."

"They'll be alright" I tell her, "the cops are not after them".

"Shit, who cares... Fuckin' rich kids, spoiled rotten... I'm sick 'n tired of being everybody's momma, Leo. I got my own kids to worry about. If I can get them back..."

Couldn't be self-pity. She is just discouraged.

"You will" I tell her.

She ponders it in the dark. The night is almost

warm. The wind rustles in the aspen.

"You're sweet" she says.

We leave the car at the Forest Service lot and walk slowly to the bridge.

"I'm going to hike back up" says Serena. "You take the car".

She must be sensing my reluctance:

"Go ahead" she says, "park it at the Jerome. I'll come down for it tomorrow".

"Why can't I stay with you?"

"The cops are watching the place. They don't know you, you better stay out of it".

"But..."

"No buts, Leo".

"Just for tonight".

"Nothin' doin'. You can't stay up there".

I try another tack:

"Why don't you come with me then?"

"Come where?"

"Anywhere".

She shakes her head slowly.

"Get real, Leo" she says. "I'm old enough to be your mother. I got five kids to worry about. And now Gary".

"For all the good he's done you".

But she stops me right there:

"Don't" she says. "Don't ever talk about what you don't know".

"What's there to know?" I tell her. "I've seen the way he treats you... Shit, you've told me yourself..."

"I've told you nothing" she says.

I reach over and, ever so gently, remove her shades, something I have wanted to do all evening. She lets me. Even in the dark, the angry dark splotch surrounding her right eye is clearly visible.

"Gary?" I ask.

"Yes".

"When?"

"At the motel... We were having a fight in the bedroom when the cops kicked the door in".

"See?"

Serena replaces the shades.

"Fuckin' big deal" she says. "They all do that, every one... You will too if you stay long enough. Just the way men are".

"Not me" I tell her.

Serena nods slowly.

"Maybe" she says. "It's no use, Leo, so just lay off-- shit, I almost forgot, here..."

She pulls a crumpled piece of paper out of her pocket.

"Mad left this for you... the Boz called. You're supposed to call back, number's in there".

"Mad..." I say. "Shit, I plumb forgot... Where is she?"

"Took off. Her Mom got a bigshot lawyer from Denver to fly in, put up bail for her, got her sprung in two seconds flat... She should be back in New York by now..."

"No shit".

"Cute little dish, that one".

I would rather not talk about Mad.

"Well, I don't know" I tell Serena.

"Cute enough for Gary".

"What do you mean?"

"What do you think?"

"He told you?"

"Didn't have to. Why do you think he sent you up to Boulder?"

Share and share alike, *kemo sabe*? I am astounded how anyone could dream of two-timing this gorgeous creature standing next to me.

"You don't mind?" I ask Serena.

She chuckles mirthlessly.

"You should have seen *his* shiner" she says.

"You *do* mind then?"

"Sometimes. Sometime I don't" she says, "long as I know where he sticks it. It's the ones I don't know about that get me worried, clap and that... It's all under control now..."

I stuff the paper with the Boz' number into my back pocket. I feel like crying. For Serena? For myself?

That's when she takes me by the hand, turns and starts walking. I hold on to her warm, rough palm, following her blindly down the steep bank all the way to the creek. We grope our way into the pitch dark under the bridge. The water is rushing through in a low gurgle that reverberates off the cement arches. Serena is pulling me after her. I follow.

Presently she stops and leans back to the rough concrete.

"One for the road" she says.

There's a wild chuckle in her voice.

I hike up her skirt and drop my pants, all in one sweeping fevered motion. Soon I am back in my private Eden, where she treats me for the last time to her perfumed garden of celestial delights.

We fly in ecstacy for what seems a whole eternity. Serena's knees are thrust over my shoulders, her back pressed to the wall. I am weighted down with her delicious mass, suckered all the way into her and then some. Or is it she who is wrapped all the way around me? Reckon, both. Though we are way beyond where the puny details matter.

Afterwards she kisses me for the last time, a slow, tender kiss that lingers on and on and, like a delicate echo, hovers above our now-exhausted passion. Then she pulls away, darting out and scrambling up the bank. Before I have pulled up my jeans and zipped my fly shut, she is gone, melted into the dark void beyond the pale boles of the aspen.

4. The Lower Depths

(New York City, August 1968)

In the near dark, I feel for the buzzer, recessed to the right of the door. I hit it twice and wait. Dim light creeps in through the cobwebbed pane high above the third-floor landing. The plaster in the stairwell is chipped. None of the lighting fixtures work. Coming up gingerly in the semi gloom, I step over a giant cockroach. Splat.

A rumble of knocks and scrapes comes from the inside, suggesting heavy locks being undone one by one. Whoever is responsible for this methodical unbuckling may or may not be checking me out in the unblinking peephole.

At long last the door is thrown wide open.

"I was wondering what took you so long" says Mad.

Shit.

But I had better backtrack.

• • •

Of sheer necessity, I travel light. Whatever possessions that had survived my magic trek with Serena are consigned to oblivion in the defunct coal shed of High

Noon Mine. I park Serena's old dinosaur at the airport's long-term lot and make my way to the lone counter of Aspen Airways. The ticket my mom had pledged is there. The first available flight, however, doesn't leave till seven in the morning.

I thank the tired counter lady for my seat assignment, walk back to the car, retrieve the key from its magnetic shelter under the back bumper and crash in the back seat for the balance of the night.

In the early dawn, I am roused by the cold. The car windows are frosted from the inside with the condensed vapors of my dreams. I kick off the assorted rags that served for my bedding, limp back to the terminal, find the pay phone next to the silent luggage ramp and put a call through to Berkeley.

The Boz's sleepy voice comes on line after the fifth ring:

"This better be good".

"It's me" I tell him.

"Leo?"

"Yup".

"The fuck you doing calling at such an obscene hour?"

"You tell me".

The Boz doesn't take long to shift gears sliding seamlessly into his business mode:

"You got enough money on you?" he asks.

"Hardly".

"Didn't you get paid?"

"That was ages ago".

"Three weeks?"

"I had some expenses".

"You had enough left for a ticket to New York".

Am I being interrogated?

"I didn't buy the ticket, Boz".

"I know".

"Don't you want to know how I got it?"

"I know all about your mom, Leo. Now, how long's your stopover in Denver?"

I pull out the ticket and try to make out the faint print.

"Fifty minutes, maybe".

"Good enough" he says, "just barely. You'll need to haul ass".

"What for?"

The Boz is surprisingly patient with me.

"You awake, Leo?" he asks.

"Sure. Why?"

"Then shut up and listen, and don't write anything down. There's a souvenir stand on Concourse C in Stapleton, just this side of gate 4. Guy'll have two keys for you. Got any ID?"

"Just my California driver's license, which is not exactly safe..."

The Boz cuts me short.

"For Christ's sakes will you shut up? Guy's not a cop, he's expecting you. Take the keys, zip over to the lockers next to gate 23, find locker 19, one of the keys'll open it. There's a suitcase in there, that's your check-in luggage. When you retrieve it back in New York, go to the United counter out in front. There's a cards-and-candy shop just behind it, on the right. Show the old lady your ID, she'll give you an envelope. It has instructions, also your cut".

Like all the Boz's deals, it sounds like a piece of cake, a walk in the tulips.

"I don't know, Boz" I say into the phone. "I mean, what would you've done if I hadn't called?"

At the other end, the Boz is swearing under his breath:

"Christ..."

Following which he dresses me down like a father would his dim-witted son:

"Tell me something, Leo".

"Yes?"

"Have I ever shitted you?"

"Well, no..."

"Ever stiffed you on your cut?"

"That's not the point..."

"Think I'm an idiot using a fuckin' amateur like you, Leo? Think I'd be doing this unless I absolutely had to?"

I wait as he spells it out for me:

"Now, just say yes or no, OK?" he says. "Big Injun's out of commission, right?"

"Yes..."

"Bad Viking bought the body-bag farm, right?"

"Yes..."

"Big Mama's got the kids to worry about, right?"

"Yes..."

"Little cunt you shacked up with is gone, right?"

"Yes".

"But life goes on, hey? Now don't it?"

The Boz pauses, letting the frugal sanity of his perspective sink in.

"So just do what Uncle Boz says, willya, Leo. I'll make it up to you, promise".

Why do I cringe?

"And Leo?"

"Yes".

"Stay off the merchandise".

I am about to protest, but the Boz has got his hook firmly in my gills. I am not exactly thrilled by the prospect of hightailing it back home penniless, bowing and scraping my way up the river, deflated prodigal son oozing contrition.

The line goes dead at the other end. I hang the receiver and run to catch my flight.

●   ●   ●

I blink twice and open my eyes wider, and Mad is still standing there in the door. Neither the oversize pink house robe nor the spiked purple hair sticking out at random tufts make her identity all that transparent. A smell of curried cauliflower chokes the stairwell, making the open door an inviting haven.

"Won't you come in?" she says.

For a moment I think Mad is about to throw her arms around me in a welcoming embrace, a gesture I would be loathe to reciprocate. Then I realize her passion is directed at my suitcase. She grabs it with both hands, hoists it up and turns, retreating into the sparsely furnished living room that smells of cat piss and industrial Lysol.

"Lock the door behind you, willya" she calls over her shoulder. "All of them... This is not exactly a safe neighborhood.... Got the key to this thing?"

"Yeah".

"Lemme have it".

Mid-way across the room, she drops the suitcase to the off-green linoleum floor.

"Shake a leg, Leo!"

"What's the rush?"

"There's a sweet incentive bonus in there for little Maddie" she says. "She's been a good girl, now she gets her candy".

I dig out the key and hand it over to her. From my perch on the lone chair that has seen better days, I watch Mad tear into the suitcase with the zest of a starved hyena. She pulls out a brown paper bag.

I look around me.

"This your place?" I ask her, just to make conversation.

"Neat, huh?"

The room is a sorry mess, but Mad doesn't seem to mind. Indeed, she seems altogether oblivious to her surroundings as she retreats at full trot to the dark posterior recesses of the flat.

"It belongs to a friend of mine" she says. "Rent control deal, I'm the house sitter. You're welcome to stay".

•   •   •

The most obvious solution to one acute problem invariably engenders another, often more acute. Having dodged the prodigal son's contrite peregrination upriver to face the music in Salt Point, I am embarked upon a joyless ride to nowhere. Slowly, methodically, I plumb the nether depths of the Lower East Side, where I am trapped in Mad's third-floor dive.

In our growing disenchantment with each other, the two of us have declared a truce, an armistice-of-convenience sustained by the reiterated ingestion of hard-core pharmacopeia. And so we dose ourselves morning noon and night with whatever the moment has dredged up. We cook it, sniff it, smoke and shoot it. In the course of our frantic rush to oblivion, we make the occasional passionless love--technical, detached, forlorn, a sad feast of the doomed.

I have no clue what Mad is running away from and little inclination to ask. Nor am I anxious to plumb my own depths. Let sleeping dogs lie. The long list of my private demons is topped by an all-too-corporeal memory of Serena's phosphorescent glow as she looms over me in slow ecstasy, her wild hair dripping sulfurous mist in the moonlit Conundrum pool. Serena in the scented mesquite. Serena backed up to the cedar trunk under Soldier Summit. Serena on the dead Plymouth's warm hood at Thompson. Serena in the pitch dark under the bridge.

Only rarely am I sentient enough to contemplate, in the briefest flash immediately extinguished, calling home.

●　　●　　●

It is eleven in the morning. I am still half dazed from last night's chemical feast. In anticipation of a quick relief, I am making ready to dope myself some more. There is a loud knock on the door.

I freeze, having just tied off below the elbow with the rubber tube that serves as my tourniquet, having just selected, after careful inspection, a vein that looks promising-- puffed, blue, throbbing. On the low coffee table, the syringe is lying at the ready, five cc's of pure snow, dissolved and sparkling.

I am pumped up to the gills with anticipation. For a fix about to be had--imagined, craved, ached for--is almost as good as the fix itself. At the very least, two for the price of one.

Hot Jesus, what a wretched timing!

Mad is spread on the couch, limp and inert, her dulled eyes scanning me without curiosity. She has already had hers, the intrusive knock hardly impinge on her satiation.

I hand her the syringe and whisper:

"Here, hang on to it just in case... Quick, the bathroom! Lock up and listen through the door..."

She is lying there, hooded eyes looking past me.

"Goddamn it Mad, d'you hear me?"

She nods weakly.

"Okay, listen--if anything sounds wrong, flush it down. The whole thing, y'hear?"

"Sure Leo darlin' ".

She nods several times, emphatically now.

I wait for her to get up and tiptoe to the bathroom. When I hear the lock click behind her, I roll my sleeve down and walk to the door. I stand and listen, checking to make sure all the bolts are in place. Not much use if it's the fuz.

"Who is it?" I ask.

"Got a Leo Swenson up there?"

A man's voice; sounds out of breath.

"Who wants to know?"

"This is the super. There's a man downstairs with a telegram for you. Says you'll have to come sign for it. Says he ain't coming upstairs."

"Okay" I say "tell him I'm coming".

I listen as the footsteps recede slowly. I can refuse the telegram, seeing as how I think I know who it is from. I wonder briefly how they got the address.

I walk back to the bathroom and bang on the door:

"Mad? It's me... It's alright, I'm going downstairs, be back right away. Hold on to the stuff. And don't shoot it yourself, y'hear?"

I walk back to the door and undo the bolts.

The man in front of the Super's flat wears a Western Union uniform. I observe him from the landing, seems authentic enough. I make my way to the bottom.

"Got something for me?"

"You Leo Swenson Jr.?"

"As of last report".

The man eyes me skeptically. I ignore his disapproval.

"Got an ID?" he says.

"I suppose".

I hand him my California driver's license. He scans it briefly, hands it back and whips up his clipboard:

"Sign here, please".

I sign, he hands me the yellow envelope.

I wait for the man to take off, then I tear the envelope open. I raise the cheap yellow paper up to the light, squinting at the faded capitals:

DRAFT BOARD LOOKING FOR YOU STOP CAN'T STALL MUCH LONGER STOP IMPER YOU COME HOME IMMED STOP MONEY AT WESTERN UNION STOP DAD

I read the faded type once, I read it twice. I crumple the paper into a tight ball and toss it in the corner, then I turn and hurry upstairs. I will have to call this time, but first thing first. I take the stairs two at a time, I stumble and crash across the second floor landing. I curse, get up and rush on.

Back in the flat, out of breath and sweating, I see Mad is back at her station on the couch, supine, eyes shut.

"Quick!" I call to her, "give it to me!"

"Why, Leo..." she says.

Her voice trails off.

"Quick! Where the fuck is it?"

She seems comatose. I turn and rush to the bathroom and throw the door open. The syringe, my fix, is lying on top of the toilet tank. I pick it up and--Holy Mother of God--it is empty. All gone, sucked dry.

"What the fuck!..."

I rush back into the living room.

"You shot up my wad!" I scream at her. "Shot up the whole thing! You fuckin' fiend! You addict!..."

In my desperate need, I am frothing at the mouth as I approach Mad, who is laboring heroically to keep her eyes open.

115

"Why, Leo..." she protests, "I was only..."

"Get up!" I scream at her.

I am shaking uncontrollably. My skin is clammy, my breath labored, the room has turned unbearably cold.

An expression of innocent alarm blossoms over Mad's haggard face.

"Why Leo" she says, "I was sure the guy was busting you... didn't want to just flush the stuff down..."

Apparently, she means it.

I look down at her. My tremors are worse.

"I couldn't just let it go to waste, sweetie" she says. "Why, you'd have been the first to scream bloody murder... Had to get rid of it real quick, right?... Seemed like the right thing to..."

My rage at Mad is tinged in no small measure with self-recrimination. I shouldn't have left her alone with the stuff. But, however good a culprit Mad may make, what I need right now is my fix.

I look at her drooping frame on the couch. Her eyes are wide open. The gravity of her situation has begun to register.

"Leo honey..." she says.

"Don't honey me!" I bark at her. "Just go get me something! Anything! Quick, before I lose it!"

I contemplate bodily harm, but will she take me seriously? I have never beaten anybody. Well, except for that cop in Berkeley.

"But I don't have any money..." she says.

"Neither do I. And its your turn to score, I don't give a shit how you do it".

"But..."

Her voice is barely audible, she is about to nod off. I grab her by both shoulders and shake her vigorously:

"Git!" I scream at her. "No sleep for the wicked till you come back with something".

And I keep shaking her till she drags her malnourished frame off the couch and yanks her quilted coat off its peg near the door. The last thing she says is:

"You'll b e sorry..."

I will be. But that's then and now's now.

I bolt the locks behind her and listen to her receding steps. Then I settle down for the wait. I turn the TV on and watch old re-runs. Seductive well-coiffed blondes insinuating themselves to nattily-dressed interns and stock brokers. I lean back and try to hold off the tremors.

I am about to give up and go fend for myself when I hear her steps approaching. I rush to the door and fling it open. Mad is dragging herself up the stairs, one hand gripping the rail the other holding a brown paper bag.

I come out to meet her:

"Quick!" I reach for the bag.

She lets go, it drops to the floor. As I go for it, I scan Mad's face long enough to take in the red eyes, the slack mouth. She must have been crying. But I am in a rush.

"Thanks, babe" I mutter as I rush back inside. My fingers are groping for the bottom of the paper bag, where they makes contact with the slim glassine envelope.

"What did you get?" I call back over my shoulder.

"Meth".

"Shit".

Not what I had in mind. For a fleeting moment, I contemplate sending Mad back out to score a better product.

"Nevermind" I tell her.

And I race back to the bathroom, the slim baggy in my hand. I tear the glassine open and pour the sparkling crystal dust into a glass. I can only pray it is not tainted. I pour an inch of tap water on top and swirl the luminous crystals around, watching them dissolve. I put the glass down, grab my syringe and suck it full, then lay it on top of the sink and roll up my sleeve. Forget the rubber tube. I aim for the old vein but miss.

"Christ..."

It hurts like the devil, must have hit a sinew. I try again and this time nail the sucker. I boost the entire load in one smooth stroke, then pull the needle out. An anemic-looking drop of blood wells out slowly at the point of exit.

When I step back into the living-room, Mad is once again sprawled on the couch. Her coat is still on, her head drooping. The purple tufts of her spiked hair are gleaming faintly in the dim light. Her eyes are wide open, tho.

I drop to the floor next to the couch and watch her with fascination, letting the meth take hold slowly. I am back in control.

"How'd you get it?" I ask.

Time for a truce, maybe a quick roll in the sack for old times' sake.

"C'mon, Maddie" I cajole, "how'd you score?"

"None of your fuckin' business, creep".

She is going to be difficult.

"Knock it off" I tell her. But my tone is conciliatory, I feel magnanimous, almost ready to forgive her.

"Sorry I was hard on you, babe" I tell her, "but I really counted on that last load".

Still no answer.

"Maddie, I said I was sorry".

The meth is finally hitting. I am wide awake, charged, relentless.

"Listen" I tell her, "listen... I gotta go downtown to Western Union, score some bread. Wanna come? Buy you a blintz on the way back".

"What bread?"

At least we are on speaking terms.

"Well, my dad's sending me some, says so in this telegram..."

I stop. Mad's eyes boring into me. There is genuine note of incredulity in her voice:

"You mean, you sent me out there to hustle for your

fix and all this time there was this money sitting waiting for you?..."

In spite of her lethargic state, Mad manages to sound outraged. She makes a stab at getting up and almost succeeds, but then pitches sideways, barely missing the hard edge of the couch. She has little control of her muscles, but there is nothing wrong with her hectoring voice:

"Why you son-of-a-bitch no-good cock-suckin' creep! You lousy bastard! Motherfuckin' leech! You made me go hustle for your lousy booster bag and all the time that money's sittin' 'n waiting at Western Union?!.."

"Now take it easy, babe" I tell her. "The money may not be there yet. Besides, it'd have been a two-hour trip... Here, lemme show you..."

My hand dives into my pocket in search of my dad's telegram, coming out empty. Too late I remember pitching it in the hall downstairs.

"Shit, fuckin' telegram" I say, "let me go down and..."

But Mad is not about to let me finish:

"Fuck you!" she screams at me.

She has finally managed to pull herself up on her wobbly legs. She turns on me, her mouth spewing invectives:

"Creep! Louse! Motherfucker! Get out of my house! Get out! Get ooooout!..."

And impaired as she is, she takes a swing at me with her balled fist, losing her balance so that I have to step in and

120

prop her or she would have crashed face down. Which doesn't stop her from flailing and spluttering some more. Before I know it, she grabs my hand and sinks her teeth into my knuckle.

I scream and slap her with my free hand.

She lets go, teeters, then takes another swing at me, and I shove her to the couch, where she crashes on her side, face upturned. Her eyes are locked on me, she is breathing hard and feeling for her face, one finger tracing a slow circle around her split lip.

Which is when, with nary a warning, my junior partner in crime and punishment begins to stir, inexplicably.

"Hey babe..."

I should know better, but my colossal hard-on is driving me bonkers. Soon we are back at it, thrashing joylessly, with Mad's unblinking eyes fixed on my face.

I must have fallen asleep in spite of the meth. When Mad rouses me up, I am a tad disoriented. She is standing over me in her bathrobe.

"What's up?" I groan.

"Come" she says, "I wanna show you something".

I am about to object but then think better and let Mad guide me to the door. She opens it just a crack:

"Come take a look".

I peer cautiously out onto the landing. In the dim light, I see a dark pile at the top of the stairs.

"Go ahead" Mad urges me, "take a look".

I start toward the pile, and that is when she shoves me out with both hands. I pitch forward, stumble and crash head first. Behind me the door bangs shut and the bolts click in, final as gunshots.

"What the fuck!..."

"Stay out, creep!" Mad's voice screams from behind the bolted door. "Your stuff's all out there. You ever come back, I'll call the cops".

My right knee is throbbing, the heels of both hands are badly grazed. In the dank gloom of the landing, I fumble for my ill-assorted possessions. I work my way slowly through the pile, pulling out a T-shirt, crumpled shorts, my lone pair of tattered jeans. Thank God, my wallet is still there. I fish out a pair of ripe socks, my perforated sneakers, the Navy surplus pea-coat.

I sit on the top stair and dress myself slowly. I find my green canvas bag and cram the rest of the pile in. Then I go back and bang on the door:

"Mad!..."

No response.

"I'm outa here" I advise the blank peephole. "I'm leaving my stuff near the door, I'll come and get it as soon as..."

"It won't be there when you come back".

"Whatever" I tell her, then turn and walk down and out of the building into the blinding afternoon haze.

My blood is humming along at a high pitch. I feel

122

relieved and light hearted, fancy free and supremely competent, up to anything life may dish out. A sated bug in prime garbage, on top of the heap, invincible. I cast Mad out with no further thought, flying high in all my splendor. Just when I am ready to intone my departing mantra--*fuck the cunt, no big deal*--I hear the window squealing open three floors above, then a descending object swishing through the air.

I look up just in time to leap aside and dodge the missive that crashes next to me on the pavement with a thud, accompanied by the thin ring of broken glass. My army surplus bag is lying on the pavement next to my mangled paraphernalia.

I step carefully around the debris and pick up my bag.

"What the fuck" I say aloud, "bitch's gotta have the final word".

●   ●   ●

A sharp maritime drizzle is blowing straight into my face. It is downright invigorating, a reminder of the changing seasons after a year in California. I take a deep breath, look both ways, turn up my collar and march toward Avenue B. The prospect of money waiting at the other end keeps me warm.

In the Western Union office, I go to the window, produce my ID, scrawl my signature and collect the tan envelope. I tear it open. Two ten-dollar bills are mocking me. Just enough for the train fare upriver, hardly enough for a midget-size fix. Someone is determined to keep me on a short leash.

I step out, scout for a bench, and sit down. My ears are ringing. The drizzle is falling harder. My hair is soon soaked and plastered to my skull. Water is seeping under my collar.

I am waiting for a sign.

An elderly man carrying a chessboard under his arm walks by on his way back from Tompkins Square, driven away from game and camaraderie by the monsoon weather. He is neatly dressed, his tweed cap pulled down over his brow.

"Hi" I call out softly, just as he passes.

In spite of the drizzle, he stops to chat. That is, he chats away while I try to keep up. Sweet old man, no care in the world, nobody to go home to but the cat. Maybe an old wife with a list of grievances that go back to their honeymoon in Atlantic City, which he can't remember, or won't.

"What're you up to, young man?" he asks.

"Nothing much" I tell him, "got the time?"

He digs under his coat and pulls out an old pocket watch.

"One fifteen".

"That early?"

"Think so?"

"Who knows? Thanks, tho".

The old man departs. I get off the bench and walk toward Fifth Avenue. I go past a corner luncheonette, I should be hungry. I walk back and shove my way to the counter. My bag gets tangled behind me, I turn to apologize, then order a coke. It is slammed hard in front of me. The guy's eyes are unforgiving.

"Quarter" he says.

"Here".

I drop my last quarter to the floor.

"Sorry..."

I fumble under the counter, my neighbors don't make it easy. Someone steps on my pinkie. When I come up with the quarter, my hands are shaking.

"Here" I tell the guy and drop the quarter on the counter. "Sorry..."

His hard-boiled eyes fix me, I gulp down my coke. As I squeeze out, I catch a glimpse of myself in the mirror. I look like shit, scruffy beard sprouting in uneven patches, dank curls framing a stranger's gaunt face. The people at the counter will trade uncharitable comments once I've gotten out of earshot.

I am fifty yards a way when I remember my bag. Fuck it.

A freak among the hale and upright, I could use some rest, some solace, some TLC, someone to share my misery. A most inopportune moment for my father's alert, clean-shaven face to pop out and float in front of my eyes; but pop it does, beaming its omniscient benevolence.

I shudder and chase the apparition away. *Lay off, dad, let me be.* I look furtively over my shoulder to make sure no one is listening.

I turn and walk north. Time to throw in the towel? Walk over to Lexington Avenue, catch the uptown subway to Grand Central, hop the train up-river, get off in Poughkeepsie, dial the all-too-familiar number, then wait for the ride? Concede, face the music?

A bare residue of self-respect says *fuck it, not yet.*

I turn around and walk back south. I hurry past the luncheonette. My bag is gone. Good riddance. A few storefronts later, the old-fashioned poster catches my eye. Uncle Sam in red-white-and-blue stovepipe, his craggy Lincolnesque visage tilted to one side, bushy eyebrows hanging low over the ice-blue eyes. His finger is pointing directly at me:

I WANT *YOU*!

I stop. An Army recruiting post. I scan the other poster:

WANT TO BE A LEADER?

LET US MAKE YOU ONE

TODAY'S ARMY BUILDS CHARACTER

Next to Uncle, a crew-cut Cousin Sam in sparkling uniform squints at me. His clean-shaven face, incongruous next to my own gaunt reflection, is oozing true grit. *Whoa!* Who is this oddly familiar wraith that has just joined us, smack in the middle between me and Cousin?

"Far fuckin' out!"

Apparition or revelation?

"Could do worse" says the voice right next to me.

I turn:

"Christ, Boz, you scared the shit outa me! What are you doing here?"

"Looking for you".

"But how the fuck...?"

"Been trailing you for three hours. You're not exactly inconspicuous. Here--"

The Boz dumps my bag at my feet.

"Gee, Boz" I say, "thanks..."

"I reckon it'd be too much to assume you've made your way here by sheer design" he says.

"Whatever..."

The Boz squints at me:

"Damn, I should've known".

"What?"

"You're zonked outa your fuckin' gourd, Leo" he says. "Haven't I told you not to sample the merchandise? Hell, I might as well be talking to a blank wall... Say *yeah* if you actually understand what I'm saying".

"Sure, Boz..."

"Shit. What are you doing here, Leo?"

I look around. Cousin Sam's severe visage on the poster is boring into me. Nothing to lose by telling the truth.

"Damn if I know, Boz".

"Good. Have you ever considered signing up?"

I examine the Boz carefully. He seems the same. He couldn't be serious.

"Me?" I ask. "Build character?"

My incredulity must strike the Boz as funny. I have never seen him smile before, makes him look like a different man.

As I scan the triptisch in the window again--the crew-cut Cousin Sam, the brooding Boz, my own scruffy self--the comparison is unflattering.

"Far fuckin' out..."

The Boz nods his assent:

"This is your chance, Leo".

"That so?"

"Just think--the Alameda County cops are still looking for you, last I heard. There is an APB out with your mug-shot on it, courtesy of the Colorado narcs. Got anything to lose?"

I think of my parents in their cozy house up-river. I think of Mad in her roach-infested flat. I think of Serena trying to yank her kids back from the Pitkin County child services.

"Shit no" I tell the Boz, "you're right". And I turn and push through the door.

The place is narrow, sparsely furnished and almost empty. The lone upright figure sitting at the desk sports sergeant's stripes on an olive-drab sleeve and a chestful of ribbons. His severe crew-cut is speckled with grey, belying the taut, smooth, young face.

If the sergeant is shocked at my appearance, his crisp gray eyes reveal nothing as he takes it all in. I keep my hands deep in my pockets to hide the tremors.

We face out in silence. At long last, the sergeant says: "May I help you?"

His eyes are strangely hypnotic, almost impossible to withstand.

"Quick" I blurt out, "take me before I change my mind".

The sergeant inspects me coolly, pulls out a form and hands it over.

"Fill this one out" he says, "read carefully, be sure you really mean it before you sign".

"I do, I do".

"Still. You can't take it back once your John Henry is on there".

"Wonderful" I assure him, "I've been looking for just this kinda setup all my life. Got a pen?"

He passes me one in silence.

I squint and plow my way through the form, scrawling in my name, my parents' Salt Point address. The narrow slots keep switching places, I have a devil of a time confining my hand to the designated space. I shake my head to clear up the cobweb.

"Having trouble?" says the sergeant.

"Nothing I can't handle".

"You wear glasses?"

"Never have".

"We'll check you up once you're in".

I do my best. The sergeant's opaque gaze stays on me. He must be wondering.

I hesitate over the section asking for details of my education. The space is much too small. I finally settle for Berkeley, sign, and hand the form back.

The sergeant scans it.

"You signed" he says.

"I did. You gonna give me some tests?"

"Later" he says. "You can still change your mind. I'll tear up the form if you like. Next bus to Fort Hamilton doesn't leave till tomorrow. Got a place to bunk off for the night?"

"Nope".

I am mildly indignant, I'd like to get going. No way is he going to dump me now. Not that easy.

"Besides" I tell him, "it's now or no deal. Take me while you can. A night's an awful long time, anything could happen".

"I see" says the sergeant. "Tell you what, Mr. Swenson, you stick around, I'll take you down myself, soon's I close. Ft. Ham's on my way".

"Fair enough" I tell him. "Got a pay phone anywhere?"

He points to the corner. I amble over, only to discover I am out of change. I go back to the desk:

"Spare a dime?"

He looks at me evenly, then pulls open a drawer and hands me a quarter.

"Thanks" I tell him.

"You bet. Good luck".

•   •   •

My dad's long-time receptionist picks up the phone after two rings.

"Dr. Swenson's office. May I help you".

"Hi Hazel, this is Leo".

"Leo! Where are you? I thought you'd be here by now".

"It's still under discussion" I tell her. "Hazel, is his eminence available?"

"Now Leo you better behave yourself" she says. "Let me see... He's expecting a patient in five minutes... Hold on, let me see if he can talk..."

We both know my father will take the call. Hazel is privy to the most intimate recesses of my father's daily life. I have no secrets from her either, no need to pretend. She knows at least as much as my mother, with whom she has managed over the years to sustain an amicable *modus vivendi*. The spoils of my dad's time and attention are divided--how equitably I will never know--between the two of them in a friction-free manner that remains a mystery. It won't surprise me if it turned out the two of them have been comparing notes all along, adjudicating the fine print. Neither my father nor Hazel's husband, a mild-mannered CPA, have much say in the matter.

My father's measured, urbane voice comes on line: "Leo?"

"Hi Dad".

"Where're you calling from?"

"The city".

"Did you get the telegram?"

"Sure. How did you find the address?"

"Wasn't easy. Let's say I got hold of one of your associates. Your mom got worried when you didn't show up. The airlines said you used the ticket".

Associates?

"You got the money, Leo?"

"Got that too, Dad. Thanks".

"Never mind. Are you alright?"

"I'm fine, Dad, real cool".

Even from afar, I can sense his trained ear scanning my voice for false notes, for masked traces, hedged denials, deep-buried clues.

"Good" he says. "When shall we expect to see you then?"

"Well, that's what I'm calling about, Dad... Thing's

are still kinda up in the air, you know. I was thinking..."

"This is serious, Leo, are you listening? Your draft board's getting impatient. They've been sending registered mail to your Berkeley address and getting it back unclaimed. So they called me, a personal courtesy. I'm on their medical review board, you know".

"Yeah, I guess so, Dad. That's cool tho, I'll take a look at whatever they send..."

"Hold it, Leo, that was just the beginning. When they called me, they said they've received a note from Cal telling them you've failed to maintain your minimum course load. The university's dropped you off the rolls, Leo".

"They have?"

"They said you never took your finals this spring" says my father. "Is that true, Leo?"

"Well yes, dad... but you see, classes were cancelled, finals pushed back. I couldn't just hang on there forever and..."

"Leo, are you listening? This is serious. The draft board is going to revoke your deferment. You know what that means, don't you?"

"Yes".

Vietnam.

The unspoken word is humming silently on the line between us, wafting lush odors of lethal jungle.

"It's cool dad" I tell him, "no sweat, I'll take care of it".

"When?"

"Soon".

"Leo..."

The urgency in his is downright unprofessional:

"Here's what I want you to do. Drop everything and go to Grand Central, buy that train ticket and come up straight home. Your mom'll pick you up at the station in Poughkeepsie..."

"Dad--"

"You hear me, Leo? Just do it, you..."

Hazel's voice is on the line, *Deus ex machina*:

"Dr. Swenson, your three-thirty's here".

"Thanks, Hazel, send him in... Leo, we expect you here this evening. I have to run now. Goodbye".

"Bye, Dad..."

But the line has gone dead.

Back at the desk, the sergeant is pulling on his jacket. As he maneuvers around the desk, I notice his limp. I let go of the phone and walk to meet him half way to the door. His right shoe doesn't quite match the left one, the pant leg seems empty. Having noticed my gaze, he stops:

"Want a peek?"

"Well, why..."

"Here".

The sergeant bends down and hikes his right pant-leg upward. Above the shoe, a gleaming stainless steel tube extends upwards.

"All the way to the femur" he says, "just above the knee".

"Wow".

I can't take me eyes off the polished metal rod.

"How did you get that?..."

The sergeant drops the pant-leg.

"Landmine. Nam" he says, "the delta, my third tour. Should have known when to quit, hey? Makes a good recruitment poster though, don't you think?"

"Gee, that's awful".

"Not so bad, really" he says. "Took a bit of getting used to, 's all. Wife's happy, says I'm easier to get hold of this way... You can still change your mind, you know. It ain't no picnic out there. Go back to school. Seems a shame to quit so close".

I shrug and say nothing. Birds of a feather, he and my dad.

"Well, we better get going" he says.

I grab my bag and follow the sergeant out to the grey Chevy with the blue *disabled* plates. It occupies a clearly-marked *no parking* slot.

"Fringe benefits, hey?"

He chuckles and opens the back door for me. I throw my bags in, then join him in front. As we pull away from the curb, I turn to look back. The street is deserted, no sign of the Boz. The rest of our trip to Ft. Hamilton, we are both silent, savoring the incongruity of our brief association.

II: **SEADOCK**

5. The Real Leo Swenson

(Ft. Gordon, GA; September 1969)

It is a beastly fall in Ft. Dix, NJ. The cracking asphalt roads are trimmed with frozen slush. The vast parade grounds, where we spend countless hours shuffling to and fro, doing about-face and being yelled at, is glazed over with black ice. Long before Christmas rolls in, I know I have made a dreadful mistake.

I drift through Basic Training in a daze, shorn of my long curls, clean shaven, crew-cut and olive-drabbed. Like the other fifteen hundred homesick adolescents in whose company I goose-step from point A to point B and back, I wonder why I am there. The Leo Swenson I used to be is gone. In his stead, a stranger drags his feet across the frozen asphalt, his oversize fatigues chafing his shrunken crotch.

Whatever else the Army has wrought, it has restored me to prime health. I haven't been this trim and fit since my junior year at highschool, before girls and dope derailed my varsity tennis career. And going cold turkey has done the trick. I am clean as a whistle, reborn, drug free.

The downside to coming clean is, your mind catches up with the rest of you. Having survived the double whammy of cold turkey and sleep deprivation, I am assailed by the utter folly of what I have wrought upon myself.

Christmas at home, my first furlough. My mother is overjoyed to have me back, crestfallen though she may be about my *situation*. My father is equally discreet about my *prospects*. They are yet to recover from the shock of my re-emergence in the alien dominion of the US Army.

I tell them I'll think of something, nothing irrevocable has happened. The dread name, Vietnam, is never broached, except perhaps in the privacy of their master bedroom.

I am woefully devoid of plan B but unaccountably serene. I listen and nod as my father makes barely-veiled references to *a better deal*. He is not, I gather, beyond pulling strings when it comes to his lone offspring. All I have to do is say the word.

I do what I do best--feign and prevaricate.

"Let me think about it" I tell him.

Back in Ft. Dix, I put off writing the requisite letters, assailed by a strange blend of leth and obstinacy as I slide, slowly and inexorably, nearer the yawning maws of the dread Moloch.

●　　●　　●

Prospects turn to virtual certainty when I am shipped out, right after Christmas, to the Armored Infantry Training school at Ft. Knox, KY. I am being sucked deeper and deeper into the belly of the beast, with the point of no return rapidly approaching.

It is this galloping inevitability that propels me, in late January, to take the OCS aptitude tests. Not that I have any intention of becoming an officer. I have seen enough by now, it is not my bag. But a leisurely three-day mid-winter break beats trampling the countryside in thick mud breathing heavy armor fumes.

As I had hoped, the OCS test delays my final classification. What is more, it is also responsible for my unsolicited session with an Army shrink, on an unremarkable day that begins like all others.

We are in the midst of falling in on the parade grounds, having just staggered back from a ten-mile jog with full gear. The lukewarm breakfast porridge, consumed at five AM, is a heavy lump in my stomach. It is eight-thirty sharp when Sergeant Bushnell walks over and the platoon flunky barks:

"At-ten-tion!"

We are a sorry lot, having had no time to clean up, the sergeant views us with open distaste. He fishes a scrap of paper out of his bulging breast-pocket, where life and death hang in the balance. He scans it, clearly irritated, holding the paper at arm's length.

"Swenson!"

"Yessir!"

My military survival strategy, honed to a fine edge

over the fall and winter and so far remarkably successful, boils down to making myself inconspicuous in the crowded ranks. Being called out at parade is cause for alarm.

"To the hospital, on the double".

He hands me the crumpled yellow slip. I take it, execute an awkward about-face, throw my rifle into port-arms and beat a hasty retreat. The guys are watching me.

Out of range, I slow down to a leisurely stroll. I sling my rifle over my shoulder, undo my helmet strap, and take a good look at the faded form in my hand. It consigns me to a nine AM appointment with Major E. Creighton at the base hospital's east wing, Room A-117. No further clues.

I wander through the gray maze of the hospital's ground floor. The next blind corner I bump head on into an Army nurse who has just turned the bend with a tray of glassware. It crashes to the floor, scattering in bright shards.

"Fuck!" she says, "what a clod..."

Her voice is hoarse, she sounds tired. We kneel down in silent unison to pick up the wreckage, and I take the opportunity to inspect her from close quarters. Whatever hair visible under the white cap is honey-blond and silk-fine. Her up turned nose, doing its best to snub me, is sprinkled lightly with darling golden freckles. Something familiar tugs at my heart's sleeves, vague, fleeting. In the disorienting aftermath, I spy the brass insignia on her white collar.

"Sorry, Lieutenant" I mumble.

She dismisses my belated stab at military etiquette with a curt *humph*. I have dropped my rifle and helmet to the floor and am sweeping the broken glass with my bare hands.

"Don't be an idiot" she says. She is yet to look up.

Then she grabs hold of my hand, on which a bright red splotch is rapidly working its way to full bloom.

"My, are you clumsy".

"It's nothing" I tell her.

But the blood belies my words, spurting away out of my soiled middle finger.

"Hold it" she says.

As we rise together, her petite frame becomes evident. Hardly a giant at five-nine, I fairly tower over her. Without looking at me, she pulls a band-aid out of her pocket and, with clinical efficiency, applies it to my finger. She slaps two more on top, then steps back to survey her handiwork.

"There" she says. "Now, would you please step out of my way while I clean up your mess? And *please* don't try to help. Some people shouldn't bother".

I could take offense, but her freckles are utterly disarming. Out of the blue, I say:

"I'm Leo".

My heart is pounding. I know I am breaching Army etiquette. My companion seems unfazed.

"Another Leo" she says, "I should have guessed. Never had any luck with you guys".

"Actually I'm a Virgo".

"Just as bad".

I wait, the broken glassware is swept clean. Tray in hand, my companion rises, nearly bumping me in the process.

I execute a mock would-be pratfall and am rewarded with a brief smile, an instant flash of radiation that disappears just as quickly.

Something clicks inside my brain again.

"Well" she says, "nice bumping into you, Leo the lion, but I gotta split. Good thing they were all empty or, between your clumsiness and my sleep deprivation we would've started a new Black Plague".

"That'd be fun".

"Hardly".

She eyes me with a half-frown. Utterly irresistible.

"Hey" I say, "you haven't told me your name"

"I haven't".

"How about a date?"

I can't believe I have just said that.

Neither can she, apparently.

"Leo the lion" she says, stretching to her full five-two frame, "for a clumsy oaf in urgent need of washing, you sure got the nerve".

"How 'bout it?"

"Not in the cards" she says. "Some other place, some other time, maybe..."

"I mean it, Nurse".

"So do I, Soldier. Now will you please step out of my way".

I watch in awe, her resolute trajectory suggests a compact battle-tank. I haven't looked at a woman like this since Serena.

I step aside and watch her march down the corridor. I watch her heart-wrenching ass swish away in her tight white uniform. I listen to her heels tap-tapping. I wait for the stainless-steel door to slam shut behind her. Then I stand there, alone, entranced. A strange echo is buzzing inside my head, just under the radar.

●　　　●　　　●

Room A-117 is tucked away in the basement of the east wing, the hospital's psych ward. They stop me at the guard station, vet my ID, confirm my appointment and relieve me of my rifle and helmet.

On the door of A-117, a prominent plaque identified the occupant as Major Emmet T. Creighton, MD, PhD. Just my luck, another shrink.

I knock and brace myself.

"Come in" says a deep baritone.

I open the door and enter. A prematurely grey man sporting Major's brass is slouched low behind a cluttered desk, book in hand. His feet rest on top, his tie is loosened.

"Yes?" he says without looking up.

"Pfc Leo Swenson reporting, Major sir".

I execute a truncated hatless salute, which goes unreciprocated. I have, however, managed to pry the major loose of his book. He surveys me with curiosity. From near by, his face is tired and finely lined.

"At ease, soldier... Now let's see..."

I hand him my yellow form, which he takes gingerly, as if fearing contagion.

"Sit down" he says, gesturing toward the inevitable couch near the wall. I shuffle over and sit awkwardly on the edge. His office setup is remarkably like my father's. I am on my guard.

"Seems we have an appointment" says the major. "Leastwise, the army says so. Now if you could just give me a minute..."

Major Creighton's desk is littered with paper, whose proliferous chaos he now takes on with a singular lack of relish. The better part of ten minutes elapses, during which the major seesaws between muttering and cursing. When he resurfaces at long last, his hand is brandishing a thin manila folder, a trophy he regards with a mix of disbelief and regret:

"Eureka. There. Sorry to have taken so long time. Now, Swenson, Leo Jr...."

The major casts a thoughtful look at me, then immerses himself in my file. I occupy myself with a survey of his office. A great number of flow-charts are pasted to the metal-grey walls. The three bookcases are crammed to capacity. A framed color enlargement of a dark-haired woman next to a skinny pre-teen girl is tucked away safely on one of the top shelves. Framed diplomas adorn the wall behind the desk, too far to read.

The major fishes a single page out of the file and lays it on top.

"Here" he says, his face beaming triumphant. "I knew I left a note to myself somewhere in there..."

I wait.

"Well" says the major, "well... Swenson, Leo Jr., Pfc.... I wonder if you know why you're here?"

"No sir, Major sir".

"Dr. Creighton will do. Please?"

"Yes sir, Dr. Creighton sir"

The major eyes me with exasperation.

"Nevermind" he says. " Let's cut the bullshit, Leo, shall we?"

"Sir?"

"I know about your college career".

The temperature in the room has just dropped. Until now, I have managed to keep my academic career, checkered as it is, strictly under wraps. I have no idea what game Dr. Creighton is playing. He is yet to reveal his hand.

"In that case" I tell him, "you also know I never graduated".

"Seven years, six colleges, never graduated. Some stretch, hey?"

"I didn't know it was part of the records".

"Naughty naughty" says the major. "Shall we say this is not yet part of the records either? Shall we say it's just between you and me?"

"Like doctor-patient, Dr. Creighton sir?"

"If you like".

Dr. Creighton eyes me benevolently.

"This is not really what I wanted to talk to you about" he says, "so why don't you just take it easy, hey?"

"Yessir".

"Good. Now here's the deal, Leo. There are certain, uh, shall we say, curious discrepancies in your file that might have gone unnoticed forever except for one thing".

"What's that sir?"

"You took the OCS test last month, right?"

Shit. I knew it was a stupid mistake, should have resisted the temptation. The price of those three days of leisure has just shot up.

"Yessir, Major sir".

"Christ, soldier" the major explodes, "will you cut the shit and listen? When they sent back your OCS test scores, someone spotted a large discrepancy between your IQ scores at Fort Ham and the OCS test-scores last month. An order-of-magnitude leap".

"Oh?"

"Now, this can happen... fact, it often does. Sampling error, random variation, mood swings, whatever... Shoot, some people actually show a slow learning curve over a lifetime, if you can believe that..."

"Yessir".

"Yes indeed. Well, the darned thing is, Leo, in your case the lag time was less than a year, and the sampling variation, if that's what it was, is of a startling proportion. A quantum leap in your IQ. Other aptitude measures too. Now, how the deuce are we going to account for that?"

Major Creighton is looking at me, his face crinkled. When in all earnest, I have noticed, an engaging lisp creeps into his speech.

"Your guess's as good as mine, Major sir" I tell him. "Must've been some mixup..."

"Must've" the major agrees, nodding, "must've. But where?"

Major Creighton smiles benevolently. Too late, it dawns on me I am not dealing with a slow-witted hick.

"You see" he says, "your scores from Ft. Ham are at the bottom of the heap, borderline moron. Had they not lowered the cutoff point two months before, against our loud shrieks, mind you, you'd have been summarily rejected. Or at least re-tested".

"That a fact, sir?"

"Sure is. Now, here's the real doozie, boy. Your OCS scores on the same test, and on all the others... those are

149

much more comprehensive than the ones given at induction... were way above average. So, from borderline moron to disgustingly normal in eleven months... Some progress, hey?"

I nod my melancholy assent, for I know where we are heading.

"Now" says the major, "one of the least offensive parts of my job here is to go over and certify the OCS test-scores. So what with the name, I got curious and pulled out your file. Now how are we going to account for that discrepancy, Leo?"

"Beats me, Major sir".

"Care to hazard a guess?"

"Your scorer could have goofed".

"Could, but didn't. I've gone over the raw data myself. If it was you who wrote the OCS test--your signature is on it, 'case you care to check--then you're far from the moron the Army had pegged you to be. Now you tell me, which one are you, Leo?"

Desperation is the mother of ingenuity.

"Maybe you've got the wrong Leo Swenson" I tell Major Creighton. "It's a big country, sir".

"Another Leo Swenson, Jr.?"

"Why not?"

"Of Salt Point, New York? Born 1943 in Poughkeepsie? Poughkeepsie Highschool 1961? Shall we go down the list?"

"Well..."

Dr. Creighton shakes his head.

"Gotta give it to you, boy, you don't quit. That's the spirit. The damn thing is, there *is* another Leo Swnson. You know who, don't you?"

Endgame. The major has got me by the balls and is having gentle fun. I wait.

"Leo Swenson, Sr." he says, "MD, PhD, Salt Point, New York. Past president of the New York State APA, distinguished professor of psychiatry at the Albert Einstein Medical College, adjunct at Cornell Medical School, Vassar board of trustees, Honorary Doctor of Science from Yale, Princeton, Vienna... Shall I go on?"

"You mean, *Dad*?..."

All that information has never been in my file. Just my father's name.

"It didn't occur to you I knew your father?"

"No, sir".

Major Emmet Creighton, MD, PhD chuckles.

"Well let me tell you something, Leo. Your dad was my chief residency supervisor at Cornell Medical. My analyst. My guru. My Godfather in Freud".

"Hot damn... sorry, sir..."

"Hot damn indeed, ainit now?" says Major Creighton, "Your father was kind enough to let a hick kid from Mobile into the fraternity, a dumb redneck who had no business aspiring to the high altars of Vienna... A friggin'

Baptist *goy* who stood out like a sore thumb among all them city slickers who could spew out reams of Goethe, Heine and Hölderlin at the drop of a hat... Your father vouched for me, Leo, he made me who I am. Now isn't that something?"

Life is an obstacle course strewn with random hurdles, a procession of rolled dice. Of all the military shrinks I could have drawn, I wind up with one of my dad's acolytes. Fuckin' far out.

I look at Major Creighton. I am defeated, deflated.

"So" he says, "*another* Leo Swenson?"

As hard as I rack my brain, I see no alternative to the plain truth. I look into the major's sunny visage. What the heck.

"Dr. Creighton sir" I tell him, "this is in confidence, like? Privileged communication, the doctor-patient thing?"

"You got my word".

"Well, in that case I might as well tell you. It was the crystal, I was shooting meth the day I signed up, topping off the heroin I was doing just before that..."

"Meth over heroin?"

"Yessir. See, we ran out of smack and Mad... that's the girl I was crashing with... she went out and scored some meth... I was loaded to the gills when I signed up. Then this guy at Ft. Ham had some pills..."

The major is squinting at me:

"Go ahead, anything else to top it off?"

"That's it. 'Cept for the weed".

"Might be worth a note to the Annals" he says, "the effect on metamphetamines on IQ scores... Shoot, someone's probably done it already".

"If you say so, sir".

Dr. Creighton shakes his head.

"Never mind" he says, "we're sliding off the subject. Did you really mean it, going for OCS?"

"Not really. Thing is, sir, I took the test just to have a breather".

"I see. Why don't you sign up anyway? I'll recommend you. Don't you want to be an officer, Leo?"

"No sir".

"Why not? There's a premium on college boys now, you'll be a cinch".

"I didn't get a degree, sir" I remind him.

"Seven years, hey? Most colleges would've dropped you by the fifth. It takes real talent to stretch it the way you did, don't you think?"

"Not much, sir" I tell him. "Well, maybe just a little... Tho in my case it was mostly luck. See, they lost my records at Bennington. Then both Williams and Emory were in the middle of switching to a new computer system just when I was flunking out... And from Oberlin on it was easy, everybody was doping, I don't remember a thing... And then at Reed, someone burned down the Registrar's office. Got me off my last probation... Then Cal, I was actually close to graduating for once. Then People's Park came along. Must be my karma..."

"Must be" the major agrees. "Still, what've you got against being an officer? The pay is better, so's the food 'n digs".

"Nothing really, sir" I tell him. "Thing is, I'd feel funny telling other guys what to do. It don't come natural. They've made me Pfc and even that's way too much..."

"Fear, maybe?"

"Could be, sir. More like, who am I to tell all the rest of them guys how to run their lives? Half the time I'd feel like gigglin'. The guys will laugh me off the parade ground".

Major Creighton, MD, PhD, removes his glasses and wipes them with a piece of tissue he pulls out of his desk drawer. He put his glasses back on and eyes me over the lenses perched low on his nose:

"You ain't funnin' me, boy, are you?"

"No, sir".

"Full of tricks, aintcha?".

"Just trying to stay alive, Major sir".

"Ain't doing half bad neither... Well, look at it this way. OCS is six more months stateside. Otherwise you ship out to Nam. Guaranteed".

"So what's the big deal, six more months and then Nam? You know what the fatality rate is for Lieutenants Junior Grade down there?"

154

"So you've heard that one too? Why the heck didn't you hang on to your student deferment then?"

I have no answer to that, as Dr. Creighton knows. We wait. After a while he says:

"I'm not here to judge you, Leo, I'm just trying to help. And it's my job to tell you you're better off going to OCS. It's not safe to let someone like you hang on as a buck private, Nam or no Nam. People like you gets the officer corps demoralized, sooner or later you'll get into trouble. There'll always be someone gunning for you".

"I've managed so far, sir".

"Must be luck. Still, they'll flush you out one of these days, you'll wind up refusing a dumb order under fire, some jerk will throw the book at you, court martial, brig, the works... I get kids like you all the time, the ones that managed to stay alive 'n wind up in the loony bin... So, how about it?"

The major's argument makes perfect sense. My antennae are buzzing. I am the lone progeny of two people who've always made perfect sense.

"Dr. Creighton, sir" I say

"Yes?"

"Did my father have anything to do with this?"

"Shoot, boy, I haven't seen Dr. Swenson in years".

Seen. There's always the phone.

"Honest?"

"Honest. Think I ought to give him a jingle now?"

"Wouldn't that be unethical, sir?"

"Guess I won't do it, then. Will you take my word on that?"

I regroup at the line of least resistance.

"Okay" I tell him, "I'll think about it".

"You do that, Leo. You might even get to like it, once you get past the bullshit, that is".

"Oh, I don't mind the bullshit, sir" I tell him, "that's easy. It's just this business of giving orders".

"You'll be surprised how fast it grows on you. You'll develop the knack, trust me".

Major Creighton seems pleased with our encounter. I'd like to keep him happy.

"I tell you what" he says. "You fill out the forms, send them through channels, start the paper mill grinding. You can always withdraw, change your mind. And I'll keep all the rest to myself. Fair enough?"

"I guess..."

We both know I have little choice. Still, the major is being gracious:

"Now, now" he says, "let's not put such a dim face on it. Being an officer is a privilege. Leastwise, it used to be..."

An officer and a gentlemen.

With this we part. Major Creighton escorts me all the way to the front, where he brushes off my feeble attempt at a salute and instead shakes my hand:

"Good luck, Leo. And say hello to your father for me next time you see him".

"Thank you, sir, I will".

He watches me from the door as I retrieve my gun and helmet and retreat down the corridor.

●　　●　　●

I fill out the requisite forms and drop them on the sergeant's desk, then settle down to wait. When the dust settles, I find myself--from early March through late July-- biting the dust on the prairie near Fort Sill, Oklahoma.

The first three months of OCS, I am too busy to worry. But then the Army's inscrutable hand deals me Forward Artillery Observer training. FAO, a slippery slope to Hell tho at first you hardly notice. You traipse all over the countryside, fiddling with your wireless dials and minding your own business. You hassle no one, no one hassles you. Tailor-made.

Except for the war. For your bucolic outpost is planted in the midst of no-man's land. That's if you are lucky. More likely, behind enemy lines where you are perched on the tallest landmark in sight--a barren hill, a tree, a charred ruin-- naked prey to enemy snipers.

Yes, a chopper is on hand to pluck you out in case the going gets rough. But your chopper has to beat the other guys, who are trolling for you mad as hornets. For they've got the same radio-fix on you as your chopper does, and their CO back in the rear is breathing sulfur down their ass, screaming for them to nail you before your artillery totaled his new bunker.

Urban legends? Harly, it's all in the training manual. Tho I get it second hand, by way of a captain just back from an FAO tour near Pleiku. We have one beer too many one evening at an off-base cowboy bar. The captain is awaiting reassignment to a training unit. He sports a chestful of ribbons and a Purple Heart with four oak clusters. Once we have gotten sauced, he pulls off his shirt and shows me his magnificent collection of scars, front and back. He says he is one of the lucky few. To celebrate his good fortune, he drinks me under table. We part bosom buddies under the pale morning stars. My prospects are dimmer than ever.

● ● ●

The deuce of it is, there *is* another Leo Swenson. Well, Swen*sen*. Honest to God and cross my heart. The poor sucker may have saved my life, tho he may not live to tell the tale or take the credit.

The day we get our commissions, the entire platoon is routed to Fort Bragg, which is as straight as you can get to Nam. I alone am shipped out to Ft. Gordon, Georgia. Nobody tells me why, nobody knows, nobody gives a damn.

The next day, just off the buss, I wander about for two hours, casing the joint. It seems innocuous enough, a series of connecting grass-covered clearings carved, like sausage links, out of the Georgia pine ten miles out of Augusta. I spy no platoons charging about on the double. A portent?

I am feeling leisurely, having left my packs for safe-keeping at the main gate. My papers remand me to the custody of Colonel Sprague, Army MP School. Nothing in my training qualifies me for MP duty.

Another baffling thing: my orders are addressed to *Captain* Leo Swenson. The serial number is mine, so the Army must have made a simple mistake.

The MP sergeant at the front desk takes my papers and delves into his filing cabinet, resurfacing with a thick file. He charges a corporal with escorting me to my next destination. We proceed along a shaded exterior patio that loops around the low-roofed building, at long last arriving in front of a door that identifies Col. S. Sprague as the School's Adjutant.

The corporal knocks on the door, goes in and reemerges almost immediately:

"The colonel is expecting you, sir".

I enter and find myself facing a large mahogany desk behind which a balding man in his late fifties is squatting low astride a swivel chair. I am in civvies and thus cannot salute, so I give him my best posture. The colonel does not seem to mind.

"Captain Swenson? At ease, at ease, grab a chair, sit down, we've been expecting you... Was quite a job squeezing you out of Third Army's grubby hands, you better believe it... Had to pull some strings, cash in some heavy chips... Did you have a pleasant trip back?"

Not only my unaccountable promotion, but also other details are odd. Third Army? Trip back? I had better set the record straight.

"Yessir, thank you, sir" I say. "Er, Colonel sir..."

"Swell, swell" says the colonel, "we've got big plans for you, Captain. Our entire training program is bogged down for lack of qualified personnel... I mean people with real field experience like yourself... The usual crap from Army, Vietnam is sucking away every officer who's any good... Fuckin' bottomless pit, you ask me... Soon as we spot a decent one, they ship him out. They've got pick of the litter ever since Tet... We're lucky to get anybody, let alone a man of your qualifications... Seen your digs yet?"

"Not yet, sir". I had better try again. "Colonel Sprague..."

"Why don't we let you get settled down first, huh? I expect you'll find no reason to complain. We're going to treat you real good here, Captain, now that you're finally on board. Anything you need, just ask. The greens have just been redone, I had the pro from Augusta National come over 'n take a look... Gave us a clean bill of health. Swell guy too, I think you'll like him... Got your bags with you?"

"I left them at the gate, sir. Colonel Sprague, there's..."

But the colonel's joy at having me aboard is overpowering. Whoever Captain Swensen may be, he is missing a giant ego boost.

The colonel grabs the phone:

"I'll phone the gate, have them send your stuff over... While we're at it, Captain Swenson, hang on to this file..."

The colonel hands me a thick blue folder:

"It'll fill you in on the kinda setup we have in mind, I could use some feedback when you have a min--"

Mid-word, Colonel Sprague shifts gears and barks into the phone:

"This's Sprague... Yeah, give me the gate, willya".

To while the time, I take a peek at the file. The first page consists of Col. Sprague's command chart, whose bottom nodes are labeled with indecipherable acronyms. Across the vast desk, the colonel is issuing staccato directives over the phone. When he is done, his face is beaming:

"Your stuff's on its way. Ready to roll, Captain?"

Time to lower the boom.

"Yessir Colonel sir" I tell him. "Only thing is, there's a problem..."

"A problem?"

161

"Well, a mistake".

"A mistake?"

A note of apprehension creeps into Colonel Sprague's voice. It is the voice of a man who has had the rug yanked out from under him once too often.

"What mistake, Captain?"

"Well, sir" I tell him, as gently as I can, "you see, I'm not a captain, just a lieutenant, jg".

For the first time since I came into his office, Col. Sprague pauses and takes a good hard look at me.

"Lieutenant jg? What the fuck, you ain't a captain, we'll make you one, no big deal... Here, grab these!"

Out of his desk drawer, the colonel pulls a worn-out set of captain's field insignia, tossing them at me across the vast expanse of his desk:

"There you go!... used to be mine...Put them on, Swenson, we'll square it off with the CO as soon as I've got a spare minute... Say, you *are* Leo Swenson, aren't you?"

"Yessir. Lt. Leo Swenson--that's S-W-E-N-S-O-N-- Army artillery".

"Artillery? Now lookie here, Swenson, is this some kind of a joke? This file here says you're Captain Leo Swensen--S-W-E-N-S-*E*-N--Army MP, back stateside after two years at Third Army HQ, Heidelberg. Right?"

The colonel's face has grown ruddier. I can only hope he doesn't have a heart condition. I try to put it to him as delicately as I can:

"I'm afraid not, sir, not quite..."

"Not quite? What the fuck does that mean? Who the hell are you then?"

"Lieutenant jg Leo Swenson, sir, with an *oh*" I tell him. "Army Artillery, Ft. Sill, Oklahoma".

Colonel Sprague's face does a slow collapse as its owner plops down in his swivel chair, a pneumatic doll whose valve has just sprung a leak. I stand at full attention, waiting. A moment of silence elapses. The colonel's eyes are shut firmly. When he finally speaks, his voice is unaccountably soft, almost contemplative, as if talking to himself:

"Fuckin' bastards... imbeciles... did it to me again... stole my Captain Swensen..."

For a moment I think Colonel Sprague is about to pass out. He is slumped low in his chair, head hanging over his chest, lips working soundlessly. Should I phone for the medics?

"Colonel sir" I say, "are you alright?"

"Am I alright..." he echoes, "am I alright..."

Then, just as abruptly, he undergoes another metamorphosis. He springs to his feet, wild eyes boring into me, native red color restored:

"Lt. Leo Swenson, Army artillery!" he screams. "For the love of our Lord Jesus Christ, where were you *supposed* to be shipped to?"

"I don't know, sir. Most of the guys in my platoon went to Ft. Brag. That's N.C., sir..."

"I know where Ft. Bragg is! Now what did you train for at Ft. Sills?"

"FAO, sir, that's Forward Artillery Observer".

"My God, but that's straight to... The nincompoops have gone shipped my Captain Swensen over to Nam! The motherfuckers!... Five months of hard work--seven cases of bourbon, three golf carts, one Olympic featherweight--all down the tube...They've gone shipped *my* Captain Swensen to fight lousy gooks in Nam!..."

Colonel Sprague yanks the phone off its cradle and barks into it:

"Sprague! Get me AC-of-S, on the double!... What? He's what?... Track him down then, imbecile!... Yeah, send a jeep to the club!... Sure it's an emergency, you dumbshit cocksucker! I said so, didn't I?... Yeah, I'll take the responsibility, yeah!..."

The phone slams down. Like the avenger zeroing in on his quivering prey, Col. Sprague turns back to me. His face is fairly burnished with stroke-grade crimson:

"Swenson!"

"Yessir".

"Get the fuck out of my sight! Beat it! On the double! Scram! Get lost!"

I step back, away from the compressed violence pointed at me.

"Where am I supposed to go, sir?"

We eye each other for a tense moment across his desk. I pray silently the colonel's despair over losing the real Leo Swensen has not rendered him irrational or, worse, vindictive. His beef is surely with Army personnel, but they are not the ones frozen in front of his desk ready to shit their pants.

"Sit down, Swenson" the colonel says at last.

I let out my breath.

"What exactly is your training, Lieutenant?"

"OCS, sir. Then Artillery. Then FAO".

"What'd you do in civvies?"

"I was in college, sir, seven years. No degree though..."

"Where'd you go to school?"

"Bennington, then Williams... Emory, Oberlin... St. John of Santa Fe, Reed, Berkeley..."

"Berkeley! When?"

"Fall of '67 to spring of '68".

The colonel eyes me coldly. Will he start yelling again? When he speaks, it is with the measured tone of a man who has just come to a reluctant decision:

"*Seadock*" he says. "Get your sorry ass out of here, Swenson, go back to the main office and tell the sergeant to re-route you to Seadock".

"What's that, sir?"

"Never mind. Just get your skinny college ass out

of my sight. You'll find out soon enough".

The colonel pauses, his red-rimmed eyes boring into my chest:

"And Swenson?"

"Yessir".

"Stay out of my way if you know what's good for you".

"Yessir, thank you sir".

"Get outa here before I change my mind".

I click my heels, execute a sharp 'bout-face and run for dear life, with Col. Sprague's rancor fairly boring into my exposed back. At the main office, the sergeant relieves me of the old captain tags. The colonel has just called.

6. C. D. O. C.

(Ft. Gordon, GA; September 1969)

I trace my way back to the gate. I am in no hurry, having no clue where I am headed. What is more, I am not alone in my predicament. The guard at the main gate is equally baffled:

"They sure keep changing their minds about your bags, sir" he says, "had us send them over on the double, then five minutes later called back and canceled. Had poor Joe here coming and going, good thing he hadn't unloaded yet..."

His buddy nods. The two of them seem intrigued at my unfolding saga, a pleasant break in their routine.

"Sorry, guys" I tell them. "Think you can hang on to my bags a bit longer?"

"Sure, sir, no sweat".

"Thanks. I'll be back".

"When would that be, sir?"

"Your guess as good as mine, soldier" I tell him. "Soon enough, I suppose. Have faith".

The guard nods.

"Know where you're headed, sir?"

"Place called Seadock" I tell him. "Ever heard of

it?"

"Seadock? Sure, it's clear to the other end of the base. I can roust up a ride for you, sir, if you just wait a sec".

"That's alright" I tell him. "I'd rather walk, case the joint. Is the PX somewhere on the way?"

"Yessir". The guard points. "You just follow that-a-way, can't miss it. The flat square with all the cars parked in front. Officers' club's right across, 'case you need to go there".

"And Seadock?"

"Further down. You just keep going, sir, can't miss it".

"Thanks a mil" I tell the guard. "See you later".

"Yessir. You take your time, we'll keep an eye on your bags".

●   ●   ●

After a late lunch of edible Southern-fried at the PX, I launch myself in search of the elusive Seadock. Leaving the main complex of the MP School behind, I thread my way through the Signal Corps compound clear to the end of the base. Only a single block of tan quonset huts is still ahead, squatting at the edge of the dark pine forest that stretches to the east and south as far as the eye can see. A small sign says:

C. D. O. C.

168

Seadock. On the main office door a modest hand-printed note spell it out:

CIVIL DISTURBANCE ORIENTATION COURSE

Underneath in smaller print yet:

Lt. Col. R. Manners, CO

My appointment with Col. Rodney Manners, Army Corps of Engineers, is mercifully brief. A large man in his early fifties, the colonel oozes varsity football. His close-cropped grey hair is going bald on top, his face is tanned and lined like old leather. His demeanor is noncommittal.

"Swenson? Sit down".

I take the lone austere chair to the left of the colonel's grey metal desk. The bulk of the room is taken over by a large drafting table covered with charts, blueprints and cardboard models.

We eye each other wearily, me propped on the edge of my metal chair, the colonel comfortably if correctly in a high-backed upholstered antique *chaise.*

"Welcome to Seadock".

"Thank you, sir".

"All in one piece? Baggage arrived?"

"Yessir, thank you, sir".

"Good".

With which the colonel has apparently exhausted his need--or is it his capacity--for small talk.

"Now, about your service file..."

That again.

169

"Sir?"

"Your paper trail. Where is it?"

"I wouldn't know, sir".

With my heart skipping a beat, I watch Col. Manner's placid demeanor undergo a baleful transformation:

"Goddang it, I should've known, another basket case".

I blink and try to make myself smaller.

"Now, you level with me, Swenson" says the colonel. "Man to man. Where's the catch?"

"Sir?"

"I'm a busy man, Lieutenant--"

The colonel gestures toward his drafting table:

"--ain't got all day to squeeze the truth outa you. Out with it".

I hold my tongue.

"Listen" says the colonel, "Sprague wouldn't be sending me a fresh lieutenant out of the clear blue sky unless there was a catch. A gift horse from Sprague is guaranteed to have a mouthful of rotten teeth".

I still don't know what to tell him.

"Let's see" says the colonel. "Did the old goat sew a time-bomb up your ass? I can scan you, y'know. So why don't you save us both the agony and fess up".

I am out-ranked and out-gunned. Col. Manners appears to be a seasoned player at whatever game it is that we are engaged in. As a last resort, I gamble on the truth.

"Well, sir" I tell him, "there was a mixup. The colonel was expecting an MP Captain Swensen--with an *E*-- out of Third Army HQ in Heidelberg. A golf pro, I think..."

I let my voice trail off, but Col. Manners has caught on quickly:

"And instead he got you, Lieutenant Swenson with an *O*, right?"

"Yessir".

"No golf clubs?"

"Never been on a course, sir". Well, I once layed a girl on the fifteenth-hole green in Poughkeepsie.

Col. Manners' somber face transforms itself into a visage of mirth:

"Shoot" he says, "I wish I could've been there to see old Sprague stew!"

I wait.

"You a lieutenant, Swenson?"

"Yessir. Jg".

"What kind of training?"

"Artillery, sir, FAO".

"That so? Wonder why ol' Sprague couldn't find a spot for you... His staff sergeant made it sound real personal, said to make sure 'n keep you down at this end, said never to let you wander over there... *Loiter*'s what he actually said. Betcha he was quoting Sprague, just his style, bugger's meaner than a treed coon. So just what *did* you do to the

171

old goat to piss him off, Swenson?".

"Well, I'm not sure, but the colonel seems to think the Army's sent *his* Captain Swensen to Nam. In my place".

"I'll be skewered!"

I wait.

"So that's where your file is, Swenson" says the colonel. "Gone to Nam, drowned in the Mekong, napalmed in the highlands. Guess we can ask Army HQ for a duplicate. Takes at least a year in peacetime. Might as well find you something to do. Artillery, you said?"

"Yessir. FAO".

"Any drafting experience?"

"None I can think of".

"How old are you, son?"

"Twenty six".

"Thought so... Too young to've amounted to much out there... You a college boy, Swenson?"

"After a fashion, sir".

"Where last?"

The colonel seems to have gotten my number.

"Berkeley".

An audible *ouch* escapes Col. Manner's lips. He grimaces in distaste and then quickly recovers, as if determined to exorcize a ghost.

"Tell you what" he says. "You go down the hall, find Major Herskowitz, tell him you're his, he'll take care of you. The two of you'll get along just fine. Got your dig digs yet?"

"Not yet, sir".

Col. Manners jots down a few lines on a scrap of blue-lined graph paper:

"Leave this with the staff sergeant on the way out, he'll find you a bunk. Anything else?"

"No, sir".

"Good. Go find Len Herskowitz. Good luck".

"Thank you, sir".

"You bet. And Swenson?"

"Yessir?"

"Stay out of my hair, willya?"

"Yessir. I will".

I leave Col. Manners' note with the sergeant in front. I think I know what a ping-pong ball must feel in the midst of a wicked rally. Everyone I have met so far at Ft. Gordon seems anxious to hand me over to the next sucker.

I locate the right door. The sign says:

Major L. Herskowitz

DEMONSTRATIONS

I knock. No one answers but the room is definitely occupied, to judge by the loud voice that filters out through the thin plywood wall. I knock again, then settle down to listen.

"--well I don't give a minced prick what the other *golems* did, Speiser!" A voice caugh t in mid-harangue. "You missed your cue again, and once you fuck up your end, that's it! Fuckin' scene's too goddam complicated, everything's tied up to everything else, or haven't you noticed? You're the crux of this gig, Speiser, the center of gravity, *capish*? You don't come on cue, damn it, who will? Ask your girlfriend if you don't believe me, Speiser. It's all in the timing!"

"But Len..."

Tentative, apologetic, definitely younger. And not being given his day in court.

"Shut up and listen Speiser, I ain't finished yet. You know what happened to us last Friday?"

"Well..."

"Will you shut up or do I have to tape your kisser? Lemme tell you what happened--we bombed out in Fort Gordon, that's what! In front of a live audience. Not somewhere in the boonies or New Haven or summer stock, but right on Broadway! In front of the *crème de la crème*, the New York critics!... Wanna know why? 'Cause you were too goddam high--God only knows on what *chazerei*--to get your cue right!"

A loud snort follows. The second voice then takes another disheartened stab at mounting the case for the defense:

"But the National Guard opened fire before they were supposed to, Len. I couldn't--"

To no avail.

"You're the one who's supposed to give them their cue, Speiser, remember? No, don't start that again, shut

174

up!"

In the silence that follows I take my chance and knock again. My timing is irredeemably off, for like the hapless victim inside, I must have bungled my cue.

The knock must have carried through this time. From inside the room, the first voice belts out angrily:

"Come in, goddamit!"

I brace myself, open the door and step in.

A thin, dark-haired ascetic man in a major's uniform is slouched behind the desk. A red-faced lieutenant is standing in front.

"What is it?" says the major.

"Major Herskowitz?"

"Got *that* right. Who're you?"

"Lt. Leo Swenson, United States Army, reporting".

The major turns his bemused gaze back to his young companion:

"This something I ought to know about, Speiser?"

The lieutenant, having detected a surrogate victim, is nimble on his feet:

"Never seen him before, Len, I swear on the Good Book".

"Oh shit! Blasphemy will get you nowhere, Speiser. Pipe down".

He turns back to me:

"Tell me all about it, Lieutenant. Make it sound good. I need some cheering up".

I swallow hard. The major's wiry face remains impassive. His intense eyes fix on me with scorn. The only ripple in his air-tight deadpan is his left eyebrow, which has shot up in a quizzical arch.

A comic? A sadist? With my luck, both.

"Colonel Manners sent me over, sir" I tell him. "He said you'd know what to do with me".

The major mulls over the information slowly, rolling it over his tongue like a delicate wine. Both eyebrows are arched now, which for some reason suggests a thin ray of hope. The major's fingers are drumming slowly on his desk. He is sucking in his right cheek.

"Well, now" he says, "let's find out".

He turns back to the lieutenant:

"Scram, Speiser, willya? I'm through with you for now. Just remember--you screw up one more time, you're out. On your bum 'n straight to Nam. Now get outta my face".

We watch in silence as the crestfallen lieutenant slouches out of the room. Major Herskowitz shakes his head:

"I don't know about that one. Don't seem to get through. Well, I may have knocked the fear of God into him, maybe. Sit down, Lieutenant".

He motions me over and I join him across the desk.

"Nam's the magic word around here, case you haven't noticed. Gets respect, gets action. Hate to spring it like this

176

on poor Speiser, but how else would you get the *schlemiel* to mind his cues? Now, hold on a sec..."

Major Herskowitz pounces on the phone:

"Gurley? This's Len... Give me the chief, willya?... Hi Rodney, Len... Yeah, he's here alright... What the fuck... What?... He did?... That so?..."

The major's eyes alight on me briefly.

"Yeah..." he says into the phone, "sure, if you think so... Sure, I'll find out... right-oh, Rodney... bye".

Major Herskowitz lays down the phone and turns to me:

"Well, Lieutenant, now you're beginning to make sense. Ol' Rodney says you went to Berkeley. That a fact?"

"Yessir".

"Better lay off the yessirs before you drive me crazy. Name's Len. What'd you say yours was?"

"Leo Swenson. With an *O*".

"Good. Now Leo, were you at Berkeley during the riots?"

"Which ones?"

"The Free Speech Movement?"

"That was before my time".

"How about the Dirty Speech Movement?"

"Still before I got there".

"People's Park?"

Ouch. The image of me and Mad on the fence under the harsh glare of the Oakland PD cruisers revisits me.

177

"Yes" I tell Major Herskowitz, "I was there".

"Good enough. Ever seen Savio in action?"

"Couldn't help it, sir, even before I got there, guy was all over the tube".

"Shit, yeah, saw him on TV myself. A natural, real flair. Not much discipline tho, gets carried away, over-projects..."

The major rises and walks slowly around the desk, his eyes appraising me speculatively. I can't help but notice how much shorter he is than I had expected, given his deep baritone.

"Shit..." he says. "I'll be damned... hold it!"

He turns abruptly, walks over to a filing cabinet behind his desk and pulls out a fuzzy dark bundle.

"Here" he says, tossing the quivering mass to me, "try this on for size".

I fumble with what turns out to be a dark long-hair wig. I look up at the major.

"Go on, put it on" he says, "gotta see you in your natural flora".

I hold the wig up, pull it on and brush the long curls off my face. The musty smell is overpowering. When I turn to look back, the major's eyes are glued to my face. I know I must be blushing. The long locks feel alien after a year of crew-cut. Major Herskowitz's eyes, however, are kindled with pleasure.

"Much better" he says. "Ever worn it this long?"

"Longer".

"Yeah? Well, I think we've just solved our Speiser problem. Leo, right?"

"Yessir".

"Len. Here..."

Major Herskowitz saunters forward, offering his hand:

"Pleasure to have you aboard, Leo".

His hand is warm, the grip vigorous.

"Welcome to Seadock, your home away from home. You can take off that silly rug now, the rest of your costume isn't quite right. Ever done any acting, Leo?"

He is walking back around his desk.

"A little bit" I tell him. "I took a couple of theater courses, way back..."

My brief tenure as a Theater Arts major, a spur-of-the-moment tack that chagrined my father to no end but delighted my mother, came to an abrupt end when I flunked out of Oberlin.

"Where was that?" asks the major.

"Oberlin".

"That so? How far back?"

"Gee" I say, "let me think... Must be four years... nineteen sixty-five maybe".

"Good".

A brooding smile dances across the major's face as his eyes shoot in two opposite directions and his mouth cracks wide from ear to ear. The effect is so unexpected, I burst in laughter.

Major Herskowitz is enjoying himself.

"How're you fixed for digs, Leo?" he asks.

"The sergeant said he'll find me something".

"Gurley, in the front office? I better get after his fat ass or you'll wind up rotting in some basement. Where're your bags?"

"I left them at the main gate".

The major consults his watch.

"Come" he says, "we've got just enough daylight left to give you the grand tour. We'll pick up your stuff on the way back. Better hurry, she looks real spooky around sunset, wouldn't want to miss that".

"Beg your pardon?"

"Nevermind, just come along, you'll see. I don't want to spoil your fun"

●   ●   ●

There's a black giant slouched in the driver's seat of the open jeep. His hair spreads out in a lush Afro that is barely contained under a knit red-white-and-blue Tam-o-Shanter. The sleeves of his army-issued shirt sport corporal stripes. As we stop on the passenger side, the massive head turns around slowly, eyes blank behind the dark shades.

Major Herskowitz motions me brusquely to the

back seat, then climbs in next to the driver.

"Get goin', Chalmers".

Nothing happens. The opaque shades keep glaring at the major.

"Oh shit, sorry--Abdul Hameed. Now get going, willya?".

The black giant shrugs.

"Sure thing, Major Len suh" he says and starts the engine. "You ain't gonna introduce me to your new main man, Major suh? Wassa matter, you 'shamed of him or somethin'?"

"Sorry again".

Major Herskowitz' deportment with his driver is unaccountably meek. He turns back to me:

"Lt. Swenson, this is Corporal Abdul Hameed, formerly Wesley Chalmers, the 3rd... Abdul Hameed, meet Leo Swenson. Just joined us".

I endeavor to break the ice:

"Nice meeting you, Abdul Hameed".

The driver rasps back:

"Wa'ss happenin' man".

From my vantage point behind Major Herskowitz, something in the black giant's half-profile is vaguely familiar. He maneuvers us briskly out of the parking lot.

"Say, your majesty" I ask, "haven't we met before?"

The answer I get, when I finally get it, is oracular and laced with street-savvy menace:

"All black cats look the same to honkey".

I've heard this pearl of wisdom more than once on the Av. A white body lies down and whimpers and, being a good sport, radiates good will to all the wretched of the earth.

"You bet your big black Afro" I tell the driver. "Wa'ss with them shades, man?"

The driver chuckles.

"Got yourself a smartass whiteboy, Major Len suh. Better keep an eye on him 'fore he gets hisself 'n you into a heap of trouble".

"Thanks, Abdul baby" says the major, "I'll keep that in mind. Now step on it, willya".

"Where we goin' to, Major suh?"

"Down to the set".

"Yessuh, Major Len".

The Major and his driver have no doubt been polishing their routine for a while. I would love to hear more, but my immediate concern is our Jeep, launched as it is upon a high trajectory as we hit a nasty bump in the narrow red-dirt road heading straight into the pine. We crash back to earth in a shallow puddle. I hang on to the roll-bar with both hands. My two companions seem to take our wild ride in stride.

To our right, the sun is perched low over the horizon, the clouds streaking a riot of reds and yellows. The scented air is blowing in my face. Our driver negotiates a sharp curve where the road cuts into the breast of the hill. The jeep's front-right wheel plows into the sandbank.

"Dammit, Abdul Hameed" says the major.

" 'Scool, Major Len suh".

With a flicker of his wrist, he brings the Jeep back to *terra firma*. We skid to the left, then to the right. I hold onto the roll-bar for dear life and close my eyes.

The jeep screeches to a halt, the engine is turned off. In the warm evening breeze, a choir of cicadas shrieks is cacophonous unison. I open my eyes.

We are parked right where the dirt road transforms abruptly into paved blacktop. A small clear-cut valley lies in the midst of the pine. The lower slopes of the surrounding hillside are covered with sparse grass. At the bottom, just ahead, are two rows of two-story structures spanning three city blocks along a narrow street.

"Say..." I stop.

The blacktop leads down to the urban grid at the bottom, but the grid itself leads nowhere, dissipating at both ends into the grassy dunes. The serene urban panorama nests incongruously in the palm of the piney hills. Except for the deafening clamor of the cicadas, no sound. Nothing moves, no one in sight.

"Here we are" says Major Herskowitz as he alights from the jeep. "Ain't she a dream?"

"Well, yeah..."

I scramble off the jeep and hurry on to catch up with

the major. The driver remains behind.

As I come down the slope closer, the buildings turn out to be skeletal erections over unroofed stud frames, like a movie set, three city blocks' worth of painted façades. From up close, most of the structures are storefronts. A couple of restaurants, a small supermarket, a bank. I take it all in as I follow Major Herskowitz into the middle of the street, one block from the edge. From this vantage point, the illusion of an urban block is almost complete.

"You like?" says the major.

Something is disturbingly familiar about it.

"Hey" I say, "hold it!"

But Major Herskowitz is already sauntering toward the next intersection. I hurry after him. Together, we reach the white-painted zebra crossing and stop. The major turns to me:

"What do you say, tiger?"

Both street signs are visible now. The cross-street says *Haste St.* The main drag says *Telegraph Ave.*

"Far fuckin' out!"

From where I stand, I can see the entrance to the Safeway across the street to the left. The Piccolo is further down to the right, with the Boz's lace-curtained windows directly above it. It all looks incredibly real.

"Neat, ain't it?" Says the major.

"No shit".

We are standing in the middle of a life-size replica

of the Av just below campus, from Dwight through Channing and Haste up to Durant. Store-front for store-front, in living colors. Only the denizens are missing.

Major Herskowitz is beaming at me:

"Rodney Manners' dream baby".

"The colonel? He built this? But how?"

"How? He's Army Corps, ain't he? This is child play for them. After thirty years of dams, bridges and barracks, Rodney can do this in his sleep".

"But why Berkeley?"

"Aha! Rodney's private revenge. A shrine, really".

"A shrine to who?"

"Darling Cindy" says the major. "Or rather, darling Cindy's hymen".

I step closer:

"Cindy?"

"Ol' Rodney's daughter, his onliest, apple of his eye. He and his wife made a horrible mistake... well, Cindy sweet-talked them into it... sending her to Cal. Got into debt to pay her out-of-state tuition, she was going to major in Applied Social Anthro, whatever that means... First term she comes home for Christmas with a dose of the clap. Her mother almost died, wasn't fashionable then... Second term she draws four F's and gets put on probation... Third term, Fall of 1964... and yeah, you guessed it, she turns political. Nothing serious, just a bit of red-blooded all-American street theater... So she joins the roused rabble and gets clubbed on the head by the cops, scooped up with the great unwashed and thrown into Santa Rita. Ever made it in there?"

A quick shudder runs down my spine.

"Not all the way, no..."

"Nasty place, I hear... Well, to top it all off--now, this only comes out a coupla months later after poor Rodney bails her out and re-deposits her at Athens, chastised but unrepentant--she turns out pregnant. Claims it happened in jail, one of her fellow revolutionaries... Poor Rodney almost flips his top, sends her all the way to Copenhagen to get an expensive abortion... Takes some doing too, Cindy wants to carry to term, says it's gonna be a true revolutionary baby..."

"Scores of those all over the countryside".

"Sure, by now... Well, Rodney prevails, so there's one less of those running around looking for daddy. But sweet Cindy is still Rodney's precious. So when it comes to this set, he was like Ramses the Second building the fuckin' pyramids..."

The silent Av is indeed a thing of beauty.

"But why?" I ask the major. "It would only remind him, don't you think?"

Major Herskowitz surveys the empty street, his eyes lit up with the last rays of the setting sun.

"So we can burn it down".

I know I heard the words right, the major is just next to me. So maybe it's just too obvious. The Army pays to build it, then they burn it down, I see the symmetry but not much else.

"I must be missing something" I tell the major, "but I don't get it".

"Good. You will soon. Just keep an open mind, I need your fresh perspective".

"I'll try" I tell him. Ignorance must still count for something. "How about a hint? Like, where do *I* fit in?"

Major Herskowitz's large hazel eyes squint at me from close-up, almost level with mine. His lithe frame is stretched up, a rooster about to crow. His smile is beatific:

"Why, Leo my boy" he says, "you're my ace in the hole".

●　　　●　　　●

I am, it appears, stuck with Henry. Lieutenant Henry Speiser, that is, who is driving me bonkers. I can't help feeling sorry for him, he is dying for us to have a *tête-a-tête*. But all my attempts to draw him have bounced off his reticence. We are, each, after something. For my part, I am desperate to find out what Seadock is all about and where I might fit in. What Henry is after remains a mystery.

"You want something, Henry?" I ask.

He has been following me around the flat like an imprinted duckling.

"Well..."

He is working up his courage, but it's been three days and I am beginning to feel dizzy.

But I had better backtrack.

I have been granted the week off to set up housekeeping, having moved into the flat I now share with Henry. The arrangement, as Major Herskowitz has hinted in Henry's presence and to his manifest chagrin, is temporary.

"And never mind Speiser" the major tells me, "he'll love you".

After Boot Camp, OCS and FAO training, my new digs are the lap of luxury. Two rooms, a kitchenette, our very own bathroom. Henry insists I call him Hank tho nobody else does. We settle for plain Henry, who has absorbs my invasion of his privacy with little resentment, offering to let me have the bedroom. It is a tempting offer which I refuse out of sheer guilt.

I unpack my meager possessions near the hide-a-bed in Henry's erstwhile living room, after which he volunteers to take me on a tour of the base. The large three-story cinder-block fortress on the way to the PX is the hospital. We circle it leisurely. I wait for Henry to unburden himself.

Thursday after lunch finds us both in the living room. I am browsing through Henry's record collection, while he is flipping restlessly through the three available TV channels. He is clearly on edge. I wait.

"Say Leo..."

"Yes?"

"You're pretty well fixed up on Len's good side, aren't you..."

"Who?" I say, "Major Herskowitz?"

"Yeah".

"I don't know, Henry, I've only met him".

"He seems to like you".

"Let's hope he does".

I have yet to fathom the major's enthusiasm for my presence at Seadock. Henry's awkward probing, however painful to him, may shed some light on the topic.

"I haven't seen the major since last Friday" I tell Henry. "I'm off till tomorrow, some special event every Friday, right?"

"Yeah, we do the demo every Friday".

I wait for more, but Henry is back to his obsession.

"Did he..." he says, "Len, I mean..."

"Yes, Henry?"

"...say anything about your job?"

"Not a word. He wants me to stay ignorant till tomorrow. Fresh mind, no prejudice".

"I see".

He is plainly discouraged.

"Should I start worrying?" I ask him.

"Oh no... Has he, Len... Did he mention me?"

"Not that I recall".

"I was afraid..."

Henry's face begins to crumble.

"This's the worse thing about working for Len" he says, "you never know where you stand".

He must be coming to the point:

"Nothing about the show either?"

"Zilch. Oh, well, he did drag me down to the set".

"He did?"

"Yeah, he knows I went to Cal. But I still have no idea what he's got in mind for me. I expect I'll find out after the demo tomorrow".

"I see".

"You alright, Henry?"

"Well... nevermind".

"Shit, come off it, Henry, I can't read your mind. And you're giving me a headache".

"I think he wants you to take over my job".

The cat is out of the bag.

"That's preposterous, Henry" I tell him. "I don't even know what your job is".

"I act" he says, "I'm in the show, in Len's production".

"Well, then you have nothing to fear, acting ain't my forte, not since I blew the big Theresius scene in Antigone back in highschool".

But Henry is neither deflected nor consoled. And once the dam of his diffidence has been breached, his

190

pent-up paranoia is gushing out unchecked.

"It's been sheer hell working for Len" he says.

"Why? I thought he was a big-shot Hollywood director".

God only knows where I got the idea, but this is my turn to trawl.

"Oh that..." says Henry. "Sure, he was in the movies, worked on DeMille's last project, I forget the name..."

"*The Greatest Show on Earth*? The B-and-B Circus flick?"

"I guess... Thing is, I hate acting. I'm no good at it, everybody knows, and Len's always after my ass, says I miss my cues... The dialog's no problem, he doesn't care what I say, says nobody'll hear me over the ruckus... We use the jumble button on the mike, see, so all you can hear is garbage..."

"Sounds easy enough".

"Sure, but the cues... Len says I have to come on time... But the other guys always mess up theirs and nobody ever tells *them* off... 'sides of which, they don't give a damn. Half of them've already been to Nam, so he can't send them back... The other half are heading there anyway, he's got nothing on them either. So he takes it all out on me..."

"Sounds pretty grim, Henry".

He is looking truly miserable.

"That's not the worst of it" he says.

"Oh?"

"The worst is the hippie stuff".

"Say what?"

"Well, I'm supposed to wear this smelly long-hair wig, put on dirty clothes, pretend to be an anti-war hippie scum, talk trash, cheer for Uncle Ho, light up a *Mary-wana* cigar..."

"Sounds like fun".

Henry is pacing the floor, agitated:

"I hate it!" he says. "That darn wig gives me a rash every time I put it on... I would've asked for a transfer ages ago, but Len keeps saying it's either this or Nam..."

He is on the verge of tears.

"Shit, Henry" I pet him on the arm. "I bet Len's just joshin', no way's he gonna send you to Nam. He's human, ain't he? Besides, he's probably anti-war himself, fuckin' East Coast pinko like the rest of them Hollywood Jews, y'know..."

"He told you that?"

"Don't be silly. But it stands to reason, don't it?"

"Well... yeah... I suppose".

Henry shakes his head dubiously.

"See?" I tell him. "So you can relax".

"I wish I could" he says. "I wish I could believe you. Half the time I don't know what to think anymore".

We both lapse into silence. Henry's predicament is

real enough, but I had better find out where I stand. I pick up an old Sinatra 78 out of Henry's vast collection and put it on. The cheerful optimism of *I Did It My Way* fails to dispel Henry's gloom.

"Say" I ask, "how did you wind up at Seadock?"

"Sheer fluke. And Len knows".

"Knows what?"

"About the computer glitch... I was doing the ROTC at Case Western Reserve, getting my BS in Zoology, taking pre-med, thinking about Med School..."

"That so? Why, Henry, that's wonderful!"

"Think so?"

"Sure".

"Well, I thought so too, I loved it... Anyway, I was doing my thesis on some immune reactions in paramecium. Ever heard of ciliates?".

"Vaguely. Aren't they the guys with the tail?"

"Cilia, rather. Those other ones are flagellates... Anyway, you can make antibodies that will coagulate only with the cilia, they've got that specific protein, you can't find it any other place on the surface of the paramecium.... So I was working out a way to separate the cilia fraction from the rest of the paramecium. You put a whole paramecium culture in a blender, run it real slow, say 27 on the Variac... Three minutes, you filter the stuff through glass wool and the cilia come down in the filtrate. Then you spin that at two thousand, decant the fluid and re-dissolve the pellet in saline. Now all you got left is pure cilia, which you inject into the rabbits... Oh heck, I'm boring you, Leo".

"Hell no, Henry. It sounds like real fun".

"It is. Or was..."

Henry's face clouds again at the recollection. I urge him on:

"What happened, then?"

"I graduated".

"Bad move".

"Exactly. I Got my thesis published, got accepted to Med School, got my commission too. I was sure they'd defer me, get me after Med School. So I go back home to Cleveland for Christmas, Jenny and I were talking about getting married... then I get a letter from my draft board saying since I'd graduated and wasn't going on, my deferment's lapsed and I am called in. Darn Selective Service computer told them I was rejected for Med school".

"Shit, that's terrible, Henry".

"Yeah, well... So I was stuck with an Army commission and no deferment... You can guess where I was heading".

"Straight to Nam".

"What with the attrition rate for second lieutenants... Well, my uncle Rudolph has a friend from the Big One, WW-II... so he called him and the guy pulled some strings... Turns out he'd known Len Herskowitz from Hollywood, used to write scripts together, and Len owed him... Well, they were just putting Seadock together, had top priority, even over Nam.... So Len put in a req form for me, got me shipped over here..."

"What a lucky break".

"You'd think so" says Henry. "Except, Len's been on my case ever since. He keeps threatening to ship me out to Nam".

"I see" I tell him. "Can I ask you something, Henry?"

"Sure".

"How long have you been about".

"And you're still here, right?"

"I guess..."

"And Len owes that buddy of your uncle Rudolph, right?"

"Well, yes..."

"You want my honest opinion? You've got nothing to worry about. If Len had really wanted to throw you to the gooks, he'd have done it by now".

"You think so? Honest?"

"I do".

"I wish I could believe that... Thanks anyway, Leo".

"You're welcome, Henry".

•   •   •

It is quarter to four when Major Herskowitz stops by

to pick me up. Henry has left hours ago, mumbling about urgent chores. I've been hanging around the apartment, having yet to be assigned office space.

The driver, tho black, is not the same one.

"Hey" I ask Major Herskowitz, "where's the sultan?"

"He's in the show. You'll spot him, he's not exactly inconspicuous".

We drive to the edge of the base and follow the same red-dirt road. As we hit the first bump, Major Herskowitz looks at his watch:

"Just in time. I've tried to spare you most of the rah-rah, I want you real fresh".

The set is still there in the cup of the hills, just as incongruous as before. We roll down slowly, flank the left edge of the Av and pull to a stop a hundred yards behind the grandstands. We park behind the Army busses and flag-rank limousines.

It is a full house, ten jam-packed rows. I follow the major up to the top of the grandstands. We take the last two seats in the back row.

"Curtain time in three minutes, *boychik*" says the major. "Check out the audience. Ain't they something?"

The stands below us are crammed with all manner of brass. I count seven three-star generals, four two-stars, nine one-stars, fifteen full colonels, before I give up. Army, Navy, Air Force, Marines. A smattering of dark-suited civilians.

To the right of the stands, three bartenders next to a catering truck are doing brisk business mixing and dispensing. A crew of spit-and-polished black waiters in formal antebellum garb are scurrying up and down the stands, serving and taking orders.

"Who are they?" I ask the major.

"The three services.... Pentagon, Quantico, Langley... National Guard, Reserves, local PDs, county sheriffs, state troopers, military attachés... You name 'em, we got 'em. You like?"

"Heavy brass. Are they here just for the show?"

"Yes and no. They come for a whole week, lectures, demos, pep-talk. But we're the *pièce de resistance*, the icing on the cake. This is where it all comes together, my boy. If they remember anything from Seadock, they remember us".

"No shit".

The major surveys the audience with sardonic pride.

"What you got here, Leo" he says, "is Seadock's student body of the week, primed 'n thirsting for knowledge-- sedition, disruption, subversion, rebellion, you name it... This is their last stop, they go back tomorrow".

"With a colossal hangover?"

"Bingo".

"How come I didn't see them around the base? They're not exactly inconspicuous"

"You don't expect them to mingle with the scum, do you? Nah, they've got their own quarters and classrooms clear at the other end, near the golf course. Sprague is happy to keep them there, last thing he wants is for them to stray over to Seadock".

"Why?"

"Our personnel don't take too well to the brass. We try to keep them apart".

"How come?"

"A long story. Some other time".

The major consults his watch again.

"Ought to start 'bout now" he says.

Which is when a hush falls over the audience and an Army captain rises up at the base of the stands to the right. He stands hatless and trim, his close-cropped hair a neat dark bristle. There is something vaguely familiar about his demeanor. Though from where I sit his face is a blur.

The captain raises his hand up and speaks into a portable mike:

"Gentlemen" he announces in a sonorous baritone, "we're about to start. Those of you who need refills, now's the time. There'll be no bar service for the next forty-five minutes".

I have heard this voice before.

I lean over toward Major Herskowitz:

"Who he?"

"Captain B.? Protocol, PR. Keeps the visiting brass happy. The B. man is Sprague's golden fixer--golf, booze, broads, whatever these VIPs want in line of R'n'R, Captain B. will procure. Rumor has it he can score dope too, hey?"

Major Herskowitz' elbow digs into my ribs.

"That a fact?"

"Rumors".

"I see. How long's he been here?"

"Six months, a bit over, maybe. Why, you know him?"

"For a moment I could swear... His voice... I wish I had my glasses".

I squint furiously but the face is still a blur. Then the deep baritone reclaims the crowd's attention:

"Okay, we're on. What you're about to see, gentlemen, is a slightly compacted version of a genuine urban riot. As you well know, it always starts with outside agitators moving in. So, on a typical Sunday afternoon, a small town in America, same kind many of you must have grown up in.... As you can see, the place is peaceful. Everybody's going about their business..."

I know this voice so well it is driving me crazy.

Below us, the Av is empty no more. People in their Sunday best are strolling up and down the Av. Mothers push their baby prams, stopping to chat and visit. Young couples linger under the awnings, window-shopping, their arms twined discreetly. A few old geezers, over-dressed for the stifling Georgia summer, shuffle about, taking the late afternoon sun. No longhairs, no street people, no blacks. The Av has undergone a startling facelift, morphing into Main Street Disneyland.

"As you can see, gentlemen" Captain B. intones into his mike, "the town is tranquil. Everybody's going about their business cheerfully. Now..."

I can't stand it. I turn and whisper in Major Herskowitz's ear:

"What does the B. stand for?"

"What?..."

"Captain B.... What does the B. stand for?"

"Bozeman.... Like Montana".

"No shit!"

"You know him?"

"Well... it makes no sense... What do you know about him?"

"Nothing. They say he's from some hush-hush outfit, on special assignment. We don't see him much this end except once a week for the show. On formal occasions his chest's fuckin' loaded with ribbons... Can't read most of them except for the silver star and the purple heart with two clusters... Must've been to Nam. Ring a bell?"

"I don't know".

"You should see him at the piano, at parties" says the major. "Belts out a wicked Ragtime like he been raised in Saint Louie..."

"No shit?"

"Another coincidence?"

"Yes".

I am thoroughly confused, but something is stirring across the valley. From beyond the hill comes the labored sputter of an approaching vehicle, which soon emerges from the pine and descends toward the set. Nearing the peaceful tableau of the Av, it suddenly accelerates to break-neck speed.

I squint. It is a vintage VW van with its top lopped off. Loudspeakers are fitted at the van's four corners. The entire body is painted in loud psychedelic stripes. A blood-red peace sign dominates the front panel. An assortment of red stars, hammers-and-sickles and flowers crowd all other available surface. A large Viet Cong flag trails from the back.

As the van comes to the edge of the pavement, a sonic boom of loud Acid Rock explodes from all four speakers--the Dead's *Dark Star*. Inside the van, a dozen or so bodies stand packed together like canned sardines, wild hair flying in the wind. Two king-size Afros are conspicuous among them.

The audience greets the intruders with a salvo of whistles and boos that are all but drowned out by the music. The van roars up the Av to the front of the grandstands, where it comes to a screeching halt. The music ceases abruptly, all doors are flung open, and the occupants eject into the street. Garbed in tattered jeans and tie-died shirts, they brandish picket signs and red Vietcong flags. The two Afros carry, somewhat incongruously, standard issue M-16s.

As the intruders fan out on the Av, a slightly-built young man sporting wild dirty-brown locks and a matching *Fidelista* beard remains behind. He hops back onto the van, propels himself upward and re-emerges on top with a cordless microphone in hand. Before the audience has had time to adjust their bearings, the *barbudo* launches into a wild harangue, aimed at his cohorts who have by now reassembled around the van. His speech, overlaid with loud static and muffled grunts, is near incomprehensible, tho every so often a lone word crashes through the sound barrier:

"Burn!... Fuck!... Establishment!... Mothers!... Vietnam!... Shit!... Capitalism!... Bank!... Imperialists!..."

The longhair band cheer their leader boisterously, waving their flags and picket signs. Some raise their fists in the Black Power salute, others flash the peace sign. They are, it is clear, having a blast.

The townsfolk stand rooted to the pavement in small clusters, gaping at the intruders with distaste. A tableau of two native cultures in stark conflict.

Then, from somewhere in the bowels of the framed scenery, a small contingent of raunchy-looking blacks materialize and join the longhairs near the van.

I turn to the major:

"This for real?"

"You tell me".

"Fuckin' far out".

"Surreal's the word".

At the bottom of the grandstands, Captain B. resumes his running commentary:

"As you can see, gentlemen, the folks are responding to this unprovoked invasion with dignified disdain and shock. Only a few malcontents--professional malingerers, drug addicts, welfare queens--join the outside agitators".

I turn to Major Herskowitz:

"Who wrote this fuckin' script?"

"Hush, just watch, let's have the commentary later. Remember, no preconceptions".

As faithfully as I can, given my utter disgust, I recast an old bit of the Cratylus into contemporary jargon:

"Reality is one fuckin' preconception".

"A delicate point. The Master would have approved..."

"The Master?"

"Antonin Artaud... Ever read *The Theater and Its Double*?"

"Never heard of it".

"Figures. Might wanna take a peek some day. Now watch..."

On some invisible cue, the scrawny chief agitator leaps off the van, hits the pavement the wrong way and crashes head on. Regaining his feet, he is limping awkwardly. The audience in the stand taunts him with salacious observations about the less-exposed portions of his anatomy. As the man scrambles to join his cohorts, the loudspeakers resume their broadcast of Dead rock with the elegiac strains of *Saint Stephen.*

"At least you got the music right" I tell the major.

"Good. Now watch".

I do. I watch the *barbudo* lead his troupe in a rock-throwing, stick-swinging, obscenity-laced assault on the town's startled populace. I watch them scatter and retreat in disarray. They are, however, saved by the proverbial bell as the music ceases abruptly and the scene freezes again into a hushed tableau, over which Captain B.'s voice resumes the narrative:

"As expected, gentlemen, the townsfolk react with restraint to the unprovoked attack by the pinko rabble, who have now switched--as you might have expected--from verbal agitprop to violent intimidation. In the interest of preventing a major eruption, the town's mayor comes out to remonstrate with the intruders. He is accompanied by two members of the media exercising their constitutional right".

From the alley left of Pacific First National Bank, a stocky balding man strides into the street. He is suited up in bankers' grey, a gold chain dangling across his vest. Two guys in shabby brown suits follow in his wake, one sporting a camera, the other a clip-board.

The well-dressed man stops directly in front of the bank, from whence he proceeds to address the intruders. His words are drowned out by a blast of music. The longhair rabble advance on the helpless threesome, soon engulfing them. In a flash, the mayor is assaulted and chased up the Av and into the campus. The two members of the working press, not quite as lucky, are thrown to the ground and stomped on, their camera smashed.

Emboldened, the longhair band now go on a full-tilt rampage up and down the Av, chasing the townsfolk away. Then they reassemble in front of Pacific First National Bank. The music ceases, all action freezes, the comforting voice of Captain B resumes:

"As you see, gentlemen, all venues of peaceful resolution have been exhausted. A confrontation is now inevitable. The town's police, woefully outnumbered after years of liberal budget-cutting, rush over to guard the bank, the outsiders' most likely target".

Gingerly, three uniformed cops take their stand under the white colonnade of Pacific First National. To the acid strains of *Death Don't Have no Mercy*, the chief agitator, his limp more pronounced now, leads his marauders in a frontal assault on the bank.

The three policemen are clubbed to the ground. The raiders leap over their prostrate bodies, smash the plate-glass door with bricks and clubs and disappear inside. In the marauders' wake, the Av is a bleak desolation. The townsfolk are nowhere in sight, the three policemen are writhing on the ground. The van's loudspeakers burst into the lead cut from the Jefferson Airplane's *Surrealistic Pillow*.

When the silence returns, Captain B.'s reassuring baritone is back:

"At this point, gentlemen, the town's mayor, on the advice of his Chief of Police, calls in the National Guard Reserve, who have quietly assembled two blocks away at the Armory".

I turn to Major Herskowitz:

"What Armory? There ain't no Armory in Berkeley. Besides, they would have first called in the Alameda County Sheriff. Those goons love to come on campus and bash pinko hippie heads..."

"You are blessed with a literal mind, my boy" says the major. "Does it really matter?"

"If you want to give them the real thing".

"Real what?"

"Berkeley, the way it was, still is".

"Who the hell gives a fuck? Certainly not these rubes--"

The major's hand traces a wide circle, taking in the audience on the stands below.

"Just think of it as Berkeley of the mind, Leo my boy. Not your mind, *theirs*, hey?"

"Shit" I say. "Sorry, never mind".

But Major Herskowitz is conciliatory:

"We can fix up the little details if it really bothers

you, do a post-mortem. Why don't you take notes?... Now watch. The best is about to come".

Down below us, the longhair band with their local cohorts are pouring out of the bank and back on the Av, where they proceed to ransack the stores, hauling out liquor bottles, appliances and clothes. Out of nowhere, the two gun-toting Afros materialize on top of the bank, out of which dense smoke is now pouring. The brass in the stands erupt in angry boos and whistles, leaping on top of their seats, screaming obscenities and shaking their fists. In the midst of the rising pandemonium, the van's loudspeakers come back to life, spewing out--my God--the Seventh Cavalry's trumpet strains. The Duke to the rescue in the nick of time.

I can't believe my ears. To my left, Major Herskowitz is sporting a wide grin. We are the only ones left sitting.

"Son of a gun" I tell him.

"Ainit?"

The audience slowly regain their seats. Now they are stomping their feet to the beat of the martial fanfares. From both ends of the Av, National Guard platoons are rushing in, the dark visors of their crash helmets lowered. Carbines at the ready, bayonets unsheathed, they move to entrap the longhairs.

This is when the two Afros on top of the bank commence firing at the troopers. Three guardsmen fall to the ground, writhing dramatically. Hemmed in between the two Guard contingents, the longhairs begin lobbing Molotov cocktails into the storefronts on both sides. A car next to the bank is overturned and set on fire.

The Guardsmen retaliate by training their guns on the Afro snipers, plucking both off the roof. Their spectacular dive into the adjoining alley and out of sight is cheered wildly.

The smoke from the burning bank is slowly spreading, wafting toward the front rows, where the audience is coughing. The wail of an approaching fire-engine can be heard, punctuated by the *puk-puk* of a Guard helicopter, which soon makes two low passes and then dives toward center stage, where the longhair contingent is now corralled between two Guard phalanxes. A small object drops on the pavement and bounces between the contending forces. It rolls over erratically, coming to rest at the curb, where it commences spewing thick white fumes.

"Tear gas?" I ask the major.

"Johnson and Johnson".

Below, the longhair band is making its last stand, pelting the guards with rocks, screaming obscenities and flashing the peace sign. Two hippie girls strip off their tie-dyes and taunt the guardsmen with their bare boobs.

"Is this in the script?" I ask the Major.

"What do you think?"

"Shit".

"Does it matter?"

"Something might go wrong".

"Like what?"

The sight of young breasts drives the crowd to frenzy. They are hopping up and down and screaming at the beleaguered longhairs, tho whetherobscenities or encouragement it is hard to tell.

Our view is again blocked by a solid wall of roused uniforms. I look at the major, he winks:

"Ever seen such audience participation? If only Mimi could see this. She'd have an orgasm".

"Mimi?"

"Rosencrantz".

"Who she?"

"My old guru back in L.A. Ever heard of *Instant Theater*?"

"Nope".

"Second City? The Living Theater? The Provos?"

I shake my head.

"Shit, we gotta do something about you education, *boychik*. Make you a deal. You tell me about the real Berkeley, I'll teach you impro".

Down below, the pandemonium has simmered down. The exhausted brass are back in their seats, flushed with victory. On the Av, the Guards have corralled the longhairs into a tight ring facing the proscenium. Torn shirts and bloodstains are in ample evidence.

Right in front of the stands, two burly guards, their

dark visors reflecting the setting sun, are holding the bearded chief agitator between them like a trophy. Stripped to his waist, he faces the audience, arms raised up to shoulder height, chin lolling on his chest, blood-caked curls streaming down his shoulders. A tall black Guardsman is towering behind him like a tree, propping him up by the scruff of his neck.

The chief agitator's eyes are shut tight. His gaunt ascetic face bears a strained dignified smirk. The only thing missing is the crown of thorns.

"My God" I almost scream at major Herskowitz, "that's Henry!"

"Shush. I hope you've been watching him".

"Watching what? This is fuckin' blasphemy! It's in the script too?"

"You expect Speiser to come up with such a beauty on his own?"

"He wouldn't dare. He's scared to death of you".

"Didn't stop him from missing his cues again. Three that I counted. For the last time".

The major looks at his watch.

"Shit, the sprinklers better come on" he says, "let's go down and check. Pay attention to where the valves are".

I follow Major Herskowitz down, we loop back behind the grandstands and duck under the scaffolding in the back of the storefronts that line the Av. The sprinklers are on, spouting away. We make our way slowly under the frame all the way to Durant, where we re-emerge and cross the Av.

"Watch now" the major says.

We stop.

In front of the grandstands, a parade is passing in review. The chief agitator and his longhairs are in the lead, followed by the mayor and townsfolk and their out-gunned police force, now resurrected. Two Guard platoons bring up the rear, followed by an armored personnel carrier that has joined the procession out of nowhere. The helicopter is circling above. In front of the stands, Captain B. is addressing the audience, tho we are too far away to hear his denouement.

"Wow" I tell the major, "wowie zowie".

We circle behind the set, cross the street and duck under again to check on the rest of the sprinklers. When we are back out on the Av, the place is nearly deserted. The cast and the audience have decamped. The rubble-strewn Av is spewing away the last plumes of smoke. A work detail of five servicemen in coveralls are tending to the dying fires.

We stroll past the deserted stands. The limousines and busses are gone. Major Herskowitz' jeep is where we left it--with Abdul Hameed puffing on a cigar in the driver seat. His Guard uniform is still on, the visored helmet slung over his shoulder. For once, his ubiquitous shades are off. It is the helmet that finally click it all into place--it still sports the Alameda Country Sheriff green-and-red emblem.

"Shit, Wesley" I tell him, "you playing the Man this time around?"

"Just followin' orders, Leo my main man".

A grin flashes briefly across his face.

The major looks from one to the other in disbelief: "You two jokers know each other?"

Abdul Hameed nods:

"Me 'n whiteboy here goes a long way back, Major Len. We been to the liberation struggle together. Tha's right, Leo my man?"

"Right on. You been in Ft. Gordon all this time, Wesley?"

"You kiddin'? The Man got hold of my black ass, shipped me straight to Nam. Whole fuckin' year there. Man said either that or the slammer".

"What're you doing at Seadock?"

"Long story. How 'bout you? Been to Nam yet?"

"Not yet".

"How come?"

"Long story too".

"Whiteboy luck?"

Wesley-Abdul Hameed shakes his head slowly.

"Shit. Still got them gloves?"

"Yup. I see you got the helmet".

"Come in handy".

"Either side of the barricades?"

Which is where the major finally cuts in:

"We better haul ass, Abdul Hameed" he tells his driver.

"Yessuh Major Len".

In the eerie calm that has settled over the narrow valley, with the dampened fires wafting their gentle plumes into the scented evening sky and the cicadas screaming their heads off, we bid farewell to the Av and rumble our way up the sand dunes and into the pine.

7. Gretchen

(Ft. Gordon, GA; September 1969)

      I am trapped in the coiled bowels of a dark conspiracy. Too many coincidences and strange maybes, a dearth of explanations. I had better find out what is going on before I lose my mind.

      I could peruse the Ft. Gordon phone directory that is sitting right on top of my desk. I could pick up the phone, dial and say:

      "Captain Bozeman sir? Uh, this is Lieutenant Leo Swenson and..."

      "Yes, Lieutenant?"

      "I have a delicate question that..."

      "Yes?"

      "You see, sir, there's this guy I used to know..."

      "Are you planning to get to the point sometime soon, Lieutenant?"

      "Well, yes, sir... Thing is, sir, are you by any chance the Boz?"

      "Beg your pardon?"

      It is Saturday morning, and my tired brain has been running through multiple permutations ever since last night. They are all equally depressing, a tad more every time I try another one for size.

Like:

"Sir, I have been wondering..."

"Yes, Lieutenant?"

But why should the captain be interested? And how do I cover my ass just in case?

Like:

"Captain Bozeman?"

"Speaking".

"There's an urgent matter I'd like to bring to your..."

"Who's this?"

"...an urgent matter..."

"Urgent to who?"

In the end, my predicament is resolved for me. I get up late and dive into the shower just to avoid talking to Henry, who is laying in wait in the kitchen, brooding and twitching. I am in the middle of a spirited rendition of *Sitting on the Dock of the Bay* when Henry knocks on the sliding-glass door:

"Leo..."

Could he be that desperate?

"Yes, Henry?"

"Phone call for you".

"Coming!"

I wrap a towel around my waist, rush to the living room and grab the phone:

"Hello?..."

A deep baritone says:

"You awake?"

"Who's this?"

Not that I need to ask.

"Cut the shit, man. Meet me down on the set in 20 minutes".

"Hold it! Is this--"

But the phone has gone dead in my wet hand.

I towel myself hurriedly, put on my track suit and sneakers and race downstairs and out the door. The base is largely deserted, I jog past the last drab structures, down the dirt road and into the pine. A light breeze is blowing in my face, the dense vegetation on both sides rustles pleasantly. An early rising meadowlark is trilling his sweet courtship song, an uncanny rendition of the opening bars of Mozart's 40th. I whistle back and am rewarded with musical company all the way down to the little bowl in the dunes. The poor thing must be worried sick of an impostor poaching on his turf.

A lone figure in grey Army-issue gym suit is seated half way up the grandstands. I slow down to catch my breath. He waves me up to join him. I plop down in the seat next to him.

"Shit, Boz" I tell him, "you sure give a body the shivers! Kept me awake half the night trying to talk myself into believing it wasn't you".

"Pipe down, Leo. Who else could I be?"

"They could get you for impersonating an officer, you know. Not to mention all those fuckin' medals. Where the hell did you get hold of them? Central Casting?"

"Nam".

"You mean them things are for real?"

"Anything weird about that?"

"Captain?"

"Beats lieutenant any time".

"Bozeman?"

"Close enough. What's in a name? Or haven't you noticed? Swenson with an Oh?"

I feel light in the head.

"Now let me get this straight, Boz. You were in the Army in Nam?"

"Who said Army?"

"Then what?"

"Let's say special stuff? Recon, intel, spook games. Three years. Came back Christmas sixty-seven, barely missed Tet".

"And Berkeley?"

"On assignment".

"Runnin' dope?"

"Deep cover. Know any better?"

I am trumped.

"Besides" says the Boz, "business is business. What do you think we were doing in Nam? Saving the world for democracy?"

I am not exactly shocked. I flash back to Gary and Troy. It almost adds up, but not quite.

"What the fuck are you doing at Seadock, Boz?"

"Taking care of business".

"Right here in the Georgia pine?"

"Ain't nothing wrong with Georgia pine".

"What does the Army say about that?"

"Army don't know, Army don't say. Besides, they need my expertise. Longhairs and dope are in, Leo, case you haven't noticed. The Army's hot for guys who know the scene".

"Meaning what?"

"For starters, what are *you* doing here?"

"I got sent here".

"Why?"

"Army fuckup. My records got mixed up".

"Oh?"

What the Boz is insinuating is preposterous, fuckin' far-out. I get up and turn and look down at him. He is flopped back in his seat, relaxed, his arms spread out over the back of the seats on both sides. His long, tapered fingers are drumming an intricate pattern on the grey Army-issue metal.

With a start, I flash back to the musical bravura I witnessed that early afternoon in the sun-drenched flat above the Piccolo, watching the revolution go sour from behind the Boz's lace curtains.

"You had something to do with the switcheroo, right?

219

With poor Captain Swensen going to Nam?"

"Let's say I didn't lift a finger to stop it. Army's got plenty of professional fuckups sitting in their little offices messing things up".

"But this is fuckin' crazy!"

The Boz' dark, doleful, eyes survey me from under his corrugated brows. The sensuous curled lips twitch ruefully. After a while he releases the air in a soft whistle.

"Why?"

What do I know?

The Boz shakes his head slowly.

"Don't you understand, Leo?" he says. "You've been my star operative. You're a fuckin' natural. Even Troy--poor devil, may Odin let his harsh Norse soul into Valhalla--said so. Grudgingly. Sucker didn't take to you all that much... But boy are you reckless! Fucking your way across the West with the Sarge's old lady--where was your head while your prick was dippin'? That big Red Injun could've carved your skinny ass to pemican strips, could've made moccasins out of your soft white hide, hang your curly scalp on grandma's tepee back on the Rez... Would've done it half asleep too, without giving it another thought! Shit... Then getting strung up on smack 'n taking it out on poor Mad. Can't you get it into your thick skull, man--we *sell* the fuckin' stuff, we don't *do* it. Shootin' dope's for the suckers who pay..."

Do I need the Boz to tell me I'm an unregenerated fuckup? My mom and dad could have told him, all he's got to do is ask.

"Yeah, that one was bad" I tell him, "stupidest thing I ever done... Oops, take it back, signing up was probably worse".

"You kidding?" says the Boz. "Signing up was a fuckin' inspiration, the smartest thing you ever done, Leo. Why, I was there, I couldn't believe my eyes--zonked out of your fuckin' gourd 'n you still gone 'n done something that smart".

"Don't be absurd, Boz".

"Listen--"

The Boz leans forward, glaring right at me:

"The White Plains draft board was after your ass, registered letters, right? Even daddy couldn't get you off the hook this time. And don't tell me he didn't try".

"How the fuck would you know?"

The Boz shakes his head slowly.

"I make it my business to know, boy. Recon, intel, remember? Shit, Leo, signing up was a fuckin' master stroke. You got out of the loop just ahead of the narcs, got the Army to de-tox you for free, got yourself a warm bunk, three square a day, plenty of exercise, fresh air. It would've cost your daddy twenty grand, bottom, to detox you at some posh Catskills facility, even with the discount from his med-school buddies. And the fuckin' Army would've still gotten you in the end".

The Boz's intense, incredulous eyes scan me for hints of residual intelligence:

"I suppose" I concede.

"You betcha".

The Boz is right on the money. What with the Army's insatiable appetite for young flesh to propitiate the Molloch. I plop back in my seat. In the silent mid-morning, the Boz and I contemplate the surrealistic Av below, from which faint plumes of smoke are still wafting. My eyes glide over to the window above the Piccolo, where the Boz's real-life lace curtained would have been. How strategic.

"Sure was a good gig, hey?" the Boz says, as if privy to my innards. "While it lasted..."

A faint note of regret?

"Sure was".

"Was bound to blow up tho, like all good things. But here you are, Leo my boy, back in Mother's womb where one can keep an eye on you, make sure you stay clean".

"Gee thanks, Boz".

"Don't go sarcastic on me, boy. Besides, I need you".

My antennae, lulled into sleep for a moment, register a harsh jolt.

"Need me? What for?"

The air is heating up. I rise and take off my sweat-shirt. In the deserted grandstands, I now receive a compressed overview of the Boz's new world order.

"The times they are a-changin' " he says, his brooding eyes fixed vacantly on the dummy façade of Pacific

First National across the street. "Everything's in a flux. As the ol' boy said, *panta rei*, even a moron can see that. Grass's still a sweet turn-on, mind you, I like to get high just like the next guy... Does weird and wonderful things to music, things you'd have never guessed. Ever tried playing Scarlatti stoned?"

I have never tried playing Scarlatti period.

"Absolute sendoff, fuckin' blast. Drills down into your inner core, all the way back to where the Greek and Arab roots of the Spanish Partitas pop out and merge. You oughta try it sometime, Leo, never mind the playing, just listen..."

"I'll be sure to do that".

The Boz ignores my crack. For a while he is lost to the world around him, no doubt soaring among the gleaming strands of harpsichord and lute *arpeggios*.

At long last he shakes his head:

"Nevermind, this's personal. What I mean is, the market's changing. You gotta go with the flow, roll with the punches, adapt, evolve... Weed's too bulky for what it gets you per kilo. Takes a ton to turn serious profit, something that'll begin to tickle your retirement account. Fuckin' stuff's a mess to package, mess to ship, mess to sell, mess to hide... Plus, who're we selling the stuff to? Our customer base? Buncha kids on a weekly allowance? Highschool dropouts and slackers? Jazz-club blacks down on their luck? Fried-brain misfits and blissed-out hippies at Rock concerts and love-ins? Penny-ante stuff, man, ain't worth the grief. Worse--it's an entry-level market. Just think--guy tries the weed, 'fore you know it he's craving something stronger, goes on to the hard stuff. They all do. So that's where the real growth is, the future. That's where all dope-heads wind up, sooner or later".

I am having a devil of a time following the Boz's logic.

"You mean smack? Heroin?" I ask.

"Nah. Smack's got a bad rep, wherever you look around, all you see is fuckin' losers--addicts, mainliners, jailbirds, niggers. Glassware alone scares off most people, then you gotta worry about infection, sterilization... Only the nutcakes mainline, Leo. You been there, you know how it is".

I am blushing.

"Now you take meth" the Boz goes on. "That's better, but only by a hair. Mostly rednecks, goofy kid stuff, one notch above sniffin' glue. High volume, low per-unit profit, not all that different from grass, tho a bit easier to push..."

"What, then?"

The Boz looks at me pensively.

"Coke" he says.

I am not sure I heard it right.

"Cocaine?"

"Yup".

"But..."

The Boz holds up his hands.

"Just listen" he says, "and think, like crank up that unused processing capacity that must be stashed somewhere in your thick skull, hey? Coke's the rich man's turn-on, too expensive for the kids, too exotic for the rednecks. Doctors-and-lawyers stuff, bankers and brokers, accountants and young execs, guys on the make. People in the fast lane, up-and-comers, movers and shakers--judges, politicians, movie stars. You can smoke it, shoot it, snort it... Christ, you can even butt-fuck it!"

"You're kiddin'!"

"I'm not speaking from personal experience if that's what you mean".

"But isn't it kinda hard to get hold of? I thought you had to go all the way to South America..."

"Didn't I tell you the times they are a-changin'? World's getting smaller. Grapevine says a new crowd is taking over south of the border. Young hip *chicos*, know about ranching, know about labs, know about business--shit, lots of them got Harvard MBAs... Dudes think finance, think production, distribution, protection--especially protection. Story is, they got whole private armies down there protecting their investment. Story is, they pay top dollar, practically own three fuckin' governments... Ever heard of a place called Medellin?"

"Colombia?"

"Bravo, you get an A in geography... Well this new

crowd owns the place. Got their big *fincas* all over the
province, run them like military camps... Well, they're looking
for a reliable hookup at this end. We come in with them
right now, start on the ground floor, catch the growth curve...
We're talking serious moolah, man, riding a fresh bull
market to the top. Five years tops, then retire with no care
in the world..."

"And sit back play Scarlatti?"

"Whatever turns you on. You still with me, boy?"

"How do you know all this, Boz?" I ask.

"Recon, intel, remember? I'm still in the loop, I get
the latest scuttlebutt, Langley, Quantico, hush-hush stuff...
Guys come down every week with envelopes. Why do you
think they pulled me back up here?"

"To set you up in the drug trade?"

My voice must betray my incredulity. The Boz eyes
me with undisguised scorn.

"Don't be an idiot, Leo" he says. "The US Military's
going into the drug interdiction business, into the counter
insurgency business down south. Ft. Gordon's the staging
grounds, it all comes and goes through here. The hub, where
it all connects, where all supply and demand lines cross. The
vortex. So we hitch a ride. Big ops, lots of slack. Get my
drift?"

What the Boz is telling me is mind boggling. If
true, it is no cause for cheer.

"Now listen, Boz" I tell him. "I'm barely keeping my

226

head above the water as it is. Fuckin' Army might discover my lost file any day now and haul my sorry ass down to Nam. Last thing I need is a drug-traffickin' bust on an Army reserve".

The Boz shakes his head.

"You still don't get it, do you?" he says. "I'm your ticket out of Nam. Long's I say so, your papers stay lost".

"You can really do that?"

"Can? Where do you think your service file is?"

"How should I know?"

"Care to have a peek?"

I look at the Boz. I have never known him to brag. If he says he has my file, he most likely does.

"I don't think so" I tell him.

"Any time" he says, "just say the word".

What I think I've just heard depresses me.

"What do you want me to do?" I ask the Boz.

"Nothing, for the moment. Just keep cool, stay out of trouble, don't fuck up. Think you can manage that? We're phasing out of the grass business, unloading the last of the old stock. Here, let me show you something--"

The Boz rises and hops down two rows at a time. I follow him to the bottom, then on across the Av to the Piccolo. We stop in front of t he fake painted door and the Boz pulls out a set of keys. Before I know it, the door is open. Out of nowhere, the Boz produces a flashlight.

I follow gingerly into the dark cavern under the

scaffolding, a forest of studs and cross-beams. The flashlight dances upon a solid plywood wall that rises into the shadows above. We follow the wall slowly an d turn the corner.

"Hold the light, willya?" says the Boz.

I take the flashlight. In the dancing yellow beam, the Boz produces his keys and opens another door.

"Here" he says, "come take a peek".

I give him back the flashlight, and he shines it into the dark beyond the door. I see a piled-up heap covered with sheets of black plastic.

"You got the stuff stashed right in here?"

"What's left... Once we finish moving it, deal's over".

"Just like that? Here in Ft. Gordon? On the set?"

"Know of a safer place?"

"Suppose they find it?"

"No big deal. Most of it has been sold, so we write off the rest as tax loss... Nothing in here that says who owns it".

"But it's practically exposed!"

"Hide in plain sight, hey? Besides, the place's being watched day and night. Your roommate Speiser, he's in charge of posting guard, rotation, the works".

"Henry's in on this?"

"You a nut or something? Henry's innocent as a sucklin' pig, blood of the Lamb, low IQ to boot. Guess who he reports to".

"You? I thought you're PR".

"And security. And drug interdiction".

"This's all for real, Boz? Honest?"

"Have I ever lied to you, Leo? Once?"

Would I ever know if he did?

"What do you expect me to do?" I ask him.

"I already told you, nothing, for the moment. Just keep your eyes open, don't fuck up. When things fall together, I'll let you know".

The Boz locks up the inner door, than the outer. We are back on the Av in front of the phantom Piccolo.

"Race you back to the base" he says.

Before I have a chance to decide whether to take him up on the challenge, he is fifty yards ahead, pumping away up the sand dune like a gazelle heading for high ground. I break into a run but never catch up. The gap between us widens as I huff and puff over the crest of the hill. When I finally make it back to the edge of the base, I am out of breath. The Boz is nowhere in sight.

• • •

Monday at ten Henry Speiser and I present ourselves at Len Herskowitz' office, where it is all made official--I am to take over Henry's job, with a two-week overlap to assimilate the routines. After a brief lunch break, the two of us retreat to Henry's--soon to be mine--office,

229

where he drones on and I take incoherent notes.

No amount of reassurance will convince Henry he is not bound for the next troop ship to Nam. And I am the agent of his demise, the usurper, snake in the grass. His paranoia is infectious. That night, I have bad dreams.

Tuesday, my first day on the set, is fraught with ominous revelations. Stripped down to its bare skeleton, our production is a Rube Goldberg monster. Its interlocking parts, grafted onto one another in great clutter, are controlled by a myriad hair-trigger cues. Like an over-designed ambush, Len Herskowitz' directorial masterpiece is strewn with booby-traps.

When I query the proud *auteur* about this mind-numbing complexity, I am deflected with an enigmatic smile and the gentle assurance:

"Relax, *boychik*. Everything's gonna be hunky dory".

"But Len" I tell him, "there's too much here that can go wrong. Can't we simplify just a little bit?"

"A true work of art is like a Swiss clock, Leo. You muck up one part, the whole goes haywire".

"Exactly".

"You gotta think holistic, Leo. Gotta think Tao. Trust me".

"Not to mention accidents".

"Accidents are the essence of great theater" he says. "The more the merrier".

"Let me guess. Artaud, right?"

"Bingo".

I can see now how Henry Speiser comes by his paranoia.

Nor are my trepidations assuaged Wednesday and Thursday. Our cast is a mix of hard-core veterans and revolving-door temps. I can count on the former, interspersed as they are in each contingent--hippie marauders, townsfolk, national guard--to know the drill. But can I count on their good will?

Seven nurses from the base hospital comprise our female corps. Five of those make up the fair-sex auxiliary of the townsfolk. The other two, strictly volunteers, play the bare-breast hippie nookies.

I am the lone Seadock staff in the marauding band, over which I preside in my best Mario Savio panache. The National Guard regulars are split down the middle, black and white. The former, ten strong, are crew-bossed by Abdul Hameed. Like their white brethren, they are all veterans of the Big Red One in Nam. Trained killers. Are they sane enough to see the advantage of killing time in Georgia over killing gooks in Pleiku?

The balance of our white Guard contingent are fresh grunts, as are the bulk of my marauding longhairs. They rotate through Ft. Gordon for a three-week tour of duty between basic training and Nam.

Black and white come together on the set. Otherwise, they keep apart. When I mention this to Len, he shrugs:

"Say it's a coincidence".

"Black and white?"

"Army says it is. Army blows mysterious like the wind. Haven't you noticed?"

"But..."

"Grow up, Leo, willya. This is the sovereign state of Georgia".

At the end of my first week of apprenticeship I lose Henry Speiser to terminal depression. From the bedroom, into which he has retired, subdued strains of Paul Anka and Frankie Avalon emanate day and night. I know I should worry about him. Except, I am more worried about Len Herskowitz.

For, it appears, the major has cast me adrift. Having withdrawn from direct supervision by the end of my second week on the set, he is invisible. A badge of his confidence? Cruel desertion? He is still at the top of the stands every Friday for the show, and Monday for our joint post-mortem.

The gloom that hovers over our flat has become unbearable when, on the second Thursday of my ascent to stage glory, the winds again shift abruptly. Captain B. is out of PR. With Len Herskowitz's blessing, Henry steps in.

What God has taken with one hand, God giveth with the other, in abundance. For with Henry's new job come Captain B.'s digs and office. Which leaves me in sole possession of both our flat and office.

What is more, I am absolved. Henry drops by to apologize for having maligned me unjustly. I assure him all is forgiven. Perhaps, but not forgotten, for I am now the object of Henry's boundless gratitude. My personal intercession with Major Herskowitz, he swears, brought about his last-minute deliverance from certain doom.

While Henry savors his good fortune, I am in the hot seat, and am being set up, no doubt here, for an certain Fall. Once again I am the lamb, *Agnus Dei*, fattened for the altar. Having inherited Henry's job, flat and office, I am now heir to his bleak destiny.

Worse yet, I am as lonely as an orphaned kitten. And horny. And I miss Serena something fierce.

●　　●　　●

It is the third week of my reign as the chief outside agitator, our cast rolls through the drill like old pros. Grateful, I let them be, having appointed a good ol' boy from Alabama, Corporal Donner, head honcho of my white regulars. I communicate to my charges strictly through channels, Donner and Abdul Hameed, having resolved to slap both with their third stripe as soon as opportunity beckons.

The two corporals are my chain of command. All beefs and gripes seep up through them. As far as I can tell, my black and white contingents function like ancient tribes, by elusive consensus with which I had best not tamper.

Friday finds me with my band of long-hairs, raising hell in front of the bank. We are midway through our assault on the Mayor, and my current batch of draftees, in their first week on the set, have proven exceptionally obtuse. During rehearsal Wednesday, they charged prematurely, scuttling the Mayor's grand soliloquy. Chastised and upbraided, they bent over backward on Thursday and let the two newsmen escape unmolested.

The grandstands are laden with our weekly quota of boisterous brass. I am on edge. But--third time's the charm-- the guys deliver with class. Sprague's chief accountant unleashes his supplication, his shining pate gets properly clubbed. The two newsmen lie on the pavement in feigned agony. To the loud fanfares of *Honky Tonk Woman*, I lead my marauders in a spirited chase of the populace up the Av.

Once past Durant, we are invisible to the stands. The playbook now calls for the townsfolk to melt away into the storefronts, then wait out the endgame. My marauders are to rush back down the Av now and lay siege to the bank.

I am in hot pursuit of one of the ladies, who has somehow neglected to let go of her baby pram. The damn contraption slows her down, I am gaining rapidly. She reaches the corner of Durant and, in exasperation, pushes the offending vehicle back in my path.

I leap aside to duck the lethal missive. My prey resumes her flight, heading for the safety of the storefronts.

My blood is pounding in my head, a set of old atavistic instincts takes over. The woman plunges into the dark gloom under the awnings of Schwartz's. In spite of her small frame and ankle-length blue dress, she executes her sprint with great agility and grace.

The relevant lobe of my hunter's brain cannot help but register the lush backside--red flag--she wiggles at me as she dashes for cover. Under the chaste white bonnet, her honey-blond hair is pulled up in a bun, revealing a tanned neck set delicately, like the lily's anthers, in her round white-lace collar. He hair begins to unravel, wild strands of honey trail like the tails of a soaring kite. I am right upon her, mesmerized by the fine-etched detail of her backside, when--deep in the shade under Schwartz's low awnings--she stops abruptly and turns around, eyes blazing.

Hot Jesus!

I break to a screeching halt, alas too late, and bump frontally right into my query, who greets me with the terse observation:

"Fuck! What a clod!"

I draw back and fight to regain my balance, and my breath. Two undaunted blue eyes peer at me with undisguised scorn from under the almost-dislodged bonnet. The eyes preside over the most enchanting field of golden freckles, strewn over the flat bridge of a darling upturned nose.

We are both panting hard as we face off under the awnings.

"Why, Lieutenant!..." I gasp in a flash of implausible

235

recognition.

She frowns and squints, peering up at me quizzically, her head inclined forward. This is when I get my first hint of how near-sighted she is.

"I know you from someplace" she says. "Your voice. Hey, you're the one who took over from Speiser, right?"

"Bingo".

My troops are way down the street, about to lay siege to the bank.

"Shit, gotta run!" I tell her. "A favor? Stay right where you are! Be back in a jiffy".

And I turn back and sprint.

"You got some nerve!" she calls after me.

"Please pretty please?..." I scream over my shoulder.

If she has responded, her voice is lost in the ruckus raised by my rudderless cohorts, now set to polish off the town's token police force. I rush to join them, only too conscious of Len Herskowitz high up in the bleachers. I'll hear all about it Monday at Post Mortem.

The last fifteen minutes of the Battle of Berkeley are a hissing black hole into which all shards of memory have been sucked. I go through the motion, dazed and panicked, blotting out both my final crucifixion and the audience's jeers. All I can think of is--will she still be there?

As soon as the closing parade is over, I rush back

to Schwartz's and--Blessed Virgin--she is there, sitting on a charred cinder block. She appears even more petite, her lace bonnet off, her hair down to shoulder length.

I gasp.

"Thanks for waiting..."

From her low perch she says:

"I don't know why I did".

"Nevermind" I tell her. "You're here. And don't worry about fraternization, I'm a lieutenant now. Jg, in case that matters".

"Don't be silly. So, you replaced Speiser".

"Not by choice".

"You're in the Army now. Wonder what happened to Captain B."

"Called away to bigger and better".

"And Henry got kicked upstairs?"

"More room at the top".

"Good for him, good for you, good for the show".

"Do I takes this as a compliment?"

"You *are* a much better actor".

Catching herself, she adds:

"Don't let it go to your head, tho".

"Easy to outshine poor Henry, that's it?"

"I mean, you're still a clod and I still can't figure out where I met you".

"Previous incarnation?"

"You're not *that* lucky".

I squint down at her.

"You really don't remember?"

"I don't have my glasses on" she says. "And you still got that silly wig on...".

"Oh shit..."

I pull the offending rug off my head and kneel down next to her. Her proximity is making me dizzy.

"How about now?"

The blue eyes above the sweet field of freckles spark in recognition:

"Fuck, it's you. I should have known. Leo the lion...".

"You remember! Christ, what are you doing here?"

"Got transferred, two months ago".

"But, how?"

"Dr. Creighton got reassigned, some hush-hush research project at the hospital. He requisitioned me".

"Just like that?"

Then it dawns on me:

"Oh shit, don't tell me you two are..."

"Don't be silly" she says. "Emmet's happily married. I know his wife and kids, for God's sake!"

"Glory be!"

"I'm not so sure".

But she is mollified

"I still can't believe you waited" I tell her.

"Me neither".

"You've never told me your name".

"I'm still not sure I should".

I look closer and, for the first time, detect the mischievous glint in her eyes.

"Have a heart" I plead, "don't you see I'm desperate?"

"That's what worries me".

"Please?"

She relents:

"Gretchen".

I savor the name, rolling it over my tongue, half intoxicated already.

"Gretchen, Gretel. Can I be your Hansel?"

"I thought you were Leo".

"I'll change it just for you. It never brought me much luck ".

"With that silly wig, more like the bad witch".

"Guess I'm stuck with Leo" I tel l her. "At least you remembered".

"Don't make too much of it. I'm cursed with total recall. The minute I heard your voice, I knew I'd met you before".

"But I will, I will. Let me clutch at straws, please? And I adore your gorgeous total recall. The rest of you too, come to think".

The last bit escaped me wholly unbidden. Never in my life have I been so brazen. But I am giddy with lust and don't need a mirror to know I am blushing.

"Whoa, lion" she says, "too fast".

"Am I making a fool of myself?"

"Royally".

"Damn. Sorry, can't help it. How 'bout we stop fencing?"

"Oh, is that what we're doing?"

"Feels like it from this end".

"What's the matter, lion, you not up to it?"

"It's been a long day, I've been on this stupid set since nine in the morning. And now you've taken my breath away".

"That so? I've been up since four. This is overtime, case you wanna know".

"Good" I tell her. "I mean, I'm tired, you're tired, how about getting outta here? Like dinner maybe?"

"Whoa again".

I rise and give her my hand. Her small palm in my grip is firm and warm. I pull her up, then I turn and walk to the middle of the street and on toward the grandstands. My knees are wobbling. The place is deserted except for the fire crew.

"Let's walk back" she says. "I don't go back on till eleven".

"You mean, after all this you're still on night-shift?"

"Yup".

"Don't you get release time for this?"

"You kidding? We were volunteered, even Dr. Creighton couldn't get me off. We are the only officers that are pressed into this bullshit".

"Me too" I remind her.

"As overload?"

We follow the now-familiar upward curve of the hill, trudging in the dry grass as the slope rises to meet the pine. Near the top, the sun breaks out of the clouds briefly, now low over the horizon. It is a scented warm evening, with just a hint of the coming rain. I cannot tell whether the fragrance is Gretchen's or the sweetgrass wafting over from the wetlands downriver.

She takes my hand, and my heart leaps into my throat. I am choked with desire. Gretchen's warm fingers squeeze mine ever so gently.

"Sorry I gave you a hard time" she says. "Chuck it up to sleep deprivation. Plus, I really don't know what to do with you".

"Who says you have to do anything?"

"You do. You practically insist".

"That's because I'm desperate".

"Tough. I don't like to be pushed, not even by a lovable rake. Know what I mean?"

"I'm not sure".

But of course I do. Tho coming from her, it doesn't sting that much. She has pegged me just right, which is both a relief and a worry. Till now, my mom has been the only woman who's gotten my number. But she had earned her spurs with years of intimacy, gallons of empathy and, yes, love. Critical but still unconditional; smoldering, irrational, boundless love.

Well, almost the only one. For without meaning to, my mind loops back upon itself and comes up with Serena and her disconcerting flashes of dark knowledge, coming out of nowhere, cutting to the chase. But did Serena care? Really really? It all seems so long ago. And will this diminutive waif holding my hand do the same? Will she short-cut through the requisite waiting period and drill straight to my core? Can I let her skip the customary pain and suffering? Skip paying admission to Leo's circus?

Hey, I say to myself, watchit boy. Two in a row, you're losing your touch, your patented golden inertia.

As far back as I can remember, women--these magical beings I worship and pray to, like this gorgeous runt standing next to me--have found my quiescence irresistible. *Mysterium mundi.* For all I've ever done is smile and go along, and it drives them to ameliorative frenzy. They see me flawed and wanting--sweet Jesus, they ain't stupid, my kinks are out there for all to see--yet eminently fixable. Then, with relish, they take charge of my rudderless life, reshape my drifting persona, re-route my rudderless soul.

And I rise to the occasion. I accommodate, concur, give way, go along for the ride. Mostly, I feign and dissemble and hide. My brief interlude with Serena notwithstanding, what has come over me now is unprecedented. As I stand next to Gretchen on the cusp of the low hill, the two of us bathed in the rays of the setting sun, I am overwhelmed by a sharp sense of transparency. I feel naked.

Gretchen is gazing upon the valley below, but I am the one under the microscope. I am waiting for her verdict, for the other shoe to drop.

"Well" she says at last, " at least you're honest about it. Maybe semi-honest..."

Pierced through the heart. Was I talking aloud?

"Most guys" she says, "are oh so fuckin' sympathetic. Like of course they know. Like of course they understand. Whatever it takes to barrel and bully their way into your heart... The warm glow, the tenderness, the courtship--the whole obstacle course taken on the run and then, zip, they're in your pants. Hooray for the main event. Know what I mean?"

"Unfortunately" I tell her, in not-so-fond memory of all those countless other times, other places, other loves.

"The meaningful glance" she says, "the soulful sigh, the pining... The laying of siege, if not of hands... Total sensory stalking. Someone's eyes are always there to meet yours till you don't know where to turn... Shit, Leo, what have we done to deserve this? Honest, you tell me".

How could I?

"Know what it feels like from this end?" she says. "Shall I tell you?"

I nod.

"Like a prey, like having to dodge, always. Are you stalking me, Leo?"

Am I?

"I hope not" I tell her, "not my style, as a rule... Maybe it's just the long deprivation. I haven't visited inside a woman for over a year".

"Why do I find this hard to believe?"

"It's much worse, really".

"What could be worse for a man?"

"Falling in love".

"Oh?"

The joke is on me, still I find myself laughing with her.

"Out goes the fun, in comes the pain" I tell her.

She turns to looks at me, squinting against the gathering wind. We have stopped at the very edge of the woods and are facing the narrow valley that cups the set. Gretchen has dropped my hand. I haven't attempted to recoup.

"Another trick of yours? Star-crossed lover? Give me a break, Leo. Think up something more original".

"Ain't all that easy to improve on the truth".

"You playing for sympathy?"

"Shamelessly".

She shakes her head:

"You're wasting your time, kiddo, I'm not the sucker I used to be. I think I've finally discovered something I could learn from my mom. She used to fall for every basket case that washed up on her doorstep. You got a half-decent sob story, she'd take you in. Boy how I used to hate them all... My mom's a great believer in the redemptive powers of pussy... Or was. Haven't seen her in years".

"Don't knock redemptive powers".

"Don't count on a cure".

"I'm not a sob story".

"Why all the desperation then?"

"You want it straight?"

She nods.

"Honest?"

"That would be refreshing".

"Okay" I tell her. "Truth is, I don't really know. The only explanation I seem to come up with is I'm in love".

"Well then act like you are".

"I thought I *was*".

She shakes her head. In the distance I hear the rumble of an approaching storm. The wind is blowing harder, whipping Gretchen's honey hair across her face.

"A girl is not a castle, Leo" she tells me. "You don't need to lay siege to me".

"I won't".

"No plotting? No campaigning?"

"You got it".

She pauses. Then:

"One more thing?"

"Name it".

"Stop being so fuckin' agreeable. You're driving me crazy".

We eye each other like two roosters in the barn, except there's no audience to egg us on.

"You've just put me in a double bind" I tell her.

"Terrific. I got you where I want you".

I am about to apprize her I am all hers, lock-stock-&-barrel wherever and however she would care to take me, whenever she would deign to stoop. Wisely, I refrain. Not least because the clouds have settled over the small basin and a sharp bolt of lightning has just exploded over our head, striking down a scrawny acacia just thirty yards away and spiking the air with the pungent smell of ozone. The lightning is followed almost immediately by a crashing, deafening thunder.

I grab Gretchen's hand.

"We better get off this hill before we fry".

We sprint back down toward the back of Pacific First National. We almost beat the rain, but not quite. The large drops, driven by the gusting wind, are flailing at our backs as we reach the tangled frame and plunge headlong into the darkness.

"Here" I tell her, offering my hand.

"Well" she says, "I don't know..."

She sounds reluctant. She takes hold of the proffered hand, only to stop and tug at me.

"What's the matter?" I say.

"Better stop".

I am peering into the dark two-by-four jungle criss-crossed with shafts of light that filter in through multiple gaps in the unfinished structure.

"Not much privacy in here" she says. "In case that's what you have in mind".

I am about to protest when I detect the two prone bodies on the ground, next to the far wall.

From behind me, Gretchen calls out:

"Sorry, Cynthia. I tried to stop him".

"Oh, that's alright, hon" comes a woman's voice. "We're just about done".

Squinting, I make out the two of them lying on a mattress near the wall, tucked under a blanket.

"That you, Donner?" I ask.

" 'fraid so, sir".

"Anything to report?"

"All quiet, sir".

"I see. Carry on, Corporal".

I retreat after Gretchen, who is already at the gap, her back turned to me, watching the rain dancing on the grass outside.

For a long while we stand in silence.

"This going on all the time?" I ask.

"What do you think?"

"I don't know. Who's Cynthia?"

"My roommate. You'd have recognized her except for the blanket. She plays one of your strippers".

"That so?"

"Intrigued?"

"How'd you know she was there?"

"Ain't a big secret".

"How about the other buildings?"

I gesture toward the Av.

"Shall we go and inspect?"

"Nope. You ever come here yourself?"

She takes her time.

"You really need to know?"

"Oops, maybe not".

In the dark next to her, I am blushing.

"You ain't made it into my bed yet" she says, "and already you're into ownership".

"Sorry".

"You better be. Just remember, retroactive horns ain't as much fun as the real ones".

"I said I was sorry".

Too late. She explodes right in my face:

"The hell you are! You practically made up your

mind to drag me here for a real quickie before... So what stopped you?"

A good question. Especially in light of the hard-to-ignore erection sprouting between my legs.

Another zero-sum game. Shit.

I steel myself as best as I can for the inevitable rejection, cussing bitterly inside for blowing it, again.

Gretchen is still next to me.

"Let's go back" she says.

We leave the set, plunging into the steady drizzle, cutting back home across the woods. A zillion frogs, revived by the storm, are croaking their lungs out. I am deflated, I seesaw between stoicism and self-pity.Blew it. Gretchen's resolute silence underscores my defeat.

Her costume is drenched and clinging to her lithe body, her damp hair streaking across her face. We reach the outskirts of the base. I am about to offer to escort her back to the hospital, a considerable ways across, when she says, matter of fact:

"I could use a hot shower. Are your digs at this end?"

"Just around the corner".

"You got roommates?"

"Nope, Henry's just moved out. Why?".

In gratitude for his narrow escape, Henry has left me his furniture, sound system excluded. I declined all but the double mattress and the kitchen set.

"A bit more private, not to mention warmer, don't you think?" she says.

"Well..."

I can't believe my ears.

"Lead on, lion" she says.

Her rapid mood swings are giving me vertigo. Like a yo-yo, I hurtle precipitously across my inner space.

"Wow..."

She turns to me, the trace of a smile across her face:

"Surprised?"

What do you think, gorgeous being?

"Astonished" I tell her. God's truth stark and unadorned.

"Would you rather I just said 'mine or yours'?"

"Isn't that my line?"

"Well, you've been bungling the script all day long. I should report you to Major Len".

"Might as well wait till there's more to report. How about coming up for supper?"

"Is that the current euphemism? *Coq au vin*?"

"Ouch!"

"A man who can actually cook?"

"Try me".

In my mind, I am running feverishly through the few provisions in my fridge. Truth be told, I have been subsisting on a near-monastic diet--eggs, bread, cheese, olives, tomatoes, onions. No wine, how inauspicious. Still, this is not shaping up to be a classical seduction scene either.

"Spanish omelet?" I venture. "I could run and do some shopping while you're taking a shower..."

"Nevermind" she says, "Spanish omelet will do fine. I'm so hungry I could eat wood chips".

"I think I can do better".

"Good".

The drizzle has finally stopped. Her hand in mine, I lead her up to the flat. We are both in a hurry. By the time we get upstairs we are out of breath. I can only hope she hasn't noticed my hard-on.

We stumble in and she takes a beeline for the bathroom, turning back to me after a brief inspection:

"Vintage Army issue, just as I thought. Reckon it'll do. Now, if it were a bit bigger..."

"I'll work on it" I tell her.

I scurry over and rustle up a clean towel and my old bathrobe. She receives them with a nod and disappears. I strip down and dump my wet clothes in the corner, slip on a sweatshirt and shorts and go over to inspect the fridge. As I feared, the choice is meager. I pull out the last three eggs, a carton of milk, the lone tomato, a shriveled half-onion, the molding tail end of a hunk of cheddar. Not exactly a banquet.

I beat the eggs, chop the onion, shred cheese, and am about to scout for the skillet when Gretchen reappears.

251

She is lost inside my bath robe, the towel wound around her head like a turban.

"Your turn" she says.

I turn to go, but am transfixed by her smell and drawn to her like a hapless magnet to its true pole. Before I know it, we are standing next to each other in the empty living room, our shadows dancing grotesquely in the meager light filtering in through the kitchen door. The tension is unbearable. I am entranced, I can't take my eyes off her. She looks up, smiling faintly. Her head seems so small under the turban. We sigh simultaneously.

"Darnit" Gretchen says, "there goes dinner".

Then she is in my arms and stretching up the length of me in one fluid motion, her head turned up, her lips proffered. As I lean down to kiss her, her arms latch around my back, her feet slide on top of mine.

We stand there coagulated in a kiss that runs from here to eternity. Gretchen's tongue slithers inside my mouth, driving me to blind frenzy. My knees are about to buckle when she detaches herself.

"Come" she says, dragging me down to the mattress, "I don't want to take responsibility for your early demise... You were going to collapse on top of me in another minute... A girl can hardly expect supper under the circumstances... Might as well de-fang you first, maybe you'll remember how to cook then".

I follow like a lamb to her scented altar. My hands

fumble with the robe as she stops near the mattress, almost tripping. I grab for her clumsily.

"Clod" she scolds me. "Here, let me do the honors...".

She drops her robe to the floor and undoes the towel. Her wet hair swats across my burning face as she turns to me. She slides her hands under my sweatshirt to ease it off.

"One thing we do learn at the hospital..."

She kneels down next to me and pulls my shorts down.

"Wow" she says, "what've we got here?"

My junior partner in passion has risen to full attention. I don't see how I could hold back much longer. I am inflamed to the point of blacking out.

"Impatient?" she says, taking hold of me. She has the surest hand. I manage to croak weakly:

"Better watch out or I'll pop..."

"Primed to go *bang*?... We better slow you down then... Here, come sit down with mama..."

She pulls me next to her and pushes me gently on my back, where I lie prone, dazed with desire.

"Let's see what we can do to help" she says.

Her hand resumes its exploration. Having satisfied herself it's all there, she swings atop and mounts me, easing me up into her sweet eternity. She is slow, gentle, incredibly self-assured. Her head is bowed down, flinging damp hair in my face. My hands reach up in tandem to meet her small breasts. God, I pray-beg silently, let me expire right now, go straight to Heaven.

Well, not quite. For I surrender beforehand, give in and try not to blow it too soon. Tho there's little that either of us can do as Gretchen's control melts away with mine, amongst the rhythmic undulations, shrieks and moans.

Together we hurtle into the void where neither control nor space nor time matter. Everything vanishes in a sweet explosion of multifarious white light--and once again we hold onto each other and tumble in free fall... Hey, *once again?* The last sliver of my conscious brain wants to know. *Once again?* Has there been another time?

Mercifully, the last vestige of rationality dislodges itself, careening wildly. A feeling of incredible peace comes over me. I hold on to Gretchen, who has at long last collapsed on top of me. For dear life.

●　　　●　　　●

We are both soaked with perspiration. Gretchen is glued to my flank, her head nesting in the crook of my elbow. My face must be radiating with the silliest smile. She is stroking my hair with her free hand.

"Wow" she says.

"Wow you".

"Someone has been there before..."

"Just one?"

"Silly Lion. I don't mean a head count. Well, whoever she was, thank her for me. She taught you well".

"Couldn't be I'm a natural?"

"Fat chance. I've never met a man who was. I can tell the marks left by a kind predecessor".

I think of Serena, but am not about to pursue the matter. Most women, I have found, swing eternally between morbid fascination with their precursors and a desperate need not to know. They must be the onliest. Men are not all that different.

"You are not exactly ignorant yourself" I tell her.

"Women are different" she says. "We are born natural, or we have a sure-fire way of learning. From our mothers".

"You do?"

"I did".

"About sex? How nice. I learned nothing from my parents. Zilch".

"You mean, they never talked about it"

"Just the other way around. They talked about it *ad nauseam*. Embarrassing stuff, or so I thought at the time..."

"How interesting" she says. "Where'd you grow up?"

"Place called Salt Point. Small town up the river, upstate New York. You probably never heard of it".

"Bet you were an only child".

"How can you tell?"

"You got a bit of the orphan in you".

"I had two live parents, still do".

"I didn't mean you didn't. You were lonely. It shows".

"Wouldn't you be with a dad who's a professional intruder and a mom who's anointed you as her life project? My mom was a nurse by the way, case you wonder. She quit early tho, after my dad finished his residency. Used to say I was her thesis".

"Your dad's a shrink, right?"

This is getting to be a habit.

"How the hell did you know?"

She strokes my chest reassuringly.

"No trick there. I work for Dr. Creighton, remember? He told me about your interview".

"Shit. No privacy in this man's Army".

Then I see it:

"You asked him!"

She smiles.

"Don't flatter yourself, lion" she says. "Let's just say I can put two and two together".

"So you knew I was at Ft. Gordon?"

"Dr. Creighton did".

"How could he?"

"You better ask *him*".

"Shit".

I have to think about this. Gretchen senses my agitation.

"I'll ask him for you if you like" she says.

"Nevermind" I tell her. "I don't think I want to know".

I am alarmed. But Gretchen's hand has migrated from my chest downward. Before I have more time to brood, I am hopelessly distracted and we are having a wild go at it all over again. This time slowly, deliberately, with Gretchen encouraging me to take charge but still, I am convinced, retaining the responsibility for the long, controlled multiple combustion.

●   ●   ●

We are sated. I am enchanted.

"How about you?" I ask Gretchen.

"How about me what?"

"Where did you grow up?"

She takes a deep breath, must be a long story, perhaps one she would rather not revisit. I wait.

"Nowhere" she says. "All over".

I persist:

"Any place in particular?"

"California. Arizona. New Mexico. Oregon. Colorado. Points in-between".

"Wow" I say. "Sounds more like a tribal migration. Were you an Army brat?"

"Try again".

"Stolen by Gypsies?"

"Not quite that colorful".

"Well, you're too old for your parents to have been hippies".

From the slight skin reaction I know I scored.

"Think so?" she says.

"Serious? Tell me".

"Well..." she says. "My mom was the original article, long before they had a name for it".

"Your dad too?"

"Shit no, not him. But I hardly knew him, they split when I was three".

"She raised you alone?"

"Hardly. I got five brothers".

"Wow. You must have been the youngest".

"Oldest".

Now the complications.

"You mean, she remarried?"

"Shacked up's more like it. My dad was the only one she actually married, the only one who was square enough. I guess she must have been too, then. She was only sixteen when they go t hitched. Had to, with me on the way..."

She pauses.

I wait. I would like to unvail the natural ontology of her sweet blend of reticence and take-charge. It is buried somewhere in there.

"I had a bunch of step-daddies" she says, "serial, they'd come and go..."

"Oh?"

"Yup. Each one left me a brother. By the time I was fourteen, the incumbent was trying to crawl into my pants. That's when I split, went on the street, crash pads, communes... Didn't talk to my mom for four years. By then the incumbent was out again, back in his own pants, if he had any to his name..."

She smiles in reminiscence.

"That's incredible".

"Just your run-of-the-mill tribal lore. I made peace with her though, just before I signed up for nursing school. Mom's OK. Real funny, just got a rotten deal with men. She says it's her karma".

"Serial bad karma?"

"Who knows?"

"How about your dad?"

"He's alright too. Terrific, in fact, once I got to know him. He's an aircraft engineer in Seattle, remarried. I got two sisters there... I looked him up when I was sixteen. He's the one who sent me back to school, paid for my first two years in college, before I signed up... I suppose he'd always felt guilty... Made me call my mom too".

"He did?"

"Stuck the phone in my hand".

"Sounds like a cool guy. Did he leave your mom?"

"Nah, she dumped him"

"Why?"

"Who knows? Got bored, I guess. My dad's so fuckin' reliable, must've drove her nuts... Hard to say why she does things. She just up 'n does them, sorta like a tornado if you know what I mean".

"I'm not sure".

"Well, you'll just have to meet her".

"You'll have to meet my mom too".

"Hey, not so fast".

But it is clear this turn in the conversation has pleased her.

I don't pry any further. We have just discovered, simultaneously, how hungry we really are. And it is near ten o'clock and Gretchen is due back at the hospital at eleven.

My protests are summarily dismissed as she takes over the kitchen. The eggs, bread, cheese, lone tomato and chopped onion I had left near the stove are belatedly combined. We share a mammoth omelet. After which Gretchen puts on her still-damp clothes which we have forgot to hang up, and I see her to the door. I watch her hurry down the gravel to the corner, where she disappears beyond the next quonset.

8. Notes from the Underground

(Ft. Gordon, GA; October, 1969)

I love her. We have been shacked up for two weeks now in near-conjugal bliss. She still stops by her apartment every morning to change and keep up appearances. Her roommate is delighted with the extra privacy which, Gretchen says, is being put to good use. Messages are jotted down faithfully and relayed to my flat.

I am amazed, and somewhat alarmed, at how sweet and easy our cohabitation has turned out. All I do, it seems, is yield to this tidal wave of female competence. I play the *yin* to her *yang*. Is that what love is all about?

Like all of them since mom, Gretchen has taken a quick measure of my potential and deemed me corrigible. Like a homing pigeon, she trains her sights on the inner child lurking underneath my deflectant surface. Having found me redeemable, she takes charge. And enchanted tho I may be, I wait--force of habit--for the other shoe to drop. In the meantime, I enjoy every minute of my resurrection.

Sex is not everything, just almost. From the start, there is a disturbing if subtle symmetry between my growing obsession with Gretchen and my fading memory of Serena. As one wanes, the other waxes. I say nothing, I hang onto Grtetchen for dear life. I watch her eyes grow misty, then cloud up as the delicate pleasure-pain web around them crinkles, then tenses up, then gradually dissolves in incredulous relief.

We are in the delicate throes of sated post-coital bliss. My battlements have been breached, I am ready to throw in the towel. Then the phone rings.

"Fuck".

"Let it ring" says Gretchen. We are soaked to the gills in each other's bodily fluids. It is early evening, I am off duty. No cloud on my horizon. Except for the nagging premonition that this bliss is just too good to last.

"I better see who it is" I tell her. "Might be Len".

"Let him rot" she says with surprising vehemence. "Fuckin' control freak got you roped and twitching, just like poor Henry".

Still, she releases me from her sweet trap and I roll off the bed and go groping for the angry phone.

My forebodings are not altogether irrational. For the quality of my weekly romp as chief agitator has gone into sharp decline ever since Gretchen. The day of reckoning is bound to come.

"Yes?" I growl into the phone.

"Lt. Swenson?"

"Speaking".

"This is Captain Nederlander".

"Beg your pardon?"

I rack my brain but come up with no hint.

"I don't expect you know my name" the voice concedes. The resonant, rasping southern drawl of a seasoned public speaker.

"I'm sorry".

"No need to apologize, most people at Seadock don't know I am here. Sometimes I wonder myself".

The note of ironic self deprecation succeeds, if that has been the caller's intent, in pushing my button.

"I'm still new here" I tell him. " What can I do for you, sir?"

"Well, I'd rather not conduct this over the phone, if it's all the same to you".

"Oh?..."

His paranoia or mine?

"What I mean is, I wonder if I could steal a little bit of your time. Say tomorrow?"

"Well..."

"Lunchtime? My treat?"

Whoever Captain Nederlander is, it appears he will not be deflected.

"Gee" I tell him, "you don't have to, sir".

"My pleasure. Want to stop by my office?"

"Sure. Where is it?"

"Know where the chapel is?"

"I'm afraid not".

The silence at the other end palpates with multiple readings.

"Tell you what" says the voice. "I'll come fetch you at your office".

"You know where it is?"

"I do. Shall we say twelve fifteen?"

"Sure".

"Thanks, Lieutenant".

"You're welcome, sir, Captain, er..."

"Nederlander".

"Sorry again".

"Never you mind. See you tomorrow".

I shuffle back to bed, where Gretchen is sitting in her glorious nakedness, casting about fo r her slip.

"What was that all about?" she says.

"Damned if I know" I tell her. "Ever heard of a Captain Nederlander?"

"I don't think so".

She has risen and joined me.

"His office is at the chapel. That ring a bell?"

"Could be the chaplain".

"Shit. You think so?"

"You'll soon find out, right?"

She flattens her full length against my back. Her skin sticks to mine like congealed syrup, I think of dark-gold buckwheat hotcakes, and am consumed by a an irresistible urge to lick the sticky goo off her golden pelt. But Gretchen wards me off.

"Save that thought, lion. Yes, whoever it was sure ruined a perfectly good fuck. Must be a Reverend".

With this, she goes for the light while I dive back

into the bed and console myself with her lingering scent. Buckwheat.

•   •   •

We are seated in his surprisingly well-appointed basement office underneath the nondescript flaking-grey clapboard chapel. Captain Frederick V. Nederlander, US Army, is Reverend indeed, non-denominational minister to Ft. Gordon's sundry spiritual strays.

"I was ordained into the Southern Baptist ministry" he volunteers as we stroll back along the dusty tree-lined street toward his basement lair.

The Reverend is lean and gaunt. In his field uniform, he towers over me like a drab-olive giraffe. He moves with manifest dignity and a lurching, energetic gait, his deep-set blue eyes piercing the horizon with irrepressible enthusiasm.

Scanning for the odd lost sheep?

Having just been treated to a wicked double-cheese-and-fries at the officers club, my defenses are down. Without warning, the Reverend Captain launches into the strictly personal:

"Are you a church-going man, Lieutenant?"

"Well..." I say. "My parents are Christian..."

It is a considerable stretch of God's literal truth.

"It that so?"

"Well, sort of. Baptized".

I come by my denominational ambivalence most naturally, through a family of confirmed renegades. Confirmed, then reneged. My father from the constricted High Lutheran rite of his Swedish forebears, my mother from the myrrh-scented rites of the Spanish Carmelite nuns. This mix of opposites hatched an explosive but irresistible union, one of whose incongruous loose ends being me. For in the *geist* of their times if not mine, my parents had contrived to induct me into the mysteries of Darwin, Marx and Freud. This ungainly trinity is, I suspect, just as offensive to my host as either one of my ancestral High Rites.

"I see" says Reverend Nederlander. "As I said, I was ordained Southern Baptist, though I would like to flatter myself I have transcended my sectarian roots, or at least mitigated their severity, if you know what I mean".

I wait prudently while the earnest blue eyes scrutinize me, a pair of avid searchlights.

"There's a saying where I come from" says my host, "that it is not enough to worship in a Christian church, you must worship in the *right* church".

On cue, I join him in his inviting cascade of chuckles and mirthful brays, waiting for the punch-line to come. But the Rev. Captain Nederlander restrains himself.

"Whatever rite you follow, Lt. Swenson, is your private affair. You still come highly recommended".

"Oh?"

"Yes" says the Reverend. "Captain Bozeman sends his regards".

The incongruity could not have been greater if my host had intended it. I have seen neither hide nor hair of the Boz since our sunset interlude. For all I know, he reigns now over a lush cordillera south of the border.

"He does?".

"Yes".

Abruptly, the Reverend sits up.

"I take my vocation seriously, Lieutenant".

The blue eyes pin me back into my seat. My teacup rattles in alarm.

"There's plenty of lost souls in this man's Army" he says, "to keep me busy from here till doomsday. But this--"

My host gestures around him in a wide arc that takes in the floor-to-ceiling bookshelves lining all four walls of his study.

"--this is my true passion. My avocation, if you will. And this is where Captain Bozeman says you might be able to help".

"Me? You mean college stuff? Books?"

"Berkeley".

The accursed disyllable, Seadock's red flag.

"Captain, sir..."

"You may call me Reverend. Everybody else does".

"Well, Reverend..."

Steady, my boy. Prudence.

"Sure, I was there, I hung around for a spell. But I might as well tell you..."

"Modesty does become you, Lieutenant" says my host. "But I've been watching your performance for over a month now, and the change you wrought in the part--why, in the whole show, ever since you've taken over from poor Lt. Speiser--is nothing short of miraculous".

"Really?"

"Honest. I've told Major Herskowitz, I felt compelled to congratulate him on such an inspired casting. Why, the flair, the pace, the audacity! But above all, the incredible realism of your performance!"

I am once again victim to my intoxicating fluency. Here comes the day of reckoning.

"Why, Reverend, thank you".

The light blue eyes under the polished high brow gaze upon me with stupefying benevolence. Captain Nederlander's near crew-cut cannot hide the incipient baldness that is creeping across his narrow skull. He appears to be in his late forties but could easily be older.

"Most convincing" he says. "And as I said, Captain Bozeman sings your praise. In fact, he suggested I call upon your, er, unique expertise".

"The Bo... I mean, Captain Bozeman gets carried away sometimes".

"We all do".

The Reverend's eyes are fixed upon me, urgent, compelling. Their hypnotic gaze must have, in its time, rounded up and dragged down to the pulpit throngs of sinners, drunks and fornicators, blasphemers and backsliders who, hard as they might, could not resist the piercing sincerity of these twin grey-blue lasers. Shoot, they must have sprinted down the aisle, eager to repent and declare for Christ just to escape this dazzling glare.

Like Mauglie in the *Jungle Book* musical, I am about to be sedated by Kah's hypnotic siren song. I had better snap out.

"The thing is, sir" I tell the Reverend, "my credentials are a bit thin. I was just an observer, a hanger on. See, I was too busy with classes for all the crazy stuff that was going on..."

But my host is relentless..

"Remarkable" he says.

I squirm in discomfort. Abruptly, the Reverend lets me off the hook:

"More tea?"

"Please".

The Rev. Captain Nederlander pours refills for both of us, steering the cream and sugar in my direction.

"Help yourself" he says, "I have to watch out, anymore. Diabetes runs in the family, my cross to bear".

We sip in silence, in my case a silence mingled with apprehension, for I have begun to get the measure of my host. Once he sinks his teeth into quavering flesh, he won't let go. I still don't know what he wants, so I scan the room for clues. On a patch of wall not occupied by bookshelves, I spy my host's framed commission-- Lieutenant jg, USMC, 1950. Must have made Korea just in time. Framed next to it are his ordination papers, issued in 1955 by a Baptist denomination in Tulsa, followed by the requisite DD scroll on burnished wood. Just below that, a small US flag is pinned with a generous spray of ribbons and medals. The poster of a recent Campus Crusade for Christ, with the Reverend Frederick Vandevere Nederlander's name featured prominently.

My host's eyes sparkle with amusement.

"Like my trophies?"

"You been places, sir".

"You might say that. In my youth, as you can see, I used to render unto Caesar. It is only later that I came to know the Lord. Nowadays I find myself rendering unto both in equal measure, tho on occasion, I confess, the Lord gets the short end of the stick".

"The Lord is surely capable of putting up a fight".

"The Lord is indeed more than equal to the task" says my host. "Although right now His and Caesar's work are mercifully compatible. You'd be surprised, Lieutenant, what a punch the Lord and Caesar can deliver once they pull in tandem. Don't you think?"

"I wouldn't know" I say prudently but truthfully.

"Caesar's been keeping me busy".

"Terrific" says my host. "The work you're doing, Lieutenant, the work we are doing here at Seadock, cuts both ways. I'm sure you can see how both Christ and Caesar have come under siege, under a disciplined, well coordinated attack, by the hosts of darkness. The same drug and sloth and filth and free-love conspiracy is undermining the foundations of our Christian republic. In the unfolding Armageddon, the devil-worshiping, mantra-chanting children of the Antichrist, the Armies of the Night, have joined forces with the drug-pushing, sex-crazed anti-war hippies and subversive Black-Power commies. They all one and the same now, sworn enemies, ready to tear us all down".

"I see".

The thin ice I have been skating on seems to have gotten thinner.

"Now listen" says the Reverend. "You've been living among them. For seven years you've been one of them, so Captain Bozeman assures me, before you repented and rejoined the Armies of Light".

I make a mental note to thank the Boz for this revisionist rendition of my military career.

"Just think, Lieutenant" the Reverend goes on. "Who's in a better position?"

"Well..."

"Precisely. It takes no great genius to see how people like myself are badly handicapped when it comes to your, er... peculiar generation. We're much too old. We cut our teeth on the depression, came to knowledge in WW II. And--let me tell you something, my boy, may I call you Leo?"

"Sure thing, sir".

"Good. In Hannibal, Arkansas, Leo, the depression was no joke. It was just yesterday".

"I see".

"I doubt you could, y'all are so lucky... Then there's the sad truth, y'all are like aliens to us. We've been watching you, horrified, from the sidelines as you've turned on, tuned in, dropped out..."

In spite of myself, I cannot but smile at this unexpected whiff of my generation's beatific mantra. The Reverend is right there with me.

"You may laugh" he says. "I know my Leary, been reading him over 'n over looking for clues. Evil man, tho keen as a whip. Would've made a fine preacher".

I nod. I have always thought so.

"Still" says the Reverend, "truth is, we've never been out there in the streets with y'all, burning Old Glory and screaming obscenities at the police, waving the Viet Cong flag in one hand and, er, a *joint*--that's how y'all call your Mary Wana reefers, right?--in the other... tearing down the very foundation of this Christian republic just when the Ruskies are at our throat... So you see, Leo, your expertise is of unique value to us here at Seadock".

272

"You think so?"

"No question about it. We need you. We're backed to the wall. How 'bout lending a hand?"

As is my habit, I opt for the muddled middle.

"I suppose..." I tell the Reverend. "Though I'm really not sure what I can do..."

Capt. Nederlander's torrential gratitude cuts me short:

"Terrific. I knew I could count on you. Here, come with me"

We rise in unison. I am led across the room to a locked door. My host pulls out a crowded key-ring on a retractable chain, selects a key and does the honors.

Utter darkness greets us. Captain Nederlander steps forward and switches on the light. The room is small and windowless, the air is stagnant. It looks like the reference section of a small library--glass-covered display cases, floor-to-ceiling book shelves around the walls, an index-card table at the center. Books, magazines. A steel cabinet in the corner.

"Come see my treasures" says my host, beaming.

I step forward gingerly. My trepidations soon turn into delight. The room is a cornucopia of the underground press, a treasure trove of the counterculture.

I spot the biggies first--The Berkeley Barb, The Tribe, The Village Voice, The L.A. Free Press, Good Times, The Venice Beach Head, Georgia Straights, Armadillo News,

Dock of the Bay. The far left is out in force--Mother Jones, Ramparts, Muhammad Speaks, The Black Panther, El Grito del Norte. The fag rags are there--One, The Advocate. As are the fringe greens--Mother Earth, Back to Nature, Clear Water, Tree People, Rainbow Nation.

All lovingly catalogued by tribe and tribulet, psych and porn. From Playboy to Horseshit to The Realist-- beginning with issue #1, a prized collector's item. I spot the earnest harmless: The Society of Friends, The Catholic Worker, Forward.

The book collection is another *tour de force*-- Kerouac to Brautigan; Alan Watts to Ram Das; Kundalini to Tai Chi Chuan; Beckett to Artaud; Guevara to Marcuse; Jung to Laing; the Anarchist Cookbook, the Whole Earth Catalogue.

The Reverend, towering discreetly over me, says: "What do you think?"

"Far out" I tell him, "outa sight! You got everything, the whole kit 'n caboodle. How did you, I mean... You must have spent a fortune on this!"

The Reverend clears his throat apologetically.

"Well" he says, "not reall. It all started real small, I stumbled upon it... It was a parishioner who first alerted me to these, er, materials... Must've been five years ago. Took me a while to realize it was not just standard Enemy trash. Mind you, it *is* repulsive, this filth. At first I could hardly touch the paper, my skin would crawl. Know what I mean?"

"Sure".

"Then I got to thinking. Hey, I said to myself, Satan ain't gonna go away just because we ignore him. Just the opposite, the Evil One thrives on inattention, loves it... Plus, I kept discovering more and more filth, all over the place, right here down South. Fellow ministers kept me posted... So I started buying all I could. Pretty soon, I knew I had a tiger by the tail, a big one, too big for my lonesome frail hands. There was just too much of it, and it kept coming... So when I came to Seadock, I saw my opportunity. I prevailed on brother Rodney--that's Colonel Manners--to start a regular budget line for subscriptions and acquisitions. We charge it to Army Intelligence, Capt. Bozeman has been most helpful. It's been building up ever since".

"You mean, the Army pays for this?"

"Sure. Just think, Seadock's stated mission, once you strip off the jargon, is counter insurgency. That is, from Caesar's end. Well my own calling, it so happens, is counter insurgency too--from the Lord's end. This evil filth is subversive either way, right? So once again, God and Caesar have joined forces".

"But what do you do with all this stuff?"

"I read it".

"All this?"

I gesture around the room. The Reverend nods.

"As much of it as I can stand" he says, "as much as I need to, to understand. Reckon about half, enough so

I can teach others about it".

"Wow" I say, "you must be and expert..."

The Reverend Capt. Nederlander shrugs with delicate modesty.

"I guess" he says, " you might say I've become well versed, leave it at that. Pride is a deadly sin, so let's just say I do my darnest, given my handicap. Once you wade through enough of this filth, you get a feel for what's significant. You see, some of this is absolutely vital to the security of these United States"

"You bet".

"Though at first" says the Reverend, "I had a heck of a time getting our distinguished visitors, my students, to take it seriously. They used to smirk, thought it was a joke. I have them for only two hours, y'know. So I've had to learn how to sell it to them. Took a while, but I think I've got most of it down now. After two hours with me, most of them come out true believers. They go back to their units, to their cities and police departments, they start their own libraries, subscribe to what's out there near home. They send me new stuff, they send in testimonials, too..."

What escapes my lips is a tad irreverent:

"I suppose the editors thank you for the boost in subscriptions..."

My host is nothing if not gracious:

"I like that" he says. "You got a sense of humor, Leo. Rendering unto the Lord without a sense of humor can be

276

a chore, sometime a downright pain. You are my kind of a man, Leo. The two of us can work miracles together".

Co-opted once again. I am in a bind, not unlike the one I experienced with Major Herskowitz or the Boz. An age-old conundrum, damned if I do, damned if I don't.

"I see" I tell my host. "At least, I think I do... Like, it's nice to know what your enemy's up to, hey? But these guys you're tracking, they're out in the open, they couldn't keep a secret if they tried. The whole bunch of them-- Ginsburg and Leary, Abby and Jerry, Hayden and Savio, Newton and Cleaver--are a bunch of media freaks. They act out everything, they crave an audience... Not many secrets in there, it all hangs out front. Like, what you see is what you get."

My host bides his time. His brows knot, his head tilts to one side, the alert bright eyes assess me thoughtfully. I get a whiff of what may lie in store if the Rev. Captain Nederlander ever mistook me for one of *them*.

"That's an interesting point" he says. "You know, I've wondered about that myself... These guys seem to broadcast everything they're about to do, like a dare. But the way I see it, Leo, that's just a con. The Evil One does that too, steps out in the open and dares you. So think a minute--who are we really dealing with here, really?"

I study the Reverend's earnest face for a hint.

"I don't know" I tell him. "A bunch of hippies, I suppose, green college kids, angry blacks, white trash trying to crash the scene... Animal lovers and tree huggers, fags and dykes outing themselves in the mirror, libbers and knee-jerk do-gooders, a bunch of lost pilgrims looking for a warm tit... That's about it. A mixed bag of nuts..."

"Yeah" says the Reverend impatiently. "But what's under the surface? Who's behind it all?"

"You tell me, Reverend".

"It's always the same, Leo, the same one. The Arch Enemy".

"You mean, the Russians?"

The Reverend shakes his head at my denseness.

"Satan" he tells me, "Beelzebub, Pazuzu, Lord of the Flies, The Spoiler, The Snake in the Garden. The Enemy, Leo. They're all fronting for him".

The Reverend's hand sweeps a wide arc over the shelves:

"What you see here is his latest slight-of-hand, what he wants us to see, so surely there's got to be something hidden underneath. It's gotta be in there, somewhere... This is how the Sly One casts his net to snare the innocent... So if I can't see it, and if you can't see it--and you used to be one of *them*--then it must be in there in code. So here's where I need your insider's eye, Leo my boy, desperately".

The Rev. Captain Nederlander, having warmed up to his subject, is pacing up and down among his prize exhibits. He picks up an ostrich-feather duster and, tenderly, sweeps the dust off a crowded shelf.

278

"I've been having enormous trouble" he confides, "teaching our visitors how to interpret this literature. It demands a monumental effort of translation, like a foreign tongue. I think I've gotten the hang of it now--with one exception. Which is where you come in".

We are standing in front of the bulging California underground press section.

"This is where I first stumbled upon it" he says. "Though once I knew what to look for, I found it in all the others too. All in code, remarkably uniform. The very same in New York, Chicago, Detroit, Atlanta, Miami, Philadelphia. And I can't for the love of me make heads or tails of it... Here--"

The Reverend pulls out a two-year old copy of the Berkeley Barb.

"Take a look" he says, leafing through the discolored pages. "The messages are usually scattered inside the *personals*, *services offered*, or *wanted* sections. Here, this one--"

The stale pages of the Barb, showing the smudged evidence of repeated perusal, are carefully folded up to the middle of the unclassified section of small personal ads, home of the true weirdo. The Reverend's finger guides me toward a half-inch item.

I squint at the small print and make out the three lines:

W/M 28 skg BI/M or BI/GAY cpl

3 way or voy or you say

call Steve 775-4806 be cool

I can't bring myself to read the stuff out loud. Is he pulling my leg? I am blushing under the Reverend's intense scrutiny.

"Go ahead, read it out loud".

"I'm not sure I can".

"Why not?"

"Don't you know what these are?"

"Not a clue".

My host must be serious, tho how can one tell?

"Well" I tell him, "they're kinda tricky".

"Meaning what?"

"Well..."

The Rev. Captain Nederlander shakes his head impatiently:

"How about this one then?"

He is pointing at another three liner:

W cpl, PROF, ext wl end, skg

BI/F for AC/DC, rm & brd pos

wr & lv #, pobox 415, Palo Alto

"Well?"

"Seems just as bad. You really don't know what this is all about?"

"All I know is it's in code, the same code all over the country. How do we decode it, Leo? It's urgent. How about this one?"

He is pointing at a slightly more elaborate item:

B/chk 22, wl end slv

skg mstr same, pref w lrg

dog, no irsh sttr please

snd phot, hrry am hng

Glenda, Oak 775-9644

"Enemy code, right?"

He is almost pleading.

"Well, in a way..."

"How about it, then?"

I gulp hard. I see no alternative, I am cornered.

"These are all sex ads, Reverend sir. Kinky sex mostly, lonely people making connections, making dates, fixing to get together for mutual gratification... Most likely less than natural, but still between consenting adults... Absolutely constitutional, my guess..."

A long incredulous silence follows. I wait. The Reverend is squinting at the page.

"That's preposterous" he says.

"You betcha. But as far as I know, it's the truth".

"Show me".

"If you insist, sir... Though they're all kinda sleazy. I'm not sure you'd like it, really..."

But my host will not be denied.

"Go ahead, Lieutenant" he commands me. "I've been fighting the Sly One all these years. If he's got tricks I haven't come across yet, I had better find out now, don't you think?".

"Well" I tell him, "here goes... Lemme see... Here are some basics. Capital W stands for 'white', B for 'black', M for 'male', F for 'female'... tho lower-case *grl* or *chk* would mean the same... The number directly after B/M or W/F is usually age. Capital PROF stands for 'educated middle class' or 'professionally employed'. Except when it comes in lower-case, usually with a negative. Then it most likely refers to pros, like whores or male prostitutes, like in *no pros pls*. You following, sir?"

"Go on".

"Let's see... BI in capitals stands for 'bisexual', you know, people who swing both ways, like they go for either male or female?..."

"Go on, please".

"Then, capital G stands for 'gay', like queers, homosexuals, of either gender. You still with me, sir?"

"Yes".

"Well, then... AC stands for the French way of doing business, DC for the more conventional one. Does that ring a bell?"

"Never mind. Please go on".

"Well... Then there're the less-frequent stuff, like *wl end* or *wel endd* or just plain *hng*... These stand for 'well endowed', which works for either gender, or 'hung', which is specific to males..."

"Specific to what, exactly?"

"Well, the size, er, proportions of, er... the natural equipment. Shall I elaborate?"

"I think I get the picture".

"Well, then there's a problem with *wl hng* when it comes as just plain *hng* or *hung*. That's where it might mean something else, especially in the combination *am hung*, which usually means 'am hungry'. Though the same meaning is often rendered by either *hrn* or *lnl*... Best way to resolve this is, look at the context where these expressions come... Say a guy introduces himself as W/M 35 BI/G. You see *hung* after that, it means part of the description, he's pitching his equipment. But if *hung* comes toward the end, it is more likely to denote a state of mind, like 'hungry'. It's really simple... Same thing with lower-case *sm*. If it comes after the initial description, in combination with *skg*, like *skg sm*, then it means 'seeking a person of the same description'. But capital SM is something else altogether, sado-mass, that kinda thing... And sometimes it's not clear whether skin color also falls under 'same'. Last few years, people've gotten kinda sensitive about that, you know..."

"People've been sensitive about that ever since Creation" mutters the Reverend, "you just read your Bible, boy".

"I guess they have..."

We are, after all, right next-doors to Augusta, GA.

"Anyway" I go on, "if *sm* comes later on in the ad, it might mean 'same activity'. That's usually the third part of the ad, where you find descriptions like AC/DC. But there are others too, like *3wy*, which stands for 'threesome'. This often follows an earlier mention of *cpl*, meaning 'couple', quite often with BI. Tho if a dog is mentioned earlier..."

I stop to cast an anxious look at my host.

"That's about the size of it, sir" I tell him.

"I see".

"It's really plain ol' dirty sex".

"Hmmm".

The Rev. Captain Nederlander is clearly disappointed, and would have been happier with an alternative exegesis of the text. Same enemy, a different department. I am sorely tempted to go along. My standing at Seadock is shaky, I could use an ally.

"Of course, maybe I'm all wet, sir" I offer, "maybe it's something else".

My host sighs.

"Jeepers creepers" he says, "I don't know what to think. I may have to send some of this off to a friend in Cryptography. They've got those new electronic gizmos, he says they can crack just about anything... At any rate, you've been most helpful, Lieutenant. You are, if I may say so, incredibly well versed. I can see why Capt. Bozeman speaks so highly of you".

With luck, I am out of the wood. But the Reverend is

not yet done.

"There's another matter" he says. "Something I've been puzzling over. I wasn't going to bother you with it, but I might as well".

"Yessir".

"It's materials I've found in this publication".

The Reverend pulls out two-inch worth of *The Realist*.

My heart sinks down to my lower gut.

"This is the most curious publication" he says. "At first you'd think it's just plain filth. But then you keep reading--morbid curiosity, know thy Enemy--and it dawns on you there's more to it, heaps more. For starters, you never know whether they mean it or not. Then, their politics is utterly unpredictable. Why, half the time I can't tell whether they're for or against the war, I keep wondering if somebody's pulling my leg... You ever had this feeling?"

"Shoot, Reverend" I tell him, "that's Paul Krasner, that's just the way he is, always worried people might take him seriously".

"But they ought to" the Reverend says. "Anybody who can come up with such a mix of filth and fantasy and still sound like an innocent... shoot, they ought to be taken dead serious. Now you take this issue, number 84, November 1968. The lead article is on what they call *groupies*, by one Ellen Sander... Just plain disgusting to begin with, till you get to page 14 and find the quotation from a musician call named Frank Zappa. You ever heard of him?"

"Sure, Zappa and The Mothers, awesome stuff..."

"Never mind the band. The point is, these groupies--they call themselves *The Plaster Casters of Chicago*.... You keep reading on and it becomes more and more fantastic, till on page sixteen it finally hits you--the whole danged thing must be a spoof! No Rock star in his right mind would put up with this indignity of having their, er, you know, their privates, cast in dental cement by these total strangers, young females to boot... See this picture?"

The Reverend's accusing finger is pointing at a faded black-and-white photo of a series of sculpted projectiles, some of which bear an unmistakably penile cast.

"Shoot" I tell him, "everybody knows it was a spoof, like half of the rest of the stuff in there. Mind you, Rock stars are an unpredictable bunch, I've heard weir stuff..."

"But how do you know?"

"Well, that's the whole point of *The Realist*. You never know, not for sure, not with Krasner".

"But that's utterly subversive!"

"Sure. That's the point".

But the Reverend is already on to the next issue, pointing to one of Krasner's most celebrated scatological *oeuvres*:

"How about this utter--" he says, "in this issue, about President Johnson abusing himself over the dead corpse of his predecessor on the plane back from Dallas, November 23 1963?"

"That was a dead giveaway" I tell him.

"But how do you know? Really?"

"Well, you don't, not really. But that's the whole point, if you know Krasner. Everything in there is just plausible enough, it *could* be true, just a tiny little fleck of a chance it could..."

"You see my point, then?"

"See what?"

"How clever this really is? Can't you see The Evil One smacking his lips, roaring his lungs out? Only *he* could have dreamed up such a nefarious web of insinuations, off the record stuff, innuendos that can never be checked out".

"Yes, I see".

I have always suspected Paul Krasner couldn't tell the difference either, not with all the stuff he was abusing.

"Good" says the Reverend. "Then I can count on you, right?"

"Count on me for what, sir?"

"Count on your insider's perspective, Lieutenant. You've been lost out there. Now you're back in the fold. Shall we say, you've been called?"

"Well, sure, sir..."

What else could I say, squirming under the Reverend's searing gaze?

"Agreed, then. You're going to be my interpreter, my guide. Together we'll study this filth, crack the code, devise strategies, dream up counter-measures. The Lord's hand has delivered you onto my door, Lieutenant. Are you with me, boy?"

"Yessir".

The Rev. Captain Nederlander walks me to the door and shakes my hand. The vise-like grip of his bony palm almost cracks my metatarsus. His red-hot enthusiasm cradles me like a rising tide all the way across the base, back to my office, which has just become a tad more lonely.

9. Post Mortem

(Ft. Gordon, GA; November, 1969)

The show must go on, but the show is going stale. And guess-who is to blame.

"We had better dream up something, *boychik*" says Major Herskowitz.

It is Monday, our weekly huddle in his office. The major is pacing about restlessly. I am doing my best to shrink into my chair.

"The way your National Guard *nebisches* give chase" he says, "shit, they look like a flock of hopped-up weed heads storming out of an Istanbul flop-house in search of better-grade hash..."

He's got a point. For the thespian zest of my troupers, veterans and grunts alike, has nosedived precipitously over the past few weeks. Even in my current blissed-out state I can notice the downward trend.

Major Herskowitz gives up his pacing and plops down into his seat, fixing me with his lively blue eyes:

"You haven't noticed more smoking on the set, have you, *bubele*?"

My first impulse, I play dumb:

"Are we off-limit to cigarettes?"

The major is not buying.

"For chrissakes" he say", shaking his head in disgust. "Don't you go cute on me".

"You mean, the good weed? Gee, Len, how would I know? The guys don't exactly welcome me into their confidence..."

The major's brow is furrowed.

"Cut the shit, willya, Leo? This is not a court martial, it's only me, Uncle Len, remember?"

Sure, but whose ass is in the sling?

"Honest, Len" I tell him, "I haven't noticed anything. 'course, I haven't been looking. Would you like me to?"

"Nevermind ".

He doesn't sound all that disappointed.

"Truth is" he says, "I don't give a fuck about what's going on on the set all week, long as it doesn't spill over into Friday afternoon. I don't want to know. It's your oak patch, Leo. Your ass too, 'case you forget. So for Chrissakes, get your guys to show some spark. The show's beginning to look like an Eskimo funeral".

I promise to do my best. And I do, I run the guys through their paces, I rehearse them into the night. If anything, it gets worse. For I have am heir to Henry Speiser's old conundrum--plenty authority, no leverage. I brandish neither a carrot nor a stick. And so, improbably, the ambience on our fake Av has come to resemble that of the original.

Thursday is upon us. I call a lunch break and head over to the shade for my lunchtime rendezvous with Gretchen. I share my grief with her as I munch through a ham-and-Swiss hero. Mustard is dripping down my fingers on Gretchen's starched lap.

"You'll think of something" she says. "You always do".

"Thanks for the vote of confidence".

I am fresh out of tricks, nothing seems to work. I let out an involuntary sigh. Gretchen leans over and is about to console me with a succulent Klamata olive, when the tread of heavy boots intrudes on our idyll.

I sit up and squint. Pfc Johnson, one of our regular black troopers, is doing a credible rendition of the vaudeville shuffle. Stumbling to an abrupt halt at the edge of the canopy, he executes an exaggerated salute.

"Lieutenant suh!"

A thick cloud of dust rises in the wake of his combined maneuvers.

It is no use getting mad at Johnson, who is the squad clown. Besides, he is not there at his own behest.

"Cut the crap, Johnson" I tell him. "Wha'ss up?"

"Mista Big, suh. He wanna see you suh".

"Mista Big wants to see me?"

" 'S what he say".

"And who's he?"

It takes two to play dum".

"Sergeant Abdul Hameed, suh".

"You mean Wesley?"

"Same-self one, suh".

"What does he want?"

I wait for Pfc Johnson to go through a complex head-scratching routine.

"He ain't sayin', suh. He jus' say to go get the man".

I turn to Gretchen, who is doing her best to suppress a giggle.

"Sweetheart, I think I better go check this one out. Just hang on to my lunch, I'll be right back".

As Gretchen nods, I rise and follow Pfc Johnson across the somnolent Av. His shuffle gets more pronounced as we approach his home base, the back side of the Safeway next to the bank.

I follow gingerly into the bowels of the two-by maze. Soon we are inside an inner clearing at the core of the structure, where the wooden frame has been vaulted into a high dome. Shafts of light pierce through the plastic panels above. A Romanesque chapel? More like a mosque.

I peer around. Our entire black contingent is gathered in a circle, reclining over mattresses and large pillows of bright satin. They are eating lunch, guns and helmets strewn about like discarded toys.

At the top of the circle, seated on a large velvet pillow with his back against an eight-by-four plywood sheet, is Sgt. Abdul Hameed. His eyes are concealed behind his large wrap-around shades. He is sipping coffee out of a small porcelain cup. A steaming copper *finjan* is resting on a mahogany stand beside him, next to it a smoldering copper-and-glass hookah. A large poster of Malcolm X is pinned to the plywood above his head.

Pfc Johnson and I come to a stop at the edge of the circle. Everybody look up, then go back to their lunch. I count at least five joints making the rounds. In the still air, the pungent scent of high-grade weed proclaims itself unabashedly.

From his throne, Sgt. Abdul Hameed issues a salutation:

"Lieutenant Leo, wha'ss happenin' man. *Karibuni, karibuni, hapa hapa..*"

"Beg your pardon?"

"Oh, pardon my Swahili. S'down, s'down".

Sgt. Abdul Hameed gestures majestically with his arm. Then he leans over toward the man seated on his left and whispers in his ear. The trooper rises and departs. Sgt. Abdul Hameed turns back to me:

"Here, s'down, Lieutenant. So glad you could join us. Hey Johnny, bring the lieutenant some coffee. Hope you don't mind Turkish, Lieutenant".

"Wha'ss the matter, Wesley, y'all out of espresso? Jus' kiddin', my man, jus' kiddin'. I loves Turkish".

I lower myself to the cushion next to Abdul

Hameed.

A small gas stove is hissing in a dark corner to the right, propped on an ammo crate. An ornamental hammered-brass pot is steaming on the burner. Pfc Johnson, his shuffle gone, brings me the small cup over a china saucer.

"Thanks, Johnson" I tell him.

Sgt. Abdul Hameed leans over, fetches the brass *finjan* by the long handle and fills my cup. The sweet aroma wafts over, tickling my nostrils. I take a cautious sip, then exhale with genuine pleasure.

"Hey, tha's some *kahwa* you got there, Wesley" I tell Abdul Hameed. "Your health..."

I raise my cup to him, then take another sip.

"By the grace of Allah the bountiful" says Abdul Hameed, "may He shower his infinite blessings on his faithful. *Inshallah*".

"Restricted access?"

The ghost of a smile visits Abdul Hameed's mouth. His eyes are inscrutable behind the dark shades.

"Hey Johnny" he says, "go rustle up some smoke for the lieutenant".

In the ensuing interlude, Pfc Johnson and Sgt. Abdul Hameed dead-pan each other. Then Johnson shrugs, pulls a plastic bag out of his pocket and re-loads the glass hookah next to Abdul Hameed, who proceeds to light it, take a deep toke, then pass the tube over to me.

In the sudden hush, I am conscious of how

everybody's eyes--however casually averted--are pinned on me. I take the red plastic mouthpiece from Abdul Hameed, drag a couple of quick ones to prime the ember into glowing red, then take in a slow drag and let the harsh smoke sear my bronchi. I top it off with some air, then pass the tube back to Abdul Hameed. I sit back and savor the all-too-familiar yet nearly forgotten industrial-strength *sin semilla*. I sit holding my breath. When at last I exhale, I turn to my benefactor, who is towering ove r me like a ebony totem:

"Tha'ss some heavy shit you got there, Wesley my main man".

It has been more than a year since I have last indulge in the good weed.

"Wow" I say, "Maui zowie?"

"Thai. Allah provides".

Sgt. Abdul Hameed pauses to suck on the hookah.

"No shit" I say.

"Compliments of Captain Boz Man. He wishes to be remembered".

"That for fact?"

Before alighting to parts unknown, the Boz put Abdul Hameed in charge of the storage bunker in the bowels of the Piccolo. I wonder what he expects to find when he comes back.

"You had your lunch, Lieutenant Leo?" inquires my host.

" 'Bout half of it" I tell him, " 'fore your majesty stooped to send the summons..."

I accept the mouthpiece again, stock up, then pass it back to Abdul Hameed.

"Whooshy whooshy" I tell him, "I sure needed that... Shit, Wesley, this stuff is fuckin' dynamite. We better get down to business before I'm too smoked out to do you any good. Wha'ss the beef?"

"Shee-it, Lieutenant Leo, I's jus' comin' to that... 'cept we better wait... hey, here they comin'..."

Abdul Hameed turns back to me:

"Like I's sayin'..."

The trooper who was dispatched earlier now reappears at the head of the circle. With him is Sgt. Robert Lee Donner.

I shoot a quick look at my host. Abdul Hameed greets our visitor:

"Hey wha's happenin' Bubba Lee?"

"Howdy, Abdul Hameed... Howdy Lieutenant".

"Hi, Donner".

Sergeant Donner seems perfectly at ease. Still, my compromising presence can be easily stretched into blackmail and far beyond.

Across the circle, the troopers make room for Sgt. Donner. A cup of coffee is passed his way, together with a freshly-lit joint. I wait. Presently Abdul Hameed puts down his cup and turns his dark shades on me, opaque as an anciet ancient oracle.

"Thing is, Lieutenant Leo, the brothers here at Seadock--"

Here comes.

"--the brothers, they been havin' a problem needs took care of..."

The troopers around the circle nod their assent. Abdul Hameed takes a fresh drag on the hookah and passes it on to me.

"Yessuh, Lieutenant Leo suh" he says. "The brothers they been havin' a real problem. Tha'ss why we done invite Bubba Lee here, so he could testify how this here be a legit beef, jus'n case you be wonderin'... Tha'ss right, Bubba Lee?"

"Tha'ss right, Abdul Hameed".

The troops around the circle punctuate the exchange with grunts and nods. Abdul Hameed goes on:

"Now you 'nstand, Lieutenant Leo, them whiteboys, this ain't their beef. But that don' mean they ain't got sympathy... Tha'ss right, Bubba Lee?"

"Tha'ss right, Abdul Hameed".

"Good, good... Now Lieutenant Leo, it be lots of problem the black brothers havin' in this whiteman army, most of which I ain't gonna bother you with, seein' as how it ain't nothin' you can do about it nohow... You 'nstand, Lieutenant Leo?"

"I think so" I tell Abdul Hameed. "And say, I'm

mighty thankful to you for sparin' me the gory detail..."

"Good, good..."

Sgt. Abdul Hameed pauses to take a drag on the hookah, I get it again and nod my appreciation. We eye each other in silence. I am all too conscious of the circle of dark faces watching. Even more so of Sgt. Bobby Lee Donner.

"Now then, Lieutenant Leo my man" Abdul Hameed says. "This one little problem, it better be took care of 'fore it grows into a big one..."

Abdul Hameed pauses. The dark eyes around the circle are lowered casually.

"Yeah" I say. This is where the shit hits the fan.

"Yeah" agrees Abdul Hameed. "'S an ol' problem, Lieutenant Leo, as old as time. Sweet ol' ass".

"Beg your pardon?"

"Ass, Lieutenant Leo" he says, "like piece of, like cunt, like pussy?"

I keep my silence. I know my host is barely done with the warmup.

"Now the brothers here" he goes on, "they got certain 'spectations, on 'count of bein' come back from Nam where it be plenty ol' pussy to go 'round... Local pussy, sweet pussy... Too, their money back in Nam ain't got no color written on it, it be jus' good ol' green... Well you lookee 'round this base, Lieutenant Leo, it ain't no black sisters 'round to keep company to the black brothers, 'cept for the old washer ladies live off base... Well that don' look good, Lieutenant Leo. The brothers they ain't happy..."

It finally dawns on me I had better butt in.

"Now you just hold on to your horses, Wesley" I tell Abdul Hameed, "lemme get this straight... Y'all hot for pussy, tha'ss it? Well this base's got a hospital crawling with pussy. So after hours, you go for it just like everybody else... Hell, I sign your passes too, don't I? So it's up to you, man. You don't expect the Army to pimp for you, now do you, Wesley my main man?"

In the dead silence, I notice with alarm how the weed has finally hit me full blast. Not the best of times to engage in rational discourse. Not when, try as I might, I cannot repress the phantasm of Sgt. Abdul Hameed seated on his gilded throne, under the silken canopy propped up by wrought-silver poles, his head wrapped in a bejeweled turban, his viziers and courtesans--myself included-- scurrying about to do his bidding.

For our jerry-rigged hideout has transformed itself into a spacious woolen tent, pitched on the shore of a palm-shaded lagoon, a small oasis in the bosom of the white dunes. All that is missing are the troupe of bikini-clad beauties undulating in the satin-draped ring in front of the Sultan's throne, to the slow beat of a *Saz* band--the reed flute, the booming *Oud*, the sweet seductive *Saz*, the intricate *Kanoon*, punctuated by the soft beat of the *Tamboura*.

I suppress a king-size giggle that would have

stripped me of the last vestige of my dignity. I watch the colorful lower drapes of the tent flapping in the dry desert wind. I inhale the sweet aroma of Afghani hash wafting away from the gurgling hookahs. I lust after the plump dancers as they grind their lush hips. With my restraints crumbled, I let out an involuntary yelp:

"Whoopie-doo!... *Aman-aman...*"

Next to me, Sgt. Abdul Hameed leans over, his large eyes peering at me over the dark shades:

"You a'right, Lieutenant Leo my man?"

"Never been better, oh illustrious Sultan. Just had me a sweet vision... tell you 'bout it some day... Where was we, man?"

Abdul Hameed shakes his head in mock reproach.

"I better keep the good weed away, Lieutenant Leo" he says, "seein' as how you losing you grip on the main event... Le'ss see... Last thing I hear outta you 'fore we got side-tracked be pimpin', ainit? Like, nobody seen the Army doing a shit-load of pimpin' for the high brass tha'ss comin' in to watch our gig every week? Tha'ss fact, Lieutenant Leo? You done forgot Captain Boz Man 'n your ol' roomie Mista Henry Speiser?"

"Shit, Abdul Hameed, that's top-side brass out there, them are Col. Sprague's prize turkey... You don't expect the colonel to provide same kinda pimpin' for the enlisted men, do you? Let alone for a bunch of Army niggers come back from Nam?"

300

Dead silence. I can only hope I haven't overstepped my bounds.

"Christ in Heaven, Wesley my main man" I go on, warming up to the subject, hoping to defang my *faux pas*, "the Army ain't pimpin' for Sergeant Donner 'n his men either. They all make do on their own... Us chickens all do..."

Abdul Hameed turns to Bobby Lee Donner, who does not appear all that pleased at having been interjected into the front line.

"That so, Bubba Lee?"

"Tha's fact, Abdul Hameed".

"You doin' a'right tho, Bubba Lee, or so I hear".

"I'm doin' jus' fine, Abdul Hameed".

Sgt. Abdul Hameed turns back to the hookah, thoughtfully emptying the dead ashes.

"I sees" he says, "I sees. Now Lieutenant Leo here, he ain't doin' half bad either, I hears tell. 'Less it ain't no Army nurse I just seen feedin' him lunch in the shade... Tha'ss fact too, Bubba Lee?"

Sgt. Donner keeps his council. Abdul Hameed goads him on:

"I hears tell she a roomie to you ol' lady, Bubba Lee".

"Well..."

I know I should intervene, if only to let poor Donner off the hook. But Abdul Hameed is not yet done:

301

"It be plenty o' Army pussy to go around for Army whiteboys" he says, his eyes once again concealed behind the dark shades. "But nothin' for pooa' Army niggers. Ain't no black Army nurses in the Ft. Gordon hospital. Ainit so, Lieutenant Leo my main man?"

"But that's just..."

I stop. Abdul Hameed turns back to Sgt. Donner:

"The lieutenant seem to've gotten slowed down by the good weed" he says. "Reckon you better 'splain to him the fac's o' life down Georgia way, Bubba Lee?"

Sgt. Donner tips the growing column of ashes off his joint, then passes it on to the next trooper. He exhales slowly.

"Reckon" he says. "Seein's how you's a Yankee, Lieutenant, hailin' from up North, so maybe you don't know how things work down in Georgia... Them Army nurses, there ain't no colored ones around the Ft. Gordon hospital. There ain't that many white spare ones either that ain't spoken for..."

Bobby Lee Donner clears his throat, looking down at his boots.

" 'Sides..." he says, "there ain't no way a colored Army man could take out a white gal, Army nurse or what. Not in Georgia, sir".

I nod. I am stoned, but not stupid.

"I understand" I tell Abdul Hameed. "Still, I don't know what I can do about it".

"It be more" he says. "Way things' shapin' up, the brothers they don't want nothin' to do with white pussy no more. The brothers they think 's 'bout time the Army got some black pussy in uniform. All the brothers wants for the Army to do the right thing. You 'nstand, Lieutenant Leo?"

"I see".

And I do. For the zeitgeist has filtered all the way down to Ft. Gordon, Georgia.

"How 'bout all them black chicks in Augusta?" I tell Abdul Hameed. "Seem like half the town's pitch black, last time I peeked. Oughta be enough stray pussy to go around, hey?"

Abdul Hameed looks at Sgt. Donner. They both shake their heads, lamenting the incredible lack of horse sense this white-ass Yankee boy seems to exhibit. Abdul Hameed leans over and passes the mouth-piece to me.

"You better suck some more on the good weed, Lieutenant Leo" he says, "might knock some sense into you whiteboy ass, jus' might".

I take the proffered tube and drag away. Might as well indulge while I still can.

"Augusta..." says Abdul Hameed. "We's got a problem there too... Town's got enough black pros to go 'round. But thing is, Lieutenant Leo, the brothers they had nothing but pros for a whole year down in Nam. Plus, back there, prime pussy go for a box of PX cigarettes, a bottle of Army rum... Shit, maybe a pack of chewin' gum throwed in for good faith... So the brothers they kinda spoiled. Them black pros in Augusta they don' measure up... 'sides of which, the brothers they'd like to pass time with some reg'lar black chicks for a change. Quality black chicks, you 'nstand?"

"Sure" I tell him. "Well, what's stopping them?"

Abdul Hameed turns to survey his troops, crouched around the circle.

"It be a little problem there too" he says. "See, black chicks down here in Georgia, they kinda prim 'n proper, know what I mean... They church-going black chicks, they sittin' in the pews ever' Sunday all dolled up, they's mama watchin' over them like a hawk, ain't 'bout to let they's sweet girls have nothin' to do with these Army niggers... On 'count of they all badass ghetto niggers from up North just come back from Vee-Eight-Nam... Hell, not without some serious collateral, like, put a 'spensive ring on they's little finger, take a long walk down the aisle in black tux with the chick's daddy and three big brothers watchin'... You 'nstand, Lieutenant Leo?"

I do.

" 'Sides" says Abdul Hameed, "the brothers here they can't walk down that aisle even if they wanna, on account of they all Muslim now, see? So them proper black chicks down in Augusta they ain't gonna wanna wed them nohow... You hearin' what I sayin', Lieutenant Leo my main man?"

I can nod my sympathy, an officer and a gentleman,

but Abdul Hameed is still not done.

"And 'course the brothers" he says, "they aint' in no mind to walk down no aisle even if the blessin' be done by a proper Mullah. They just back from Nam, got they's head messed up real bad. They needs to get their shit together, get back in proper balance. All they wants's have 'em a little ol' black fun 'tween the white sheets, you 'nstand?"

The dark circle of faces look at me like I got the answer. I take a deep breath, my head is stuffed with fuzz.

"Lemme see if I got this right, Wesley" I tell Abdul Hameed. "You're tellin' me there ain't nothing can be done. Then you're tellin' me I better do something about it. That so?"

I get no response.

"Tell you what. Suppose I put in a requisition for twenty black Army nurses... Fill it out in triplicate, run it up through channels... Yessiree, that means first to Major Herskowitz, then Col. Manners, then Col. Sprague... Then we can all sit around on our fat asses 'n smoke the good weed 'n wait for the Army to grind its wheels, come up with a reply... That good enough for you, Wesley my main man?"

I am greeted with a curtain dark silence. I take a deep breath. Time for God's truth.

"Christ, man" I say to whoever would listen, "I'm just a fuckin' lieutenant jg, remember? Too far down the

305

totem pole to count for a piddlin' shit, case you need remindin'. Now them big guys upstairs, they get my letter, they all gonna think I gone plum crazy. They gonna ship me off to the loony bin for observation... Ten days, they certify me fit for Nam. Then 'fore you know it, y'all get yourself a brand new spit-n-polish West Point freak, someone who really gives a shit... Think you'd like that better?"

In the silence that surrounds our impasse, fresh joints are passed around. People are nodding in reflective silence. Abdul Hameed and I pass the hookah back and forth. Our lunch break must have stretched beyond all reasonable bounds, Gretchen must have given up on me long ago.

"Shit, Wesley" I tell Abdul Hameed. "This weed's fuckin' dynamite. This the Boz' Bangkok stash we're stonin' on?"

"Part 'n parcel, Lieutenant Leo. Man can't live by bread alone. Muhammad says".

"Ain't that the fuckin' truth".

We nod at each other and contemplate life's mysteries as we pass the hookah back and forth.

"Lookie here Wesley" I say at last. "I'll go talk to Len, okay? But I have no idea what he'll say, he ain't a free agent either, y'know".

"Major Len's a'right" Abdul Hameed concedes. "For a Jewboy".

"Yeah" I say, "the major's a righteous dude, but he can't do much on his own either. Now suppose, just' suppose

suppose, we can get some black chick in the cast. Where you gonna cast them? Len can't change the script just to put more black folk on the Av. Shit, the whole fuckin' point, if there's one, is there ain't none. We're talkin' Main Street USA, remember?"

Abdul Hameed nods.

"I digs, man, I digs".

" 'Sides, Len'll have to clear it up with Col. Manners..."

"Colonel Rodney he OK too" says Abdul Hameed. "Shit, he only interested in the real estate".

"That's right" I say. "But still he's gotta thin k of Col. Sprague 'n his fat-cat guests, right?"

Abdul Hameed nods again.

"Now tha'ss one righteous pig right there".

"A sty-full of them. And they ain't gonna like seein' *their* Main Street USA trashed with stray niggers. Gonna make them feel funny".

" 'S true, my man, 's true".

"Well, see now, Wesley my man" I tell him. "We got us a real problem".

Sgt. Abdul Hameed stretches his hulking frame slowly, joining his arms above his head and cracking the joints one by one. *Pop, pop, pop.*

"We sure do, Lieutenant Leo" he agrees. "Thing is, I got faith in you, my man. I knows you can deliver, if you jus' put your mind to it. Very least, I 'spect you gonna try".

"I will" I tell him, "I will bust my sorry whiteboy ass. But what if I can't swing it?"

I need to buy insurance.

"Well" says Abdul Hameed. "I don' know. Thing is, the way the brothers been feelin', all kinda acciden's can happen, stuff I ain't got no control over my own self..."

Abdul Hameed's voice is sweet reason. But I heard what I just heard.

"Accidents?"

"Shit" says Abdul Hameed, "y'know, kinda stuff used to happen back in Nam".

"Like what?"

"Like" says Abdul Hameed, "s'pose a brother had him a real bad day... S'pose he jus' lost his last paycheck playing Chinese poker in one of them dives in Cholon. Maybe didn' get his fix when he shoulda, maybe a local Vee-Eight-Cong whore led him on and then ditched him in a back alley where her comrades were layin' for him with their Kalashnikovs, get his feelin' hurt real bad... Shit, maybe the brother he out there in the swamp, he just missin' his mama's sweet home-cookin'. Now s'pose it be this hardass honky secon' lieutenant been ridin' the brother's ass extra hard all month, ever since the bugger got shipped over to replace the one bought the farm on patrol near My Phong... Shit, Lieutenant Leo my main man, s'pose the brother he jus' forget to unload the bullets out of his M-16, maybe he jus' not careful with his hand grenade so the pin ge's loose. You 'n'stand?"

In spite of the dense fog inside my head, I understand only too well.

"We ain't talking fraggin' by any chance, Wesley my main man?"

"Yeah, som'n' like that... Yeah, you got it right this time, Lieutenant Leo".

"Sounds like fuckin' blackmail to me" I tell Abdul Hameed. " Sounds awful like it. So I was hopin' maybe you be only joshin' me".

Sgt. Abdul Hameed sucks on the hookah in inscrutable silence. He passes the tube back to me. I load up good and proper and sit on it as long as I can. One more fuse has just been lit under my poor white Jg ass. The glistening black faces around me seem friendly enough, smiling in genuine pleasure, like conspirators who have just inducted a new member into their cell.

In the twin worlds we inhabit, together but mostly apart, I have just been allowed a peek. They got me by the balls, they know they can squeeze any time. They bear no grudge, nothing personal.

The coffee pot is making the rounds. Fresh joints are passed out, the good weed is a great equalizer. Someone has switched on a portable radio tuned to a local R&B station. In our dark peaceful conclave, voices are calling out:

"Yeah man..."

309

"Right on, bro'..."

"Sock it to me, sweet mama..."

Next to me, Sgt. Abdul Hameed stretches to his full sitting height.

" 'Course" he says, looking down at me, "I might be jus' kiddin', Lieutenant Leo. I might be jus' pullin' you skinny whiteboy leg, seein's how the brothers they kinda like you, on account of you bein' cool. For a honkey 'n an officer, you 'n'stand..."

"Gee, thanks, Wesley".

"My pleasure, Lieutenant Leo my man... 'Course the brothers they don't know how you 'n me go a long way back. Reckon we sit on it, hey?"

"Reckon".

"So the brothers, they cool about you, Lieutenant Leo. Maybe not so cool 'bout them big fat honky brass come see us playin' a Berkeley riot every Friday. Way the brothers figure, them's the same-self brass used to give 'em a heap of white shit back in Nam. You 'n'stand what I's sayin', Lieutenant Leo?"

"I do, Wesley, I do".

"Good... Still, the brothers they needs to know somebody care, they needs to know somebody with them, somebody tryin' to put things right".

"I told you I'll do my best, Wesley".

"I knows you did, Lieutenant Leo. An' I knows you will. Tha'ss why I just wanna make sure it be no accident.

You 'n I we wanna keep it sweet, wanna keep everybody happy..."

Abdul Hameed turns to Sgt. Donner.

" 'S right, Bubba Lee?"

" 'S right, Abdul Hameed".

We seem to have arrived at a consensus.

"I'll try" I tell him, "I'll talk to Len next thing tomorrow morning".

"That's all we askin', Lieutenant Leo".

It has finally occurred to me to check my watch. Almost five.

"Shit" I tell Abdul Hameed. "I better go and see what's happenin' out there in the real world. Say we're done for today? Might as well send the guys home. Same thing, Donner. See y'all tomorrow at ten".

I pull myself up with difficulty and wobble around the circle. I stumble twice. I right myself. The me n nod at me all the way out, a cheerful homage to my handicap.

●　　　●　　　●

When I emerge into the gathering dusk, the set is deserted. Gretchen is nowhere. I am still floating in scented haze. I walk off the set, cross the little valley and climb towards the base. At the edge of the pine, a surge of fresh breeze whack my face. I stand with my eyes closed, letting the air caress my burning face. I cannot shake off the

311

phantom Turkish music, whose simple, controlled strains have acquired the kaleidoscop hues of medieval tapestry. I try to make the vision go away. Soon it does. With a sigh, I plunge into the pine.

Back in the flat, a note is tucked under the phone, in Gretchen's meticulous hand:

Mom called. Had to go see her. Back Sunday pm. Good luck tomorrow. Loveya, G.K.

I read and re-read the terse lines. This is the first time she has alluded to recent contact with her mother, who thus acquires an instant, invasive reality. Before long, I seesaw between feeling alarmed and being royally pissed off. I want to talk to Gretchen about Abdul Hameed, I need to share my paranoia. My righteous indignation fairly boils over when I discover I can't even call her. I don't have her mom's number, I don't know her name, nor where she lives. I mope around in utter dejection, falling asleep in my smoke-scented clothes.

In the morning I catch Major Herskowitz at the office before rehearsal. I relate to him Abdul Hameed's story, expurgating only the most incriminating detail. The major listens, nods at the right places. He seems distracted but not surprised.

"I'll look into it" he says.

Does he understand how tricky this is? I leave his office a nervous wreck.

The dress rehearsal Friday morning is an

unmitigated disaster. My troops shuffle about listlessly. Two of the women are brand new. Come show time, I am desperate. I give up on the script and let serendipity take its course. What ensues is a near-riot. Chaos reigns, my apprehension goes ballistic. I see Len Herskowitz leaving before the end of the show. There will be hell to pay come Monday.

●　　　●　　　●

Sunday evening past eight, Gretchen isn't back. I dial her apartment again but get no answer. At ten, I get a busy signal that lasts for an hour. I finally get Bobby Lee Donner, who sounds like he's still on cloud nine.

No, Gretchen is not there. Yes, she did stop by briefly, just before ten. Yes, she and Cynthia went on their shift together. I ask Bobby Lee to jot down a note for Gretchen to please call. I hang up, royally pissed, finally alarmed.

I have a heck of a time falling asleep. When I wake up Monday morning, the sun is bathing the living-room in Georgia gold, it is almost nine. I grab whatever clothes I can get my hands on and sprint out, stumbling and cussing my way down the stairs.

What is waiting for me in Len's office is a tribunal. The three of them are huddled around the desk, one chair accusingly empty. I am unshaven and hatless, my eyes are but a slit, my wrinkled shirt half tucked in.

They look at me in silence, Len nearly dwarfed between the two others--Col. Manner and the Rev. Captain Nederlander, whose presence is unprecedented.

I execute a limp salute that no one returns. Three pairs of eyes skewer me in silence.

When Len Herskowitz breaks the silence, it is almost a relief, uncoiling like a whip:

"For Chrissakes, Leo, can't you ever be on time?"

"Sorry, I..."

He cuts me short with an exasperated grunt:

"Nevermind. Sit down".

The other two glower beside him. I take the hot seat across. Dispensing with the preliminaries, Len Herskowitz punches the start lever of a small tape-recorder lying on top of his desk, then leans back and closes his eyes.

A series of mechanical squeals pour out of the machine, superimposed over a background of Acid Rock--Zappa and the Mothers in a singularly noxious romp out of *Three Hundred Motels*.

The extraneous noise sounds suspiciously like a four-piston engine groaning in terminal labor. Periodically, loud bangs interpose into the soundtrack, only to subside and allow the bare hint of muffled human voices, laughter and grunts. A high-pitch *continuo* underscores the impenetrable whole. It persists for a steady minute, during which I steal a furtive glance at the blank-faced triumvirate across the desk.

314

A series of heavy crashing sounds ensues, followed by a male voice:

"Fuck!"

The engine noise dies out abruptly. In the hush, the male voice observes:

"Well whadaya know! A whole acre of shit-ass cock-suckin' mother-fuckin' liquor-soaked brass... So why don't y'all drag your lousy hippie corpses outta this jalopy and let's sock it to them with real honest-to-God zip for a change, willya guys? Come on, shake a leg, show some life!..."

A cacophony of undecipherable noise follows--heavy boots grinding on metal?--then a short pause with nothing but a steady hiss. Someone clears his throat right into the microphone. A few loud knocks follow. I wince, for I know that voice.

An amplified stage whisper exhorts:

"OK you stiffs, let's get this show on the road!"

My signature sendoff.

Abruptly, the volume shoots up. The voice, now in full-bore screaming mode, goes into a rant:

"Comrades! Downtrodden masses! Let us take up arms and rise against the tyranny!..."

Loud screams from a small if determined cheering section. The male voice returns, this time in its natural register. Garbled by an overlay of extraneous clamor, it is perfectly intelligible:

315

"Now listen you miserable grunts! Those mo'-fuckers out front expect you to act up like dumb-shit dirty hippies... An'body ever seen a live dirty hippie?... Shee-it, never mind, folks, le's sock it to them! Le's lay it on them mothers real thick! Le's freak 'em out, hey!... Whassa matter, too much dope last night? Loosen up willya! Chrissakes, ain't you ever been to a peace demonstration?... Now listen, after the next one give me a real howl, okay? Something to be proud of! Something to write home about!... C'meon you miserable subversive pinkos!..."

The full-bore amplification switches back on. The voice screeches:

"We've come to tear this joint down, loot 'n burn it, right?!..."

The small chorus roars its assent. It screams, it howls, it whistles. Then the voice:

"Fuck the establishment!..."

The chorus erupts. When it tapers off, the voice returns, unamplified:

"Tha's the ticket, guys, le's fuck it, fuck it real good. If we could only find where it hides its goddam pussy..."

The voice guffaws in evident satisfaction, then:

"Say, while you're at it, don't forget the dudes that gave you Nam!... Them's the ones sittin' up there in the bleachers... Take a good look, you hippie scum, you lousy cannon-fodder!... Lookie them unregenerated shit-eatin' likker-guzzlin' tobakkee-chewin' redneck pigs... So le's sock it to them, hey? But first this message from our sponsor..."

The volume is on again, the voice blaring its exhortation:

"Get our boys out of Nam! Johnson a mass murderer!..."

On cue, the chorus launches into its red-flag *responsorium*:

"Hey, hey, El-Bee-Jay! How many kids did you kill to-day?!..."

After the requisite reprises, the choir pipes down. The voice is back, unamplified:

"That was purty darn good, mah fella 'Merkuns... Purty darn good for a bunch of lousy civilians just ready to ship out to Nam... Now when you get there, boys, just remember what this is all about... And please don't forget to kill women and children and burn hamlets and flush the slimy gooks out of their tunnels with liquid petroleum jelly!... Tha's *Nay-Palm* for you buggers, remember!... And hey, when you slither in the muck down them rice paddies, your skin crawling with lice 'n your sorry ass sproutin' fat juicy leaches, why, don't you forget who sent you there, y'hear!... So hey, let's hear it now, loud and clear, for the drunk mother-fuckin' brass out there..."

The volume goes back on. The voice bursts in rapid-fire expletives:

"Fuck the draft! Screw General Hershey-bar! Shit on

317

Robert MacNamara!..."

The chorus responds. Another harangue follows, then the unamplified voice:

"Purty darn good, you guys. You's gettin' the hang of it... Now listen good, you commie low-life... When we go into the fuckin' bank next, let's not get confused by the enemy sittin' up there screamin' holy terror... Them foulmouth mothers's too sloshed to appreciate the fuckin' fine points of good theater anyhow... So let's make it short 'n sweet, hey? And loud, for chrissakes... And keep it cool, willya? Le's have fun down there, like forget about all them fat creeps, hey?... Oh, one more thing--watch out, they throw rocks, glasses, bottles too... So duck, willya? Don't pay no mind to them pigs, just do your thing 'n cool it, hey? Then we can all go home, you 'n'stand?... Al-right, here she come... After the next one..."

The amplified voice is back on:

"Fuck the oppressors! Expropriate the expropriators! Workers of the world unite! On the bank! Let's burn the sucker!..."

A loud crash ensues, then silence. Then the steady low hiss of the turning tape. Major Herskowitz leans over and punches off the machine.

The three of them watch me in silence from across the desk. The recording, I must concede, was made with surprising fidelity. The chief culprit would have a devil of a time disowning his voice.

318

The silence lingers. My eyes are firmly planted in my lap, where my fingers are twined in a tightly wrought wad. After a seeming eternity, I look up at Major Herskowitz:

"Am I supposed to say something now, sir? Or have I missed my cue again?"

The major nods in visible discomfort:

"Don't you think you'd better?"

"I reckon" I say. "Can I ask who made the tape?"

Major Herskowitz shrugs and turn s to Col. Manners. A quick exchange of looks, a shrug. My question hangs in the air, till it is resolved by the Reverend Captain Nederlander:

"I made provisions to obtain the tape, Lieutenant".

The grey-blue eyes bathe me with stern compassion.

"Reluctantly, I might add".

"I see".

My fingernails are chewed down to the cuticles.

"I assume you had authorization, sir?"

Into the ensuing silence, Col. Manners interjects himself for the first time:

"He did".

"I see".

I turn back to Capt. Nederlander:

"Must've been those new girls from th e main office, right, Reverend?"

"Well, actually..."

"Figures" I say. "A sudden switch, no nurses available... I don't expect you could've gotten any of our regulars to do it. They would've come to me first".

My observation is left unchallenged. I turn back to Major Herskowitz.

"I take it you were not in on it, sir?"

The pained expression on his face is eloquent enough. His brow is crossed with jagged furrows, he is fiddling with a boxful of paper clips. Between the twin *goyim* towering to his right and left, his wiry frame has visibly shrunken.

Into the awkward silence, Col. Manner interjects himself for the second time:

"How the tape was made, Lieutenant" he says, "is not at issue here. What we were hoping to hear from you is some sort of explanation".

I look at the colonel. I can't tell which way his wind is blowing. His clear gray eyes are alert, neutral. I bounce the ball back into his court.

"An explanation of what exactly, sir?"

"Of this tape".

"I thought Captain Nederlander's already explained that, sir".

An inelegant gambit, that. For, *mutatis mutandis*, I am damned if I do and damned if I don't. At this delicate juncture, Col. Manners may be in a bind. What I need to know is, is the Reverend holding something over the

Colonel's head? I have been in the Army just long enough to get a whiff of its arcane codicils. One dumb guess, a slip, the wrong inflection--and there goes my ass. The dread wings of Vietnam are flapping at my neck.

Colonel Manners' voice reveals little:

"We would still like to hear your explanation, Lieutenant" he says. "That is, if you have one. And let's quit pretending you don't know what I mean".

"What exactly do you want me to explain, sir?"

The Reverend Captain Nederlander leans across the desk to catch the Colonel's eye:

"May I, sir?"

The colonel nods.

Captain Nederlander turns to me:

"As you must have surely noticed, Lieutenant, there are two separate, alternating performances captured on the tape you've just heard. I am sure I am not misrepresenting the colonel and the major when I tell you none of us see anything wrong with the amplified segments. I understand from Major Herskowitz they closely follow the script, give or take some unavoidable poetic license. A rousing performance indeed--as far as it goes".

Captain Nederlander pauses, looking to the others. Having detected no dissent, he turns back to me:

"It is the other voice--the other *persona*?--that is at issue here. The one intended only for the servicemen in the cast. I'm still at loss how to characterize it, I keep wavering between *shocking, obscene, insulting,* perhaps all the way to *seditious* or *treasonous.* So I wonder how *you* would characterize it?"

I keep my eyes firmly glued to the floor. Captain Nederlander goes on:

"How about utter disrespect, Lieutenant? How about crass vilification of the Armed forces of the United States? Demeaning the officers corps? Debasing your own commission?"

I maintain my resolute silence.

"You see" Captain Nederlander goes on, "the loud aspersions you cast on the Secretary of Defense and the Commander in Chief are part of the script. As much as we all hate to hear them, they represent what they were intended to represent. But the rest? Gratuitous, vile obscenities? Mutinous insinuations? Seditious imputations? Shall I go on?"

I shrug and keep my silence.

"I must tell you, Lieutenant" says the Rev. Captain Nederlander, "I find that portion of your performance utterly incomprehensible, coming as it is from a uniformed officer on active duty".

I see an opening, however slim.

"Reverend sir" I say, "I wasn't in uniform, was I?"

Capt. Nederlander scoffs:

"You are now".

"You don't hear me saying those things now, sir, do you? Those segments were private speech, sir. They were not intended for an audience. They're constitutionally protected".

I have succeeded in getting Capt. Nederlander mad. Downright livid:

"Constitutionally protected?" he fairly hollers at me. "An officer on active duty speaking to his subordinates? In the course of carrying out his military duties? You call that private speech?"

"I was laboring under the delusion it was. Sir".

The Rev. Captain Nederlander snorts in derision:

"The tape makes that abundantly clear".

I look at him, I look at the other two. I suppose they are both curious to see how I propose to crawl out of the hole I have dug for myself. To their credit, I can detect no trace of malice in their eyes. There is no malice in Captain Nederlander's eyes either. Can he be reasoned with?

"Look, sir" I tell him. "All I've got there is a bunch of miserable, angry grunts. Kids, half of them just back from Nam 'n waiting to muster out. They've seen it all, they don't give a hoot. They hate the Army, say so to my face. I have no leverage on them, zilch. But I still need their good will or else they'll wreck the show, might frag me in the bargain too... Now the other half, they're fresh draftees waiting to ship out. Lost their deferments, or they're too poor or too dumb to've gotten one. They've left their girlfriends behind, they're lonely, resentful, scared shitless--sorry Reverend..."

For the first time I see the trace of a smile creep over Len Herskowitz face.

"I have no leverage over those guys either" I tell my tribunal. "What can I threaten them with that's worse than what they're heading for?"

I pause. Nobody intervenes.

"They've been acting like real stiffs, dragging their heels, slouching, moping about the set. Why, Major Herskowitz has told me himself... So you tell me, Reverend, how do I goad them into acting like a mob of anti-war hippie scum? How do I get them riled up enough to scream and yell and jump up and down and give the peace sign and raise their fists in a Black Power salute? How?"

"With blasphemous sedition?"

"With whatever it takes, sir. Or would you rather I read them the Lord's Prayer?"

A low blow, that. But it is my funeral, and--*mysterium mysteribus*--I am warming up to it. I am beginning to enjoy myself. What is more, if I am not mistaken, the audience--or at least two members--are beginning enjoy the show.

Not the Rev. Captain Nederlander, tho.

"That's ridiculous" he observes. "Gratuitous, too".

"Right you are, sir" I tell him. "Most of them probably don't know it. So I better use what will get the job done. The straight ideological garbage in the script ain't gonna turn these guys on. So I ad-lib.... Christ, it's not like

I think this stuff up in advance, it just comes to me, pops out right there when I'm standing in front of them trying to get them riled, get them real pissed..."

Too late, I realize I have made a tactical error, perhaps a fatal slip.

When Col. Manners finally intervenes, what he has to say confirms my fears:

"That's what worries the captain, Lieutenant" he says.

The colonel's eyes pin me back to my seat, careful, even, abstract.

"And, I might add" he says, "it worries me too. You've just said it yourself-- it comes to you too darn natural--sorry, Reverend. So one cannot but wonder whether you haven't already crossed the line between impersonating a dangerous agitator and being one yourself".

The dead silence reverberates in the small room. I have underestimated the colonel.

"You do understand what I am saying, Lieutenant?" he says, "don't you?"

"Yessir".

"Well, won't you agree then that the Reverend's concern has some merit?".

I keep resolutely, demurely silent.

Col. Manners waits.

"You see, Lieutenant" he says, "Captain Nederlander first came to me with his worry. He told me how impressed he was with your performance, your extensive knowledge of the vast un-American conspiracy we are charged with fighting at Seadock, with how well-versed you were in the seditious underground... Shoot, that's why we got you here to begin with, Lieutenant, for your Berk-- Shoot, nevermind, for your experience. I told the Reverend you were not a draftee, that you volunteered. Still, given your background, he was worried. I admit I was reluctant, but still, I went along. So now we've got this tape, and it seems to corroborate the Captain's worst suspicions".

The Rev. Captain Nederlander nods vigorously. Major Herskowitz's face is alert, his eyes fixed on me.

I wait.

"Lieutenant" says Col. Manners, "this is a serious breech, even granting the material was aimed only at your cast. So I'm taking this under advisement, and may insert a note in your service file. Major Herskowitz here tells me you are a gifted performer and have a way with the troops. That's more than obvious. I suggest that from now on you confine yourself to the script and refrain from extraneous offensive language".

There is more coming.

"Now" he says, "it's clear to me that the delegation of authority in this unit, without adequate supervision, has gone far beyond the bounds of prudence. So till further notice, both rehearsals and performances will be closely monitored. Len?"

"Yes sir".

The colonel nods.

"Good" he says. "I hope you're taking this seriously, Lieutenant".

"Yessir".

"Captain?"

There is a discernible if well-tempered tension between these two, and thereby may lie my salvation.

"Well..." says the Reverend.

I brace myself.

The Rev. Captain Nederlander clears his throat:

"Sir" he says, "I think some discipline is in order. Perhaps Col. Sprague ought to be..."

The cat is out of the bag. The pull the Reverend has--must have--comes from upstairs. The good news is immediately confirmed by Col. Manners:

"Let's leave Sprague out of this, shall we? No need to alarm him, he's busy enough as it is. Shall we assume Lt. Swenson's immediate superior will take the appropriate steps?"

"Yessir" says Major Herskowitz, "he certainly will".

With relish.

"Excellent".

Col. Manners turns back to the Rev. Captain Nederlander:

"Captain?"

Reluctantly, the Reverend falls in line:

327

"If you think so, sir".

The colonel nods.

"Thank you, Captain" he says. " Any more questions?"

A note of mischief creeps into Col. Manners' voice, as he once again turns to address the Reverend Captain Nederlander:

"I assume there are no other copies of the offensive tape, Captain?"

It is a neatly laid trap, into which the poor Reverend now steps, open-eyed and visible chagrined. He is trumped by a skillful bureaucratic infighter, and he knows it.

"No sir" he says.

"Splendid. In which case, I suggest the matter is closed for the moment. This tape stays in my safe, just in case we need to refer to it again. You did an excellent job of investigating, Captain. I appreciate. Needless to say, it will be noted in the appropriate file".

The last bit of inspired ambiguity leaves the Rev. Captain Nederlander little choice but gracious concession:

"Thank you, sir".

"You bet, Captain".

Col. Manners draws a long breath, stretching his arms upward slowly and twining his hands behind his neck. His eye are focused at the wall across, just above my head.

"I'm glad we've had a chance to clear this up" he

says to the three of us at large. "Because there's some real business we need to take care of, and it would've been bad if we had let things fester".

The colonel lowers his eyes just a trifle, for a brief moment locking them with mine.

"This coming Friday, the show had better be something special, above and beyond the call of duty. Col. Sprague's got some high-ranking guests flying in, top Pentagon brass. He'd like to bring them down to the show. So he'll be there himself, together with the C.O. Which means I'll be down there myself, with Mrs. Manners. I take it you'll be there, Len?"

"You betcha, my wife too. Plus, it just so happens I've got out-of-town visitors who I'd like to come see the show. That is, if it's okay with you, Rodney".

The colonel nods his assent.

"Sure. Now Reverend, you've got guests coming too?"

"I might".

In my state of disgrace, I don't expect to be asked.

"Well, good" says Col. Manners. "In this case, we all appreciate even more how this Friday's show must be a special effort on everybody's part. So whatever needs to be fixed, you've got a whole week to fix it. You understand that, Lieutenant?"

"Yessir".

"Len?"

"You bet, Rodney".

"Good. Now, Captain Nederlander has a suggestion he'd like to bounce off the two of you. You had better explain this yourself, Captain".

"Well, sir..."

Once again, I am struck with how Col. Manners is much keener than his good-ol'-boy façade lets on. What is taking place now is the handing out of a consolation prize.

"Gentlemen" says the Rev. Captain Nederlander. "I've been thinking... We've got a show that is profoundly instructive. But still, it lacks a certain..."

Je ne sais quoi would have come in handy.

"We've got all the negatives out there" he says. "A rampaging Red mob, blasphemy, sedition, riot, lewd and lascivious behavior, consorting, miscegenation... Then we've got the heroic forces of law-and-order coming to the rescue, courageous and, for once, unrestrained by phony constitutional scruples and sharp East-Coast lawyers. But still, there's something missing--a positive note, an inspirational theme, a clear moral message the audience could take home with them. Something to remind them what this is all about. Now, in my experience as a man of the cloth, I've noticed a similar problem with many of my fellow clergymen. Their sermons are mostly about Evil--hell and damnation, fire and brimstone, sin and depravity. But neither love nor charity nor grace nor redemption. My esteemed colleagues get their flock scared out of their wits--but what then?... See what I mean?"

The three of us nod solemnly. I have no idea where the Reverend is heading.

"So I've been wondering" he says, "if maybe a inspirational note cannot be tacked onto the very end of our show, something that'll make its deeper significance more apparent..."

Len Herskowitz and I exchange a brief look. The silence stretches on. Finally the Col. Manners says:

"Go ahead, Reverend".

"Well" says Capt. Nederlander, "this may sound a bit simple minded, but--I've been, for a number of years now, the spiritual director of a fine Christian congregation in Augusta, a congregation blessed with, it just so happens, one of the finest inspirational choirs this side of the Mason-Dixon line. Now, what would be a more fitting end to the show than--right after the National Guard has finished mopping up--our choir coming from, say, behind the bank, to give a rousing rendition of one of their prize-winning numbers, say *Amazing Grace*, or even better, *The Battle Hymn of the Republic*? If we tack it on to the very end, there'll be no need to tamper with the script. And it will still endow the whole affair with a lasting aura..."

The Rev. Captain Nederlander pulls a large white handkerchief out of his pocket and proceeds to dab his brow. Col. Manners is the first to stir:

"Len?"

"Well, I don't know, Rodney. It's not exactly a natural fit, if you get my drift".

"Well now" says the colonel, "It's not a major shuffle, you wouldn't even need to rehearse it, would you? And as long as the Reverend takes care of getting his choir behind the scenery before you start, make sure they stay out of the way... Why, it couldn't hurt, now could it? Len?"

"I suppose...".

Major Herskowitz has finally gotten the colonel's drift. Still:

"How do you propose to guarantee their safety during the final bash, Rodney? Standing there behind the scenery with everybody fighting it out around the bank?... I suppose we could stash them behind the stands to begin with, then let them sneak around the very last minute? Maybe arrange themselves near the bar? Yeah, that ought to keep them out of range, but still close enough to deliver their inspirational message. What do you think, Lieutenant?"

I am startled out of my reveries.

"Sure, yeah, yessir... Sure, that ought to work".

Col. Manners turns back to the Reverend:

"Settled then, Captain. You put in a requisition for a bus to ferry your choir over to the base Friday. Leave it on my desk. Anything else, Len?"

"I don't think so".

We watch the two of them depart in silence, the Rev. Captain Nederlander deferring to Col. Manners, the colonel striding out resolutely.

Major Herskowitz is drumming thoughtfully on his desk. I wait. Presently he looks up:

"Really, Leo".

"Sorry, chief" I tell him, "I goofed, landed you in deep shit, right?"

"What do you think?

"*Mea maxima culpa*. How could I know the fucker'd play such a dirty trick? A Reverend? Chrissakes, he came to me asking for help!..."

"Make you wonder, don't it? A man of the Cloth..."

"Cloth my dick".

"My sentiments".

Major Herskowitz swivels in his chair and looks out the window. Has it occurred to him his own office may be bugged?

"Don't kid yourself, *boychik*" he says, swiveling back to face me. "You're all the way up shit creek, no paddle in sight. Tho maybe, just maybe, it's not terminal. Not if Rodney keeps the tape locked up in his safe. Better yet, at home, which I have a hunch he will. It's your sheer good luck he despises the Reverend, loathes him, really. But that ain't going to save your sorry ass unless you find a better way of channeling your frustrated passion for Mark Anthony's Funeral Oration... Or at least be a bit more

333

discrete about it. Christ, that was some stunt! Where the fuck was your head? Do I need to beat your dense *sheygetz* brain into pulp to get you to stay on task?"

"I'm trying, Len, I really am".

Major Herskowitz shakes his head.

"Well fuck it, man, try harder, willya? I hope the Reverend wasn't lying about there being only one copy of your caper..."

"Guy's real devious".

"Snake in the grass. We better keep our fingers crossed".

I decide to take a chance.

"Seems like he's holding something over the colonel's head" I tell him, "over yours too, for that matter..."

Major Herskowitz squints at me for a long moment.

"Oh that..." he says. "You can sum it up in one word---Sprague".

"How come?"

"I'm not sure".

"The colonel seems to have handled him rather deftly".

The major is again looking out the window. The khaki shirt on his wiry back is dark with perspiration.

"Don't ever underestimate ol' Rodney Manners" he says, "just because he's just gone out of his way to save your sorry ass. You put him in a rather awkward position, case you haven't noticed".

"I said I was sorry".

"Sorry will get you nowhere, *schmuckele*. But, it just so happens, Rodney despises Sprague almost as much as he does the Reverend. Your dumb *goyim* luck again. Not that you're scot free. Fact, consider yourself confined to quarters till further notice. You can go to the PX, go to work. Otherwise, you're grounded. And this goes into your file too, case that should bother you".

"I understand" I say. "Thanks, Len".

I am not about to remind him that my service file is yet to be found.

"Thanks for nothing. Don't stretch your luck, *sheygetz*. What the fuck were you trying to do? Get to Nam on the fast track?"

"Heaven forbid!"

"Up yours".

Our last exchange has dissipated the tension. Len Herskowitz rises and stretches, his compact frame unwinding like a liberated spring.

"Listen, *bubele*" he says, "I ain't saying it was not a good schtick. Shit, you've got the knack for impro, that's more than obvious. That's why I'm glad you're finally going to meet Mimi. Speaking of which, listen real good... This Friday is special alright, and it's got nothing to do with Sprague's Pentagon brass, or Mrs. Manners, or the Reverend's inspirational choir. We've got a real VIP coming down Friday. So we're going to put our best foot forward for the lady, *capish*?"

"The lady?"

"Mimi Rosencrantz".

"Your *Instant Theater* guru lady?"

"The one".

Of his various and sundry meanderings in the stucco jungles off Hollywood Boulevard, long before landing a steady job directing tobacco commercials, Len Herskowitz still counts among his most cherished career peaks, he tells me, the three-year run of the rigorously--fanaticall--improvised *Instant Theater* at the Horseshoe on Melrose. Off Sunset, he insists, 1963-1966, at the end of which the outfit imploded in a rancorous round of free-for-all eye scratching over communal ethos an d Equity minimum.

"No shit" I say.

"Damn right. Now, this is one sharp lady, Leo. She sees through the trickery and artifice, cuts through bullshit like she's got laser eyes, not to mention a razor tongue. So we're going to have us pure live theater for once, you understand what I'm saying? It's gotta click. It's gotta sparkle. It's gotta swing and pop and sizzle. We gotta unleash all that energy, kid. You better get to those miserable grunts of yours, get to the niggers in the Guard unit, get to the lousy nurses too... And not the way I hear say you've been getting to one of them either, *schlocker*... You gotta get them to shape up, get them motivated, get them channeled and then released!..."

It is a safe bet what I'm hearing is the impro lady's motivational rap.

"Shit, Len" I say, "that's just what I was trying to do last Friday".

"Wrong turn, boy. Sure--talk to them, goad them, plead, scream... Dig into their anger, get under their skin... Get them to channel their fury, transform it into a creative frenzy, into an apocalyptic eruption! Christ, haven't you ever heard of Stanislavsky?"

"You mean, the *Method* dude?"

"Yeah, the Method dude".

Major Herskowitz shakes his head in exasperation.

"Nevermind" he says, "just do it. There's something else too. You're going to have extra props. Rodney's made some suggestions. He too thinks the show needs a bit more zip".

"Like a second inspirational choir?"

"Don't be cute, *bubele*. Rodney's right, tho. The show could use some fine-tuning. So he's sending us another fire-engine, another chopper too, just to show he cares".

"Gee that's sweet".

But Major Herskowitz is on to me:

"None of your sarcasm, *sheygetz*. Anyway, I'm going to be on the set for rehearsals every day this week, just to make sure. The thing is, Leo, just between you and I, you *are* on the right track. You woke those zombies up last

337

week, you got them mad. So keep it up, except for the *sotto voce* stuff, hey?"

I stand vindicated, partially.

"You got it, chief" I tell him.

"Good" says Len. "Now listen real careful. You're on double shift for the rest of the week. Henry Speiser's got the mumps, been hauled off to the quarantine ward this morning. So you're subbing for him at Protocol, effective immediately, till Thursday".

The news is truly alarming.

"But Len" I protest, "don't you think--"

"No use telling you what I think, Leo. It's out of my hands. Colonel's orders. So you swing by there after rehearsal, which you run--on schedule, mind you, with me breathing down your neck--from nine AM till three PM with half an hour for lunch. You'll be late today, that's obvious. By the way, have you had the mumps?"

"I must have".

"Good. Get your ass over to the hospital and see Speiser. He'll brief you. I'm phoning ahead for your authorization".

"Yessir".

Still, I cannot resist one more stab at the obvious:

"If you're really sure I am the one to do PR..."

"It's out of my hands, Leo, you've been snatched away from under my protective wing. The Powers that Be have called for you... *Fershteyst?"*

338

"Shit. I mean, yes"

"Good. Now scram. And for Chrissakes, stay out of trouble".

"Yessir. Give my love to Ruthie".

"I will. Now fuck off, willya".

●　　●　　●

I take a bee-line to the hospital. Not to see Henry Speiser, who could wait. It is past eleven and I am drained. I aim to catch Gretchen before she goes off her shift. I haven't heard from her since that cryptic note Friday. I ask for her at the nurse station. The duty nurse doesn't know for sure but thinks Gretchen may have gone down to the lockers to change. Dr. Creighton might know, she says, Gretchen may have gone back there first.

I proceed to Dr. Creighton's office and almost bump smack into him pacing his outer perimeter.

"Hi there, Lieutenant" he says and stops, offering his hand. "How ya doin'?"

"Oh hi... Alright, I guess".

My hand feels awkward in his warm grip.

"I'm looking for Gretchen" I explain.

"You've just missed her. She's gone on down to change. Wanna sit and wait?"

He gestures toward a chair.

"I shouldn't" I tell him, "I need to catch her before

339

she takes off".

"Better go down then... By the way, I've got a piece of news that might interest you".

"News?"

"Dr. Swenson" he says, "that's your father, is going to be here Friday".

I find it impossible to keep the sharp note of increedulity out of my voice:

"My dad's coming here? But why?"

"I've invited him for consultation. Been talking to him about some of the guys in the ward, the shell-shock cases back from Vietnam... Your father is interested in them. Said he might want to take in your show while he's here".

"Oh shit... Sorry, sir, I didn't mean to... It's just that... oh, never mind. I gotta run. Talk to you later".

I tear off down the corridor with Dr. Creighton looking after me, baffled. I find the staircase and go two floors down, where I park myself in front of the nurses' locker-room and wait. I am utterly exhausted from lack of sleep and the drubbing received this morning. Could it get worse?

I lower myself down near the wall across from the door, hoping there is no other exit. I am almost asleep when Gretchen comes out in her dress uniform. She seems preoccupied and is about to pass me when I call out:

"Gretch".

She stops.

"Oh, it's you" she says.

"Yeah, me. Remember?"

"Go away".

I pull myself up. I wonder what the fuck is going on. I know I look like a bloody wreck.

"What was that again?" I ask her.

"You heard me. Go away".

She turns her back on me and starts walking away. I trail after her in total bafflement:

"Getchen, stop. Please".

But she continues down the corridor. I run after her:

"Honey!" I please. "Slow down!...When did you come back?"

"Last night".

She still wouldn't slow down.

"Why didn't you come over?"

Silence.

"What's wrong? I was waiting..."

"I needed some sleep".

"Oh".

Something is terribly wrong. She is not herself.

"How was your trip?"

We are marching into the dim stairwell. She still hasn't relented.

"How's your mom?"

Gretchen stops:

"She's fine" she says as she turns to face me. "Fact, she said to say hi".

"Gee, that's nice".

We are eyeing each other at close quarters now. Even in the dim half-light, I can tell she is seething.

"You didn't tell me you knew her" she says.

"Knew who?"

"My mom".

"How the fuck would I know your mom?" I explode. "I've never met her, remember? Christ, Gretch, you've never even told me her name!"

She looks at me. Her eyes are dark with rage.

"Serena" she says. "She says you knew each other in Aspen".

"You mean Serena is..."

I look at Gretchen and now, at long last, things click into place. The nagging elusive resemblances, the scent of *deja vu*, the odd coincidences. The inspired, explosive lovemaking. It all stands out like a sore thumb.

"God in Heaven..."

Gretchen's voice cracks at me like a whip:

"You slept with her!"

She spits the words at me. I step back, the sheer vehemence of her voice is overpowering.

"Don't bother to deny it too!" She screams. "I know my mom, I've watched her and her men all my life! Why do you think I ran away? Every fuckin' man she's ever had tried to crawl into my bed!... Christ, I was only eight when the first one did... You think that would have stopped him? I bit half his nose off..."

"But..."

I stop.

"Oh, shit..."

"Shit exactly! And don't bother to deny it, Leo!"

"But honey..."

The sheer unfairness.

"Don't honey me, you bastard!" she shrieks right into my shocked face. "You sex maniac, you incestuous creep, you child molester, you...!"

In a flash, Gretchen is transformed from a raging tigress into a grieving child.

"Shit..." she wails as she collapses on the concrete steps, burying her face in her hands. "Shit, shit, shit... I was so happy with you, Leo. For once, it felt so right... Why did you have to go and do this to me? Why? The two of you..."

"Do what?" I ask. "Do what? I met Serena--if she's really your mom--more than a year before I met you. How could you possibly accuse me of..."

I am not about to get a fair hearing.

"You did it!..." Gretchen sobs, "the two of you... Why couldn't she just lay off what's mine? I've been busting my ass all these years trying to shake loose of that *woman*... Oh shit Leo, now it's all back, she's done it...

343

Why couldn't she just let me be?... Why? Why? Why?..."

I wait. Gretchen wails inconsolably:

"Shit, shit, shit... Every single one of them was lusting after my ass from the time I was barely outta my pampers... I had to fight them off, she wasn't much help either... I had to scratch, bite and scream and finally run away... Didn't talk to her for years... Now she's finally gone done it, she's finally got me to sleep with one of her men..."

Gretchen's tears are pouring out uncontrollably. Her tiny frame is racked with bitter sobs as she sit there, utterly forlorn, hugging her shoulders in total despair.

I lower myself down next to her on the cold cement. Slowly, cautiously, I place my arm over her shoulder. She shudders violently but doesn't repulse me.

I am just as shocked as she is.

"Honey" I say, "this ain't your childhood anymore. And Serena hasn't passed any of her men down to you. How could you expect either of us to tell the future? Christ, my bumping into you a year ago was a sheer accident, don't you remember? So is your transfer to Ft. Gordon, so is my being here... Can't you see?"

But she is inconsolably. I put both my arms around her and let her sob away. In a while her tears subside. She is nestled in my arms, heaving. Finally, not looking up, she says:

"Besides, it wasn't an accident..."

"What?"

"My transferring here, I knew you were here, Dr. Creighton told me".

"So who's seduced who now?"

"Shut up, you creep" she says. Then: "Let go".

She searches through her bag, coming up with a box of Kleenex, which she proceeds to apply to her puffed face.

"It's much worse" she says. "She's coming down to visit".

"Serena? God! When?"

"This Friday. She's coming to see the show. And me. And you...."

Gretchen's voice trails off. For a moment I think she is about to start wailing again.

"Christ" I say. "The last straw..."

"What do you mean?"

"My dad's coming too" I tell her, "as Dr. Creighton's guest. And Len Herskowitz' mentor lady, Mimi what's-her-face. And Rodney Manners' wife, who's never seen the show. And the Reverend Nederlander's church choir. And Sprague is flying in a whole flock of high-polish Pentagon brass. And I am up shit creek without a paddle and in everybody's dog-house, and God is working double shift to give me a hint, like maybe it's time to bump myself off..."

Gretchen's tear-streaked face it turned up to me:

"Oh poor baby... Oh, I'm sorry, I'm sorry..."

She is hugging me. Before I know it, we are kissing--voraciously, ravenously--as if there is no tomorrow.

Only a faint residue of prudence succeeds in prying us loose of each other, off the stairwell and in a desperate dash back to my flat. Where, rushing upstairs and pulling the blinds down, we claw at each other's clothes, then sink onto my still-bedless mattress. Though not before Gretchen pulls a joint out of her purse and lights up.

"Mom's stash" she says as she passes the thin stick on to me. "She says you might like it".

"Shit".

But I drag on it hungrily:

"Shit, shit, shit..."

We tumble and careen and tussle and indulge. We couple and de-couple and delve and partake. It takes the longest time, but at last we wear each other out. In the blurred aftermath, with my hair wild and my innards deliciously scrambled, with Gretchen breathing contentedly next to me, the voice of reason resurfaces. In a flash of rare clarity, I remember Henry Speiser and his mumps.

And so, an hour after the fact, with Gretchen in deep slumber, I disengage, stretch the cover over her, pull my clothes on and sneak out, back to the hospital in search of the quarantine ward.

10. **The Last Battle of Berkeley**

(Ft. Gordon, November 1969)

"My God, Henry, you look awful. How the fuck are you?"

Speiser's face--the portion visible above the bed-sheet--gives only a hint of the pear-shaped rest. Swollen bags adorn his eyes, which are shut to thin red slits.

"I feel awful..." he croaks.

In spite of the stern admonitions from the head nurse, I lean down closer. Before leaving us, the nurse brushed off my claim to lifetime immunity:

"It's not you I'm worried about, Lieutenant, it's the whole dang base. We're trying to save it from collapse".

If I understand her correctly--and there is nothing ambiguous about this old harpy's gruff demeanor--there is nothing more detrimental to the morale of a military unit than a mumps epidemic. It is, she tells me, a throwback to primal fears that have racked the male of the species ever since Creation.

Henry appears to have the entire Officers Quarantine section to himself.

"It's nice of you to come, Leo..."

His voice rasps like a death rattle. I experience a

347

surge of sympathy.

"No big deal, Henry" I tell him, "always a pleasure to see my old roomie".

"Thanks for the candy too..."

The box of bonbons I picked up at the PX is resting on top of Henry's bedside chest, yet to be opened.

"How long you figure on sbeing here, Henry?"

My concern for his well-being is in part mercenary. I dread the prospect of taking over his PR assignment, what with Gretchen still shaky and a bevy of visitors descending upon us.

"They don't tell me anything... The way I feel, I could be here forever..."

I must have winced.

"I've taken the liberty of preparing this list for you... Everything's in here, schedule, places, names, emergency tips..."

Slowly, he pulls out a stapled sheaf of pages from under his pillow.

"One of the nurses typed this up for me" he says. "Here..."

I take the damp pages, imagining instant contamination.

"Gee, thanks, Henry".

"You're welcome...Sorry to leave you in a lurch... I think you'll have no trouble following... They treat me real good here, one of the nurses took it down for me..."

"That's nice, Henry".

What I have in my hands is five pages typed single space.

"This is terrific, Henry" I tell him. "I'll take a good look later. For now, just tell me what I need to worry about first? Like, where and when?"

Henry's face is blank.

"I mean, how soon do I have to be somewhere this afternoon?"

"Oh... You have a summary there of *their* schedule on the last page, with all locations checked... Their last Monday class ends at four, so you've got half an hour to--"

Oh me God.

"It's a sensitive assignment, Leo... You better watch your step, these guys, you know, they're all majors and colonels and generals... they can..."

"Thanks, Henry" I tell him, "I know. They can sign my ticket to Nam. Don't worry, I'll handle it, somehow. Now you just lie there and let those wonderful nurses take care of you, hey? But for God's sake, get well quick. I've got to go back to the show full time by Thursday afternoon. That is, if I last that long".

"I ought to be up by then. Tho the way I feel right now..."

Henry Speiser sighs in resignation.

"You have a problem, Leo" he says, "anything, you come back and ask me. Promise?"

"You betcha, Henry. And thanks a mill for the tips. Gotta run. You take it easy now, y'hear?".

He is sporting a brave smile as I turn and walk out.

●　　　●　　　●

I make it to the classroom behind the Officers' Club just in time to hook up with my new charges. Their last class is *History of Civil Disorder in the US*. I am doing my best to sneak in quietly, but their teacher, a stocky captain I've never met, intercepts me.

"Ah--your guardian angel, gentlemen. Pinch-hitting for Speiser, Lieutenant?"

"Yessir".

A roomful of greying crew-cuts turn to inspect me. No way will I pass muster.

"Gentlemen" says the captain, "this is Lieutenant--"

"Swenson, sir".

"Good. Lieutenant Swenson is subbing for your regular escort, Lieutenant Speiser, who is confined to sick bay. Nothing serious, I hope?"

"Just the mumps".

Cool eyes are assessing me.

"Ouch" says the captain.

The room dissolves into laughter.

"The lieutenant" says the captain, "will answer all

350

questions pertaining to the base facilities, after-hours activities, entertainment... You name it, gentlemen, he'll know and will be delighted to go to bat for y'all, anywhere, any time. He's here to make sure your stay in Ft. Gordon is not only instructive but also enjoyable. Right, Lieutenant?"

"Yessir".

"In that case, have a good evening, gentlemen".

As the captain departs, I march forward, bracing myself for the onslaught. Henry's memorandum, clutched tightly in my hand, opens with the suggestion:

P.R. IS LIKE CANDID CAMERA: SMILE

I spend the next fifteen minutes practicing Henry's prescient advice as I sort out majors from colonels, three brigadier generals and a lone rear admiral. I tell them how to find the PX, where the club is, the john, the post office. I make a host of rash promises--as soon as possible, sir--to bring extra copies of the weekly schedule. I undertake to replace a malfunctioning TV--I'll take care of it right away, sir. I pass along Henry's carefully assembled tips about the golf course--this might prove useful, sir--hoping none would ever discover how utterly out of my depth I am. Most of them have brought along their putters and slicers and seven irons. They are rearing to tee off.

Before they depart, I remind them of the CO's cocktail reception in their honor Tuesday evening. Soon the bulk are gone, drifting in twos and threes into the scented early evening. A few stragglers surround me now. The worst may be over, I am looking forward to a quiet evening with Gretchen, who is, for once, off the graveyard shift.

It is not meant to be. An Army major, two National Guard full colonels and the Chief of Police of El Monte, CA, prevail upon me to join them for a round of drinks at the club. Before long, we are back at their quarters playing poker and swilling bourbon.

It is past midnight before I pry myself loose and make my way back to the flat. Gretchen makes me gurgle with baking soda before she lets me into bed. She refuses my kisses, and I wind up taking her from behind, which she finds a turn-on.

"All in the line of duty" I explain, as I slither clumsily into her.

"Yeah, tell me..." she says. "Now, this is more like it... aah...oooh... speaking of line of duty..."

I do my best. When we are both sated, I drift off into quasi-sleep, racked by a gargantuan pre-battle anxiety.

•　　•　　•

Tuesday I barely make it to the classroom, having been rehearsing the whole morning and early afternoon under Len Herskowitz' watchful eye. As my charges scatter for their nocturnal destinations, I am cornered by a Marine captain who wonders aloud whether a tour of the night-life of the great Confederate metropolis of Augusta could be arranged. Could I point out the house where Rhet Butler dumped Scarlet O'Hara off the staircase?

"That's Savannah, sir" I murmur discreetly.

"Same difference, ain't it?"

A group of newfound buddies, the captain intimates, are loaded for bear and rearing to see the sights. I excuse myself and call the quarantine ward at the hospital. The duty nurse says Henry has lost his voice altogether and cannot be disturbed. I am about to go back and offer myself abjectly, and may the blind lead the blind. Then I remember I am still confined to base.

My excuse is ironclad, but I am reluctant to come back empty handed. In a flash of genius, I call the Reverend Captain Nederlander.

For once it is a relief to hear his voice:
"Yes?"

"Reverend, sir" I say, "this is Leo Swenson.

A short silence, then the booming pulpit voice:

"Hell-low, Lieutenant, what a pleasant surprise. What can I do for you?"

One thing he cannot do for me is take my confession. Not any more.

"Well" I say, pacing myself gingerly, "I've got a little problem, Reverend".

"Shoot".

"I'm restricted to base, since yesterday".

This ought to cheer him up.

"I'm sorry to hear that, Lieutenant".

"Oh, it's no big deal, sir, I never go out anyway. It's just that, sir, I've got this group of visiting officers... I'm subbing for Henry Speiser at PR, you know... Well, they'd like me to take them on a tour of Augusta..."

"When?"

"Tonight, sir. This evening, I mean, like right now. Which I'd love to do, even though I don't know the town all that well. But as it is, seeing as I'm confined to base..."

"I see" says the Reverend.

"Well... I've been wondering if, sir, just in case you yourself are going to town this evening... if you wouldn't terribly mind letting these officers tag along. Just for starters, y'understand, till they get their bearings. They seem a tad lonely, sir, y'know, family men away from home..."

To my great surprise, Captain Nederlander accedes:

"Be glad to oblige, Lieutenant. As it happens, I was just fixin' to drive down myself. If you could just bring them over to my office. You remember where it is, don't you?"

"Sure do, sir".

"Why don't you just walk them over, then".

"Well, they've got their own vehicle, sir, so they don't need to impose on you for a ride back to base. If you could just point them at..."

"Be delighted to, Lieutenant. I've been ministering

to lonely soldiers for a while now. Say, why don't we do it this way--you tell them to just wait at the club. I'll come over, we'll take it from there".

"That's wonderful, sir" I say. "I really appreciate..."

"My pleasure, Lieutenant".

A long pause.

"And Lieutenant?"

"Yessir?"

"I'm glad you don't take it personally. I mean, yesterday".

"Oh, I couldn't do that, sir. You were only doing your duty".

"That's the spirit, young man. Thanks all the same".

"Thank *you*, Reverend".

I go back in search of my charges, who have repaired to the club and are busy priming the pump with fresh rounds. When Captain Nederlander arrives, I make the introductions. As I take my leave, I make a mental note to avoid these officers tomorrow. My hunch is, they'll make it easy for me. I'll take it one day at a time.

●　　●　　●

Thursday morning, on my way down to the set, I stop by again to visit Henry. He gives me the bad news: He is greatly improved. His voice is restored, tho it is still hoarse. His spirits are up, only a residual swelling around his neck. However, the doctors say he will remain infectious till Monday. So he must stay in the ward, *hors de combat.*

"They say there might be complications" he confides, "I'm supposed to take it easy. Gee, I'm so sorry, Leo, I don't know what to say..."

"You do what they tell you, Henry".

I see no point in piling more shit on the poor dear. I take my worries to Len Herskowitz, who tells me it will all be taken care of.

"You've done your gig, *schmendrik*" he says. "From all I hear, commendably. Sticking the Reverend with a night on the town was an inspiration".

"You think so?"

"Story's making the rounds, got it from Rodney himself. One of the colonels had to be sprung from the local jail. Sprague got the call, had to cash some blue chips..."

"Oh shit".

"Don't worry. For once it wasn't on your watch. Just trust Uncle Len, we'll find someone to take over P.R. for today".

"And tomorrow" I remind him.

"Don't push it, *goniv*. And start without me, I've got to pick up someone at the airport".

I run them through their paces and, thank God, Len has done a superb job with the fresh batch of draftees. They come on cue, running through the drill with remarkable elan. Their rendition of the final riot is a gem. Could some of

356

them be hard-core Movement?

The two secretaries from the main office are still with us, tho their cover has been blown. The dark-haired one sticks to me like glue, she must be still wired.

Somewhere during the assault on the bank, I catch a glimpse of Len Herskowitz at his customary upper corner. The tall figure seated next to him is shrouded, head to toe, in a dark habit. Monastic? Tuareg? The face under the flopping hood is shielded behind a pair of magnum shades.

I take my lunch with Gretchen at Schwartz's. We are both looking forward to a whole night together. Gretchen's mood is clouded by the prospect of Serena's arrival. We make a date for right after the show.

After lunch we go through the whole drill uninterrupted. Like clockwork, everyone on cue. Even Abdul Hameed's Guardsmen, ordinarily indifferent if not downright oblivious, seem to have discovered a new *esprit de corps*.

I should be pleased. Instead, I am worried sick. For I am my mother's son, and like her a firm believer in the *malojo*. Things are going too well.

I check back with Len Herskowitz after the last run. He has nothing but praise:

"Keep it going, *sheygetz*" he tells me, "you're doing fine".

He is in high spirits.

"Main thing is, stay loose, stay focused... Look out

for the brief flash that exposes the pulsating vein, the slit in the soft underbelly of reality that opens up to the infinite freedom underneath... Then go for broke, *boychik*, grab serendipity by her throat and squeeze..."

It all sounds like dubious metaphysics. Artaud again?

"I'll do my best" I tell him.

"You gotta pull out all the stops, Leo. Gotta let go, release your dammed energy. Let things happen of their own accord. Be creative, be suave, be audacious..."

The major seems to have forgotten what got me into trouble last week. But I have not. Whatever hot creative juices may course my veins, I aim to consign them to the deep-freeze.

"I don't know, Len" I tell him.

"Trust me, Leo. I know you got it in you, it's all in there. Just let it all hang out, don't hold back on me, *boychik*".

I look at him in silence.

"Oh shit" he says. "Nevermind, you don't have to take it from me, might as well hear it from the horse's mouth. Which reminds me--Ruthie and I would like you to come over for dinner. Tonight, eight o'clock?"

"Gee, thanks, Len" I say, "sounds terrific. I better ask Gretch tho".

"You do that. Tell her there's a special treat".

He looks at his watch.

358

"Christ, gotta run, promised Ruthie to be back early and help. See you at eight".

As apprehensive as I may be about tonight, my fear of tomorrow is boundless. The sky, I am convinced, is coming down on my poor head.

"Lighten up, Leo" are the major's parting words. "We'll iron out the last kinks tomorrow morning. Relax".

I am about to go in search of Gretchen, when I remember. I run after Len, who is halfway to the Jeep.

"Say, Len" I tell him, "you done anything yet about that problem? You know..."

"What?"

He is anxious to split.

"You know, Wesley and his black troopers..."

"Oh shit! Black pussy. Haven't had a minute... Can it wait?"

"I don't know..."

"Tell you what" he says. "Let's finish this week's show, then first thing Monday morning I go and talk to Rodney, okay?"

"I guess".

I look after Len as he joins Abdul Hameed in the Jeep. They takes off almost immediately, a spray of red clay in their wake. I go back to look for Gretchen.

•　　•　　•

The lady is a full-blown riot. She stands near the mantlepiece in Len's narrow living room, erect, in total command, her tapered sinewy fingers clutching a long-stemmed glass of pale wine. She is almost as tall as Serena. Under the loose velvet mumu, her invisible body is as fluid and restless as a whirling snake's. It is impossible to tell whether she is skinny or stout. Above her unabashed stevedore's shoulders, shoulders that celebrate their owner's spunk, the glistening clean-shaven head rises majestically, scattering refracted light like a halo. The round, ageless Buddha face is yellowish and finely lined. The pale wide-set eyes peer out like a child's from under the puffed lids. They wheel about constantly as she talks, scanning the skyline like a chameleon's revolving occuli, following you around the room without their owner needing to turn her head.

Len Herskowitz, who is talking to her animatedly, detaches himself and comes over.

"Let me introduce you".

But the lady has already launched herself from the mantlepiece and, in three gliding strides, caught up with us.

"Loved your show" she says. "Len has been telling me about you for months, I'm so glad I could finally come".

Her voice is a low gurgle, enticingly melodious, an oracular emanation with a lingering trace of continental cadence. Her hands, tapering off the thin long arms, are as powerful as a baker's, dry and warm and crisp and soft and incredibly sensuous. From up close she appears ageless—

360

except for the revolving eyes. They smile, brilliantly, ravishingly, shining their intense blue sapphire on whatever they clasp and inspect.

Behind us, Len does the belated honors:

"Leo, my teacher Mimi Rosencrantz".

"Pleased to meet you, ma'am" I chortle.

"Pleasure is all mine, Leo".

In spite of Len standing right next to us and Gretchen and Ruthie at the table further back, the woman standing next to me appears to have crafted a private universe for the two of us. I am alone with her, bathed in the radiance of her round Buddha face.

"Love your show" she says again. "What a daunting scale! What a vast canvas for spontaneous action! Free of trained professionals and their preconceptions! Have you ever thought of throwing away the script and just letting go? Letting yourself be swept away by circumstances? Have you tried doing by not doing? Tossing off your puny will and letting things happen *to* you? Liberating your life-force from the tyranny of pre-formed dialog and stage directions? Shining your own light on? Blurting out your own sound? Wouldn't that be a gas?"

"Sure would".

"Why not just do it then? Let go. Let life express itself *through* you in its immense universal aspectuality. At long last, extract from the fenced-in little lifeling that has been you all these years its ultimate essence, its profound message, the universal myths buried deep inside you all along! All the hidden images through which we can, all of us, find the true bliss of self discovery and simultaneous oblivion! Would you dare?"

"Wow".

Whatever she means, her hypnotic cadence is overpowering. She lets the words roll off her pale full lips, lets them cascade down like the petals of a mellow tulip, caressing, engulfing, lulling you into submission.

"Just think" she says, zeroing in on me with laser-beam ferocity. "Or better, just don't".

I am paralyzed, helpless, choked with astonishment, and split wide open. She need not fear, the last thing I could do is think.

"Just imagine the magnificent scope that will open up to you, claiming the entire world as your stage! Wherever you are, whenever, right here and now as the spirit moves you! Not only on stage but ever and everywhere! Don't you see? The stages we build, the shows we put on, they're just our launching pad, our beach-head into the beyond! Life with its myriad refracting surfaces and dark crevices is our real stage! Life transformed through the prism of unbounded intuition and infinite serendipity! Life renewed, transmuted, grasped by the throat, sucked dry and blissfully experienced! Life performed in utter liberty, life to the hilt!"

Dear Jesus.

I feel like I have just blissed out on pure crystal

acid. Is Ms Rosencrantz herself floating on any booster? I think she is not. She seems utterly liberated and free-wheeling, her sapphire eyes drawing me in relentlessly.

"You see, don't you? Right?" she says. "I can tell you do, listening to your psychobabble down there this afternoon--pure, unadulterated gesture, unhinged from all premeditation! You are a rare one, a natural. All you need to do is let go. Not just of the script, but of language itself, language as we know it--pre-formed, pre-conceived, prevaricated, pre-configured, pre-fixed pre-sensed. You can, we all can, go for the pure cosmic gesture, make it the launching-pad of our infinite tongue, one that, for once, would spring from the *ultimate* necessity of all speech, not from tired, configured schemata of frozen meaning! A language whose words will jettison their tired old habits of definition and thus, left free to roam, will drift and find their situated potential! Free to assume whatever the context would demand, take on only meanings that are *truly* motivated, that are inevitable! At long last, free of the arbitrary, coercive sense-prison, of decrepit old conventions! Let us liberate our words and let them roam free! Then proclaim the language of unconstrained passion, unbridled intuition, of soaring metaphor and unabashed metonymy! We'll liberate the theater first, Leo and then life itself from the oppressive tyranny of pre-packaged concepts that paralyze our thought and arrest the eternal creative spirit! This is what the Theater is all about, Leo! Instant, lavish, liberated! Loose, explosive, emergent!"

I remember little of the rest of the evening, except for snatches of the vegetarian dinner that must have taken all of Ruthie's skills and then some. And Gretchen sitting next to me, uncharacteristically subdued. And Len goading his guest on. And that resonant spectral voice welling out and flooding the entire universe with bright visions of eternal liberation.

Walking home with Gretchen, punch drunk with Ms Rosencranz' voice, I wondered if I could ever shake it loose as it pursued me into the night, reverberating, compelling, seductive like the siren's call.

•   •   •

Late in the night, an alien mood takes over Gretchen. We are in the midst of making love, then something creeps up just below the horizon, like an encroaching cloud. Soon a shadow has drawn over us. In my arms, Gretchen tenses up. Her nails claw at my back, our easy rhythm is all shot to pieces.

"What is it, my love?" I ask.

She says nothing, but gets up and moves to the window. The near-full moon is whitewashing the kitchen floor.

I wait. After a while I drag myself up and join her, pressing myself against her. Her skin is clammy with sweat.

She shivers.

"What's the matter?"

"Nothing".

"You sure?"

She remains silent.

"Still Serena?"

"I feel weird".

"When's she coming in?"

"Sometime tomorrow, I'm not sure. She said she'll call".

"Where's she going to stay?"

"I don't know. She said not to worry, said it's all taken care of".

"Well, maybe it is". I am not sure what to say.

"It'll work out" I tell her, "don't worry".

I could be more convincing.

"Maybe it's the moon?"

"Maybe".

It takes a while to coax her back into bed, where she clings to me under the blanket and shivers away till, like a child needing to be consoled, she relents and falls asleep.

Propped on my elbow, wide awake, I hover over Gretchen, a silent guardian, fully alerted. But to what? Whatever has cast its shadow over my true love is still there.

●   ●   ●

I am standing in t he middle of the Av just in front of the Bank, having dismissed my troops early with a stern injunction to be back on the set by two. Gretchen has taken off to wait for Serena. She is still shaky. I am not sanguine myself. It is a tossup which one I dread encountering more, Serena or my dad. In my reveries, I don't hear the approaching steps till the deep voice booms next to me:

"Lieutenan' Leo".

I turn with a start. Sgt. Abdul Hameed is looming over me, still in his Guard uniform. He is wearing the Alameda County Flying Wedge Squad helmet, the one that never fails to bring back the narrow *cul-de-sac* off Dwight where we first met. Our daily commerce is never entirely free of this infringing menace.

The visor is raised over Abdul Hameed's helmet. His eyes are for once unencumbered by the ubiquitous shades. He is brandishing a riot-control club. A sawed-off shotgun is slung casually over his shoulder. Three tear-gas canisters are clipped to his belt. All part of his costume, they still give me the shivers.

"Oh hi, Wesley" I say. "Man, tha'ss a badass outfit you got there, brings out the Martian in you... Jus' kiddin', jus' kiddin' ".

"You ain't halfass bad lookin' y'self, Leo my main man. I be lookin' like this, I be worried sick The Man might catch up with me".

I am still in my hippie attire, the dark long curls

cascading over my tie-dye shirt.

"Thanks Wesley. Wha'ss happenin'?"

"Nothin' much. 'Cept, tha's what the brothers been wantin' to know, seein's how you supposed to take care of some urgent business for them".

"Oh shit..."

Abdul Hameed's exquisite timing is hardly inadvertent. All I can do is stall.

"I've talked to the major twice, Wesley. He says he's trying. These things take time, y'know, he's got to go through channels. He thinks next week maybe..."

In the pause that opens wide between us, Abdul Hameed favors me with a rare smile, a sweet affair that swoops in and lights up his deadpan--and is gone. His dark eyes are as inscrutable as the shades that normally shroud them.

"The brothers" he says, "they pretty un'standin', y'know. They patient, they been around the block 'n then some. They know you can't do everything. Still, they been wonderin', maybe you ain't got enough 'ncentive, Lieutenant Leo... The brothers they thinkin' maybe they need to give you a higher stake in the game. You 'n'stand? So maybe you be tryin' a little bit harder on they's bee-half?"

"Have a heart, Wesley. Can't you see I'm busting my fuckin' ass? Tell 'em I'll talk to the major again. Tonight, promise".

"Sure thing, Lieutenant Leo. Now, I know you cool,

you 'n'stand? 'S jus' that it ain't no sayin' when the brothers gon' decide they had enough whiteman bullshit. Don' want nothin' bad to happen, you 'n'stand?"

"Gee, Wesley, thanks for the warning".

"Jus' tryin', my man. Keep the faith. *Allahu Akbar*".

"Yeah, you do the same, Wesley".

●   ●   ●

The hosts are gathered at their staging grounds, resplendent in their respective costumes, ready to roll. I have just walked down from the saddle, where my marauder van with the hippie contingent is stashed in the pine. I am on my way to check on the townsfolk, under wrap at the top of the Av. I am also looking for Gretchen.

I thread my way slowly along the painted façade of the Piccolo, cross the Av diagonally in front of the empty stands, when a false note jiggles my attention. Someone is already there. I do a quick double-take. To the left side of the stands, all the way in the rear, a lone figure in full dress uniform is sitting in a brightly chromed wheel chair.

I pause, then walk over and almost faint. He is wearing a staff sergeant's parade-ground uniform, his chest a riot of ribbons and medals. The green beret is pulled low over the dark, lined, narrow face.

Gary.

I approach him gingerly, only too conscious of the

incongruity between his spick-and-span military getup and my own costume and wig. He sits ramrod straight, born to the chromed throne.

"Late again".

"Shit, man" I say. "What're you doing here?"

He offers his hand. I lean over hesitantly, he almost yanks me off my feet with his steel-vise clasp.

"Waiting for you".

"In this getup?"

He looks like the real thing. Under the crew-cut, the bottom back side of his head is pale grey.

"Christ" I say, "you gave me a fright. Didn't you tell me you'd already done your stint?"

"I have. Never let out good n' proper, just under wraps for a spell. They got me back now in the monkey suit".

"But..."

Gary holds up his hand.

"Easy, man, we got plenty needs talkin' about... Come, gimme a push, we need to go across for a quick inspection".

I get hold of the rubber-clad handles and maneuver his wheelchair slowly toward the Av. I wonder why he isn't using the electric drive. I hit a rough clump of grass.

"Sorry..."

"Shit" says Gary, "nevermind, man, just hold still for a sec..."

I wait. Gary adjusts his tall frame. Then he pulls himself to his feet, stretches up to his full height and saunters off.

"That's better" he says, stepping to the pavement. "Thing's a fuckin' pain".

Without looking back, he walks across the street toward the Piccolo.

"Bring the throne, willya" he calls back to me.

I push the empty chariot across. Gary is walking with a slight limp, but his stride is fluid, vigorous. I follow him to the café's façade, then under the low awning. He fishes out a key, opens the painted door and ducks into the bowels of the two-by jungle.

I leave the chair behind and follow. I recall the Boz leading me through the same dark maze. When my eyes have adjusted, I see Gary standing ten feet away. He has unzipped his fly and is taking a leak.

"Boy, this feels good" he says. "Thanks, Leo, I needed that".

"You can walk" I say.

"Fuckin' big deal".

"She said you were paralyzed".

"Never was. Just nicked the nerve".

"But the doctors..."

Gary snorts as he zips his fly, turning to face me:

"Fuckin' neurologist at Denver General used to be an Army sawbones in Nam" he says. "Takes one look at me,

370

says I'm lucky to be wigglin' my big toe. I tell him, I say, you just wait see what a big Red Injun from the Rez can do. Well guess who's right?... Next thing, the guy gets a call from one of the big talking heads in Langley, maybe DC, a four-star guy... Guy tells him which way to jump if he wants his NIH grant renewed. He jumps, says thank you sir too, fixes my medical charts just like they tell him. You think he wants to be recalled into Reserves again, draw Army National Guard duty in a field hospital in Duc Toh, say bye-bye to wifey 'n the two kids, to the half-a-mill brick castle on the golf links in Cherry Creek Village? Guy ain't stupid, so he writes me down as a paraplegic, stays put in Cherry Creek, everybody's happy. Who's gonna know the difference?"

Gary makes it sound easy.

"But--why?" I ask.

"Well..." says Gary. "First thing, that's the best way to get the Pitkin County narcs off my poor red back. They've just gone caught themselves a real live Injun living off the Rez, dealing hard stuff to all them sweet blue-eyed highschool kids, hey? They're real hot to pin a serious rap on him too... Shit, a longhair Red Man hanging out with all them dirty blue-eyed hippies on the back side of Aspen Mountain--that's the stuff of legend. What with Sheriff Brown up for re-election and runnin' scared, with that nutcake Hunter Thompson goin' against him... Shit, don't you ever read the papers, Leo?"

371

"Not the Aspen Times".

"Nevermind. Big Woman told you about Troy?"

"Yeah. I'm sorry".

"Yeah, well, them's the breaks. Goddam Viking makes it back from Nam in one piece, just barely, mind you. Trigger-happy deputy just out of police academy drops him with one lousy round. Shit, someday I might go back up there, look the guy up maybe..."

In the near dark, I can barely see Gary's face.

"'Course" he says, "it ain't really the sucker's fault.... Whole bust was a dumbshit screwup, someone forgot to patch the Pitkin County narcs in. Viking 'n me, we was scammin' the same pipeline. 'Course, from a different angle. But who knows?... So how they gonna spring me without hurting the local boys' feelings? Well, the big Kachina dolls in D.C. got into a huddle, figured a way out, passed the word down the pipe to Denver. Governor there aching to be a VP on the next Democratic ticket, fucker hates the war worse'n a hippie draft-dodger, but still, he's anxious to do the right thing. So the Pitkin narcs get a call from the AG in Denver. Who says they have to like it? Still, they know ain't no mileage in prosecuting a lousy Viet vet in a chair 'n a chestful of medals. Don't hurt he's a Red Injun either, coming from the only Rez in the State of Colorado. Shit, you shave his head real close, he's just another hero... Well by now everybody's making the Pitkin cops look silly, so the fix's on, big hush-hush, nobody knows that don't need to know.

372

That's how them big boys play... Shit, nevermind. Anyway, they blow my cover in the process. Boz says we can't tell them what the cover's all about, won't do. An Injun Viet vet in a chair with medals makes a better story. 'Sides which--"

Gary pauses and gestures toward the door and the discarded chair:

"Sucker's real slick, gets you through airport security without a search, what with the monkey-suit 'n medals. Good stash space too... So the Army gives me a new gig, I go all over the country givin' inspirational speeches to down-home folks, boost the home-front morale, what with the damn war going nowhere. Be surprised how many women get turned on by a big Red Injun in a chrome chair. So I do the rounds, I wait for the Boz to line up a new scam. No big hurry, hey?"

"I see".

While I struggle to adjust, Gary moves further into the deep shadows, heading straight for the camouflaged door.

"Stuff still in there?" He is jiggling at the lock.

"How would I know?"

"Boz says you're supposed to keep an eye on it".

"Not me" I tell him. "Far's I know, he made the arrangements with Sergeant Abdul Hameed".

"The big nigger? I hear him 'n his dudes been dippin' into the Thai. You in on it?"

"Hell no". A bit too fast.

"Hey, no big deal, ain't nothin' to me. Shit man, might's well smoke it all up. Boz says we gotta get rid of it".

"Get rid of it? When?"

"Right away".

"That's impossible!"

Gary is facing me five feet across in the deep twilight. I wonder how long it will take for him to bring up Serena.

"Boz says today" he tells me, "gotta be today. Period. Now, here's the drill: You still got that sprinkler system you turn on at the end, right?"

"Sure".

"You been doing it yourself, right?"

"Yes".

"That's what the Boz says. Okay, you lay off it tonight".

"What do you mean *lay off?*"

"Somebody else's gonna take care of it".

"But..."

Gary cuts me short:

"You're in the Army, man, remember? Shit, you even outrank me, come to think, maybe I better salute you? Anyway, the Boz outranks both of us, so he says you lay off the sprinklers, you lay off, hey?"

"Like hell I will!"

Gary towers over me. I think of the first time I saw him, doing his avian Tai Chi on the beach in Laguna. When he speaks again, he is conciliatory:

"Hey, pipe down, man, it's cool, everything's under control, we all got our marchin' orders. Shit, we better go back, you gotta get ready. I hear tell you're a real star".

"Shit".

We thread our way slowly toward the bright rectangle of the door. Once there, Gary lowers himself back into the wheelchair.

"Better push me across" he says, "case someone's watchin' ".

In the dazzling mid-afternoon, we cross the Av in silence. The chromed wheels crack loose gravel on the pavement.

"You know Serena is here" says Gary.

"Yeah".

"I hear tell we're practically in-laws, man".

A deep purple blush must be spreading across my face.

"Welcome to the family" says Gary. "Not too shabby, man, could've done much worse".

I nod.

"Hey, don't worry" says Gary. "I know you had the hots for Big Mama, used to slip it to her behind my back. No big deal, hey? I did your squaw, you did mine, all in the family, hey?"

375

I remember what Gretchen said about Serena's men lusting after her butt. I wonder if that's what Gary means.

He seems to be reading my mind:

"Don't worry" he says, "I never did Little Girl, she split way before my time. Now, if she hadn't..."

He shrugs.

"Jus' kiddin'" he says, "jus' kiddin'".

"Does Serena know?" I ask him.

"Know what?"

"About this chair scam?"

"What do you think?"

Gary's dark eyes are scanning the horizon.

"I don't know".

"Shit" he says, "she was in on it from the start, one of the few. Can't keep Big Woman out of the picture, not so long 's we're hitched..."

He pauses.

"Had to take her 'n the boys back down to the Rez, you know" he says.

"Where's that?"

" 'Bout two hundred miles south-west of Aspen. Put them on my uncle's old allotment down-river..."

I wait.

"Shit" he says, "what do you know, Big Woman really loved taking care of me, was quite a tiger up at the hospital. Says she wouldn't have minded having me in the chair back home for good. You'd think she's got enough to take care of... Them women's funny this way. Better watch out for Little Girl. Them bunch's a tricky lot, can't never figure what they'll come up with. Heck, 'fore you know it, she'd move in with you, take over, run your life for you, wimp you down to a patch of wet nothin'. Do it in nothin' flat too, that skinny runt..."

"You seem to be thriving" I observe.

"You betcha. Thing grows on you, like good dope. 'Fore you know it, you're strung up. That's why I'm telling you, man. See, this is family now, you 'n'stand? Better watch out, that little gal's got as much piss'n vinegar in her as her mama. Reckon you should've figured that for y'self by now..."

"Reckon".

Gary nods. We stand there in the dead quiet, ruminating over the vagaries of our improbable bond. Gary is the first to break the spell, taking a look at his watch:

"Shit man, you better shake a leg, everybody's gonna come down in another minute. Serena too, Little Girl's bringing her down".

"I know".

"Good luck, man. Break a leg, hey? Tha's what you stage people say?"

"That's right. You do the same, man".

As I hurry up the hill to rejoin my cohorts, I can hear the busses rounding the bend.

●　　●　　●

We   roar down the slope like raging banshees, emerging on the Av in a thick cloud of red dust and diesel fumes. The van's four mag speakers are blasting away with gut-curdling Zappa. For an overture, I have selected *Lumpy Gravy*, one of Freakdom's greatest travesties, guaranteed to blast the most lethargic mind into high orbit.

Zappa's machine-shop percussion section has been lifted out of the sound track of *300 Motels*. The sly old fox re-tracked it with an unnerving high-treble human voice, dropping the concoction into the blender at near random. A repulsive auditory bomb.

The wind is blowing in my wig, which refuses to stay   put. My face is smeared, aboriginal fashion, with horizontal streaks of stove-pipe grime. As an added sop to serendipity, a woven Guatemalan Indian strap cross-cinches my   chest   over   the Deadhead tie-die and Army-surplus fatigues. My marauding band have likewise risen to the occasion. Their painted faces run the ocher-red-black gamut from Africa to New Guinea.

We screech to a dead halt in front of the grandstands. I hit the breaks extra-hard without disengaging the engine. The old wreck obliges me with a staccato of sharp explosions. The engine diesels, backfires and belches its way to sudden death, leaving us in a cloud of blue smoke.

A quick look at the stands: Full house, standing room only. A chorus of boisterous catcalls and whistles greets our arrival. Today's crowd needs no prompting. Their audience participation would have done Pirandello proud.

The townfolk are at their assigned spots, a bucolic tableau of Main Street USA. I see Gretchen in the back with her baby pram. The diesel smoke wafts away slowly. The liquor traffic up in the stands is brisk.

Scanning from under my tangled mop, I spot Len Herskowitz in the top row. The shaven head atop the tall figure next to him refracts beams of sunlight over the mag-size shades. I spot Major Creighton in dress uniform. My dad is nowhere to be seen. But the figure to the major's right, topped up with the dark pompadour, is--Mother of God--my mom.

I blink, but she is still there, poised and diminutive next to Dr. Creighton. I tear my eyes away, then spot Gary in his wheelchair to the left of the grandstands. Behind him, in a full-length dark gown, her hair a flared halo, is Serena.

The narrator rises. Not Henry Speiser but a chestful of ribbons, Army Rangers' uniform, paratrooper wings, Captain's insignia. The Boz is back.

"Ladies and gentlemen" he says, "as you can see, the peaceful afternoon of our small town USA is shattered by an invading band of outside agitators bent on overthrowing the established order..."

The Boz's delivery is seamless, as if he has never skipped the last six weeks. The hand-held microphone is firm at the mouth, his stance regulation ramrod, his green beret tucked neatly in his left epaulet.

379

I alight, wave my troops down, then climb back to the hatch and launch into my opening harangue. Before I switch the mike back to Zappa, some of the audience are already on their feet, booing and shaking their fists. Obscenities fly as I give my marauders a last-minute *sotto-voce* admonition.

"Now you guys take it easy" I tell them. "Just do your bit, don't try to be outrageous, hey? We've got lots of special guests out there, the CO with tons of brass... So for God sake's, be cool, don't let them provoke you..."

I can only pray they got the message. Except for the two secretaries that may or may not be wired, my cohorts are all fresh grunts, with us only since Monday. I pray they don't hatch anything perverse in their harried little heads.

Last night, all three national networks carried live footage of a bloody peace demonstration cum police riot at LA's Century Plaza. The recently re-christened Muhammad Ali was there. Both my fresh grunts and my veterans, not to mention the brass and their guests in the stands, must have watched the Sheriff troopers club down clean-cut college kids and their bearded professors, while the President was dining with Hollywood fat cats thirty-six floors above the fray.

I switch the music off and have another go at the open mike. I screech, groan and grunt, I grind the mike into the metal roof of the van. A sizeable portion of the audience comes back at me with loud invective.

During the next respite I caution my troops again:

"Watch out you guys" I tell them, "they'll be throwing stuff at you soon. So just duck, hey? Just ignore them... and hey, watch me, willya? We might have to adjust the script some, play it by ear... So watch out, hey? There's more to this show than the friggin' script, there's truth and beauty to be found in the fleeting moment--if you only dare to seize it..."

If I don't check myself, that woman's hypnotic voice will come spewing out my mouth. It is not too early to start praying.

I am about ready to rise with the mike to deliver the balance of my harangue when a flying projectile strikes the van just below my perch. The side window shatters, tossing a spray of glass diamonds onto the pavement. There we go. I switch the mike back on and lead the chorus in a spirited rendition of everybody's all-time favorite:

"Hey, hey, El-Bee-Jay! How many kids did you kill to-day?!..."

This gets the house on its feet. A flying beer bottle nicks my shoulder, barely missing the tape-deck and crashing to the pavement behind my troops, where it is joined by a barrage of like missives. Above the din, I hear the punctuating obscenities.

I wonder whether the state of Georgia has ever gotten around to outlawing lynching. Under the rapidly unfolding circumstances, in a burst of true Rosencrantzian spirit, I scrap the rest of my intro and cut to the chase sequel. To their credit, the townsfolk troupers can read sign and have commenced their retreat up the Av.

Ducking and bobbing, I switch the music on, jack the volume all the way up and leap off the van. The wailing notes of the instrumental lead to *St. Steven* pierce my eardrums like molten steel.

My faithful marauders are huddled behind the van, waiting anxiously. I hit the pavement and point them north toward Campus. We make a brave dash for cover as the bombardment from the stands escalates.

My troops need no exhortation now. If anything, the audience's response has galvanized them. I lead them toward campus, aiming for Gretchen. I duck and bob, running for cover, my cohorts right behind me. I motion them to halt and stay put. Then I dash to the sanctuary of Schwartz's.

We are alone, back at the scene of the crime. As before, Gretchen has discarded her baby-pram at the curb. As before, I barely miss it as I scramble after her. She is leaning back to the door-jamb, watching me, smiling faintly.

"You okay, honey?" she says.

"God... I don't know. If I can live through this one. You alright?"

"I'm fine".

I have last seen her early in the morning. She seems cool and collected. A surge of pride washes over me.

"How's your mom?"

"Didn't you see her?"

"Only from afar. I had a talk with Gary, tho... Seems I'm family now. Did you see my mom?"

"Yes" she says. "You gonna introduce me?"

"Sure, you and everybody. Might as well throw a big reception, get them all to mix, get to know each other.... I'm not sure I can swing it, Gretch".

"You'll live, lion".

I look at my watch.

"Shit, gotta run!"

"Again?"

She leans over and peers into my eyes:

"I love you, my lion" she says.

"Thank God someone does" I tell her. "Loveya too. Stay under cover, hey? It's a mean crowd out there, might turn ugly".

"Don't worry. See you afterwards".

My hardy band are assembled next doors. The two designated blacks have joined us. Everybody is waiting for my say-so. I cross myself and lead them back toward the van from whence, God willing, we shall rally and sack the bank. The crowd has simmered down a bit. The bar service has resumed. I thank my guardian angel and the Boz's quick thinking.

Our presence reignites the hostilities. We are a red flag that to their raging bull. I switch on *Honky Tonk*

Woman, letting Jagger and his itinerants drown out the bedlam.

"...come back, come back..."

The assault on the Mayor and the trashing of the City Police draw a crescendo of boos and obscenities. Bottles and glasses are again crashing on the pavement. A black trooper, brandishing a length of pipe, grabs the Mayor by the scruff of his neck and drag him down the alley, simulating repeated strikes.

Above the din, a booming voice from the stands: "Get that nigger!"

The trooper, one of Abdul Hameed's vets, stops in his track, dropping the Mayor to the ground. For a moment I think he is going to lose it.

I rush over to intercept him:

"Don't!" I scream at him, "you'll start a riot..."

"Shit, Lieutenant, us niggas loves a riot!..."

It is Johnny Johnson, who, God be praised, retains his sense of humor. I slap him on the back.

"Right on, Johnny!"

He smiles back at me, then grabs the Mayor and drags him behind the scenery. Fresh racial slurs pour down from the stands.

With the rest of my band, I dive headlong into the Bank. In the momentary calm, I gather them around me.

"Listen, guys" I tell them. "We gotta keep this under control... It's almost over, so just hang on in there, don't blow it..."

A few nod. Most are silent. I wonder what they are thinking. We stay under wraps for the requisite three minutes. I can only hope this leaves the Boz enough time to pacify his charges.

With the action in momentary limbo, I sneak a cautious peek at the stands. The Boz is still talking, liquor service has resumed--a shrewd move or a miscalculation? God only knows. For it has finally dawned on me how the Boz' *modus operandi* bears an uncanny resemblance to Mimi Rosencrantz's.

With the audience diverted, I deem it safe to dash across the Av back to the van and switch on the Cavalry tape, my signal for Abdul Hameed's National Guard platoon to commence their upward sweep. I dash back to the bank, send the two black snipers up the ladder, and gather my cohorts. They seem strangely subdued. I decide I have said enough. I light the fire at the back of the frame and lead them back out on the Av.

The National Guard's arrival, to the Cavalry's trumpet flourishes, re-galvanizes the crowd. Soon they are back to whooping and hollering, jumping up and down and shaking their fists:

"Shoot the fuckin' niggers!... String up them coons!..."

I try to catch Abdul Hameed's eye. He is not looking my way. I order my band to commence our retreat, hoping

Abdul Hameed can hold his guys together and follow.

Once out of range, I disperse my troops and go to light the fires under the other the store-fronts. Then I turn back to watch. The two black snipers on top of the bank are done with their drop-dead gig. Thick smoke is pouring out of the building. From just beyond the dune, I can hear the fire-engines wailing. For once, perfect timing. The Av is shrouded in smoke. We are almost there. If everybody just hang tight, keep cool. I cross myself again.

I sneak a quick look at the grandstands. Pandemonium seems to have resumed in earnest. I see the Boz standing erect, mike in hand, silent. He is inspecting the scene with detachment, an artist surveying his handiwork.

At the top row, Ms Rosencrantz' erect figure looms above the crowd like a mirthful lighthouse, her mouth cracked in a beatific smile.

From the top of the Av, we are soon to begin our southward retreat. With luck, we might yet make it. I brace myself for the crucifixion scene and rejoin my loyal troops on their mad rush back to stage center. Exposed again, we are greeted with a fresh barrage of glass and invective. The smoke from the storefronts grows thicker.

This is where I should sneak over to turn on the sprinklers. I wonder who is doing the honors today. Gary said not to worry. I still do. Soon, there is no room for worry. We are hemmed in tight between the two Guard platoons. The two secretaries--my electronic nemeses--launch into their

386

striptease, taunting the Guardsmen. The last shreds of restraint are discarded. Our audience has gone into wild frenzy:

"Fuck the commie whores!..."

"Up their ass!..."

"Hey big nigger, drill that hippie nookie!..."

The last one is pitched at Sgt. Abdul Hameed who, thus far, has been playing by the book. Towering over the scene like a blue minaret, he is wading through the crowd on his way to grabbing me for the climax.

I am standing near one of the bare-chested girls, transfixed by Abdul Hameed's majestic progress. The dark-tinted visor of his Alameda County Sheriff helmet is pulled all the way down. In his left hand, he brandishes a regulation night-stick. In his right I spy--surprise turning into consternation--a glistening tear-gas canister.

A dummy?

Over the bedlam of taunts and obscenities and the wailing sirens, I watch Abdul Hameed extract the safety pin, then executes an under-arm pitch across the street.

I hear the dry *puk!* of the primer. The canister rolls on. It comes to rest right in front of the stands and starts spewing dense white fumes. Other canisters join it. A thick white cloud is rising into the stands. A desperate uproar erupts above us. People near the top are screaming and pointing across the street.

I turn. The two black snipers have resurrected.

Standing in full view on top of the bank, they train their rifles on the audience, then commence shooting.

God in Heaven! Let it be blanks!

The sheer iniquity drives the grandstands into mad frenzy. Beer bottles, pop cans and liquor glasses are raining down on the Av, scoring long-hair and Guard alike. I make a desperate dash over to try and drag the snipers off the bank. Before I am half the way across, I hear the *ak-ak* bark of the helicopter. It is swooping down, going right for the jugular--center stage.

Everybody ducks. The helicopter banks steeply and pulls back up. It circles over the set and swoops back down. At the nadir, it releases a cluster of canisters right in front of the stands. The canisters burst in rapid succession. The white cloud thickens. On the wings of the early evening updraft, a thick white cumulus engulfs the scene.

By the script I am to be racked up now between the two Centurions. Neither they nor Abdul Hameed are in sight. My eyes are smarting from the tear gas. Smoke is rising from the burning Av. I burst into a fit of coughing. I can't see a thing.

Whoever was supposed to turn the sprinklers on has done nothing of the kind. Fuck the script, I had I better get to the master valve if the set is to be saved. Under the shroud of tear-gas and smoke, half blinded and coughing my lungs out, I turn and run up the Av. I bump into people, disengage and keep going. The chopper is circling above. Both fire-engines are wailing. The audience is screaming in the thick fog. Tongues of fire leap from the top of the bank.

With a start, I remember Gretchen. I can only hope she cleared out in time. In front of the Piccolo, a general melee has erupted. I hear the *puk*s of more canisters, the dry *ak-ak* of M16s. Who is shooting who?

Incredibly, from somewhere inside the cloud, the first bars of *Battle Hymn of the Republic* sound out, their amplified choral strains punctuated with screams and curses. I wonder if the Rev. Captain Nederlander is with his flock at their hour of trial.

In a last-ditch burst of utter despair, I circle above the last block, aiming to come back behind Schwartz's. I hope I can find the master valve. I grope onward in the smoke, doubled up and coughing. I crash to the ground and claw my way blindly to what seems to be a dark opening in the smoldering frame. I cough and keep going. My knee is badly bruised and smarting like the devil. A shower of burning ash is coming down. My wig begins to hiss.

I make it to the far corner where the valve ought to be, and find the passage blocked by a tall figure in a visored Guard helmet.

"Move over!" I call out.

A deep Southern baritone says:

"Take it easy, boy".

Vaguely familiar.

"Take it easy my foot!" I bark back.

I ease down to a low crouch and squint hard. In the flickering light that filters down from the burning set, I see a tall man in shirtsleeves. Except for the helmet, his uniform does not match our Guard's. A flash of brass insignia garnishes his collar.

Holy Jesus.

The measured voice, pleasant, sonorous, calls out: "Place's out of bounds, soldier".

"On whose authority?"

"Ain't none of your business".

"The fuck it ain't!" I scream. "Move over buster, I gotta turn the sprinklers on!"

Without waiting, I hurtle myself at him, aiming for a low tackle at the knees. With the grace of a seasoned *torero*, my adversary steps aside and lets me crash to the ground. My knee screams with pain. I ignore it. I ignore my tormentor too as I fumble in the dark for the valve. My fingers grasp at metal, but it is only the blunt stem, shorn of its wheel.

"Quick, get a wrench!" I call out.

"Sure, right here".

Then, without warning, a bright light explodes at the back of my skull and the world goes blank.

III. ON THE REZ

11. Escape from Ft. Gordon

(Ft. Gordon, GA; December 1969)

My head is aching like the devil. A piercing, pounding, annihilatory pain, like someone is drilling right into my brain stem. I must be awake, for how could one sleep through so much agony?

Of course, I may be dead, and this searing ordeal may be part and parcel of Hell. It is pitch dark, at least this much seems to tally. I have no control over my extremities.

Discorporated? Pure spirit? Just in case I ever stray into Metaphysics 101: Does the mind ever feel the body's pain, or only its own cerebral anguish?

There is more. My bladder says I need to pee. Urgently. Which, if my powers of deduction have not absconded upon crossing to the other side of the river, rules out Hell. Till proven otherwise, I am not yet dearly departed.

Gingerly, I try to move my right hand. My fingers respond sluggishly, their flexion constrained almost immediately by what feels like a thick wad of rough cloth. My face too must be wrapped in the same material. A full-body cocoon? A shroud? Oh-me-God!

Panicked, I try my right arm. A crippling surge of

piercing white pain shoots up through my shoulder, scorching the back of my head. I writhe in blind agony. Then, mercifully, everything goes blank.

• • •

I must be lying on my back. That much is clear from the consistent pressure underneath. The pain in the back of my head has simmered down to a throbbing dull pulse. Time for another test?

Slowly, I try my left arm. Nothing doing. I try the right. Ditto. I try to turn my head. No go. My wrists and elbows must be restrained. Likewise, my knees and ankles. My neck must be held in a brace.

The first conundrum is settled tho, somewhat incidentally: Why should anyone bother to restrain the dead?

I give in and relax, enjoying my newly reclaimed status among the living, shifting attention to my ears. I may only be imagining this, but a faint trace of musak is filtering in through the shrouds. For my sins, someone is piping in an old medley of Percy Faith and his orchestra. Again, cause for cheer. This music couldn't be a figment of my posthumous imagination. No way--unless this is His perverse sense of humor. Living Hell?

I could probably manage to blot the sound out. But at least I can hear. Indeed, my hearing must be normal since, to judge by the sudden surge, someone has just opened a door, then closed it again.

Behind them? Someone is now with me?

Light steps approach, then stop. Gentle fingers stroke my left shoulder, drawing an involuntary twitch.

"You must be awake" says Gretchen's sweet voice. Praise be Jesus. Heaven, then?

The fingers travel gingerly down my left arm.

"Move your fingers if you can hear me, sweetheart".

I flex my fingers slowly, obediently.

"Good. Don't try to talk, just listen. Are you in pain? Squeeze once for yes, twice for no".

I squeeze once.

"Bad?"

I squeeze twice.

"Good. I have another shot for you, it should put you under as soon as I give it. Your head still real bad?"

I take a chance, eeking out a weak grunt.

"Poor darling" says Gretchen. "That was a nasty one, must really hurt. We're keeping you under sedation".

I grunt again, flexing my arms against the restraints. She make the connection right away:

"Oh, that's for your own good. You were stark raving mad when I found you. Had to pump you full of pentathol, you were ready to slug me. Good thing mom and Gary were there..."

I grunt in frustration.

"Oh nevermind. Besides, you're not supposed to be able to move. Your chart says you're in total shock from third degree burns over ninety percent of your body and pumped full of morphine. Cynthia works in the burn unit, that's why we stashed you here. You're the only burn case right now, that's another reason. The rest of them were smoke inhalation and tear-gas, a few rubber-bullet lacerations..."

I manage another grunt.

"Don't worry, hon" she says, "you're not that bad. No serious burns, just a couple of spots. It's your head we're worried about, must be killing you. I'd love to get hold of whoever gave you that nasty whack. Did you see anybody?"

All I can remember is the tall helmeted figure with the pleasant baritone and insignia. I won't tell her that.

"You're going to be alright" she says, "nothing bad on the X-rays. Tho you must be horribly concussed. So all this immobility's just what the doctor ordered. Can you stand it for just a while longer, darling?"

I try to clear my throat. Where the fuck is my voice? Must be in there somewhere. Maybe all that smoke.

"How long..." I finally croak.

"Two days".

Sunday.

I try again:

"Mom?"

"She's still here. I introduced myself, I hope you don't mind, had to tell her you were alright. She and my mom are keeping company, a matched pair if I've ever seen one".

Ghrrrrrgh.

"My eyes...?"

"Nothing wrong there, I'm just keeping you under full wraps till we can move you downstairs. Maybe tonight".

I would like to know more, but my voice has just given up. All I can manage is a weak:

"Arrgh..."

Which Gretchen interprets by the nursing manual.

"That's all for now" she says. "Gotta run. Here, this ought to keep you happy. Now, if you wake up and somebody else is in here before I'm back, just play dead. Or dumb, whichever is easier. It says on your chart you're in shock, so they ought to leave you alone".

I am rolled on my side. A sharp needle is shoved into my behind without ceremony. I am rolled back, like a log. Then a light kiss through the gauze. After which I lapse back into merciful dreamless oblivion.

•　　•　　•

They must have removed the restraints, I can flex

my arms and legs now. I would try to turn over if my neck didn't hurt so much. And someone must have cut peep-holes through

My vision is blurry, but the three white-clad figures gazing down at me over their surgical masks are unmistakable, even in the backlit glare: Gretchen's freckled nose on the right; Serena's irrepressible halo in the middle; my mom's dark pompadour, barely up to Serena's shoulder, on the left. An improbable trinity.

My heart leaps out with love and dread to my three guardian angels. What the three of them may have hatched together is beyond my imagination. I close my eyes, resigned, crossing myself inwardly.

My mom steps forward to the rim of my bed:

"Leo love" she intones in her tremulous alto. "How are you?"

"Hi mom" I squeeze out. "I'm fine".

"I suppose I had better take that on faith" she says. "For all I know, you're burned beyond to crisp underneath all that gauze".

Gretchen intervenes:

"He's not, Mrs. Swenson".

"Carmen. Please".

"Carmen... I ought to know, I'm the one who wrapped him up to start with. His clothes were something else tho, practically peeled themselves off ..."

My mom lets out an involuntary chortle.

"Yeah" she says, "he was always easy to diaper, lie down like a lamb. I suppose he still does".

I groan:

"Mom, please..."

My mother, uncharacteristically, relents. She sends a quick look back to Serena and Gretchen, both of whom have the courtesy and good sense to avert their eyes.

When the mood is upon her, my mother can be rather daunting. If you know what is good for you, you stay out of her sniping range.

She turns back to me.

"You gave us a fright, honey-chile" she says. "I had to let your dad in on it, no way I could keep him out, tho maybe I should have. For a while there, I thought he was going to go ballistic, he was fixing to call the Pentagon. Al Strapton at Army Med Corps was his classmate..."

What my mother means, I would wager, is that she herself was frantic enough to prevail upon my father to lean on one of his professional cronies. Which he hates to do, fussing about favoritism. Still, all she has to do is ask.

"Is there anybody who wasn't?" I say.

"Shush" says my mom, "don't be an ingrate. Thank God Emmet Creighton had the good sense to track down this girl..."

My mom gives Gretchen an affectionate nudge.

"Lucky there again" she say. "Can't imagine what she sees in you. What do you think, Serena? I mean, as a would-be son-in-law?"

"I'm still undecided" says Serena. "He must have his good points, I suppose".

Gretchen's freckles almost submerged in the dark blush that floods the bridge of her nose over the pale-green surgical mask. She gives her mother a hard thump on the arm.

Serena smiles down at her d aughter.

"Oh heck" she says, "most of them do, once you get over the fact they're so goddamn imperfect".

"You said it, sis" says my mom. "I could tell you some stories. Tho we might as well wait, I don't think I'd want Leo to hear those".

I find their easy camaraderie alarming. The last thing I need is my mom comparing notes with Serena. Neither I nor my dad are bound to fare too well when these two are through with their dissection.

To my relief, Serena says:

"I think we better scoot along, Carmen, let the two lovebirds have some privacy".

In order, the two of them come forward and lean down over me. My mother first.

"Don't do anything stupid, Leo" she murmurs, brushing her lips briefly against my gauzed cheek. "God knows you've done enough as it is. Just listen to this young woman, y'hear? She seems to know what's what. I expect you'll pull out of this mess. God only knows how, you ask me..."

Some comfort.

"Don't worry, mom" I tell her, "I will. Give my love to dad, tell him I'm okay".

"What else could I tell him?"

With this parting shot sailing across my exposed bow, my mom relinquishes her spot to wait near the door.

Serena steps over:

"I assume you're really somewhere in there, Leo, under all those fuckin' shrouds" she says. "Could be anybody in there for all I know".

She leans down, searching my eyes. Her wild hair flops down, like a tent under which the two of us are almost enshrined:

"No flirting, mom" says Gretchen's voice from behind.

"Hush, Gretch" says Serena. Then back to me:

"I told you she was quite a gal, didn't I? I hope you appreciate what you got there".

"I do, I do".

"You must've been born under a lucky star" she says, "all these people trying to clean up the bloody mess you keep leaving behind. The stories your mom tells..."

In the privacy of my gauze prison, I wince.

"Which reminds me" she says. "Gary says to just hang on tight. The Boz's working on it".

"Working on what?"

"Never mind, just hang on in there. Listen, I better run. You be good to my little girl or I'll come after you myself, got it?"

"Shit" I groan, "I better".

"Atta boy".

Serena steps back and joins my mom at the door, the two of them march out together, as incongruous as a statuesque Don and his compact Sancho.

Gretchen and I are alone, listening to the receding echoes of our mothers.

She is smiling.

"Some pair".

"The world isn't safe anymore".

"You said it, love".

"What's happening on the outside?"

"Nothing much. They're still looking for you. Officially, to testify in front of a Board of Inquiry".

"No court martial yet?"

"Not before they come up with some facts".

The room, now that I can turn my gaze a bit and scan it, is windowless. The walls are padded with thick gray rubber mats, the floor seems to match them.

"Am I in your ward now?" I ask Gretchen.

"All the way down".

"Dr. Creighton knows?"

"All in due time".

"How about Len Herskowitz?"

Gretchen considers for a moment.

"Well" she says, "that's what I want to talk to you about. Can we trust him?"

"Probably" I tell her, "might as well. They're going to keep looking for me. At least, you should tell him I'm okay, he might care".

"If you think so. Tho I better ask Gary. They've been looking all over, sent the MPs to search all the flop houses in Augusta. Wonder who dreamed up that one..."

"Sounds like the Reverend".

"More likely the Boz" she says. "I don't trust him either".

"Go easy on the Boz" I tell her, "you want him on your side. What do they have on me?"

Gretchen seats herself on the bed next to me. My hand, liberated if a trifle stiff, crawls all of its own under her skirt and up her thigh.

"Nobody's saying. They pulled me in for questioning, but I couldn't tell what they're after, just that they were anxious to talk to you. Said to call them immediately if I heard from you".

"Shit".

"We need to wait" she says.

Wait for what? My hand is up to her panties.

"You gotta get me out of this crud" I tell Gretchen, "I don't think I can stand it much longer. I'm itching all over, like the Devil's tickling me with a bunch of feathers..."

"Poor darling". She leans down.

Emboldened, I let my hand creep further up.

Gretchen looks down at me, her eyes narrowing:

"Better stop right there, lion" she says. "I might lose my train of thought..."

I let my hand rest on her *mons veneris*. And, entropy being irresistible, my middle finger, with a mind of its own, wiggle its way to the palpating crown jewel.

Under the loose sheets, with only a flimsy gown to hide my total nakedness, my pride-and-joy has assumed its full stature. I can only hope Gretchen hasn't noticed. But of course she has. A slow smile spreads across her face, I can infer it from the merry crinkles around her eyes.

"My poor darling" she says, "what a compliment! In your condition..."

"Fuck my condition" I hiss at her.

"Now" she says, "I wouldn't know how to fuck a condition, but maybe..."

"Come closer, I can't hear you..."

"None of your cheap tricks, lion".

But her resolve has melted away. Before I know it, she darts over to the door and turns off the light. I hear the lock click, then the rustle of clothes being shed. Then she is back next to me:

"I better be gentle" she says, "you're supposed to still be in shock".

"Shock schlock" I say, "try me".

404

And she does. She mounts me expertly and takes over while I lie there flat on my back.

I let myself be overtaken, then overcome. Shoot, woman. Holy shit, how sweet. In no time at all, she is gyrating like a seasoned camel jockey, heaving and moaning away. She leans down over me, her hair in my face, my sore hands clutching at her breasts.

Heavenly woman.

We scale the heights together, slowly, deliberately, up to near ecstasy.

"Better slow down" I tell her, "or I'll pop like a volcano".

"Might as well" she says, "we ain't got much time... I'm on my lunch break. Dr. C. would want me back upstairs. He doesn't know you're here...oooh... So don't settle in for a long one, love... oooh... Christ I needed this... You'd think we haven't fucked in weeks..."

"Sure feels like it".

"Feels like a hundred years... wooooosh..."

She rides me to heaven's gate, taking her pleasure. Then she disengages, leaving me, captive audience for once, thoroughly spent.

● ● ●

"This is fuckin' irregular" says Len Herskowitz.

He is seated on a metal stool next to my bed, eyeing

405

me in total disbelief.

"How do I know that bloody Indian ain't just feeding me a line? Jeezus, the big palooka just about kidnaped me, taped my eyes shut over the blindfold before he let me come with him... Shit!..."

The Major is seething with indignation.

"Made me push his damn chair all the way to God knows where, blind as a bat. Is this guy for real?"

I shrug. Another trick question.

"Is he really a sergeant?"

Major Herskowitz' eyes are searching mine.

"Hey, say something quick, *scheygetz*" he says, "or I'll start thinking there's nothing but stuffed gauze under the fancy head-gear..."

"He's a sergeant alright" I assure him. "And sure, it's me, Leo. I can unwrap the shrouds if you like..."

"Nevermind. I don't think want to see. God only knows what they made you look like. You don't sound like yourself either, *schmendrik*. How're you doing?"

"Not so hot" I tell him, "a little weak in the head. Is the lady R. still about?"

"Alas, gone. Said to tell you it was the most incredible happening she'd ever witnessed. Doing by doing, her very words... Said to give you her love. Said you're a rare one, a natural. That you've got a home in *Instant Theater*, if the Army ever lets go of you... "Speaking of the Army".

"Oh no..."

"Can't be helped. They're still looking for you. Scoured the whole of downtown Augusta, got zilch, naturally".

"Didn't anybody tell them I was confined to base?"

Major Herskowitz's saturnine face cracks briefly in a reflective near-smile.

"Know something? I actually did, I told them just that. But it appears I am a suspect too. Someone's been following me around. You ever been tailed, *boychik*?"

"Not that I know of".

"Weird feeling. Shit, I'm glad the fuckin' Indian blindfolded me. This way I won't be able to rat on you, even if they give me the third degree. Christ, you'd think Ft. Knox was burned down rather than a lousy plywood set..."

He lapses into deep thought.

"How bad was it?" I ask. "Really ".

"Depending which way you look" he says. "Thirty-odd high-end brass treated for smoke inhalation, tear-gas poisoning, cuts and bruises. Four generals, three admirals, Colonel Sprague himself. That bad enough?"

"Ouch".

Major Herskowitz nods.

"Ouch indeed. Old Rodney's not mad at you though, if that's a consolation. Boy seems to have learned how to smile again, doesn't seem to miss the old set. Can't see's how I'd blame him either. I was getting sick of it myself, may be you did us all a favor, *sheygetz*".

"What do you mean *did*? I did nothing, I fuckin' busted my head trying to save the place! Someone'd sawed off the sprinkler valve, couldn't have been an accident either, same person that conked me on the head, most likely. Didn't Gretchen tell you how she found me?"

"Nope. Nobody's said a thing. Story is, you just took off to parts unknown".

"Shit" I say in utter exasperation, "shit, shit, shit..."

Major Herskowitz shakes his head slowly.

"Fuckin' mess".

"Yeah. What're you going to do now?"

He whistles softly.

"I don't know. Show's cancelled. Cast's gone. Guess I'll wait for orders. I'm too old to ship down to Nam, thank God. Tho they can sure fuck me over in the six months I still have left, don't underestimate the buggers. 'Course, Mimi wants me back in LA, rejoin the troupe. Ruthie wants to go back to New York 'n start a restaurant. Jesus, I wish I knew what to tell them. Nam might be better, for all I know..."

"Perish the thought".

"I suppose".

An abrupt knock on the door, then Gretchen comes in carrying a dark bandanna and a roll of duct tape. She is in civvies, blue jeans and my old CAL sweatshirt.

"Now Major..." she says.

"Nevermind" says Len. "Just wrap me up and be done with it".

Gently, expertly, she blindfolds him, then tapes the bandanna in place.

"Hold on to me" she tells him. Then, to me:

"I'll be back".

●   ●   ●

She isn't. Instead, the door opens and the Boz bounds in. He is half way across the room to my bed when he stops, goes back and locks the door behind him.

"Fuckin' nuisance" he says. "I suppose you're sick and tired of the loony bin".

"You said it, brother. Where's Gretchen?"

"She's walking the major back to his place" he says, "Big Injun's gotta run an errand. Just as well, you and I need to talk".

"It's about time. Fuckin' place's driving me nuts".

"Par for the course" says the Boz, "seeing as how it's the psych ward".

"Cut the shit, Boz" I tell him, "and you better spring me outta here quick, 'fore I start climbing the walls".

"Easy".

The Boz's unshakable self-possession has its ususal

409

effect on me, both cooling me off and driving me bonkers. Some day I may discover how he does it. Right now, tho, I have more urgent business.

"Easy yourself" I tell him.

Warming to the subject, I leap out of bed to face the Boz. My hospital gown flies wide open to reveal the full monte underneath. I fumble for the draw-strings, blushing under my mask.

"The head-gear sure bring out the best in you, Leo" says the Boz. His eyes dart down quickly to assess my shrunken member. "You trying out for Frankenstein?"

"Fuck off, Boz" I tell him. "Dammit, you ain't gonna play me like your fuckin' piano, not any more. I'm sick and tired of your games, y'hear?"

"Well now" says the Boz, surveying me with curiosity.

"Well what?"

"Well" says the Boz, "it just so happens the game's up".

"Which one?"

The Boz is clad in his dress uniform, bright green beret stuffed under the left epaulet leaving his near-shaven skull almost glistening in the harsh neon light of my sound-proof cell. His chest is replete with his service medals and ribbons. The brooding brown eyes survey me thoughtfully from under the prominent brow, as if weighing the odds one would want to lay on me. Turning abruptly, he crosses the room and plops down on my bed, relaxing completely.

The effect is immediate, as if a deadly feline has just switched into its play mode. I stand there in my frustration, gazing down at the Boz through the peepholes in my shroud. The bellicose mood I have been working up to has just been yanked from under me.

The Boz leans back, shaking his head in feigned sorrow as he surveys my padded cell.

"Shit, you must be a born martyr, Leo. I couldn't've taken two hours in this fuckin' box".

"See what I mean? Now, would you please cut the crap and tell me what's going on?"

"Well..."

The harsh fluorescent light renders the Boz' face sallow, verging on gray. The skin around his eyes is taut, the cool glare exposing a network of fine lines that belie his youthful carriage.

"Well what?" I demand.

"Well, we gotta wind down this crap game. Gotta pull you out, for starters".

"Bravo" I say. "When?"

"Tomorrow night".

"Where to?"

"Out".

"Back to Seadock?"

"Nay. Ain't no Seadock no more. Done gone".

"Great. Where then? You can't just yank me out

411

like that, Gretch says there's a whole posse of Army MPs looking for me".

"Never mind the fuckin' Army. We'll spring you, don't worry".

"You're not suggesting I go AWOL, are you?"

The Boz shakes his head.

"Don't worry about the paper-work, kid. We'll get it fixed".

"How?"

"You don't want to know".

"The fuck I don't! I've had enough of this trust-me bullshit, Boz. I'd rather face the music than be a party to another one of your screwy deals".

The Boz surveys me thoughtfully.

"There ain't gonna be no music to be faced" he says, "so long as you do the right thing. You've done good so far, Leo, real good. I mean it. I'm proud of you. Let's see--The leftover weed's gone. Only those in the know could catch the smell, what with the tear-gas. The set's down for good. That was a must-do too, we needed to close down this sorry scam, it was beginning to attract attention. Too many screw-balls muscling in on the action, the whole Seadock deal's gone sour. Time to move on. Except for this stupid business with the sprinklers, you've done real good, boy. Might be a future for you in the Outfit".

"Fuck your outfit".

"Take it easy".

412

The Boz's brown eyes assess me coolly, genuinely curious about the murky mysteries of my innards. Like a teacher waiting for this dim-witted kid to get the point.

"Shit" I tell him, "can't you see? I'm burned out of Ft. Gordon, Army's after my ass, they want me to take the rap for the burndown. Why--"

"Oh that" says the Boz. "I wouldn't take the Army too literally, I were you. It's just a smoke screen, keep the Pentagon happy till the visiting brass get all the tear-gas out of their lungs, stop coughin' 'n wheezin' and go home. There'll be a Board of Inquiry. But, number one, Rodney Manners's all smiles, ain't nothing bothering him. So he ain't gonna file charges. Number two, Sprague, the old crook can't afford to find you. Wouldn't know what to do with you if he did. If it was strictly up to him, he'd just as soon you burned to a crisp with the set".

"He would?"

"Wake up, Leo. Remember how you got here? Papers switcherooed? Captain Leo Swensen with a *EE*, the golfer? Shit, man, ol' Sprague'd be in deep shit 'case anybody ever dug that out. He's got no more rights to you than I do. If the AAG auditors ever get a peek at those fake papers he signed to keep you at Ft. Gordon, he can kiss his pension goodbye. So, you're not really here, Leo. Never been".

"I'm not?"

"Nope".

"Gee, Boz, thanks, that's a comfort".

413

"Ainit now? Might as well relax, then".

We eye each other in silence. I am having a hard time convincing myself I am not trapped inside an elaborate sadistic fairy tale.

"Look at it this way" says the Boz. "If you're not really here, nobody'll miss you when you're gone. So all we have to do is offer Sprague a deal he can't refuse. Get *him* off the hook".

"Can you do that?"

"I'm working on it".

"Am I going to hear about it some day?"

"You don't really want to. You're better off out of the loop, case the deal goes sour".

"Where am I going?"

"Later, man. You'll just have to trust me".

"Again?"

The Boz pitches a hard glare at me from under his furrowed brow. For a brief moment, I think I can see what it is about him that makes guys jump and say yessir. And follow. Maybe to their death. A glimmer is all he lets out. Then the cool façade snaps back into place.

"Have I ever failed you, Leo?" he asks. "The Alameda County Sheriff been bothering you lately?"

I keep silent. The Boz goes down the list:

"Didn't I get you off your stupid junk habit? Got the Army to detox you for free? Made sure you'd never make it to Nam? Got you a cushy state-side gig, a sweet ol'

414

lady who thinks you walk on water... Shit, man, you even got her mother, I hear tell. Fuckin' Big Injun' could've scalped you for that, I seen him carve up guys for much less. But you're still alive, ain't you? And now that you're fixin' to become his friggin' son-in-law, he's off your case for good... long's he stays hitched to Big Mama. Am I right or what?"

The Boz waits. I say nothing.

"Seems to me" he says, "I've been taking care of you long enough without ever asking for a lousy thank you. So for God's sake, man, pipe down. Like, play ball. This is life, Leo, this is for real. You gettin' my drift?"

No great comfort being told your life for the past two years has not been your own, that you've been dangling on someone else's string. Rounding the next blind corner, would you like to come face-to-face with your puppet-master?

"Fine" I tell the Boz, "I'll do what you say. On one condition".

"Yes?"

"Gretchen goes with me. I don't want to leave her here".

The Boz rises off my bed and stretches to his trim full size. He walks to the door, then turns back.

"I see" he says, "you got conditions now".

"Just this one".

He shakes his head.

"Just this one? Two years in this fuckin' Army ain't yet taught you to shut up and take orders, hey?"

"Bottom line" I tell him. "Take it or leave it".

The Boz whistles softly, then lets out a sigh:

"You think I'm a magician, Leo?" he says. "Give the Boz your specs, he'll deliver on your favorite fantasy, fix what ails you, pull your burnt chestnuts out of the fuckin' fire? Shit, man, has it ever occurred to you everything's got a price tag on it? You ever gonna start paying?"

The Boz shakes his head. I wait. I know I am on shaky grounds.

"Well" he says, "it just so happens Little Girl's got only three more months on her stretch. Army can't make her re-enlist, she's entitled to quit. So maybe, just maybe something can be arranged".

"It better".

For the last time the Boz fixes me with his baleful stare. The long, tapered fingers of both his hands, hanging loose at his sides, are flexing slowly in soundless *arpeggios*. I wonder if he still finds time to play. I flash back to that afternoon in his loft above the Piccolo, the wild flourishes of Scarlatti, the sly romp through Debussy's *Petit Negre*, the thundering Bach-Buzoni. It all seems so far away, so out of synch with this ramrod crew-cut captain in his Green Berets uniform and chestful of ribbons.

In this alien universe, the old Berkeley street scene

416

seems like a faded fantasy. Does the Boz regret his transformations? Do I regret mine?

Next to me, the Boz sighs.

"I don't know" he says, "if it's ever occurred to you where you really stand, Leo. So look sharp and listen real careful now. There's still an open file on you in Oakland concerning the death of a motorcycle cop in May 1968. It's listed as unsolved, but they're keeping it open. Then there's this glaring discrepancy between the records that say you're a forward Artillery spotter with the 88th Mechanized in Pleiku, and your being right here in Ft. Gordon playing guerilla theater. And, incidentally, at the moment being unaccounted for and presumed AWOL. Not to mention this murky business about a near mutiny of Army troops under your command and the burning down of military ordnance. Shit, man, I've been busting my ass to cover up yours. So far so good, I think I can see my way through this mess. But you've got to give me some good reason to keep trying, hey? You gotta play ball, Leo, you gotta deliver, you gotta give me some incentive. *Capish?*"

The Boz nods in gracious recognition of my unconditional surrender.

"I think we understand each other" he says. "So no conditions, no threats, okay?"

With this, he opens the door and is gone. The lock clicks back into place as he bolts the door behind him. Once again, I am alone.

●　　　●　　　●

They come for me in the dark of the night, two pale ghosts with a gurney, to which I am summarily conveyed and strapped. My head-gear is again bound in place. A dummy IV has been inserted under the bed-sheets to simulate my condition. A real saline drip-bottle is swinging from its wheel-born stand as we glide our way in silence through the deserted corridors.

"You're supposed to be under sedation" says the diminutive ghost peering down at me over her mask. My guardian angel in her pale-green *burkah*. "So no talking till we're out of range".

Next to her, Gary is looking ridiculous in an orderly's gown that is much too small, his dark eyes squinting over the mask. The old freight elevator whines its way slowly down to ground level. We meet no one on the way.

In the hospital's dim emergency bay, the two of them load me into the back of an Army ambulance, where my gurney is collapsed into a bed and snapped securely in place. Gary hops to the front. Gretchen bolts the door tightly from inside.

A thousand frogs are croaking away their winter mating chorus across the fecund east Georgia countryside. Their love-fest is soon drowned out by our siren's mournful wail. With red lights flashing, we race through the deserted wide avenues of Ft. Gordon clear to the gate, where the sentries wave us through.

418

Three miles out of the base, Gary turns off both the siren and the flashing lights. We proceed east in total silence toward the Augusta suburbs, making frequent turns into narrow country lanes.

"Guess we're far enough" says Gretchen. "You can get up now, hon. Here, let me take the mummy wrap off your head..."

I submit. In a moment my face is exposed to the chill night air.

"How about the stupid dress?" I ask.

I am totally naked under my hospital gown.

"Robe" says Gretchen. "And you look cute in it".

"Cut it out, Gretch".

"Here".

She passes me a plastic bag.

"Put those on. I brought them from the flat, I hope they still fit".

"How about my wallet and stuff?"

"In your jeans".

In the dark, with Gretchen sitting on the gurney's edge, I slip on the cold underwear, then the jeans and sweatshirt, one of my old Berkeley riot specials. God only knows what is printed in front.

The worn old cotton feels divine on my skin. I am intoxicated with my newfound freedom. I fumble for the socks and tennis shoes. My shorn head notwithstanding, I am back in my old habit.

419

"Shit" I tell Gretchen, "you should've brought the wig".

"Last time I saw it" she says, "it was burning away".

I feel for her in the dark and pull her closer. With my other hand I grab purchase as the ambulance sways.

"Aren't you going to change?" I ask her.

"Not before we dump the ambulance. Just in case".

"Why not now?"

"You're incorrigible" she says.

"A quickie?"

"Not a chance".

"Where're we headed?"

"Damned if I know".

We turn and twist our way across the somnolent countryside. Abruptly, the ambulance screeches to a halt. The headlights are switched off, then the engine. In the sudden hush, we are again afloat in the ardent croaking of a gazillion frogs. The Savannah river must be just over the wooded rise.

Gingerly, I hop down and pace slowly around the ambulance to test my unfamiliar muscles. Gretchen and Gary get busy shucking their medical costumes. A low half moon peers out from under the fringe of the clouds.

"Let's skedaddle" says Gary.

"Where're we heading?"

"Onward".

We strike out in silence across the moon-lit terrain, circling around fallen trees and thick brush. Gretchen turns back periodically to make sure I haven't bolted. I am still wobbly. Gary's brisk pace is almost too much.

When we break through the trees, the small monoplane is squatting just ahead, gleaming faintly in the moonlight. We rush toward it on the rough-mown strip of grass. Half the way over, we cross a raised circle of fine turf cropped down to a smooth carpet.

"Jesus" I say, "a fuckin' golf course".

"Augusta National" says Gary.

"No shit. You gonna tell me where we're headed?"

The three of us are huddled near the plane. The fuselage and wing markings are visible, a jumble of dark letters and numbers on the taut silver skin. Gretchen has taken my hand in the dark, her fingers are warm and damp. We wait. Then Gary says, apparently in answer to my question:

"Back to the Rez".

After which he ushers us on board.

•　　•　　•

The monoplane glides like a nimble nighthawk over the silent terrain, somewhere below. I am strapped into the co-pilot seat next to Gary, who commands the one-engine bird as if born to the cockpit. Gretchen is tucked in the back seat directly behind me and must have fallen asleep the minute we took off. Her head is resting over her small backpack.

The auxiliary joy-stick protrudes between my legs, jerking back and forth as Gary puts the plane through its paces. The altimeter dial registers just under five hundred feet. We must be hugging the ground.

"You need me to stay awake?" I ask Gary.

"Nay. You can crash".

I let t he vibrations rock me into restless slumber.

I come up with a start just before daybreak. Gary is taking the plane into a steep bank, following the flank of a wooded hillside. We must be preparing for landing.

"What now?" I ask.

"Need to gas up".

"Where are we?"

"Tennessee".

I peer over the rim of the cabin. I can see no landing lights.

"Another golf course?"

"Nay, just a Rez".

"Which one?"

"Eastern Cherokee".

We land on a grassy clearing and taxi slowly toward the fringe of a pine-and-oak thicket. A small wooden shed is tucked under the canopy of three giant pecans. While Gretchen retires to commune with nature , I help Gary with the jerrycans. The bracing fumes of aviation fuel are almost too much. By the time we have stacked the empty cans back in the shed, I am dizzy. And hungry. And wide awake.

"Any chance of breakfast?" I ask Gary.

"Gretchen's got some stuff in her pack" he tells me. "You two go ahead and eat. I need to go see a man. Won't be long".

I watch him plunge in silence into the dense vegetation. In another minute Gretchen rejoins me.

"Boy was I tired" she says.

"Feel like breakfast?"

"I'm starved".

We picnic on the damp grass over a stained tarp she found in the fuselage. We listen to an invisible choir of birds go through their sunrise drill. The sky lights up slowly above the tree tops. Gretchen turns over and stretches, her head in my lap.

"This is divine" she says. "I can't believe it".

"Are you really out, legally?" I ask.

"I'm not sure" she says.

"Seen the paperwork?"

"Gary says it's being taken care of".

"That's what the Boz said. Sounds highly irregular".

"So is life".

I have finally done snared myself a philosopher.

When Gary reappears, just after the sun lights up the monoplane, he's got hot coffee in paper cups. We gulp down the blessed liquid and are soon airborne.

●　　　●　　　●

We traverse the majestic river someplace north of Memphis, then angle diagonally northwest across Arkansas. We munch on the apples and cheese-crackers from Gretchen's pack

In the brilliant daylight, we change course again and again, no doubt to skip the urban centers. At two in the afternoon, the gas gauge is pointing to near empty. In the back, Gretchen has gone back to sleep. We are cruising at 1,500 feet over flat country. The lush eastern forest has given way to meager clumps of scrub oak that punctuate the gray farmland at growing intervals. Empty fields stretch out to the haze-filled horizon. Desolate little towns hug the flats under the stark open sky.

"Don't you think we better stop for gas?" I ask Gary.

From behind me, Gretchen chimes in:

"And a bathroom break. Please?"

Gary is busy consulting his charts.

"We're almost there" he says.

"Almost where?"

"Indian Territory".

"What's the big deal? Redmen cornered the market on aviation gas?"

424

Gary doesn't answer.

"Pipe down, Leo" he says at last, "take it easy".

In ten minutes we are down and wheeling slowly along a packed-dirt strip. I see an old quonset, next to it a lodgepole shade-house. A lone figure is leaning to an ancient pickup in front of the quonset.

As we draw near, the figure grows into a gargantuan hulk, who detaches himself from the truck and comes forward to meet us. His raised hand is pointing to the shade-house. Under Gary's careful ministration, the plane rolls slowly between the two poles. When the engine is switched off, the monoplane rests wholly under the tangled thatch of dry cottonwood limbs.

We clamber down, I turn back to give Gretchen a hand. We duck under the wing and walk out. Just ahead of us, Gary is being smothered in a monster bear-hug by a gargantuan Indian man. Who after a while steps back, beaming. He turns to face us, his right hand rises, open palm out:

"Welcome to the sovereign Cheyenne nation".

His voice emanates from some deep recess of his mass. The fading T-shirt, pulled carelessly over the massive belly, exposes a dark centerfold topped by a protruding navel flopping over a large silver belt-buckle. Under the stained cowboy hat, two graying waist-long braids cascade down his chest. Next to him, Gary's wiry frame appears child-like.

425

"Meet my Cheyenne brother Kicking Bear" says Gary.

I offer my hand gingerly.

"Any friend of my brother Grey Eagle is a friend of mine" says the giant, almost dislocating my arm. "Got a name to go with the pale face, *kemo sabe?*"

I extricate my hand, suppressing the urge to blow cool air on it. I wonder if the metacarpus will ever mend. I can only hope Kicking Bear is more gentle with Gretchen, who is standing there like an orphan, her backpack dragging on the ground. She smiles up bravely as her small palm is absorbed in the giant's grip.

He beams his creased mahogany face down at Gretchen. The two of them are engaged in a brief silent communion.

"I'm Leo" I tell the giant, who seems to have forgotten all about me. "This is Gretchen".

Kicking Bear nods solemnly, releasing Gretchen's hand.

"You better watch out for this skinny squaw, *kemo sabe*" he says. "Them skinny ones pack a wallop, I hear. Maybe you be better off trading her to me, hey? Reckon she's worth--"

"Name's Leo" I tell him, "and you can't afford her, even if she was for sale".

"Give you one paint horse" says the giant, "prime condition, just been broke. Throw in five blankets, real

Pendelton. Give you a good deal on a fifty-gallon drum of crude. Best offer".

Next to us, the lady herself says:

"While you two barter over my skinny carcass" she says, "would you mind pointing me to the bathroom? Or there won't be much to barter over..."

"Back side of the quonset" says Kicking Bear. "It's only an outhouse. Sorry".

"I'm sure it'll do" says Gretchen, "us skinny ones are real tough".

After which she hoists her backpack and disappears. Kicking Bear turns to Gary, who has been following our exchange in silence:

"Think your pale-face friend can hang on to her, brother?"

"Reckon he better" says Gary, "or Big Mama's gonna come after me with a carving knife. That's her little girl there, case you been wondering".

"No shit!" says Kicking Bear. "This Big Mama's little girl? You mean, this *kemo sabe* is family?"

"Seems like".

The three of us seal our new-found kinship by taking a communal leak against the shimmering vast horizon.

●　　　●　　　●

"You ever gonna tell me what this is all about?" I ask Gary.

We have been airborne and flying due north-west for the past four hours. Gretchen is again asleep in the back seat, poor lamb.

For twenty minutes now, the thin white band of snow-caps has been suspended up in the distance ahead, just above the shimmering horizon. We left Kicking Bear's airstrip sometime before noon, with Gary resolutely declining an invitation to stay for the night.

He takes his time fiddling with the levers.

"One more to go" he says.

"One more what?"

"One more Rez. Jicarilla".

"Where's that?"

"North of Santa Fe, west of Chama. We're almost home, *tɨgɨvɨn*. Can't you smell it?"

"Smell what?"

"Sagebrush".

"I used to" I tell him, "long ago".

My four-month term at St. John's college, on the outskirts of Santa Fe, has never made it into full consciousness, blurred as it was in cloud of prime Afghani.

"What's the big deal about all them Rezes?"

Gary mulls over my question.

"Aside from security" he says, "we're checking out the route, gauging mileage, making sure the fuel dumps are in place... lining up campsites, personnel, the works".

"Lining them up for what?"

"Just to be ready".

"Then what?"

"Then we sit tight, take it easy, wait".

"Wait for what?"

"Wait for the Boz".

Waiting for the Boz seems more and more like waiting for Godot.

"How about my papers?"

"The Boz'll know".

"The Boz knows everything, right?"

"That's his business".

"So you just sit and wait?"

Gary fixes me with a sidelong glance:

"We been waiting you out, you *murukachiu*, five hundred years now, *kemo sabe*, case you haven't noticed. You get used to it. Take my word".

"Till when?"

"Till whenever. Need be, forever".

Must be easy for him, with five hundred years of practice. Must have waited out a thousand Bozes.

"Where's he now?" I ask.

Gary looks up briefly from his gauges. We are slowly approaching the snowcaps. He shakes his head.

"Anybody ever tell you you're a fuckin' pill, Leo?"

"Only a thousand times. Where's the Boz?"

"God only knows. Somewhere south of the border, I reckon".

"This Rez business, it's all part of his new dope scheme, right?"

Gary shakes his head.

"Man don't tell me nothing. I'm just one little Injun. I know nothin', that way I don't need to tell nobody, hey?"

"So what am I supposed to do, just wait with you?"

"Got a better idea?"

"No".

"Listen, Leo" says Gary. "You're almost family now, case you need remindin'... That little girl sleepin' in the back, you got *her* to worry about now. You got her Momma too, you got me. So, see, you got plenty to worry about 'side yourself. Christ, I'm not even sure I like you all that much, you're such a fuckup, y'know. Shit, no matter, I gotta put up with you now, take care of you. So just remember, you're not alone anymore, y'n'stand? Like you're in the hoop now. Know what that's all about?"

"Not really".

"It's about not being alone. Shit, man, you gotta learn how to be. You gotta learn how to wait. Gotta have faith".

"Faith in what?"

"Just faith, goddammit".

12. Paper transactions

We have been here for a week now. I still can't believe it. The house is a derelict old adobe tucked in a clump of pines, in a small hollow dug into the bosom of the hill at the top of the valley. Inside, a floor of compacted dirt is covered with threadbare rugs. The main room doubles up in the daytime as kitchen, living room, dining room and family space. At night it transforms itself into sleeping quarters for the five boys, who have grown so much I hardly recognize them.

Serena and Gary occupy the bedroom. Gretchen and I are relegated to a decrepit cab-over camper out in the back, under a shed of crumbling lodge-pine poles topped with rusting corrugated sheets. The twin-seater outhouse is directly behind us.

The packrats under the roof punctuate our sleep with their nocturnal bacchanals over the thin plywood ceiling of the camper. The morning sun, rising straight across the narrow valley, tickles our faces through the decrepit front door. If the elements were ever to come any closer we would be one with nature.

We spend our days walking and talking and making delicious love, under the trees, on the warm rocks at

431

midday, on top of the craggy hills, whenever and wherever the spirit moves us. We are deliriously, desperately happy, perhaps because we have no idea how long this idyll will last.

• • •

Wednesday just before dawn, we are waken by Gary, who says we have an urgent journey to undertake. Wrapped up in our blankets, half asleep and shivering, we scramble into the old Bronco--still alive--and tear off cross-country, out of the small valley then down an old dirt road that leads east to the river. There, we join the graveled county road and proceed upstream in a thick cloud of dust.

We zip past shuttered ranch houses and lodge-pole corrals, a small adobe church, sheds and old barns and rusting mobile homes. We honk away at the occasional stray cow grazing at the side of the road. In half an hour we hit the blacktop, hang a right and glide through the sleeping town of Pagosa Springs, sniffing at the corrosive sulphur fumes.

"*Paqos'ay*" says Gary, as he runs the red light across the bridge, "what the Old Ones used to call it. Stinking Sulfur. Spring's over there, just across the river. Spaniards couldn't hack the sound, changed it to Pagosa".

"That the old Injun lingo?" I ask him.

"Yeah".

"You speak it?"

"Not much. A word here 'n there".

"How come?"

Gary takes his time.

"My mom still does. I think Grandma taught me, she must have, she didn't speak any English and she lived with us much of the time when I was a little shaver... Then I went to school. That's when us kids shucked it".

"Why?"

"Shit, who knows? Didn't wanna be different, I guess".

"Don't you wish you'd kept it?"

Gary ponders.

"I don't know" he says. "It's still in there somewhere, hiding, maybe. Ain't much use tho. Grandma's gone, most of the old 'uns are gone, ain't walking about no more... Who'm I gonna to talk to? Only Mom. What's gone's gone, gotta move on, go with the flow, bob with the mob, spin with the wind, hey? Shit, I don't know..."

Just north of town we begin the steep ascent. The old Bronco growls and grinds as we hit the switch-backs. As we rise higher and higher, the sky lights up. On a level stretch just below the pass, Gary makes a sharp left turn and pulls into the scenic overlook. We roll slowly to the log barrier, where he switches off the lights and kills the engine.

We are perched on top of a jutting promontory, an

eagle's nest suspended above the the river valley. We scramble out and walk to the edge of the cliff that falls straight down two thousand feet to the river-bed floor. Gretchen and I stand together, hugging our blankets against the morning chill.

Our backs are turned to the bare parapets of Wolf Creek Pass. Straight below to the south, the upper gorge opens up into a narrow valley, snaking southward in a series of narrow spans that plunge periodically into dark granite gorges. Farther south, the river slows down gradually as it commences its serpentine meandering through the meadows. Another fork joins in from the west, then the narrow band of shimmering silver traces wide arches. It courses sedately through bottom-land pastures, where the browned remnants of last year's grass have been cropped down to the root by grazing cattle.

At the far end, under the rim of the dark-green horizon, the white plume of a lumbermill's smoke-stack curls up lazily as it drifts eastward before ascending to snare the first rays of the rising sun. The town itself is tucked away downriver.

The scene at our feet is frozen in eternal vertigo. Nothing moves. Not a whiff of a breeze.

Gary is standing next to me.

"Pretty, ainit?"

"Amen, bro'ther".

"Used to be all ours, far 's the eye can see. Ten

days ride in whatever direction to the four winds. Man had to ride long and hard to run out of Numa country... Best to lookit in the morning, 'fore you can see how bad it's all fucked up, before you can see the clear-cuts 'n fencing 'n motels... You squint hard enough, it's almost the way it used to be before you White-Eyes come 'n trashed it..."

We watch in silence, waiting out the glorious sunrise. Then we pile back into the Bronco and drive back to town. At the Elkhorn Café, we load up on carbs and skillet grease. We sit and sip coffee in silence. Then we get back on the gravel and go back downriver.

We clear the top of the hill and begin our descent. A strange jeep is parked in front of the adobe. I look at Gary, who doesn't seem concerned.

"Shouldn't we slow down, check 'em out first?" I ask.

"Nay".

"You sure?"

He shakes his head.

"Relax, man" he says. "Your troubles are over. The Boz is back".

●   ●   ●

"This is absolutely, utterly, totally insane!" I almost scream.

The five of us--Gretchen, Serena, Gary, the Boz and

435

I--are sprawled in a semi-circle on a tarp spread over the dry grass, under a clump of scrub oak tucked into the hillside. Right below us, an improbably symmetrical cone-shaped juniper stands all alone at the edge of the dry creek. A faint rut in the eroded yellow soil, the creek threads out of the womb of the hill that seals the top of the valley to the right.

The other trees in the meadow below us, an assortment of cedar, black-jack and pinyon, seem to have drawn back from the lone juniper, giving it a respectful wide berth.

"This is 7,000 feet" says the Boz, "a tad over. Your head must've gone all fuzzed up. Here, Big Chief, why don't you pass the poor boy some antidote for his altitude sickness. Go on, Leo, drag some, it'll do you worlds of good. Steady you up a bit, give you some perspective..."

The Boz has undergone another metamorphosis. Gone are the uniform and medals. Over the still close-cropped hair, an ancient off-gray ten-gallon Stetson presides in full bloom. The faded blue jeans are cinched low with a large cast-silver rodeo buckle and tucked into worn cowboy boots. The new Boz seems born to the range, much as his predecessors looked born to the Av, to the Fort. To the Delta?

Gary, who has been snorting white powder next to me, hands me the glassine envelope, together with the thin cylinder rolled out of a dollar bill. I take it, then drop it back

436

on the ground between his legs.

Next to me, Gretchen is rubbing my arm gently. Both she and Serena have likewise declined the white-powder offering. Gary and the Boz have been snorting for a solid ten minutes. Neither seems impaired.

The Boz shrugs.

"You got a better offer, Leo?"

For a while, no one speaks. Finally Gretchen interjects:

"Seems to me" she says , "asking Leo to accept this total loss of identity is a bit too much".

The Boz is in an expansive mood. He seems reluctant to break the picnic ambience.

"Who's talking loss of identity?" he inquires amiably. "It's all just paper transactions. Think Wall Street, sweetie-pie--all we're doing is de-activating one old stock issue, re-activating another. What's the big deal? He's still who he is, ain't he?".

The stack of manila folders spread on the tarp between the Boz's boots tells it all. They document the demise of one Leo D. Swenson, jr, lieutenant jg, formerly of Salt Point, NY, formerly forward artillery spotter with the 88th Mechanized working out of Pleiku; of a single bullet wound to the left torso, courtesy of a VC sniper; on top of Hill 517 along a low jungle ridge in the Central Highlands. Immediate field burial, authorized due to lack of adequate transport under heavy enemy fire; grave coordinates kept under seal in the event of future access becoming possible; dog tags and other documents attached, together with personal effects found on the deceased by the Special Forces helicopter team that was called in, alas, too late; notification of next-of-kin pending.

"You betcha!" I say. "You creeps were gonna notify my mom and dad I was *deceased*?"

The offensive word hisses out into the thin mountain air, like a deadly asp, sorely tempting my mom's *malojo*, as if the Old Goat needed a special invite to pounce on his only-too-painfully alive-and-breathing victim. Me.

"Don't be dense, Leo" says the Boz. "We're gonna let you explain everything to them first, way before the information grinds out through Pentagon channels".

"Most thoughtful of you!"

I am thoroughly disgusted. The Boz pins me with a sharp look that broadcasts his surprise, indeed hurt, at my rigid negotiating posture. For a while, he holds his peace. Gary and Serena seem to have opted out.

Not Gretchen, tho. My beloved champion who, bless her stout heart, is just as incensed:

"How about his name? What's he supposed to call himself now?"

"Why" says the Boz, "anything that strikes his fancy. Fuckin' sky's the limit".

These wide open vistas freedom fail to give me

438

comfort. Next to me, my true love presses on relentlessly:

"How about his college records? You guys expect him to forfeit all his credits?"

"Such as they are" says the Boz, who has no doubt seen my transcripts. "Nay, not if it's a real hardship. We can give him a diploma from the school of his choice, God knows he's sampled enough of them. Real authentic, hey? Ivy league? Throw in a *suma cum laude*, ought to make him happy. Go straight into their computers, case anybody'd want to ask questions. Shit, he's earned it, eight years of hanging out around those dumps... Wanna make it Cal, Leo, for ol' times' sake?"

"You can do that?"

"Guys I work for can do anything".

The Boz lets the message sink in. Gretchen is the first to recover:

"I don't know" she says, "this whole trip's getting too weird for me. I was looking forward to being Gretchen Swenson for the rest of my life. Krumm was getting a bit old, know what I mean..."

She turns over to Serena, who is curled around Gary:

"What do you think, Mom?"

"About what? Your name? You could have dumped it when I did. I don't think your dad would've minded, not that it would've done him much good..."

"Unload it and use what? And for how long

each?"

My tiger, once aroused, is in the mood to pick on all comers. Not beyond settling old scores either.

"Christ, Mom" she explodes, "I was only three!"

Serena shrugs.

"So?" she says. "Life goes on. Bless your fortune most of the real heavy shit between me 'n your dad just passed over your sweet little head. What's this fuckin' big deal about a name?"

"My point exactly, Big Mama" says the Boz. "Besides, Little Girl could help him choose, hey? Plus..."

The Boz turns back to me.

"There're some real liabilities go with your current moniker, Leo, case you forgot".

"You mean Seadock?" I ask. "I thought it's all squared off with old Sprague..."

"Sure" says the Boz, "that was the easy part. But there's still that delicate business of a dead Alameda County Sheriff deputy, crashed his Electraglide into a wall in a dead-end alley, noontime of the peace riot? Far as I know, Alameda County's still looking for a Leo Swenson, jr, former Cal undergraduate 'n petty dope dealer... Shit, wanna see the APB with your mug-shot?"

But my beloved won't stand for it:

"How do we know your fancy hush-hush outfit didn't print that? And even if it's legit, they can fix it, too. Just another paper transaction, right?"

440

Touché?

"Well..." says the Boz, clearly in his placating mode. "Everything can be fixed, it's just a question of price and priorities. Cost-benefits, supply 'n demand, that kinda stuff. As this one goes, fixing a state rap is not as easy as fixing a Fed one. Tho if it's absolutely necessary, I reckon it could be done. Anything could be done once they switch to storing their records on computer tape. That's why it's a cinch with the Feds and the Pentagon. Ol' MacNamara talked them into going off paper early on in the Kennedy Administration. So all their records are on tape. Any decent teckie can hack into their code-books, fiddle with the records, fix what needs fixin' ".

The Boz is in his element. If he chose to, I am sure he could fix St. Peter's in-list.

"You're talking Fed records, Boz?" I ask.

"Yup".

"Don't they have security?"

"Reckon. 'Course, it just so happens the guys I work for are in charge of that. Makes it more wholesome, know what I mean, all under the same big roof? Got a nice symmetry to it, like a Bach fugue, hey?"

The Boz lets his observation hang in the crisp dry air. As always, I am struck by how sane it all sounds once he has laid it out for your pea-brain to appreciate. It is so tempting to concede to the inevitable, catch the coming wave. Effortless, like entropy.

441

"Can you tell me something, Boz?" I say.

"Sure. Within limits".

"Okay. Who exactly are these guys you're working for? How the fuck can they do all that? Not to mention that new drug scam..."

Who indeed? Come to think, how can a guy be a Green Beret in Nam one day, a hippie weed dealer off the Av the next, Captain PR in Ft. Gordon, GA next, then off to South America and points in-between as a drug interdictor-importer? How indeed?

The Boz weighs my question slowly. His dark brown eyes squint against the sun that has catapulted across the narrow valley and is now grazing at the tops of the sparse Ponderosa pines on the rim of the western ridge.

Serena and Gary have reclined onto the tarp, lost in each other's company. Gretchen is tucked snugly under my left arm, content to let me carry the ball. The air is beginning to turn cold. I know she will soon start to shiver, then go to look for thicker cover. She is not yet accustomed to the rapid shift of temperatures in the altitude.

Presently the Boz says:

"Well, you're trolling pretty close to classified info there, Leo. So let's just say, guys I work for are well connected, say they're plugged in tight into the fat umbilical cord of good ol' Mother, leave it at that, hey?"

"Leave it at what? No name, just well connected?

442

Plugged in tight? That's it?"

The Boz stretches to his full height, his head bent, studying the ground.

"Back in the old days" he says, "say Nam, we used to call it Grandma. Just as good a name as any, hey? Everybody was too fuckin' busy doing their thing, nobody had time to ask questions. Outfit was kinda small then, like family, ol' boys network, everybody knew everybody... No more. Everything's gotten big now, big 'n scary, like a fuckin' business. Global's the word, interconnected, integrated, interactive, whatever. Sorta like the B Minor Mass, y'know? The Berlioz Requiem? Brahms' Fifth? Too big for one guy to take in. Fuckin' octopus with zillion legs, can't see your way across... Still, you know there must be a head somewhere, doing the reckoning for all those legs, doing the coordination, the prioritizing. It's more streamlined now, I reckon... One thing's still the same tho-- it's still like family. We take care of our own. You're in, you're in for life, got nothing to worry about, not any more. That's what I keep telling you, Leo. Shit, you gotta stop worrying. You've graduated. You made it, you're in, suckin' on mama's Big Tit".

The Boz takes a deep breath, shooting a slow brooding look at me:

"Wasn't easy, boy, I'm sure you know. There's all those times I was ready to dump you, pitch you to the wolves, let you go visit Nam see for yourself. You're such a fuckin' flake, fuckin' fuckup... But you've got something else too, a rare thing. Call it the spark, call it imagination, invention, genius, who the fuck cares? You got a penchant for for impro. You come up with totally goofy insane ad-libs... way outta left field, but still, they work. Don't ask me how, don't ask me why. This is something the Outfit appreciates, something it respects, something it can get behind. So why don't we just leave it at that, hey? Main thing, everything's under control, everything's gonna be alright".

Am I being initiated into the paradise of blessed fools? The ground under my sore feet is as slippery as ever.

"So what am I supposed to do now?"

"Nothing. For now".

"How about Gretch? We're supposed to get married, you know".

"Who's stopping you? Have you asked permission yet? It's a family thing, y'know, gotta make sure these guys accept you".

The Boz turns over and nudges Gary, who seems to be lost in Serena's halo.

"Hey, Grey Eagle, you don't mind havin' this skinny-runt *kemo sabe* for son-in-law?"

"Little Girl ain't mine to give" says Gary. "Better ask Big Mama".

Next to him, Serena stirs:

"He'll do" she says. "Long's he calls his mom right away, I promised her he would, soon's he got here, come to think. 'Sides, your Outfit might fuck up and release the info on his sad demise prematurely. So he better call right away to let her know he's alive".

"Good idea" says the Boz, turning back to me. "You can use the wireless in the Jeep, it's in the glove compartment".

" 'Course" says Serena, "you'll have to let go of him, Boz. I don't want my little girl hitched up to another dealer, bad enough he ain't got a name now. So let's have this settled, a'right?"

"Shit" says the Boz, "I was counting on the skinny runt".

"Too bad" she says, "he's spoken for, family now and you already got Gary. One's plenty, you go poach on another clan, hey?"

I look from one to the other. The three of them seem to have disposed of everything. What the fuck.

Under the crook of my arm, Gretchen stirs:

"Honey, I'm freezing" she says. "Race you down to the house?"

Without waiting, she leaps and takes off down the dry meadow. In a minute, she is lost in the cedars.

I rise and turn to the Boz:

"Anything else up your sleeve I should know about?"

"Well, now..."

There is always more.

"If you two wanna get hitched" he says, "so long's I'm here, might as well do the honors for you".

"You mean, you can hack that too?"

"Nay" says the Boz. "I can hitch you two. For real".

"How can you?"

"Easy. Just happen to be a man of the cloth. Ordained, all legit. So you-two trot over to the County Courthouse in Pagosa, you show them your new birth certificate, get the permit forms, bring 'em back. I'll hitch you two right here, s ay right under that cedar?"

The Boz is pointing straight across at the lone symmetrical juniper next to the dry creek.

"What church are you ordained in, exactly?"

"Church of Universal Brotherhood".

"That mail-order outfit out of Modesto?"

"'Good's the Pope. State of California says so".

On the blanket next to Serena, Gary says:

"Man's legit. Got us hitched too".

"Just like that?"

"Nothing to it. We'll make it a real party once he's done his gig, throw you-two an Indian barbecue, call Kickin' Bear to come in on it, case the you two hunker for something a bit more sacred. Man's a shaman, plenty ol' spirit up his ass, knows the old lingo. Make Little Girl run circles around you in a blanket..."

I look down at the three of them--Gary reclining back on the tarp, his head propped on Serena's lap. Serena bent over him, her wild-honey hair almost matted. For the first time, I notice the gray streaks in it. Her eyes are open, fixed on me. The Boz is seated next to them, hugging his knees.

"Shit" I say, "nevermind, I believe you".

"Better catch up with that girl before she changes her mind" says Serena.

I look down at the three of them. They seem to have forgotten my presence. I turn and run down to the creek bed toward the old adobe. Once I plunge into the trees, the surrounding hills are gone. The smell of sage and juniper blends together. It will soon make me sneeze. I sprint down in the dry wheatgrass after the woman I love.

In another minute, I catch a glimpse of Gretchen as she rounds a clump of scrub oak, her divine ass wiggling away at me. Her honeyed hair is streaming back, wild as the wind. I try not to think too hard as I follow her down to where the valley opens up. Where it is traversed now by the lengthening shadows of the blackjack pine high on the western ridge.

AUTHOR'S POST-SCRIPT

Many people contributed directly or indirectly to the writing of Seadock. For the Berkeley chapter, I owe much to Herman Pevner, Richard Bozolich , Jim Matisoff and the late Raya Albert. For the Laguna and Aspen segments, I am much indebted to Karin Givon, Tammy Nace, Harry Sweats and Roy Engebretsen, and their cohorts at Midnight Mine. Linda Givon read, and commented on early versions of the manuscript.

The bulk of the Seadock story I owe to Mike Lindquist, who shared it with me one evening in 1972 over a generous helping of the sacrament; and who endorsed my plan to write Seadock as a novel.

In 1997, with my curiosity still intact, I drove cross-country to Ft. Gordon, GA to inspect the scene of the crime for myself. Capt. Henry Holmes, Chief of Media Relations at Ft. Gordon, was extremely gracious and accommodating , giving me an extensive tour of the base and the defunct Seadock compound, as well as of downtown Augusta. He xeroxed for me 3-decade-old documents from the C.D.O.C.-SEADOCK files still there. Henry also directed me to Ft. McClellan, Alabama, where the US Army MP School, original home of Seadock, had been relocated. In Ft. McClellan, Capt. Herschel M. Chapman, Chief of Media Relations, was equally gracious.

The following is the official announcement of the initiation of Seadock at Ft. Gordon:

449

24 January 1968

Colonel William Schabacker
Chief Public Information Division
Office of Chief of Information
Washington, D.C., 20310

Dear Colonel Schabacker:

As you know, Fort Gordon has been handed the mission of conducting a Civil Disturbance Orientation Course, with the first class beginning February 12. This course if five days (40 hours) in length and we have been directed to conduct 12 of the classes.

The guidance we have received indicate that this course is one of the "hottest" project now being worked on in the Pentagon and, as you can imagine, it has the highest priority here at Fort Gordon.

I was directed to prepare a Public Affairs plan for this course and a copy of this plan is at Inclosure. I prepared the plan with a very minimum guidance from higher headquarters and I wish that you would review it and offer any comments or suggestions. The major concern of all involved is that there should be no press on the course, however, this thing is of such magnitude that I see no way to keep the thing under wraps. I would appreciate any guidance you can furnish me.

Sincerely,

1 Incl   WALLACE C. HITCHCOCK
as   Major, Artillery
                                    Public Affairs Officer

In the Public Affairs Plan attached to Major Hitchcock's letter, the following two sections are of some interest:

2. Although the entire contents of the course is completely unclassified, the very nature of the instruction is controversial and could be the subject of considerable interest on the part of the press and other groups.

3. Guidance received from the office of the Chief of Information, Department of the Army, states that no press release will be generated by the Army...

Seadock operated at Ft. Gordon from February 1968 through April 1969, when it was first suspended, to be resurrected in May 1970. In October 1970, Maj. Thomas E. O'Malley, MPC (PhD in Sociology, Yale 1969 and Seadock instructor) and 1st Lt. Donald A. Lund, MPC, wrote a review article titled "SEADOCK: An Overview" in the Ft. Gordon Military Police Journal, Oct. 1970 issue. On p. 6, in a section titled "Contemporary Social Unrest", the following observations are found:

...Disaffection is an attitude or state of mind of individuals who are concerned about, alienated from, or dissatisfied with the operation of the socioeconomic political system... We also have in our society those elements that feel reform will not take place unless militant action is taken to force society to change the system. Within this group--radicalism--there are those who do not want to change the system, but rather destroy it in order to build a new one. Radicalism can be

451

explained as an extreme extension of disaffection. Radicalism is studied by focusing on five ideologies of concern, the old left, the militant right, the militant black, the new left, and the new life style...

In the Program of Instruction for C.O.D.C, US Army Military Police School, Ft. Gordon, GA, August 1968, p. 4, the following description of a public demonstration class is given:

Dramatically presented demonstration depicting the teamwork, coordination, force buildup, and prior planning required to adequately cope with civil disturbances in metropolitan areas. The EOC demonstration depicts a type [of] situation in which a city EOC is opened by order of the mayor and, as the civil disturbance situation worsens, other agencies are brought in as follows: city, county, state, National Guard, federal government, and Active Army. A return to normalcy is depicted at the close of the demonstration.

The Army's concern with the media intensified after the reinstatement of Seadock in May of 1970, when the new Public Affairs Officer, Major Richard H. Lamb, wrote in a memorandum dated May 7, 1970:

a. No effort would be made by the Public Affairs Officer, Fort Gordon, to generate media interest in the course.
c. Media visits to classes in session will not be authorized...

452

In the subsequent public information release dated May 8, 1970 by the Public Affairs Office, Fort Gordon, GA, one finds the following item:

Conspicuously missing from this year's course will be the live demonstration at "Riotsville", the mythical town constructed at Ft. Gordon for the first SEADOCK series. It will be replaced this year by television and film presentations.

Concern with the media further escalated, so that on May 20, 1970, Major Lamb sent a memorandum to Ft. Gordon's Commanding General, with the subject line "CBS filming SEADOCK", opening with:

1. At 1400 hours, 20 May 1970, Mr. Zelman, CBS News, a producer of "Sixty Minutes", called this office and inquired about the SEADOCK course. He stated that they were doing a story on the National Guard as part of "Six Minutes" and wanted to include SEADOCK as a part of the training and insrtruction which guardsmen receive.

On August 27, 1970, Major Lamb produced a Memorandum of Record in which the following is found:

1. At 1600 hours, 26 August 1970, a Mr. Tim Shellhardt, Wall Street Journal, Chicago, called this office concerning SEADOCK.
2. Mr. Shellhardt had been in contact wuith the Campus Security Division, Southern Illinois University, and was greatly impressed with their noperation. They commented on the SEADOC course, thus

his call here.

3. Mr. Shellhardt's area of interest was in the attendance of campus security types at SEADOCK. He asked if I would provide him with a list of educational institutions which had securrity personnel in attendance.

In a subsequent memorandum to his commanding officer, dated October 19, 1970, Major Lamb recounted a July 6, 1970 incident concerning a visit to Seadock by a Hearst reporter, Mr. Harry Kelly, and how lines of authority were crossed and established policies not fully enforced.

Lastly, in a letter dated August 6, 1970 to the Commanding Officer of Ft. Gordon, GA, M. Howard Sienstra, a City Commissioner from Grand Rapids, Michigan, transmitted a report he had sent his Mayor and fellow Commissioners on July 28, 1970 after attending the Seadock course. His report on the Seadock staff and curriculum is most laudatory. Beginning with p. 2, however, Mr. Sienstra had the following to say about his fellow attendees:

2. I was chocked and dismayed at the narrow-minded repressive attitudes of most of the attendees. About 1/3rd were regular Army personal [sic.], 1/3rd National Guard personal [sic.], and 1/3rd domestic police officials. I was the only elected official in attendance. The Nat'l Guard were the most gungho for law and order, with some notable and delightful exceptions.

454

a. Most of the attendees have no understanding and even less sympathy for the dissidents who engage in civil disturbances. They regularly denounced the 'permissiveness' in our society which has given birth to such dissidents and which now permits them to exist. Even the Military Police School came under attack from some of the attendees because in their view instructors were not harsh enough. With little understanding of what a free and constitutional society means they repeatedly asked, "Why do we have to put up with them?"

b. Although seldom expressed openly and directly, there was a widespread sentiment among the attendees that police and military personal [sic.] should become instruments of punishment, rather than merely instruments of control. "Cracking heads" and "shooting a few" were often urged with little discrimination...

c. Civilian control of police and other control forces were clearly suspect. It was particularly denounced in those situations where mayors and college presidents refuse to allow the control forces free hand in quelling a disturbance...The restraints that the courts impose on some control force activities was [sic.] equally disdained... Many attendees seemed quite willing to suspend the right of habeas corpus and to wish that those making arrests could also arrange for punishments.

d. There was open disdain for the news media. Walter Cronkite is the current symbol to be attacked.... Some of the Guard personnel just couldn't understand the negative public reaction following Kent State. One actually asked the question about why people got so upset over the shooting of four long-hairs...

e. I discovered rather shortly into the course that as far as the attitudes of the attendees were concerned--to put it in the words of Wm. Stringfellow--"my people are the enemy." The enemy of the majority of the attendees were the people with whom I identify. My

455

people are students and college teachers and administrators and hippies and ministers and judges and Blacks and other minorities and even elected officials. All of these were the enemy at some time during the course...

What neither Mr. Sienstra in his anguished letter of July 28, 1970 nor Major Lamb in his frantic fending off of the media in May of 1970 mentions, is that the commanders of the Ohio National Guardsmen who shot the four demonstrating students at Kent State University on May 4, 1970, were graduates--attendees--of the Seadock training course. The subsequent inquiry into the Kent State massacre led to the termination of the Seadock program later that year.

In *A History of Fort Gordon Georgia*, published by the Command Historian Office (Carol E. Stokes, Command Historian, Editor; undated), chapter VII "The Vietnam War" (pp. 142-149) has no mention of Seadock .